S0-AGL-240

Spencer Hill Press

Contact: Spencer Hill Press, PO Box 247, Contoocook, NH 03229, USA

Please visit our website at www.spencerhillpress.com

First Edition: December 2013.

Wooldridge, T. J. 1978
The Kelpie : a novel / by T. J. Wooldridge – 1st ed.
p. cm.
Summary:
Eleven-year-old girl must face a killer fey horse and faery politics to save a young friend.

The author acknowledges the copyrighted or trademarked status and trademark owners of the following wordmarks mentioned in this fiction: Audi, Band-Aid, Biscoff, Blackberry, Crock-Pot, Diet Coke, Disney, Dungeons & Dragons, Facebook, Ford, iPod, Jimmy Choo, Lego, MENSA, Muppets, National Geographic, Nutella, Pepsi, Prius, Rolls-Royce, Skype, Swiss Army, Tylenol, Velcro, WD-40, YouTube

Cover design by Victoria Caswell

Interior layout by K. Kaynak

ISBN (paperback) 978-1-937053-78-9
ISBN (e-book) 978-1-937053-79-6

Printed in the United States of America

The Kelpie

T. J. Wooldridge

Cast of Characters

Heather Marie MacArthur—I'm the one telling the story. And trust me, sometimes I can't keep all these people straight!

My Immediate Family

Michael MacArthur and **Aimee MacArthur** are also known as "Dad" and "Mum."

Rowan MacArthur is my next-younger brother.

Ivy and **Ash MacArthur** are my youngest sister and brother; they are twins.

Lily MacArthur is my older half-sister.

Rose Bujoirnais MacArthur is my oldest sister, whom Dad adopted.

And there's also **Hunter Milan**, who is Rose's serious girlfriend.

The Royal Family

Prince Joseph is my best friend and either third or fourth in line to the throne. I think.

Prince Christopher is Joe's dad and definitely second in line. That much I know because it's in all the papers.

Princess Maryan is Joe's mum who's from Bahrain, but swore allegiance to England so she could marry Prince Christopher.

Princess Annette is Joe's sister, next-oldest to him, and likes being called "Annie."

Prince Richard is Joe's youngest brother.

Prince Albert is Prince Christopher's younger brother.

Other Important People

The **McInnis family** is originally from Ireland. Now they live on the castle property and they are in charge of keeping it up.

Mr. Jack McInnis is in charge of all the outdoor castle stuff, like the farm and garden

Mrs. Marie McInnis runs everything about what goes on inside the castle.

Miss Eliza McInnis is the Mcinnis' daughter who works at the castle. She is second-in-charge to her mum.

Mickey McInnis is the McInnis' son who takes care of our farm animals.

Ginny Roberts is Mum and Dad's assistant who keeps all of our schedules mostly sane.

Anita Cano is our nanny, who I'm way too old for, but who cares about all of us. Even Mum and Dad, sometimes.

Jonathan is Joe's immediate bodyguard, the *nice* one.

To Travis,
for being an awesome brother.

Chapter 1

"Kids on the telly do this sort of stuff all the time..." *Nothing could go wrong with that.*

I can't honestly say I was joking when I suggested to my best friend, Joe—Prince Joseph, eldest son of England's Crown Prince—that we could probably find something the police had missed in regards to the missing tourist children. They were all the news in my family's little corner of the Borders for the past week and a half, so of course we were interested in helping. After all, eleven- and twelve-year-olds like us did that *all the time* on the telly and in the books we read.

I also can't honestly say whether Joe was in full agreement or if he just wanted another reason to ditch the annoying guard shadowing us. It was a new guy; Joe's usual bodyguard, Jonathan, was on holiday and didn't hover so much. With New Guy close enough to hear the gory details, I certainly wasn't about to tell Joe about the hell that was the last whole month of school. Not that I really wanted to talk about it, but if there was anyone I *could* talk to about nearly getting expelled for standing up for my other best friend and then having her yanked out of school and me having to face all the other girls who hated me all by myself...well, it would be Joe.

It was also the first completely sunny and warm day since school had let out, which gave us a great excuse to want to walk the hedge maze. The hedge maze Hovering Bodyguard had never been in before.

Regardless of our intentions, we used the secret exit we'd made in the maze and ran to the stables. From there, we threw a halter and lead ropes on Opulent Majesty, Mum's Shire stallion (dumb idea number one), grabbed helmets (redeeming choice number one), and rode him bareback (dumb idea number two) down to the loch where two children had gone missing last week, while we were still at school (dumb ideas number three through three hundred).

Neither of us was sure what we'd find, but a murderous faery water horse was *not* on either of our minds.

We were almost to the loch when Oppie (you never use a horse's full name unless you're really angry) gave a little hop and a shake. It wasn't quite a buck, but he'd been trying to turn around and go back home for half the ride. It was a warning, apparently. I gripped his mane, and Joe gripped me, breathing a word I knew was a curse in Arabic. It was a long fall from a seventeen-and-a-half-hand horse.

"We're almost to the loch," Joe said. "Let's walk."

I let him slide down first, then followed.

Oppie pranced nervously, something I'd never seen him do, and curled his lips back, scenting the air. It should have been another hint about how bad our idea was, but we weren't paying attention. Instead, I wrapped his lead rope around a lower-hanging bough so he wouldn't leave us (I've lost count of what number dumb idea that was.).

We'd ridden to the loch via that route, through my ancestors' grove of trees, many times. Just ahead, we could see the glimmering water.

Joe put a hand on my shoulder and stopped walking. "You hear that?"

"What?" I smirked at the cliché.

"Yeah… Exactly," he frowned, clearly not intending any cliché. I listened, and it was dead quiet. No birds, no incessant sheep *baa*s, nothing. Except for Oppie's nervous stomping behind us. The wind was dead and I couldn't even pick up the sound of the ocean against the cliffs that were so close, we could have walked to them, too.

There was a slight smell of brine, which wasn't unusual because the nearby sea often flowed into this particular loch. The smell mixed with dead and rotting things—which *was* unusual.

Water sloshed as if someone were just getting out from a swim. Rings rippled out from a bunch of plants moving towards the shore. Those…plants…slipped from the water, stepping up, revealing the weed-covered body of a horse.

Not a horse. The nightmare of a horse. It curled its lips. Beneath the greenish black lips were sharp, shark-like teeth—not the teeth of gentle hay-eating horses.

Its eyes reflected—or glowed—red in the sun.

"Heather…?" Joe's voice trembled. He took my arm, pulling me back towards the trees.

Behind us, Oppie screamed. There was a crack like thunder, and the ground quaked with hoof beats. As he galloped towards us, his head was pulled down by the bough dragging behind him, tangled in the lead rope.

His baritone scream echoed again, and he stopped just behind us. He lowered his head, arching his back almost like a stalking cat. Nostrils flaring, he wove towards us, neck extended like a snake crawling through grass. His posture sent shivers up my spine. Despite Oppie being the only stallion in our herds, no horse on our property was gentler than he was! And now I was terrified of him.

A grunt and growl behind us yanked our attention to the other…creature. It matched Oppie's posture, twice as terrifying with its hellish appearance.

The two circled us.

The water horse charged first.

Joe yanked me out of the way, and we both fell to the ground.

I cowered beside him as the ground trembled with 2000 kilos of furious stallion. Oppie's black dinner-plate hoof planted only a breath from our faces.

Kelpie—the memory of the faery tales Mum told us and wrote about slithered into my mind. This…*this* must be a kelpie.

The kelpie reared. Oppie towered over us like a guardian monster, protecting the stupid human youths of his herd. The lead-rope-tangled limb danced as he reached the apex of his rear.

Oppie hadn't even wanted to come.

The kelpie lunged. Defying physics, Oppie twisted and hammered his back legs into the charging monster that wasn't all that much smaller than he was. The kick pounded the kelpie to the ground where it threw up dirt, flailing its own jagged hooves that were feathered with water-weed fetlocks. Oppie's momentum flung the broken tree limb, and it landed on the ground, wedging beneath a rock. The Shire lunged at the fallen water horse, but the pinned limb anchored him.

I crawled towards the limb and rock.

"Heather! What are you doing?" Joe hissed at me, following.

"He's stuck." I was the idiot who'd wrapped the lead line that had ended up tangled. I yanked the knife from my work boot to saw the rope, but a sickening crack whipped the lead rope's shattered clip at us. We dodged most of the pieces save one sharp bit that cut across my arm. The stallion jumped forward with his new-found freedom.

The kelpie reared, turning but not losing ground. It still blocked our way from the woods we'd come from. Oppie didn't charge; he stayed near Joe and me, keeping the water horse from us. Both equines, mortal and fae, paced and sized each other up.

Oppie's maneuver left us room to get to our feet without eight oversized hooves pounding around us. Though Joe was on his feet first, I followed too soon for him to even offer a hand.

"Now what?" His eyes were glued on Oppie and the kelpie.

"I…don't know."

The kelpie charged again. I could see it favoring the hip that Oppie had kicked, and it was furious. Its eyes blazed orange-red, flickering like flames. The afternoon sun gave the slick black coat a slimy green sheen. Its nostrils hissed steam, and its long muzzle angled sharply, like it'd been hacked out of wood with kitchen knives.

Oppie avoided an oncoming charge and reared to his full height, beating towards the kelpie's skull. His white fetlocks fluttered like avenging angel wings so high Joseph and I had to strain to see, even as we backed farther away in terror. The kelpie veered away and tried to circle around.

It shifted its fiery gaze from Oppie to us and sneered, revealing blood-rust, needle-pointed teeth stained green at the gums. The Shire landed, turned tightly, and pushed back at the faerie.

"Trees!" I pointed. Joe nodded. We darted that direction. The kelpie was faster. In a rollback so fluid it'd make any of my riding team—even my perfect sister—green with envy, the water horse changed direction, striking its front hooves at Oppie. As unusually athletic as our Shire was, he couldn't move the mass of his body out of the way fast enough. Blood dripped across his silver chest. Then, the kelpie charged us.

I don't know which of us changed direction first, but Joe and I turned towards the water.

Oppie's deep scream and the thunder of his gallop stopped us. Without looking, I could feel the pressure of his approach and shoved Joe to the side—and back on the ground. The Shire jumped over us. His landing resonated deep into our guts as he grunted several times. The kelpie screeched back. It must've moved faster than either of us saw because now it faced off with Oppie, hind legs in the brackish water it called home. As if drawing strength from its source, the kelpie reared again, shaking blood and salt water from itself, then leaping with unnatural grace and strength to the other side of us before Oppie, huffing and limping, could intercept.

We were between the horses again.

The kelpie came at us, pushing towards the water.

"Don't touch the water," Joe said.

"No, really?" I growled. He glared at me. Both of us searched for an opening as the stallions attacked each other again. "Maybe the bank?" I gestured with my chin to where a grassy hill crested above the sandy embankment, where the water lapped hungrily.

Joe nodded. "We can cut towards the trails in two different directions."

The path took us dangerously close to the fighting horses, but I could see Oppie's dark eyes flashing every so often. He knew where we were.

We were his herd; he'd protect us.

We edged for the bank, then darted as Oppie rushed the kelpie again. I winced seeing how much of his blue-grey chest and shoulder were red with blood. The water sparkled below us, deceptively pretty in the sunlight. Joseph took my hand and ran towards the azalea bushes growing along the embankment. They were still close to the water, some with roots hanging like skeletal fingers reaching for the fresher water that still moved with the tide.

They offered cover, though, and we could stay within them for a good part of the way home. Any other path would require us to dodge fighting horses.

At the very least, we were still smaller than the kelpie, and once we were clear, Oppie could retreat. He'd find us.

The kelpie was having none of it. Was the faery monster smarter than our draught? Psychic, maybe? It galloped away from the Shire, then turned to cut us off.

Oppie pounded to our rescue.

When the Shire was only a meter or so from us, the kelpie changed direction. Oppie turned. We could feel the heat radiating from his body. The ground crumbled beneath his back hooves. Beneath us.

We all fell beneath the shifting earth. Somehow neither Joe nor I was hit by flailing hooves, though I felt hard *clack*s against the helmet I still wore. For a brief moment, I felt every molecule of breath squeezed out of my body as Oppie rolled over me. I don't know how I wasn't killed or crushed, but I lay frozen as water pasted sand around me. I couldn't even gasp.

"Heather!" Joe was beside me, his normally dark face like a ghost, painted with splashes of mud. "Heather? God, Heather!"

A wave broke over us, but Joseph stayed close, kneeling in shifting sand even as he lifted an arm to protect his face. I heard the splashes and horse screams as if they were coming down a tunnel or through static-spewing headphones.

"Heather!"

Joe had a hand under my neck and side and the world tipped over. I sucked in air that burned my throat like razors and salt. Then, I coughed out red blood and sickly green water.

Loch weed tangled around my wrists and knees.

"Come on, Heather!" I felt Joe pulling me up. I broke away from the weeds, snapping them as more seemed to find whatever part of me touched the water. My now-soaked and muddied braids flogged my back, and mud dripped from under my helmet down my neck and face. We staggered backwards towards where the collapsed hill offered dry land. I saw even more weeds climbing and tangling around Joe's legs. He fell.

"Ow!" Joe cursed, trying to pull himself up. "Bloody rocks!" I gave him my hand and tried to yank him to his feet, but the water surged and more weeds grappled at him. Blood stained the leg of his jeans, and he grimaced in pain.

"Priiiiiiiiiiiinnnnnzzz." The kelpie stopped and looked right at us, mouth agape and nostrils flared. Its fiery eyes seemed to glow even brighter. Oppie was fighting the weeds tangling his legs as well. The kelpie took a step towards us, head lowered, smiling wickedly, predator teeth bared. "Yourr blooood. Ssmellss. Sso. Goo—"

Neither Joe nor I could repress shuddering an "aaurgh!" at the eerie sound of its voice. Its voice! The thing *talked!*

One thrash. One splash. Oppie's rear legs connected with the kelpie's jaw. Another tearing splash and the Shire was mostly free, jumping and battering the downed kelpie further into the now-cloudy red and black water.

"Come on! Move it! Move!" Joe and I both shouted, pulling each other from the now-retreating weeds onto dry ground.

We managed one breath in and one out before Oppie galloped towards us. He stopped, hooves right beside our feet, and snorted angrily, brown eyes bugging and staring at the churning water. I gave Joe a leg up onto the Shire's ginormous back and let him heft me up. His face strained in pain as he tried to grip the broad back with his injured leg while balancing my weight as I used his boot and Oppie's mane to pull myself up—as if I were scaling a mountainside.

I heard the kelpie scream from the water. And I heard more splashing.

I was barely seated when Oppie took off. I clung to his mane while Joe gripped my middle. We hung on for dear life, and it was only the strength of our utter terror that let us hold on as we flew between trees.

Oppie stumbled into a trot, nearly falling. It was enough to knock me and Joe off his back. We fell onto each other in a pile, helmets banging against each other, and grunted some choice words, but we were only scuffed and bruised.

"Oh. My. God. That…that really just happened?" Joe's eyes were wider than I'd ever seen them as he brushed mud off of his now not-bleeding leg.

I shook my head. "I…I don't even know." I was still fighting to catch my breath.

"That was…? What…what the…" Joe let loose a curse, in English, I'd never expected to hear from his princely self, "…*was* that?" He looked at me.

I swallowed hard. "A kelpie. I think. Mum wrote about them once..." I bit my lip, shaking my head as the whole scene replayed itself in my head.

"Really? I mean—"

Beside us, Oppie started coughing raggedly, leaning heavily on his left side. He barely rested his right hoof on its edge. It was caked with blood that still flowed from a much deeper wound on his shoulder. He just stared at us as we stood up.

"Oh, baby, I'm so sorry!" I didn't care that tears choked my voice. My best friend. One of my favorite horses. They both could have been... I didn't want to even think it. I felt worse than I'd ever felt in my life—and I hardly had a scratch.

Oppie just turned away and limped down the familiar trail towards our home. Joe limped, too, but didn't look nearly as disappointed in me as the horse did. I looked away, guiltily, and walked at Oppie's shoulder. Joe followed behind me, leaning just a little on the muscled and not-bleeding rear leg. He was staring at me, looking like he was still lost in thought. It took him a second to realize I was watching him over my shoulder.

"There could have been some loose horse on the trails," he quickly offered.

I nearly tripped on a branch. "*What?*" What was he on about? We'd just run into a killer faery monster that my mum wrote fantasy stories and folklore research about, not some regular old loose horse!

He pulled off his helmet, then continued, "You've got the whole park around the loch. Someone could've gone riding on a spooky horse...or maybe it had rabies and attacked? Horses have rabies? We could say it was frothy at the mouth?"

It took me a second to realize he was coming up with what we'd tell our parents. Right. Joe could do that, go and be all in-control and cool like *that*, no matter how much trouble we got in. It probably went with being royal or something. I tried to pull my brain into planning mode, too. "If there were a chance of rabies, they might put Oppie down without even testing him." I took off my own helmet and shook out the mud. My heavy braids deepened the pain in my head with each swing, so I wrapped one around my shoulders and began unplaiting the other.

"Okay, just a spooky horse then. It got a few good kicks on Oppie, we fell off, and it ran off." He paused. "By a stream of some sort."

"We're covered in loch weed."

"We can pull it off." When I didn't answer, he said, "I'm *trying* to help here, Heather."

"It's all my fault, and my stupid idea and now you're hurt and Oppie's hurt real bad and—"

"You know how American you sound when you get upset?"

"What does *that* have to do with anything?" I looked back at him again, eyes narrowed.

"Nothing." He offered me a weak smile. "Just trying to make you laugh or something. We're alive. We're okay. Even Oppie will heal up—"

"But… It almost…" I couldn't even speak the awful things I was thinking could have happened. That-that *kelpie* wanted to kill us! Wanted to *eat* us! Especially Joe, my best friend. "And it's all my fault for dragging you out here with this stupid plan!"

"If I had said I wasn't coming, you wouldn't have decided to go play Sleuthy MacInvestigator by yourself." He reached forward and pulled hair out of my face. "And we *are* okay. All right? Now, listen, we need a good story so we both don't end up *dead* when we see our parents."

I sighed and gently finger-combed the now-loose half-a-head of muddy hair. "We could've fallen in the mud, and we could use the hose to clean ourselves and Oppie off, which'll get most of the plants off us."

"Good idea. See, I knew we'd think of something. And between your mum and McInnis, I'm sure we can make Oppie right as rain, as they say, right?"

"I guess." I sighed, began unplaiting the other half of my hair, then dropped it, turning around and walking backwards so I could better look at Joe. His thick, wavy black hair stood out in about twenty directions, half-caked with mud. He smiled at me, which only ended up making me feel worse. "I'm so sorry! I am! I—"

"I know. We're all right, though. It's all right." He took my free hand in his and squeezed it, still smiling.

I wanted to believe him, but despite Oppie's limp, the horse was still rigid, ears and eyes alert. I could feel his tension beneath the water, blood, and fur; he was still ready for an attack.

I nodded at Joe, turned around, and returned my attention to my hair, which was wrapping and sticking to my fingers like the loch weed. I could feel whatever was still frightening my horse in me, too, along with an unnatural chill that I somehow knew didn't come from the wet clothes or hair.

Chapter 2

Families.
They just make everything...well...complicated.

Once upon a time, the McInnis family had lived on my family's castle grounds and worked for a great-great uncle that we hadn't known. When he saw my dad on the show *Who Do You Think You Are?,* Great-great Uncle William MacArthur sent us family records and the deed to the falling-apart castle just before he died. Since my parents fall into the "reasonably famous" category of people—and my mum was an American, of all things, the McInnises were scared of losing the land and life they'd known for generations.

My parents, on the other hand, had been worried that the McInnis family wouldn't *want* to stay with them in charge, and there was *no* way they could keep up a castle and all its grounds with just our family, no matter how cool it was to live there.

After some conversation between both parties, the McInnises, their children, and their grandchildren became extended family. Just like Anita, our super-nanny, and Ginny, Mum and Dad's super-personal assistant, who had even stuck with us as we moved from London to the "boonies," as Mum said, of Scotland.

Because the McInnises were like family, Mr. McInnis' cold regard and disapproving stare as he entered the stable stung me a lot more than it did His Royal Highness, who was used to distant "staff" in his parents' stables at the Mews. I could also tell from the look in Mr. McInnis' eyes that he knew we were lying three words into our carefully concocted stories. He said nothing, though. After all, he knew better than to accuse royalty of lying.

Only Joe's parents had that right. Joe had only come with his mum, today, but even so manners would prevent either of his parents from making a scene before non-royalty.

Where that left us after this visit, I didn't know. It just meant I didn't have to think about punishment right at this moment.

Not overt punishment, anyway.

"Heather, this is going to use up all of the tranqs in this stable and the main one, and likely all your bute—and that'll just last for today. So, 'less you want this horse in pain shortly, run down and get more from Mickey in our yard."

I clenched my teeth. The McInnis farmhouse was almost a mile from our Shire stable. And I was wearing wet clothes and jeans, which already chafed and scraped. Walking was going to hurt enough. Jogging might as well be torture.

But it was my fault this all happened, no matter what Joe said.

"Yessir," I replied and loped out of the stable.

I passed my younger brother, Rowan, on the way. I felt his dark eyes, Dad's eyes, on me for a few minutes before hearing his running footfalls and watching him fall into pace beside me. He didn't say anything, but that was normal for him. Talking still came hard after years of speech therapy. On the other hand, he could communicate more with a look than even my actor dad. He wanted to know what happened and had seen Joe and me sneaking Oppie into the stable.

"I don't want to talk about it. I just need to get bute, a med kit, and probably some extra tranqs from Mickey." My voice was almost gone and hurt as I spoke.

Rowan nodded and broke into a run, his gangly eight-year-old legs looking more ungraceful than they probably were because he basically disappeared before my eyes. One of the white peahens that someone had given us as a housewarming present (what else do you get a family who inherits a castle?) scurried out of his way with a cry (answered by a sheep somewhere). Within a few minutes, he was back with a leather duffel bag slung over his shoulder. Only obvious to those of us who knew him, the slight smile on his almost-girly lips betrayed that he was rather proud of his achievement and happy to help.

"Thanks, Rowan."

"We get each other. Me and Mickey," was all he said with a nod. Mickey was Mr. McInnis' son who had autism like Rowan—or at least, that's how Mum explained it. I never heard any of the McInnises say anything directly about Mickey except that he just had to "do things a little differently."

I nodded, and we jogged back to the Shire stable in mutually comfortable silence. He didn't say it either, but of all our siblings, I was also the only one who seemed to get him… and more often than not, he got me. Especially when I didn't have my older sister, Lily, around. A few times, when Mum wasn't home and Dad couldn't quite get Rowan down from a meltdown, I'd been able to.

Mr. McInnis nodded—at Rowan—and quickly stuck Oppie with one more needle of the tranquilizer. For his part, Oppie snorted and made a few half-hearted nips and stomps in Mr. McInnis' direction before his head started to drop.

"What happened?" Mickey stiffly strode into the stable. Rowan must've asked him to come, too. He exchanged an actual nod of greeting to Rowan and sort-of nods to the rest of us as he walked towards Oppie.

"Loose horse ran us off the trail and got into a fight with Oppie," Joe stated matter-of-factly, crossing his arms and puffing out his chest.

Outside, one of the peacocks gave another doleful cry.

"Must've been hurt." Mickey spoke almost monotone as he ran his fingers and a clean cotton wipe along the gash that went from Oppie's shoulder to his chest. He may as well have been able to do magick with the animals, but he still struggled to speak easily. He frowned at the damage, took a sniff, and plucked out the one remaining bit of plant that I'd managed to miss. "Down by the loch? Didn't—"

"No, we weren't," Joe said firmly. "Just out on the trails."

"Loch weed." Mickey stated, back still to us, holding up the offending vegetation.

"We were not down by the loch," Joe repeated, and I felt sick to my stomach.

Mickey turned a quarter of the way towards us and glared at the floor by our feet. His over-six-foot frame hunched even more than it had when he pulled out the vine. "No, loch water and weed, I need to—"

"Are you calling me a liar?"

More comments from the peafowl gallery; some sheep echoed in.

"Joe!" I put my hand on his arm. Mickey didn't know better.

Mr. McInnis put an arm around his son's shoulders, giving me a look but avoiding Joe's eyes. "Just treat it for what it needs, boyo. Let it be."

"But—"

"Does it need stitches, Mickey?" Rowan interrupted, giving me (not Joe—he never made eye contact with Joe) a really dirty look.

"It needs to be cleaned better first so it doesn't get infected," he answered. "Then stitches. A lot of cuts…" His fingers traced around just above the wounds. "Very accurate for a panicked horse. Especially here and on the face." He pointed to the other cuts that still seeped blood, then he stopped and pushed aside Oppie's heavy mane. "And a dog? A big one?"

Joe and I looked at each other.

Mickey looked at our piece of floor accusingly. "Not horse teeth marks. Sharp, like a dog."

Joe stood even taller, giving Mickey a withering look. I straightened up and gave Joe an even stronger look—and I was almost two inches taller than him.

"Just take care of it, lad." Mr. McInnis shifted his weight so he was between us and Mickey.

Mickey shot his dad a look I knew too well. Rowan had the same look when he was frustrated at a situation that he knew wasn't fair and couldn't wrap his mind around. It usually preceded a tantrum. Except Mickey was almost forty, and I almost wondered what a forty-year-old autistic tantrum looked like.

"He's hurt, Mickey, lad," Mr. McInnis said gently, more of his Irish accent coming out. "You'll help the poor boy, won't ye?"

Mickey squeezed his eyes shut a few times in awkward blinks, then turned his attention back to Oppie. Rowan held up Mickey's case. Without a word, he continued cleaning, working with methodical perfection. I reached to help clean some of the smaller scrapes along Oppie's legs, but Mickey shooed me away, so I went to stand by Joe.

"Joseph!" Joe's mother, Her Royal Highness Princess of Wales Maryan, called. She was originally from Bahrain, and you could hear it in her accent. The tabloids and news still had *opinions* about her.

"Come on." Joe took my hand.

"I—" I glanced back at Oppie.

"Go," Mr. McInnis said.

Lowering my head, I let Joe drag me out of the stable.

"Oh my goodness! What happened to you? Are you both all right?" Princess Maryan dropped the towel she'd been wiping her manicured hands with and rushed over to us, grabbing Joe by the shoulders and inspecting him. I shrank back as the two dark-suited guards flanked her, turning their dark glasses in my direction.

"Heather! What happened?" My mum was at my side just as quickly, entirely ignoring the guards. One looked firmly in her direction.

"We were just out in the trails and a loose horse—still all tacked up—freaked out and basically ran us off into the trees," Joe explained confidently. "We just got a little roughed up from falling off Oppie. He's a big horse. The McInnises are taking care of him now with Rowan."

"You're hurt! And what on earth were you doing on the trails? You know about the two children who went missing last week!" The princess's voice grew angrier as she continued. "Graeme told us you purposely lost him! I've got Alex and Josh on the trails now." The pristine knee of her fancy riding breeches dropped to the ground, and she turned him around and started peeling open the tear in his designer jeans to inspect the wound on his hip. Behind her, I saw one of the other guards type into his phone, probably calling back the other two guards.

"Mother!" Pink colored Joe's cheeks as he turned away from me and pulled himself from her. "We didn't go very far. It's fine. We're fine, and Graeme was being—"

"I don't care how you think Graeme was being. His job is to protect you! And your *responsibility* is to not get yourself—or your friends…" She gave me a mother-like onceover and turned to my own mum, who was also giving me the same eyeball treatment. "…into any danger." Her unusual green eyes were sharp. Joe shrank a bit when she returned her gaze to him.

"I cleaned it up in the loo." He took a breath, regaining his usual composure. "Really, I'm fine. We're fine. Promise." He bent to kiss her cheek.

She tightened her lips and did not return the kiss, then stood up and one of the dark-suited guards handed her another clean towel. She pressed it to her son's hip.

"Ow! Mum, I'm fine, I swear!"

Frowning, she patted it against the dirt smears on his face. "Alert the local police about the loose horse. It could be sick or injured if it was acting like that," she stated. A quick glance over her shoulder had one guard turn away to do just that. "Did it bite any of you? The other horse?" She glanced at my mum. "Aimee, if the horse was ill…"

"If there's anything wrong with Oppie, Jack and Mickey will notice and act appropriately." Now that the princess was done scolding Joe, I got *the look* from my mum.

"They're not proper vets, though." Princess Maryan's voice was tight despite the polite smile. "Doctor Rivka is coming down in a few days to check on Artemis Rose and see how the twins are developing. Why don't I ask him to look at your Shires, too? Especially your pregnant mares?"

"Dr. Caroline trusts Mickey like a colleague," Mum answered. "But extra eyes are always good, so thank you. He'll be able to find this place okay? You know how wonderfully the GPS functions around here."

Maryan laughed, relaxing just a little. As she did so, I felt Joe sigh in slight relief. She ran a hand through her perfect raven-black hair, smoother and shinier than Joe's. "If you didn't remind us each visit about that old oak, Harold might take out the front end of the Rolls. I'll make sure to give your cell to Dr. Rivka." She lightly patted my mother's shoulder and the two leaned in for delicate kisses on each cheek. "He's really looking forward to seeing your Artemis and how she's getting along with the pregnancy. I still can hardly believe you found her in one of the meat pens! The waste." She clucked and shook her head. "My father would have paid a million pounds for a mare in her line. I look forward to meeting those foals. All of them. The Shire Association has sent wonderful letters regarding your work, you know."

"Thank you." Mum answered, smiling more.

"There you are!" My dad came down the hill with another two guards and our two greyhounds, Isis and Osiris. Unaware of the moving commotion, another peacock strutted behind them, showing off his jewel-toned tail. "What on earth happened to you? You're soaked!" My dad jogged over.

"Loose horse on the trails," I mumbled as he pushed my hair from my face and kissed my forehead. That was about the extent I could say to him without feeling even guiltier for lying. Oppie had been loose on the trails, so it *was* kind of the truth.

"What on earth were you two doing on the trails?!" He stood, crossing his arms and giving me his version of *the look*. "After those two kids went missing? Heather Marie, you *know* better!" I didn't answer, so he gave me another look.

"It was just a short ride, Mr. McArthur," Joe spoke first, head lowered and looking properly apologetic. "I'm very sorry to have worried you all. We just wanted a little bit more space. I never get to see Heather, and we can't really talk about school and stuff with guards *hovering*." Joe shot a dirty look at the freckled, small-nosed guard who had followed my dad down.

Princess Maryan's eyes hardened on her son now. "You *know* there is good reason you are assigned guards. Even without the worry with the missing children. The park off this property is *public* land!"

"We're sorry, really!" I squeaked, feeling awful for the look Joe was getting from his mother. "We weren't thinking, Princess Maryan. It won't happen again."

The princess sighed, shaking her head. "We do need to be on our way. Your father, sister, and brother are meeting us in Edinburgh on the hour." She returned to brushing mud from Joseph's clothing. "You're quite the mess, and it's not like I pack extra clothes for you. You're too old for that. Harold's going to have to see to the car being cleaned out."

"I have a couple of jeans that might fit, and maybe a T-shirt," I offered. When Joe raised an eyebrow at the sparkling unicorn across my chest, I added, "The not-girly kind, even."

Princes Maryan and my mum looked at each other with furrowed brows.

"Those army pants you have are boy's pants," Joseph perked up. "You said they didn't make them for girls. And maybe just a black T-shirt?"

"You can change in Rowan's room. Come on."

Dad's hand tightened on my shoulder, and I looked at Princess Maryan, who paused a moment before nodding approval. At the slight movement of her head, Joe had my hand again and we were running to the kitchen door of the castle.

"The army pants are my favorite. You know that!" I scowled as he only just barely remembered to hold the door for me.

"You'll get them back. Promise!" he said. "It's a good reason for us to come visit again."

"They'll probably just send them with the vet or a courier."

Joe pouted at me. "I'll ask, anyway. I'm sure Mum will want to see the horses again. You should see her at my grandfather's. You'd swear she was our age the way she plays with them all. And she likes your mum, anyway."

"I guess…"

He paused on the narrow staircase that went upstairs from the kitchen and gave me a grin. "What, you don't want me to come visit again this summer?"

"No, I just… Half the time something comes up," I frowned. "You know…"

He gave me a pained look. "I know, but my family *likes* coming here. Especially Mum. And me. Have a little faith in me?"

I couldn't help but laugh.

"But of course, Your Highness." I made a sweeping gesture with my arm, which he swatted before sticking out his tongue and racing up the winding stone staircase.

"Where do you keep your trousers?" he called.

"Don't you *dare* go through my drawers!" I screamed back. "Prince or not, I'll deck you into next week!"

"What's wrong, love?" Ginny, my parents' super-assistant, hardly looked up from her computer as I passed her office later that afternoon. I was failing in my covert attempts to see if my parents had come in from the stables yet. The shower I'd taken after Joe and his mum left would only delay the confrontation, I was sure.

"Nothing." I continued toweling off my hair.

"Heather?" My dad stopped outside Ginny's office and looked at me. "Can we talk?" There was an edge to his voice. His hand was in his pocket, and I knew he was fiddling with his pill bottle. He only kept it on him when he felt his moods swinging more than usual. He hated taking them, and sometimes joked that he hoped they might work by osmosis. On a good day, I'd remind him that osmosis was only for water, and he'd say if I was going to be smart, I should put more effort into establishing world peace or something useful.

Today was not a good day.

"Sure," I said.

He nodded his head towards the office he shared with Mum.

"Heather, what happened today?" he asked as he sat at his desk near the back of the office. I borrowed Mum's chair and rolled it so I sat across from him. As I sat, I couldn't stop bouncing my knees anxiously.

"Joe's—"

"*Prince* Joseph," he corrected.

I frowned. Joe *asked* me to call him "Joe" two years ago when we first met. I was already in trouble, though. "Prince Joseph's guard wouldn't even let us get, like, four feet away from him, so we couldn't talk. We just wanted a little space. It was my idea to take Oppie because he's the best of all the horses and could carry both of us, easy. It was a dumb idea, I know, and I'm sorry."

"*Heather...*"

"We didn't go far on the trails." The loch wasn't that far, really. And I was already hating myself for thinking of taking us there after what happened! "We just...we just couldn't find any space around here."

"Heather."

"I'm sorry! It was stupid, especially knowing about those missing kids, I admit it. It won't happen again, I swear!"

He tightened his lips. "This *will not* happen again. Prince Joseph's family insists that there must be guards—"

"Dad, no!" I couldn't keep the whine from my voice. "*Prince Joseph* hates that. He just wants to be *normal*—"

"It's not up for discussion, Heather. Period. Even if you hadn't both run into the park *after two kids went missing,* Prince Joseph's *family* makes the decision, not you, not Prince Joseph, and not even me." His voice was gentler, but still firm. "But I do agree with them. If anything, *anything* happens to him on our property…you can't begin to imagine." He shook his head. "The fact he was injured—"

"It was just—" *A monster kelpie wanted to eat him,* scolded my brain, but Dad already cut me off.

"Heather, you have *no* idea!"

I folded my arms and slouched angrily. No, I didn't. And I didn't want to either. Joe liked being my friend and escaping from being royal all the time. Next time, we just had to make sure not to run into any faery monsters.

"So, next time we get a visit, if there is a next time, you will not go out alone with him without one of the guards. You *will not* leave the castle grounds—"

"What do you mean 'if there is a next time'?" I sat up. "His parents can't be that mad! It was just an accident and we're both still safe!"

"Prince Christopher is next in line to England's crown. Prince Joseph is his firstborn. If they think their child is in danger—even from accidents—they will not put him in those situations."

"Then why even bother making a stupid rule about always having guards!" I couldn't stop the tears stinging my eyes. Never see Joe again? Never have him visit? I hadn't thought of that as a consequence of us surviving.

"You're right. I don't think anyone would have brought up requiring you both being accompanied if there definitely would not be a 'next time.'. Prince Joseph's parents are reasonable. I just want you to understand the weight of the situation, Heather."

"Believe me, I get it." I sniffled and glared at the box of tissues on his desk before grabbing one. Dad had no idea how badly I *got* it! I dabbed at my nose, but still did my best to rein in the tears that stung my eyes. I was *not* a baby; I should be able to deal with this. I took a deep breath and waited for things to get worse. Mum and Dad would have talked to Mr. McInnis and Mickey by now. Mickey would have said something about the loch weeds and water.

"So, do you want to tell me why you decided to go into the park when two children disappeared last week?"

I looked up at him. His face was kinder now, and he leaned back in his office chair. I blinked. He was giving me an out, a show of good faith; I knew it, despite the angry crease that still lined between his eyebrows.

"Not really. We just wanted...to go out and just, you know, have an adventure."

Dad stared at me for a few minutes, then sighed. "Come here, love. Come here."

I stood and walked around his desk. He sat up in his chair and took my hands in his, and I let him pull me into his lap even though my legs were so long my heels dragged on the floor. He hugged me tightly, and I hugged him back, feeling more tears threaten escape. "Do you have *any* idea what it would do to us if something happened to you, baby? All of us? Me, your mum, your sisters and brothers?" he whispered. "Any idea?"

I rubbed my eyes on his shoulder. "I'm sorry, Dad. I really am." And I was. Really, really sorry.

After another hug, he pushed me from him enough so we could look each other in the eye. He still rubbed my arms, but frowned fiercely. "I want you to promise me that you will never, ever put yourself in danger like that again! I want your word, Heather."

I nodded. "I promise, Dad, I swear, I'll stay safe. I promise!"

He stared at me for a few more minutes. Squeezing my hands once more, he nodded and let me go.

I stood up but kissed his cheek once more. "I promise, Dad, I really do."

"Good girl." He glanced at his watch. "Your mum and Rowan are still down in the yard with Oppie, Jack, and Mickey. Your sister should be calling in less than ten minutes. Go round them up, okay?"

"Sure thing," I said. "And…thanks, Dad…and I really am sorry. And I love you."

He smiled. "I love you, too. Very much—and don't leave that wet towel on your mother's chair, love. She'll have a fit!"

"Right." Grabbing my towel, I deposited it in the laundry chute as I jogged back out to the stables.

"Your father talked to you?" Mum asked coolly as she watched Mickey finish up the last of the stitches on Oppie. Two more empty tranquilizer needles balanced on the nearby stall wall.

"Yes, Mum. I'm really, really sorry…for everything."

"You remember that two kids went missing last week, right?"

"We talked about that, and I'm really sorry! It was stupid to go out there."

"Did he even mention the fact you were out *on a stallion*?" She hardly raised her voice and only looked at me from the corner of her eye.

I shook my head. I knew I was already in too much trouble to protest. I hadn't even thought of that; it's not like it was a rule or anything. I sort-of got why Mum was making a big deal out of it; stallions are normally more dangerous than any other type of horse, on account of wanting to mate all the time. Stallion or not, though, Oppie was sweeter than just about anyone but Mum's own horse. He wouldn't hurt anyone! "I really am sorry, Mum, I am!"

She didn't say anything, keeping her arms folded as she watched Mickey tie off the stitches.

"Lily's going to call in about five minutes," I pretty much whispered.

Mum pulled out her cell phone to check the time. "Crap." She looked at Mr. McInnis.

"We're fine here, Aimee," he told her, giving me a brief evil eye. "You all can go on in. I'll give you a call if there's anything."

Mum nodded. "All right." She looked at Rowan and waited a minute for him to meet her eyes. "We're going in to talk to Lily. Let's go in, Rowan."

He scowled and leaned on Oppie's flank. The Shire sighed and shifted towards my brother, glazed eyes hardly open.

Mum stood taller and sharpened her voice and face. "Rowan, we're going inside. Jack and Mickey will take care of Oppie."

Rowan whined. Mum took a step forward. "Rowan."

They stared at each other until my brother looked away. Chuffing, he stood away from Oppie, scratching his side for a few minutes, then dragged his feet towards us. Without touching him, Mum herded him so he moved a little faster. She was good like that. She could almost always get Rowan to cooperate just by how she stood or looked at him.

We headed to our private library/family room where the big computers were. For the next several minutes, I felt like I was watching life on the telly; everything was so *normal* when, just off our property, there was a killer faery monster horse who wanted to eat Joe and me.

The whole of my family and our collected pets (two dogs, two cats, my six-year-old twin siblings, Ivy and Ash, me, Rowan, Mum, and Dad) had barely managed to arrange ourselves and set up the computer when the speakers announced Lily's incoming call from America. She was visiting her own mother,

Dad's evil ex-girlfriend, and part of allowing that visit was that they had to talk at least once every day. Even though I was expecting the call, I jumped at the bleeps, then felt embarrassed when Mum looked at me funny. I wasn't going to say Joe and I woke up a kelpie, and I was still creeped out and twitchy about it. It sounded mental, right? Dad leaned forward over the keyboard and mouse and opened the call.

"Hi, everybody!" A pixilated Lily was grinning hugely across the screen. She waved her hand, obscuring half her face. "Can you see me okay?"

We all waved back and chorused a "Hello, Lily!" Dad added, "You look beautiful. How was the flight? Did your mother pick you up without any problems?"

"Flight was boring, everything else great! Mum was there to pick me up, and omigod, you're not gonna believe this, Dad—"

"For Chrissakes, what the hell are you doing with camera three?!" boomed from behind my sister.

"Are you on set?" Dad frowned deeply." Your mother told me that she was done shooting. That's why we rushed to pack you up now, between films!"

"They called her back for a few more scenes. It's *fine*, Dad, really. You've had us on set—"

"With a proper caretaker or nanny—."

"I'm going to be *fourteen*, Dad, I don't *need* a nanny." She took a breath and I heard her force more patience into her voice, though she seemed to be vibrating on the screen. "And you've taught me how to properly behave on set, right?"

My sister had no idea I'd already put Mum and Dad in a cruddy mood. Yeesh, she had no idea there was a scary horse monster that had almost *killed* me and Joe only hours ago!

Lily continued, "Besides, Mum knew I was going to call you, so technically, *you're* watching me right now." She offered one of her ice-melting smiles that normally worked on just about any human being she wanted something from. "And *anyway*, don't you want to hear my *amazing* news?"

"What's your news, honey?" Mum quickly asked. Dad took a few deep breaths.

"Omigod!" Lily's calm, dealing-with-parents-who-hate-each-other demeanor exploded as she bounced in place. Even over the screen, her excitement was infectious, briefly chasing the monster horse from my mind. "They needed a teen girl for a certain part, and the one they originally cast now can't do it, so Mum had them try me out, at like four this morning, so we didn't sleep at all, and…" She took a really deep breath. "Igotthepart! My very first speaking role! In a major motion picture!"

"Oh my God, yeah!" I squealed, along with Mum and the twins (the latter just squealing). "That's *the* freaking awesome!"

With frustrated groans, both dogs left our over-excited presence and slunk to their beds by the courtyard windows, where they were in less danger of deafness or flailing human limbs.

Rowan nodded along with us and clapped his hands.

"That's—that's brilliant!" Dad said. "You tried out and got it?"

"Yeah! Omigod, I was so nervous! I mean, they needed someone, and Mum's in it…so *obviously* that helped, but there were two other kids who also tried out, and one was way prettier than me—"

"Impossible," Dad interrupted. Lily smiled even more, light pink coloring perfect cheeks in her heart-shaped face. My sister was drop-dead gorgeous, much to my aggravation. She'd had boys from our sister (or would that be brother?) all-boys school and the riding club sending her texts and Facebook messages since she was eleven or nearly twelve, my age.

"Anyway, they *just* made the decision, like, five minutes before I called, so I'm totally geeking out. I've got my script, look!" She reached around behind her and pulled up a sheaf of papers. "I mean, it's just one line, but I get to read the whole script, and it's so cool!"

"It's brilliant, it really is, love. I'm proud of you!" Dad said, and we all echoed the same. "Jess and her agent know how to handle your contract, right? I mean, you're not even fourteen—"

"Da-ad! I'm sure Mum and her agent can handle a contract for a one-line job. Just give her a chance, okay?" Lily rolled her eyes, but even that didn't detract from her beaming face.

I sighed and leaned on Mum, wondering if we'd avoid an argument on the first Skype call with this visit out to the States. Mum, for her part, kept quiet, as she usually did when it was an issue between Dad, Jess, and Lily.

"It won't hurt to ask her to fax us a copy. Alison and I have a *little* more experience in youth contracts. And underage working is definitely something that, legally, requires both our consent." Dad gave her a sweet and supportive smile.

Lily sighed extravagantly. "I'll *let* her *know*," she said with great effort and gesticulation. "Aaaaaaaanyway, want to hear my line?"

"But of course." Dad adjusted Ash more in his lap, so he could lean forward attentively. The rest of us followed suit.

Before she could start, Dad hopped a little on the couch, holding my giggling little brother, who must have also felt the vibration of his phone.

"Who is it?" Lily asked quickly.

"I'll get it later. We're talking with you."

"No, check! Is it Rose?"

With a sigh, Dad readjusted again and pulled out the phone.

"Aye. I can call her back—"

"I gotta go anyway. Thanks for the help! Tell Rose I got the part! Eeee!" And like that, she collected herself with a more "up to something" smile. "She's gonna want to Skype you, anyway. Love you all!"

"We love you, too, but—"

My sister blew us all kisses with both hands and closed the connection, her smile quite mischievous now. Rose also lived in California. Obviously, the two had met up already, and Lily knew something we didn't. Dad's phone buzzed again.

As I looked over his arm, I realized that there was nothing like family drama to keep one's mind away from horrible things.

"Hello, love… Aye, she just closed the connection on us when I said it was you calling. It was all a bit mysterious. She got the part, though. Yes, we're all proud of her… Yeah, we've still got Skype open. All right."

He took back the mouse from Mum, who settled back and let Ivy resettle, and opened the connection. Hunter, Rose's girlfriend for the last five years, was on the screen beside my oldest sister. Both of them looked ridiculously happy and tear-stained.

"Dad, Aimee, we're getting married!" Rose blurted out. She held her sparkling ring up to the camera.

"Married?!" More squeals broke from us as we all threw congratulations.

"Where are you getting married, then?" Mum asked. "And when?"

"Actually, we wanted to come home, or, I did. Hunter's got family in Ireland, too. Will your dad do…a lesbian marriage, Dad? Does the Presbyterian Church…are they okay with it?"

"I-I can find out from him. I'll call him tonight. When are you thinking of having it?"

"Whenever," Hunter said. She had one of those husky voices, like a jazz singer. "We haven't planned much of anything yet."

"She just asked me last night!" Rose made another squee noise and the two kissed, which made Dad and me turn away and blush. Rose was my adopted sister, but still my sister. Seeing her snog almost ranked up there with seeing my parents snog! Ugh!

"We'll work with whatever, really." Hunter hugged my sister tightly.

They yammered on about details, and I half-listened until something that actually concerned me came up: "…Lily's already asking about bridesmaid dresses—"

"Wait! If Lily's gonna be a bridesmaid—" I began.

Rose laughed. "I know it will be hard for you, Heather, but we were hoping you'd be all right with something frilly or maybe sparkly…."

I stuck my tongue out at their teasing. That was about three-quarters of my closet, despite playing both football and polo. If I could sew on ruffles or bedazzle my uniforms, that'd be perfect, but school, league, and horse show regulations took issue with that. "What about me?" Ivy demanded. "Can I be flower girl?"

Rose grinned at Hunter, who said, "We were just gonna ask you that."

Ivy did a little dance in Mum's lap, squawking happily.

"Aimee…I was gonna ask, too…" Rose bit her lip. "Would you be…matron of honor? I mean…you know…"

Mum's eyes got all wet, and she started to sniffle. "Of course, yes, yes! Thank you… Of course!" She kind of ducked behind Ivy. I saw her discreetly looking for a tissue, which Dad handed her. Mum hated people seeing her cry, but I knew Rose asking meant a lot to her. She'd stepped in, even though she and dad were "just friends," when he'd adopted Rose.

Dad held a tissue in one of his hands, not caring that his tears were obvious. "We're so happy for you, Rose! Congratulations."

When that conversation was ended, Lily called back and practiced her very first line ever with Dad for twenty minutes or so while the rest of us tried to still look more or less excited for her. Watching Miss Perfect practice her very first line was still better than thinking of…other things.

When Skype finally blipped closed, I sank into the couch with a sigh. Rowan also leaned back and gave me a look to remind me I still owed him an explanation about what happened this morning. I nodded my head towards Mum and

Dad. Rolling his eyes, he bounced off the couch and headed for his far corner of the library/family room, giving me a look that said "follow."

Rowan had a collection of chairs of different textures. I have no idea about the logic or reason for that, but there you go. Folding his legs with the grace of a dancer, he lowered himself into the blue inflatable one. It gave that deep squeak that only an inflatable chair can make. I picked the nice, normal computer chair. We stared at each other a few moments. I glanced over at Mum and Dad, who were playing with the twins, then blurted, "You know what a kelpie is?"

That gave him pause. He considered a few minutes, then responded, "A faery horse that lives in water."

"Aye, that's it."

Rowan waited for more of an explanation.

After chewing my lip a minute more. "That's what we ran into, me and Joe, down at the loch. It…might be what took those other kids who are missing."

"You really were down at the loch?" I thanked God that he matched his tone to mine or Mum and Dad woulda been over here in a second. Bad enough I disobeyed and got the prince hurt, but if I put Rowan in any danger, well, I'd be as literally dead as they could make me. "You're not supposed to go down there! Missing kids!"

"Yeah, I know. But we did. We thought we'd find clues, you know, maybe get something the police missed…help find the kids?"

"Oppie and Joseph were hurt. Really hurt for Oppie. And you-you could be missing!"

"I know!" I started, then stopped myself, glancing over to Mum and Dad who looked over at us. I gave them a smile. After a pause, Dad put a hand on Mum's shoulder, and they turned their attention to the twins. "I know," I growled again, softer this time. "I didn't mean for it to happen like that, and you have no idea how sorry I am or how bad I feel!"

"Did they ground you?"

"I…not exactly."

"What?"

I slouched in the chair. "Someone suggested to Dad that Joe might not be allowed back…and even if he is, we're going to have stupid suits on our heels the whole time. Which is even worse for Joe, 'cos he just wants to feel *normal* while he's here."

"Normal?"

Rowan had a point. Our family was far from "normal." "More normal than being a royal prince."

"What if the kelpie kidnapped you? Like…" He didn't finish, but I knew what he was thinking. He was only a baby when Jess kidnapped Lily for a second time—before Jess was declared a "fit" mother so Lily could visit again. Even overseas. He didn't know the whole of it, though, just that it was awful and Lily still had nightmares.

He flinched when I scowled at him. He also looked about ready to cry, too, so I sighed and leaned back in the chair.

"It was freaking stupid!" I whispered. "I know! I know! I swear, it's not gonna happen again! I'm done playing spy and detective forever!"

I couldn't read the look on his face as he stared at me.

"What?" I finally asked.

"I'm glad you're not kidnapped."

I slumped in his chair. "Thanks… Me, too."

Chapter 3

Not getting killed? Yay! Consequences of cheesing off a killer faery horse? Not so yay.

Mr. McInnis gave me a particularly scathing look as I entered the stable the next morning. He was hammering something into the post beside Oppie's stall. Oppie, for his part, had his ears pinned as he faced the farthest corner away from the banging, his butt towards the obvious aggravator.

I waited for Mr. McInnis to finish. When he looped the hammer into his belt, I asked, "How is he today?"

"Hard to say," was all the answer I got as the man turned and headed to the south entry of the stable. Setting up a ladder, he started nailing something into the beam above the doors leading into the paddock. I looked at the post beside the stallion's stall. A cross of farrier nails was pounded deep into the wood. I bit my lip.

How much did Mr. McInnis know about kelpies or faeries? That they were real or not? How much did he know about our adventure? I was afraid to ask. How much more trouble would I get into?

"Hey, handsome," I crooned into Oppie's stall. He didn't turn around. I opened the door and edged in. He stomped a foot, but his ears were only partly back. His left side wasn't very injured, so I ran my fingers along his flank until I got to his neck. Moving his head just a little, he gave me a look not very different from Rowan's look last night, like he was disappointed, scared, betrayed, and relieved all at once. As I ran my hand over his coat, it was clear Mr. McInnis had already groomed Oppie. In the corner, there was a pile of fresh hay, almost as tall as I was, which the horse now munched on. I stood there a few more minutes, rubbing his favorite spots on his neck and scratching around his ears.

Without warning, he started. All four hooves skipped from the ground and his legs locked. He looked back over his shoulder, then turned around, stumbling on his front feet. The tape over the clean bandages snapped and crackled.

"What is it boy? You okay?" *Should I get Mr. McInnis?*

"Helen! Damnit, you, get back here!" I heard the shouts from outside and thuds from the hopping of a recently escaped horse intent on taking the pursuing human on a chase. Helen was one of the shire mares we were breeding with Oppie. A few more choice words came from Mr. McInnis, and I heard the angry rattle of the paddock chain.

Oppie's nose flared, and he snorted several times. He pawed at the ground, then the door.

"Oh, no, you don't!" I rubbed the non-bandaged part of his right shoulder. "You're in here."

Raising his head so his lips reached the top of his stall, the horse stomped close to my feet and belted out a whinny that sent vibrations down my body.

"Whoa, hey, what is it, boy?"

"Sweet Mother of Christ!" The thunder of running hooves echoed away from the stable and paddocks. And Mr. McInnis didn't take the Lord's (or his Mother's) name in vain lightly. I slipped out of Oppie's stall and barely slid the door back before he forced his nose through. Latching it securely, I jogged out the door, the stallion's whinny reverberating around me.

Mr. McInnis was bareback on Chixie, Dad's thoroughbred. She danced in place, being especially witchy at the moment, but Mr. McInnis had control. "Get your mum, then ring down to my farm. Marie hasn't come up here yet, so have her send Mickey on one of our girls. Helen's out spooked and running. Last thing we need is something to happen to one of the pregnant mares."

"I can get on East—"

"No! Go get your mum. Do as I say, child!"

His sharp tone and "child" hit my gut like a rock. I held back a smart remark and ran back towards the castle at full speed, dialing Mum on my cell even as I ran.

"What's up, sweetie?"

"Helen got out, Mr. McInnis is after her and needs help. Says she's spooked at something. He wants me to call Mrs. McInnis and have her send Mickey up, too."

"I'll be right down." I could hear the clicking on Mum's computer. "Is she hurt? Why does he need Mickey?"

"I dunno."

"Well, give a call. I'm on my way down." Her voice was muffled, and I heard her heavy breathing and scrambling. I pictured her balancing the phone between her ear and shoulder while pulling on her work or riding boots.

I hung up and rang down to the McInnis house, relaying the story there. Since everyone was on their way, I ran over to our other stable. I froze as I approached. Every single one of our horses was at the fence line, facing the Shire stable, looking past it. Oppie's whinny echoed again, and our horses—East, Dream, and Artemis—all answered. From the distance, I heard Chixie and Sophia, the Shire mare who hadn't gotten away, also call.

It was eerie, all of them looking off into the distance, tails up, eyes bugging, nostrils flared. On top of that, I didn't hear any of the peafowl screams or sheep bleats that were the normal cacophony at the castle stables. Sometimes we could even hear the McInnis cock or one of their cows. Always, we could hear songbirds.

Now, there was no sound besides the snorting horses. Shivers prickled up and down my spine.

I thought of the loch, and the dripping, fire-eyed, shark-toothed horse monster.

I'd remembered to grab a lead rope from the Shire stable, so I hopped our fence and looped it around East's neck. "Come on," I tugged him towards the stable. He planted his feet and snorted. "East!" He wasn't budging. With a frown, I rewrapped the rope around his head so it was more like a halter. With control of his nose, I got him to move and follow me back to the stable. With him acting like this, I at least knew better than to ride without a proper bridle.

Isis and Osiris barked and yipped, circling around Mum and Dad as they came running. Dad was faster by far, and he got to the stable first. He gave me a firm look. "You are not riding off."

"But—"

"Listen to your father," Mum agreed as she dashed by, grabbing Dream's bridle and a long rope. I hardly saw her put it on before she was leading him out of the stable at a jog, lasso rope over her shoulders. Dream looked just as nervous as East, but he was Mum's baby and stood stone still as she hoisted herself upon onto the fence and hopped on his unsaddled back. "Isis, Osiris, come!" The two greyhounds followed her. They weren't exactly herding dogs, but they had done well enough in prior horse escapes.

Following right after Mum and the dogs, Mickey rode a thundering canter on one of the McInnises' Belgians; I couldn't tell which at the speed they were going.

Dad did not grab a horse and go riding off. Rather, he stayed with me. A firm look from him, and I pulled the lead rope from around East's head. My pony immediately returned to Artemis's side. I frowned at him wistfully. Even if I had gotten on him, I wouldn't have ridden well; I hadn't gotten any rank in the last few shows because I sat so awkwardly on him after my latest growth spurt.

Putting a hand on my shoulder, Dad guided me out of the stable, making sure the doors were secured behind us. Last thing we needed were any more escapees.

"What happened?"

"Helen just got out is all," I said. "Just, Mr. McInnis was acting kind of weird about it."

"Weird how, love?"

"Took Mary's name in vain and yelled at me." I looked away.

Dad raised an eyebrow. "He yelled at you?"

"He's…still really mad about yesterday."

Dad just nodded and squeezed my shoulder again. After a few minutes, he furrowed his brow and looked around.

"It is quiet."

I nodded. "It's weird."

"I wonder if a storm's coming in, and that's what spooked Helen and what's got Jack extra testy. The pressure, weather… sometimes it affects everything." He was fiddling with his pills in his pocket again.

"Maybe." I looked up at the perfectly clear blue sky. Two clear days in a row was pretty unusual, I'd learned since we moved to Scotland.

His phone buzzed and both of us jumped. With a weak chuckle, he reached for it.

"Aye?" His face grew pale, and I read that *particularly strong* oath even as he bit it back on his lips. He walked away from me.

I took a step to follow him. "Heather!" Rowan called as he jogged down from the back kitchen steps. "S'wrong?"

"Helen got out."

"That's all?" He frowned at me.

"Christ!" Like McInnis, maybe even more since his dad was a minister, Dad was not one to abuse the Lord's name.

We snapped our heads in his direction.

"I'll ask Marie to get the tractor. I'll drive down and get the stuff." He looked back at us, half-nodding at my brother.

"Heather and Rowan know what to look for? Right. Aye." He tapped off his phone. "Rowan, run and get your mum's truck keys. The twins are with Anita?"

"Aye, Dad. They're doing art."

"Good. Hurry." He dialed his phone again. "Marie, there's been an accident. Aimee said she and Jack need you to bring the tractor with…that lift thing for the horses. They're about half a kilometer northeast of the Shire stable, they can see the trees' edge…? Yeah, there. I'm driving Aim's truck down your way to get Mickey's whole bag of stuff… Aye, see you."

Rowan came back and tossed Dad the keys to Mum's truck. He hated the F-250 Mum had had shipped from the States, but his Prius wasn't going to make it out to the fields. With a sneer at the vehicle, he circled around the whole truck to get to the driver's side. Rowan, being smaller, climbed into the back seats—it was a full cab—and I took the front with Dad. With a *vroom*, we were bouncing down the dirt road connecting the main castle buildings and stables to the McInnis farm on our property.

"What's wrong, Dad?" Rowan asked first, leaning on the console between us.

"Buckle up!"

We heard the click. "Dad?"

"Helen's down. Injured, and…having a miscarriage, it sounds like."

Rowan and I gasped.

"Your mum thinks that she will pull through, but…it's complicated, and she was breaking up."

I heard my brother whimper in the back seat, even as I felt the same creep from my throat.

"Mickey needs his whole bag, tranqs, a bunch of bute… and…lots and lots of rags and antiseptic. And those long gloves. And…your mum said you probably would know what else."

"Aye," Rowan said. I nodded in agreement.

Dad had hardly put the truck in park outside the McInnis horse stable before Rowan and I jumped out and ran into the office. I grabbed the medic bag and unzipped it while Rowan dashed around, grabbing an armload of other things and stuffing them all into the bag. We tossed it into the truck bed and leapt back into the cab.

As we buckled, Dad said, "Text your mother and tell her we're on our way."

"Aye." I pulled out my phone again. "Done."

"Good girl."

The ride out to the scene blurred by in bumpy silence. Twice I heard Dad hiss a few more curse words—and he was the one who always glared at Mum when she slipped with language. He honked as he approached Mrs. McInnis on the tractor. She flipped her arm in a wave to let him know she heard. As we passed her, her face looked just as pale and tight as Dad's.

We stopped a few meters from where Jack and Mickey knelt over Helen. Mum was further back, clutching the reins of the other three nervously stomping horses.

Dad unbuckled, then paused to give us both a firm look. "Stay. Here."

"But—"

"No buts!"

He was out of the car and slammed the door. He jogged the med bag over to Jack and Mickey, then went to Mum. Isis and Osiris circled them, hackles up and ears pinned. Mum put the reins in his hands and joined the McInnises over Helen. The sun was rising higher, and we could see the glistening red on the grass by Helen's hindquarters. I rolled down my window so we could maybe hear. Rowan climbed into the driver's seat and did the same. Even though the wind was coming from inland, we could smell salty sea air along with the metallic blood scent. I shivered, imagining the monster horse watching us with malicious glee. Would it attack so many humans? Mostly adults?

Dad was not a horse person. He could ride, and did so in films and shows, but it wasn't his *thing* like it was Mum's, so it was all he could do to juggle the three lead ropes and try to keep the horses from bolting.

"We should help Dad," I said, but not leaving the car. I was already in trouble for disobeying.

Rowan shook his head. He kept glancing at the trees nervously.

"You see something." I tried not to sound scared.

"Just. Feeling." He gestured to the dogs, who had taken up pacing a border between all of us and the trees.

"No! Stay. Whoa!" Dad's commands were getting louder and more nervous as he yanked at reins. Mum got up and took Chixie and Dream, though her eyes hardly left the McInnises. Dad said something I couldn't hear, and she looked over to us. She gestured to the car with her chin, then looked past us as Mrs. McInnis and the tractor approached.

"Heather, Rowan, come give us a hand," Mum called, and we flew out of the car. "Here, Rowan, take Chixie; Heather, Dream. Bring them closer to the car, walk them around if you have to, but stay where we can see you. Something in the trees has them all spooked." She glared at the tree line, hand brushing her hip. Dad scowled at her mildly. One of their ongoing arguments was the UK's lack of an amendment permitting firearms. Silently, right now, I agreed with Mum on this one. A bullet might actually do something against a kelpie. Maybe. I glanced at the thin trees over the bed of the truck. It looked like shadows danced between them, blocking out the slivers and chunks of sky beyond them. Like dark ripples through water.

Rowan started walking Chixie in a figure-8, keeping one hand on her neck. Dad paced back and forth with Daisy, the Belgian Mickey had ridden. I tried to pace with Dream, but I nearly walked us into Mum's truck twice because I couldn't tear my eyes from the direction of the loch. He shoved my shoulder with his nose and pawed the ground to tell me I wasn't helping his nerves.

"Sorry, boy." I threw an arm against his big neck. Not as huge as Oppie, Dream, a Percheron cross, was still a formidable beast much taller than me. Fortunately for me, he wasn't pushy…and Mum, who was his "Mummy", was still pretty near. I gave up on the walking attempts to watch the McInnises and Mum. Dream accepted that, though not contentedly, his ears stretched out to listen for everything. Isis circled around to check on us, found us in satisfactory condition, and returned to her station with Osiris.

It looked like the fetus was out, though I couldn't see it. Mr. and Mrs. McInnis were hitching up the lift thing to help Helen to her feet. Helen, for her part, was shiny with sweat and blood, but she was pulling her feet beneath her. She groaned and cried and obviously didn't have enough strength to do it herself. Mickey knelt beside her neck, one hand on it while the others negotiated the backhoe to lift the wrap around her in time with her efforts.

It felt like forever passed by, but the sun had only risen to about noon. Helen was on her feet but still wobbly. Mickey haltered her, handing the lead to Mum as he gave the horse a quick inspection. After a nod, he took the lead rope back from Mum. Mum ran over to us and said, "We're gonna walk Helen back to the stable, but she's really weak. Marie's gonna follow us in the tractor. Can you three walk the horses back? We can come back out and get the truck later."

"Yeah, we can do that." Dad grabbed Mum's hand. "She'll be all right?"

"Mickey thinks so."

"And you?"

"I'll be fine," she dismissed, giving him a smile. He pulled her into a quick kiss. As she headed back, she shouted, "Rowan, Heather, *walk* the horses back. No riding! Ya hear me?"

"Yes, Mum!" Rowan and I called back. He looked more disappointed than I felt. As good a horse as Dream was, I knew he was in no mood to have another human on his back, especially since we were leading him further from "Mummy".

"Take Osiris with you!" she shouted.

Dad called for the greyhound, who took station circling around us as we walked, pausing to insist that Dad or one of us run our hand down his back every so often. Dad said the poor dog spent too much time with the cats, the way he liked to be petted. I felt better, though, with him circling us, and with Dad on one side, and Dream, who I knew would look out for us like Oppie did, on the other.

I felt even better when we turned away from the trees and started heading closer to the castle.

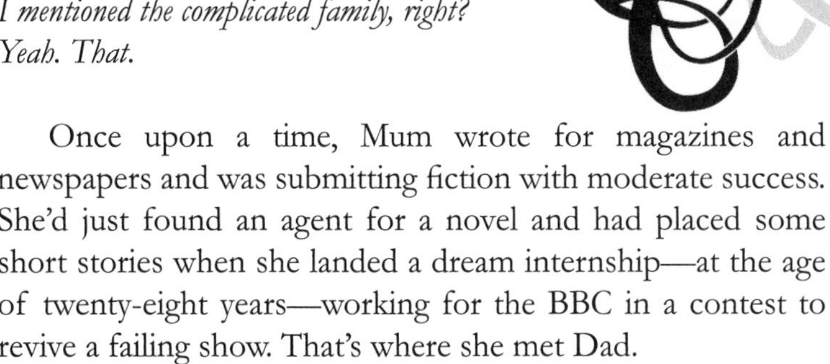

Chapter 4

I mentioned the complicated family, right? Yeah. That.

Once upon a time, Mum wrote for magazines and newspapers and was submitting fiction with moderate success. She'd just found an agent for a novel and had placed some short stories when she landed a dream internship—at the age of twenty-eight years—working for the BBC in a contest to revive a failing show. That's where she met Dad.

The show was called *The Professor,* and it was about an archaeologist who keeps finding magickal talismans and stuff, and goes on adventures with his daughter. The point of this little story is that Mum is a stickler for fact, so she would come up with plotlines based in actual folklore and history, which means that we've got a scary big collection of faery tales, folklore, myth, and history.

A good portion of it, at any time, is in piles on her side of my parents' office.

Mum knew her faery stories really well, and knew I had snuck down to the loch yesterday (I'm sure the McInnises told her about finding the loch weed on Oppie). The family spent all morning a stone's throw from the loch where Helen had a miscarriage—often thought to be caused by faery folk. On top of all that, she was snippy because she was tired and worried about poor Helen, so, well, if I asked what references were good about kelpie, she'd know something was up.

I didn't know if she actually believed faeries existed—or even what she really believed religion-wise, sometimes, even though she went to church with all of us most Sundays. But she isn't one to take such things lightly.

When Rowan was five, Mum and Dad had wanted to share a movie, *Labyrinth,* they both liked as kid. They knew Rowan had autism by then. He was already working with a therapist, so it wasn't their most brilliant parenting moment, but they thought it was tame enough, I guess.

But the Muppet goblins had totally freaked out my poor brother. He had slept in their bed for a month.

Lily then had made things worse when Rowan was pestering her some time after he was back in his bed by actually saying the line, "'I wish the goblins really would come and take you away!'"

Rowan had refused to leave Mum or Dad's side after that, even throwing a fit if only one of them was there. He'd been sure the goblins really would come and get him.

So, Mum had gone to her books and had explained to him that she was casting a very powerful spell to protect him from any goblin or faery creature. Dad had not been entirely comfortable with this, but he played along. Mum had been very serious about it, though: following the directions exactly, matching things up with the moon, and reciting the spell just like Granddad would say a church service. Mum had said she had wanted to show Rowan that she was doing everything exactly by the book because being literal was something important to a lot of autistic kids. It had *felt* like church, and Rowan believed it. He didn't need to sleep with Mum and Dad after that again.

"Heather, that's the third time you've walked by my door in twenty minutes. What do you want?"

Mum obviously wasn't working with a deadline this afternoon. If she were, I could walk by twenty times in twenty minutes, stomping, and she'd not notice. I suppose that she wouldn't be focused on deadlines after having spent the last twenty minutes on the phone making a report about some clearly vicious animal that tore up Helen and Oppie. I wondered what, exactly, was the proper authority to deal with kelpies. I knew I'd never heard of any department of evil faery monsters.

"I'm just worried, is all."

"Come in, honey."

She nodded to Dad's chair. Dad was in the library playroom with Rowan and the twins, talking about what had happened this morning. She knew I didn't like to sit on the couch after a terribly traumatic incident when I had run into the office at… an inappropriate and private moment when she and Dad were on said couch.

"What is it, really?"

I just shrugged.

"Did you see something yesterday that…was wrong? Did something happen to you that you need to talk about?"

I looked up at her quizzically. What was she worried that I had seen or that had happened to me? Probably a bunch of things, knowing Mum. She'd always been clear on teaching all of us, for as long as I could remember, not to trust any strangers, or even people we know, or even family. And if they did *anything* we were uncomfortable with that we should tell her or Dad, and we wouldn't ever be in trouble. Still, I had been out with Joe and if it *had* just been some crazy guy who'd attacked us—like who we thought had might've taken those other kids, I'd definitely have given her and the police and the papers a full report. (After Joe and I beat the crap out of him and hopefully found the missing children.) What was I supposed to say about a magick creature that most of the world said was imaginary? That wanted to *eat* us? Even if it was possible that she believed in imaginary magickal creatures or could cast spells about them? I shook my head at her questions, spoken and unspoken, but she didn't look convinced. I had to admit, she had good reason.

"I'm fine, really, Mum. I promise. I'd tell you if I wasn't." That was the truth. I wasn't hurt, in any case, and I'd have to tell her if I was.

She pressed her lips together. "The police want a full report from us, including the injuries on Oppie and Helen." Mum stared at me for a few minutes, and I dropped my eyes to my lap, trying not to squirm. She continued, "The bite marks on Oppie, the gashes on Helen… those *aren't* from a horse. What happened, Heather? The police are going to want to know."

"We fell off, and Oppie ran where we couldn't see him. He screamed and I heard the fighting…I swear it sounded like horses."

"Did you see another horse?"

"That's what it looked like, but we couldn't see it well through the trees and bushes." *I'm still not lying*, I told myself, though I still stared at my hands in my lap.

Mum's chair squeaked back, and I felt her looking at me as she considered what else to ask or say. I certainly couldn't justify asking to borrow a book with info on kelpies, not now.

"The police might stop by and do a follow-up. They're gonna want to talk to you."

Crap. "I know," I said. "That's fine."

Mum sighed. "I'm going to give Ma—Princess Maryan a call now. She should know." I looked up worriedly. Would this be what kept them away forever? Would Princess Maryan want to swoop in, take Artemis in her custody till the twin foals were born, and have nothing to do with us again? "Do you want me to ask if you can talk to Joseph?" she asked gently.

"Aye, yeah!"

Sighing once more and giving her cell a pained look, she pulled up the princess' phone number and hit send.

"Hi…uh, Your Highness, hi! It's Aimee…" Mum gave a strained chuckle, stumbling over the formalities. I hadn't actually seen her outright call the princess before. "Well, yeah, caller ID, but I figured it's better to still announce oneself, no? Anyway, Helen got out today and something, we don't know what yet, attacked her. We…we lost the foal." There was a long silence. "Thank you, and yes, I already filed a report. I mean, if you want to follow up, by all means. The more help, the better, obviously… Yes, yes, I'm sure the actual grounds are secure… it didn't happen near the stables… Over…by the loch…again." Another long pause. "Oh, and Heather is in the study with me and wanted to know if she could see how Joseph was doing?" Mum gave me a mirthless smirk, shaking her head. I could hear Princess Maryan's elevated voice but not what she was saying. Mum kept her eyes on me, and I could tell she was speaking so I got enough of the conversation. "Oh, no, but it was traumatic for them both, I'm sure. Anyway, she says that they fell off the horse and she remembers hearing horse fighting noises. She possibly saw another horse through the trees. Of course. But Joseph is all right? Good." Long pause. "Oh, yes, it would be great for Doctor Rivka to look at the injuries, too, and add to the report." An icy, tight smile stretched Mum's lips across her teeth, but managed to not affect her pleasant tone. "Yes, I'll definitely keep you posted if anything new happens, and give me a call or shoot me a text when you think Dr. Rivka can make it up here. Best to your family, too. God bless, and have a good evening."

Mum tapped the "end" on her phone several times until the screen was clear; she was always paranoid about a connection still being open before she said anything. But even after ensuring she was properly "hung up," she didn't say anything. She frowned as she tapped the phone on each edge, spinning it in her hand.

"You trust Princess Maryan's vet over Mickey?"

Mum sighed and shook her head. "I trust Mickey completely with any of our animals, but it's only fair to respect Princess Maryan's knowledge about horse care. She does adore her horses, and she only wants the best for them. And she is right that Jack and Mickey aren't vets; that's why Dr. Caroline comes out here twice a year and when things are really big. She was here this morning before you were awake and will probably stop by tonight." She furrowed her brow. "Prince Joseph is grounded, and she seemed rather surprised I'd let you on the phone as if you weren't grounded."

"I'm not *not* grounded," I sighed.

"Damn straight, kiddo. Your dad and I were going to talk about that today, anyway."

I slouched deeper in the chair, not caring as the bottom hairs were pulled when my braids stuck to the suede.

"Come on. Speaking of your dad, let's see how he's doing with the younger half of the clan." She sighed and looked much more exhausted than a few seconds ago.

"Not so well" was the answer to how Dad was dealing with my younger siblings. At least Rowan, anyway.

"Rowan, let me in. I just want to know you're all right!" Dad was struggling not to yell. As we approached, he gave Mum a look of guilt, relief, and apology. "He wedged the door closed."

"Heather, get me a ruler from…the closest place you remember seeing a ruler." She sighed. "You know the drill." She asked Dad, "How're the twins?"

I didn't hear his answer, so I looked back to see him looking even more heartbroken, shaking his head. "Thought Rowan needed the attention now… Anita is…"

I ducked into the room I normally shared with Lily. It was closer than the library, and I kept a meter stick in the closet because I needed it to open the closet's secret passage that I had neglected to mention to my parents. I knew what Mum was doing, though. It wouldn't be the first time she'd have pushed out my little brother's makeshift doorstops, so I wouldn't have to let on that I could sneak into Rowan's room if necessary.

Dad was already heading back to the library when I got to Rowan's door with the meter stick. I got down on my hands and knees and dislodged the stuffed animals and clothes that stopped the door. Mum knocked hard six times and announced, "Rowan, I'm coming in."

"NOOOOOOOO!!!!" he shrieked, making Mum and me wince, even though she hadn't opened the door yet.

"Thank you, Heather. Go put that back."

It was a dismissal. I frowned but left. *I* was worried about my brother, too! Except I knew I'd probably make things worse. He already figured it was my fault, what had happened to Oppie. It wasn't a huge leap for him to also blame me for what had happened to Helen's foal, either. I already blamed myself. It was *my* stupid adventure that went and possibly cheesed off a kelpie. Making it attack her.

After putting the meter stick away, I threw myself on my bed. From the other side of the wall, I heard Rowan's screams grow louder for a few minutes, plateau, then taper off into sobs.

I didn't stay long. What better chance would I have to sneak into my parents' office and grab the books I needed? Hopping off the bed, I closed my bedroom door and went to my closet. By now, I could maneuver the stick to open the slide latch in the pitch dark without any thought. The several inches I'd grown over the school year didn't hurt, either. I grabbed the torch I always kept in the closet and fluffed my hanging clothes to cover my retreat.

I could have just gone through the regular halls. Ginny was sure to be busy with filing and figuring out Mum's horse camp for the summer—would we even have horse camp with the missing kids? With the kelpie that only Joe and I knew about? Could I figure it out in time? In any case, Ginny surely had her hands full, Mum would have her full attention on Rowan, and Dad would be with the twins. Then again, if it took me a while to find the right books, who knew who I'd find on the way back? This way I could slip out of their office and back into my room and no one would know. Dad knew about a few of them—he'd uncovered a secret library room full of family records when we moved in, but I'd found more when I noticed the latch in my closet.

In hindsight, I think I needed to take the tunnels. And meet the ghost.

Chapter 5

Dealing with family? Okay. Scary storms? Okay. Murderous faery horse… working on it. But: I. Really. Hate. Ghosts.

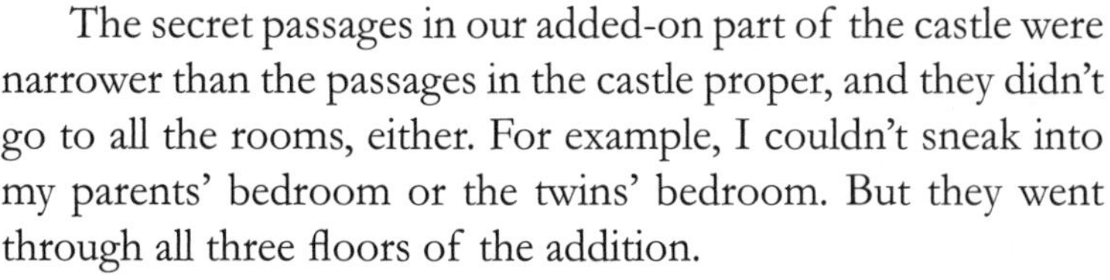

The secret passages in our added-on part of the castle were narrower than the passages in the castle proper, and they didn't go to all the rooms, either. For example, I couldn't sneak into my parents' bedroom or the twins' bedroom. But they went through all three floors of the addition.

My parents' and Ginny's offices make the middle two rooms on the first floor, just below my room and Rowan's. I've never tried to get into Ginny's office, but I have snuck into Mum and Dad's office to see who was coming to horse camp (once in a while, we actually got other royalty or nobility). Or to listen in when I knew they were discussing something, like how much trouble I was in for whatever in school.

The thing is, I usually didn't need to because they would tell me anyway. The things I didn't know, well, I probably still don't know. But something inside of me always feels the need to know what's going on.

At the end closest to the outside wall is a very tight spiral staircase similar to the stone ones hidden in the castle itself, but made of wood. There's a rope with knots in it to hold onto.

I suppose it was a good thing the ghost showed up before I got to the stairs.

I reacted before I even saw anything. At first, I felt things get really, really cold and dry. I was only about a meter and a half from my room when I started to shake uncontrollably. Goosebumps erupted all over my skin. My torch was on the stairs, and where it shone was getting brighter, but I couldn't see the stairs.

I froze.

I've never had asthma, but my possibly ex-second-best friend, Joli, who got pulled out of school thanks to one Miss Danicia Tennons and her crew, sometimes needed an inhaler. She described the attack like trying to breathe through a crimped straw. That's what it felt like. My lungs burned and strained. I tried to suck air through the crimp in my throat. My head felt like it was floating off, and my vision got blurry.

The light started to form into the shape of a person…a person who looked a lot like my sister Lily!

I felt like I couldn't breathe at all. Even the kelpie hadn't scared me this much!

"Ye can't trust faeries!" the ghost girl declared in a Scottish brogue that rivaled Granddad's when he was in a mood.

"Wh-h…" I think I managed. Her face started to come into focus, like when you're way too close with the camera setting and pull back. All I could see was how much she looked like Lily.

"I see ye 'round the castle," she said. She even sounded like Lily, except for the accent. "I know ye're not simple. Say something!"

Lily was still alive. She was safe in the States. I knew this, but my stomach started twisting and then felt like it dropped down a bottomless pit. I don't remember anything after that.

Except thunder. And having to…um…change my clothes.

Mum was too busy juggling cowering twins to notice that I was now in shorts. (After I'd gotten myself out of the secret passage, I'd discovered that all my regular jeans were in the wash. Brilliant).

And it was cold and stormy outside. Not shorts weather.

Rain pelted the courtyard windows and the skylights (a recent addition to the modern part of the family room/library). It was only early evening, but the deep grey sky was almost as dark as night—save for the huge flashes of light punctuated by thunder that made everything shake. Wind howled and screamed and made the edges of all the glass moan just a little.

Oh, and everything was lit with candles or electric torches.

Because, really, I wasn't already shaking and feeling downright sick from today.

Mum just barely stopped herself from dropping a potent cuss in front of the twins when her phone rang. "No, we're fine, really, Mum. It's just a storm… Power's out, and the computers, obviously. We're all okay…"

Dad was pacing, clutching his phone with white knuckles as he spoke with clenched teeth. "Well, when I checked online, Dad, the church as a whole didn't have a formal stand on gay marriage…it was up to the individuals…"

Rowan was on the opposite end of the couch from Mum, his expensive headphones covering most of his head, clutching his knees and rocking.

Everyone was in their own little world right now.

I sank into the couch beside Rowan. His rocking slowed, and he lessened the grip around his shins. His clothes and hair were a tousled, sweaty mess. The wrinkles on his shirt and jeans were as sharp as the wrinkles around his eyes. His hair stuck together in a chocolate faux-hawk somewhat resembling a style Dad would spend lengthy time in the bathroom to achieve.

Leaning deeper into the cushions, I closed my eyes, shivering at the thought of the ghost I was quickly trying to forget—and failing miserably at forgetting. Why? The kelpie yesterday hadn't had this effect on me. The only reason I'd had to change jeans then was because of the mud. What was *wrong* with me?

Another crashing lightning-flash lit up the room, making me jump. Beside me, Mum escaped from the twins to match pacing with Dad, who was furiously punching numbers into his phone screen. She touched his shoulder, and he growled, glaring at the tiny screen that made his face look eerie in its light.

Had there *always* been a ghost in this castle? I shivered even more at the thought. We'd lived here for over five years, and I hadn't heard anything ghostly before, never seen anything. Did I just not notice, thinking any unexpected sounds were because it was an old castle? Why was my heart hammering so hard, still?

"Are you scared, too, Heather?" Ivy pushed my arms open, climbing onto my lap.

"It's just a storm," I told her. My desire to comfort won out over my own fear of the ghost.

"I never saw a storm this big." Ash dove under my other arm with another flashing *boom* from outside. "Will the horses be okay?"

"I'm sure the horses are fine." I couldn't help it; I kissed the tops of both their heads. Their warm little bodies definitely made me feel better.

Maybe it was because the stupid ghost—the stupid ghost who looked like my sister!—still freaked me out.

"Lily, thank God, you're there!" My dad's voice was almost a shout. "No, no…we just have a really bad storm here. Electricity's out. Jack's working on the generator, which isn't cooperating, either… Just… I just wanted to hear you, and let you know not to worry when you didn't see us on Skype."

I breathed a sigh of relief. Me, too. I wanted to know Lily was okay. *Alive*. Not like the stupid ghost.

Dad talked with Lily for a few minutes, which I only half-listened to because they discussed shopping and film stuff. But she was *there* and *talking* with Dad. He informed us all that she said she loved us. I blew a kiss in his direction and waved.

Once he hung up, he let himself collapse on the couch where Mum had been sitting.

I frowned, not liking how much I could see his wrinkles and dark circles in the torch and candlelight. Or how tightly he was closing his eyes like he was in pain. I didn't see him fiddling with pills, which meant he was past that phase into the "I don't want to accidentally take more" phase. I hadn't seen him like that since the last major Jess blow-up over the last Lily-custody battle, over a year ago. She'd only gotten extended visitation rights, but Dad worried whenever Lily went too far for him to drive to get her.

And now he could only reach my sister by crappy, storm-fuzzy cell phone.

Ivy and Ash immediately started climbing into Dad's lap. Ivy planted a kiss on each cheek and started rearranging his hair. Ash started poking tickles under his arm. A lot of people forget how much kids know, but I knew what they were thinking as they pushed him for attention.

He sighed, but his lips started curling up in a smile. Dad was pretty perceptive, even with his moods, so I knew he realized the twins were trying to help. Within the minute, a tickle war broke loose on the couch.

"Help! Save me, my dearest love!" he called to Mum as he gave over to laughter.

"But you're so *cute* when you're tickled!" Mum grinned, crossing her arms. I rolled my eyes despite the smile that was creeping across my own face. It was payback for when Dad decided she was "so cute" (blech!) when *she* was tickled. Dad still managed to drag her onto the couch. Rowan leapt off, but I somehow got yanked by someone as a "Shield!"

The twins pig-piled on top of us, tickling one moment, then ducking under the closest arms whenever the storm crashed and lit our indoor horseplay. When one particular roar had each twin cowering with Mum and me, Dad slipped between us, dropping a kiss on each of our heads.

"I'm going to see if Jack needs any help. The generators should be on by now," he said.

"Don't go, Daddy!" Ivy squealed. (Ash also squealed an unworded echo behind her.) "You need to protect us from the storm!"

He paused, then gave each of us a kiss, especially Mum, who he kissed far too long in the presence of children, in my humble opinion. He solemnly stated, "I have passed to you all of my Daddy superpowers. They'll last all night, so you will be safe."

There was still some whining, but Mum interrupted with "There's a Crock-Pot curry that's calling all our names, kiddos. Let's go grab some. Last one to the kitchen helps Miss Eliza with dishes—without the dishwasher!"

And so, we went.

Dad didn't join us for dinner, but the generator came on when we started in on some chamomile tea and shortbread biscuits. He followed shortly after, soaking wet and shivering. The dogs flew from under the table to try to lick him dry.

"Honey!" Mum was right behind the dogs, with a kitchen towel she blotted on his face.

I tried not to roll my eyes. Dad looked pretty awful, so I'm sure the (freaking annoyingly cute) kiss-almost-snog Mum also gave him was warranted. But still! Kids in the room!

"There's a tree down on the main access road here. Jack, Mickey, and I cleared it. The village is pretty battered, too, and something else big is going on…but the storm seems to be messing with Jack's scanner, so I don't know what it is," he reported, leaning heavily on the kitchen counter.

"Are you all right?" She kissed him again. "You're soaked! Where's your coat?"

"Soaked through. In the hall. Wind and rain are really bad." He kissed her back. (They could stop any time now!)

"We saved you dinner," Mum said.

"I really just want to go to bed."

"Can we stay in bed with you and Mummy?" Ivy asked, cringing from the window where the storm hadn't lessened any.

I looked at my parents. My dad's face fell. I knew he was doing badly and really just wanted to be left alone, but I also knew he would never turn down one of us.

"You could camp with me!" I volunteered. "You can share Lily's bed. It'll be like a sleepover!"

"Will you tell us stories?" Ash asked.

"Sure." Besides, I had dreaded spending the night alone. Could the ghost watch me in my sleep? Not that I wanted the twins to have to deal with a ghost, but just having someone in my room made me feel better. And I was far too old to demand to sleep in my parents' bed because I was scared of ghosts.

Both my parents flashed me looks of intense gratitude, too, which definitely made everything feel a lot less scary.

Chapter 6

Because research always needs snarky talking cats.

The twins ended up glommed onto me in my bed rather than "camping" in Lily's, but that was fine.

Because the ghost didn't make another appearance. Thank *God!*

Downstairs, we met with a tight-lipped Mum who was glued to her phone screen, frowning. She had put out cereal, yogurt, and fruit, telling us Dad was still in bed (Dad normally cooked breakfast) and that she was going down to the stables to check on the animals. We were to eat our breakfasts and be good for Anita and Miss Eliza, who would "be up shortly." Ginny (who insisted no one call her Miss or Ms. because it made her feel old) was in her office, and we shouldn't bother her because she was working.

While I still worried for Dad, I realized this was an excellent opportunity to hit Mum's books about faery things to find out something about the kelpie! I all but inhaled my food and, as soon as Anita arrived to cajole the twins and Rowan into eating, I excused myself to "go read."

Mum just happened to be working on some book about faery stuff. (Okay, "just happened," is an overstatement: nearly everything she writes, fiction *or* nonfiction, is about magick or faeries or folklore because she got her degree on that sort of stuff.) Anyway, over a dozen books were haphazardly piled beside her desk, all feathered with multi-colored sticky-notes.

I had work to do. Plopping on the floor next to the piles, I grabbed the first few off the top.

I smiled a little. The top book was the one Mum had taken the anti-goblin spell from when Rowan was going through the whole *Labyrinth* issue. It was well-worn, edges softer than my Eastwood's winter coat; Mum used it a lot. The next top book was her *Encyclopedia of Faerie* with the cover almost as flexible as the pages and held on with clear packing tape. I flipped through that alphabetical listing for "kelpie."

I hadn't gotten but two sentences in when the room got freezing cold. I shivered and my stomach did a full somersault. A bubble blocked my throat as I recognized the sensation, and goose bumps roughened my arms and legs.

No! I was so not ready for another ghostly encounter!

Squeezing scratchy breath through my constricted throat, I forced myself onto spaghetti legs. I stumbled three times, clutching the books to my chest.

"Heather…" came the disembodied voice.

"No!" I wanted to shout, but barely managed to squeak. I ran down the hall and out the nearby door.

At least the storm was over and it wasn't currently raining!

Fortunately, the storm also meant no tours. So help us *God*, if there were flipping tourists! I'm *so* glad Mum and Dad could set strict rules and hours for that sort of thing. They only need so many hours to be open to the public to get national funding and stuff.

All the grass was flattened and wet, and lots of branches and leaves littered the grounds. As I failed to clear one of the larger branches, a sharp pain in my ankle nearly stopped my retreat. My flip-flop folded in half as I tripped, wrenching it more, so I kicked them off. I ran, limping and barefoot down the rest of the hill towards the stables.

Crap, my ankle hurt.

I was on the polo and football team, and one of the top athletes at my last school. I don't think I ever ran that fast, though. Especially with a twisted ankle. The very idea of seeing the ghost again freaked me out to no end. My lungs burned like I was sucking in icicles. I could hardly breathe, and I stumbled even more on the sharp stones of our drive.

I was too proud and ashamed to cry out for Mum. That could've also been related to the fact I could hardly breathe. At least I didn't soil my shorts. Or faint.

Freaking ghosts! Didn't I have enough going on with an evil faery horse?!

Barefoot—yes, it was stupid; I was on a roll with making dumb choices—I stumbled into the Shire stable. The floor was clean, but no one was around, and I didn't see any storm damage to anything. Leaning on Oppie's stall, I slid to the ground and let the books fall to the floor. In the farther stall, I could hear Helen pause in her eating.

The top of Oppie's stall was open, so he lowered his giant, silver head and chuffed directly on my hair. I didn't care about the boogeys. I reached both hands up, flexing the now-sore arm that had clutched Mum's books, and hugged his nose, feeling hot tears stream down my cheeks. I took a few deep breaths; they came out like sobs. God, I was such a baby! With an audible groan, Oppie reached further until his lips were by my face. He gently nibbled my braids, and I hugged him tighter. After a few minutes, he chuffed again and retracted his head. I looked up to see him stretch his neck up and shake a little, pained and concerned lines deep around his snout. He let his head drop again and pushed his mouth against the top of my head.

I rubbed my hands over his nose and closed my eyes until the stupid tears subsided. I wiped my eyes with my T-shirt, sighed, and picked up the books. I turned back to the "kelpie" entry in the encyclopedia when Oppie gave me another nudge, turned around, and started munching on hay. The entry didn't tell me anything I didn't know, and not a thing about how to make it leave. I shut the book loudly, sighed once again, then inspected my ankle. It wasn't swollen, and I felt the throbbing lessen against the cool mat. Chewing my lip, I stood, relieved it still held my weight.

Not limping much, I went around the corner into the office and pulled on my muck boots. I may have lost count of the dumb decisions I'd made lately, but I'd been accidentally (or purposefully) stomped on enough times to know better than to enter a stall barefoot.

Gathering the books in one arm, I let myself into Oppie's stall and leaned on his uninjured side. He looked up from his hay, nuzzled my elbow, then returned to eating. I pressed my lips together as I saw the hoof-shaped scabs across his chest, so I rubbed his shoulder in another apology. Kicking a pile of fresh pine shavings into the corner, I sat.

I started flipping through the well-worn *A Wicca's Guide to Faerie*. The book was tagged, and automatically opened, to the protection spell Mum had done on Rowan. I read through it, wondering if I could do something to make it go around the whole family. Except I didn't know if it worked on people who didn't believe in magick—or thought it was un-Christian—like Dad and Mr. McInnis.

There was another iron cross nailed to the beam above Oppie's stall now.

Mr. McInnis would likely *not* approve of anyone using Wiccan magick on him or his family. Mum had only barely gotten Dad to agree to it for the sake of Rowan's terror.

Are there banishment spells in there?

I admit it; I screamed when I jumped to my feet at the "sound" of another, unfamiliar, disembodied voice. A boy voice this time.

Oppie started, too, planting all four hooves.

"Oppie?" I whispered. He looked at me.

"Meow." Not Oppie.

Strutting along the edge of Oppie's stall was Monkey, the feral tomcat that "lived" in the big stable with the riding ring.

We called him "Mickey's Monkey," because Mickey was the only person the thing would let near him.

Oppie followed my gaze and sneezed in the fluffy cat's direction. He looked like a mix of tortoiseshell and Siamese with funky coloring. The cat gave a half-hearted hiss in the Shire stallion's direction, but returned his gaze to me. With a flick of his tail and an irritated angling of his ears, the feline began cleaning himself.

Yes, yes, I'm a cat that can communicate with humans. Your family's being plagued by a kelpie and you just ran from the castle as if all the beasts of Hell were on your tail, so you must've encountered one of the less genteel ghosts. Are you really all that shocked about a talking cat?

"I…uh…maybe?"

Oppie flipped his lips open to take a big sniff of Monkey and promptly sneezed once more, then returned to his hay, no longer perturbed. Although the cat growled louder this time, Oppie's lack of concern assured me that I wasn't likely in danger from this new development. My legs still wobbled, so I sat back onto the shavings.

So, is there one?

"Huh?" What had he asked me before? He expected me to remember past the fact he was a talking cat?

Is there a banishment spell in that book?

"Um, I don't know." I picked back up the book. "Let me look again."

Monkey strolled along the stall walls until he was right over my head. The cat peered down from his perch as I flipped through.

"Mr. McInnis nailed all those iron crosses around. Won't that help?"

It'll give me a headache the longer I talk to you.

"You're a faerie?"

No, cats regularly speak with humans. Usually over a nice tea.

I craned my neck back so I could look up at him. His voice was more in my head than in my ears, so the sarcasm was pretty hard to miss.

"Can you see my book from up there?"

I'm a cat.

Of course he was. I once thought it'd be nice to talk with our pets; I was having some serious doubts about that now. Monkey's tail swished impatiently above me, so I returned to my book.

"Would this one work?" I moved my head out of the way so Monkey could see.

To banish mischievous pixies…from a closet…maybe.

"What about this one? My mum did it to my brother and it worked." I flipped back to the protection spell. "Could I just do it on the whole castle grounds or something?"

The dark-haired one? Rowan?

"Aye." At least, I thought the spell had worked.

Hmmmm…

Monkey didn't contradict me, so that was a start. And knowing that Rowan was protected made me feel a little better.

Do you have enough salt to create an unbroken perimeter around the castle's land?

Crap. Like a few hundred acres or more? "Probably not."

Of course, that wouldn't keep anyone traveling in the park or living in the village safe either. It sounds rather selfish, if you ask me.

I glared up at the cat.

You need to banish it. Or, better yet, destroy it.

"How, exactly, am I going to do that?!"

I thought that's what you were trying to figure out.

"I *am*!" Oppie stamped a foot. I was getting loud. I gritted my teeth and growled up at the cat. "I *thought* you were helping me."

Did I say I was helping?

"Oooooh!" I squeezed my eyes shut and banged my head on the wall of the stall.

Did you ask me to help? Politely?

I glared up at the cat through slitted lids. His eyes seemed to glow amber-green down at me. I took a deep breath and blew it out through pursed lips. Manners. Faeries always required manners.

"I'm sorry, Monkey. I'm just very upset at all this. Will you please help me?"

What will you do for me?

And faeries always had a price.

I thought a moment. "There's already something in it for you," I said. "Or you wouldn't have gone to the trouble of letting me know you weren't just a cat. Exposing yourself to humans has its risks, too. You *want* me to do something about this kelpie."

Oooh, now we see she can be clever. Monkey turned himself around on the wall and sat, fluffy tail dangling from his feet like one of those furry costume boas. *What makes you think I've put myself at risk in talking to you? Or that I'm not here to spy on you for the kelpie?*

"If you had any intention of harm or were an agent of the kelpie, Oppie would be throwing a fit," I stated.

He's just a regular horse. The cat sniffed.

"He nearly took out the kelpie."

He injured the kelpie and angered it further. It wants to take over, which is why it made sure to kill the foal and not the mare. Now, it's gathering its strength, and if any of your other mares gets out—

"Why would you tell me all this if you were helping the thing?"

To taunt you. We fey folk are a proud people.

"Uh-*huh*. If you were taunting, there's a whole lot worse you'd be doing because there's a whole lot worse I can think of, and I'm just a human."

Oooh, touché. Now you're stroking my pride. Mmn. Yes, I suppose I could be a whole lot crueler if that were my goal. Still, what makes you think I have some great need to get rid of the kelpie? We're both fey—

"'Cos if you didn't, you wouldn't be trying so flipping hard to convince me you don't. So, how about this—you help me get rid of this kelpie before it hurts anyone else, and I refrain from asking why you want to help. Would that be a fair deal?"

Monkey stood up and turned around again, tail rolling back and forth as he considered.

It's an unfair deal for you. Any fey folk's motivation could be to undo the kelpie's claim to make room for something even worse for humankind. You should never give up your right to knowledge when bargaining, child. It's a foolish play.

"I..." Well, crap.

You may thank me for the enlightenment.

"Sorry..." I stared at him, confused, for a moment, but vaguely remembering something in one of Mum's books about not thanking faerie...people...things.

Most kelpies are Unseelie. They seek nothing but harm upon humans, but, like many of us, they cannot resist a good game. Particularly if it leads to the human undoing him- or herself rather than the fey being a direct influence of harm.

"The kelpie's done enough 'direct harm' by taking those kids! And trying to kill me and eat Joe and hurt Oppie and kill foals—"

Not exactly.

"What do you mean 'not exactly?!'"

It's...complicated.

"Seriously, try me." I folded my arms. My neck was getting stiff with tilting my head back to look up at the cat, so I stood and turned around to face him.

The cat paced back and forth atop the stall boards.

One of the members of Clan Arthur, from whom you are descended, was gifted this land by the crown some long time ago. It included the village and the reserve. There was...an agreement...between all parties, with the Seelie court who shared the land. In short, there was some sort of betrayal, your family lost their title, but that left the agreement in a flux...

"So, the kelpie wants to take advantage of that or something? How does that still *not* make him directly responsible for what he's done? Can I use some game or something to get the kids back?" I felt...*something*...wrong that wasn't in words coming from Monkey. "Can...can I get the kids back?"

Kelpie are culturally as much animal as anything. They don't take prisoners. They kill—as any animal in the wild would. And they will not waste the meat—

"Stop! No!" My voice was a squeaky whisper that ended in a gag. I dropped back to my knees and tried to breathe as I wrapped my hands around my stomach, pressing my head against the rough wood of Oppie's stall. I heard Oppie stop chewing and felt his eyes on me.

And the fact you brought him royal blood… The cat's tail twitched sharply.

"Shuttit! Just…just shut it!" I couldn't quite yell, and I felt like I was out of tears, so my eyes burned. I had to focus; I had to fix this. Before someone else…got killed! I turned my head, looking up at Monkey from the corner of my eye, not feeling strong enough to straighten up. My rudeness hadn't made him leave, but he was pacing and flicking his tail in irritation. "I didn't mean… But what does Joe have to do with anything?"

He stopped and looked down at me with as much disbelief as a cat's face could muster.

What does Prince Joseph *have to do with anything? Oh,* I *don't know. Do you know anything of the history of the Crown and magick? Have you any idea? No, I'm sure there's no potency in* that *blood. No statement to be made in* that *death—*

"Don't say that!" I growled. The cat growled back. "I'm *sorry!* I didn't mean—"

Of course, you didn't. But that doesn't undo the damage. So, let's focus on fixing things. He jumped down from the wall into the main alley with hardly a sound.

"Hey! Where are you going?"

Your iron hurts my head. You do your research, I'll do mine. His voice in my head was barely a whisper as I watched his silhouette stroll out. Oppie moved to inspect where I'd been sitting.

"No! No!" I ran over to him. "Back up!"

I waved my hands at Oppie's face, and he stepped back, wrinkling his nose in irritation. The immediate ridiculousness stole my concentration. I couldn't deal with all this! I couldn't! Below my feet, I saw his giant hooves had wrecked the covers of Mum's books.

"Baby, noooooo!!" I scooped up the books. The encyclopedia now sported a hoof-curved tear in the cover and first few pages while the cover of the paperback spell book was bent right in half and just clinging to the spine in a few paper threads. "Mum is gonna *kill* me!" That sounded like such a childish thing right now, but it was all I could think of. If that wasn't bad enough, as I stood up, he pressed his hay-drooling mouth right on the covers to check and see if they were food. "Oppie!"

He lifted his head and gave me an impatient, "What are you making all this noise about, human?" look.

"Opppieee!" I groaned, but he leaned down and lipped at my collar in apology and/or begging for treats. I leaned my cheek on his nose, and he sighed onto my neck. What choice did I have except to scratch his chin and face in all his favorite places? As if just doing that was a release for me, I felt more warm tears wet my face, probably streaking it with dirt. When he was tired of my attention, he went back to nosing the corner, seeking out the last few blades of hay from the pile he'd consumed during my conversation with Monkey. I patted his bum as I left his stall.

I didn't want to go inside yet. I didn't know what else to do, so I grabbed a few handfuls of treats from the tack room. On the other end of the stable, Helen leaned out of her stall and whickered. All the horses knew the sound of the treat bin. My stomach turned when I saw the deep lacerations and stitches up and down her side, and I let her finish the whole handful of horse cookies. Grabbing another handful, I said my goodbyes to Oppie, too. When he crunched the last one, I sighed and resolved to head back into the house, hoping the stupid ghost was done trying to talk to me.

What was I supposed to do?

Chapter 7

In which even the most familiar things become scary and I consider I might maybe be in over my head.

As I came from around the rose garden, trying to avoid the worst of the mud and puddles, I saw the police car pulled up in the driveway.

The ghost was the least of my worries right now.

Mum had said they were coming, hadn't she? What was I supposed to say to the police? That I knew about the kids?

I growled an oath that I wouldn't dream of saying in front of any adult and glared at the entrance to the castle's addition, where the offices were and where my parents would likely be. Maybe I could avoid them. No one should be in the main castle in midday when we were closed to tourists. I headed to the heavy main doors that led to the marbled foyer, grabbing my discarded flip-flops from the hill where I'd thrown them.

"Heather, there you are!"

I all but jumped out of my skin at my mother's voice. I gaped at her as she came from the formal sitting room. Why there? Why not the offices? Just my luck!

"Rowan found you?" I could hear that she was forcing her voice. My heart pounded.

I shook my head. "No. Just came in… I was reading outside." I held the covers of the books to my chest to avoid the yell-fest for now. Or at least to keep the strained lines in her face from getting worse.

"In the barn?" Her facial lines got worse anyway. I looked down to see bits of hay and shavings clinging to my clothes.

"It's quiet. And peaceful."

She just shook her head. "Come into the parlor. The police need to talk to you."

"Let me just put the books back—"

"Do it later. Come on." She turned and headed to the room. Quickly, I shuffled the books so the less-damaged-looking one was on top.

I stopped at the door, wondering for half a second who the strange man sitting beside my mum was. I bit my lip as his face softened in concern upon seeing me. He shifted to make room on the couch.

Dad? How could I not recognize my own dad? I swallowed hard; my brain couldn't process this!

Every line on his face, his long nose and pointed chin, looked sharper and deeper. Dark circles—darker than last night—made his uneven eyes look haunted. The stubble added shadows that didn't look right—especially bathed in the crimsons and blues of the nearby stained glass window—and his hair was truly messy (as opposed to styled "messy"). As I sat down, he clamped his arm around my shoulders and pulled me close. I leaned on him, putting the books in my lap, and tried not to wrinkle my nose. Mum must have dragged him right out of bed because he hadn't showered, either.

I could feel his hand shaking, his shortness of breath, and even his heart hammering in his chest—all of which usually happened when he was "up" and not in one of his depressed moods.

One of the officers, the younger one with ginger hair, stiffly rearranged himself in a white wing chair while the other, with salt-and-pepper hair, paced behind him. A tea service had been set, but no one was eating or drinking. They glanced between my parents and me. Salt-and-Pepper cleared his throat a few times, as if about to talk, then paused.

Jogging footsteps echoed across the great hall. Mum stood again as Rowan appeared at the parlor door. When he saw me, his eyes flashed both anger and relief. "You're here."

"Yeah, I just came in."

"Thank you, Rowan." Mum bent and kissed the top of his head. "It's okay now."

He turned narrowed eyes on her and then in the direction of the policemen. "No, it's not."

The two officers glanced at each other uncomfortably, as most people did when Rowan had that charged look that never quite met your eye.

"You're right, it's not, but I need you to go and play with Anita and the twins. Can you do that for me?"

"I wanna know what's happening!"

"And we'll tell you. We'll have a family conference. Right after this. I promise."

He scowled, mostly at me. Unable to help myself, I leaned more against Dad, appreciating the fact he was alert enough to rub my head when I did so.

"Rowan, please," Mum said.

"Can't I just go to my part of the library?"

Mum nodded. "Yes, you may. I'll come get you."

He turned and left. Mum closed the stained glass doors behind him and returned to the couch on the other side of Dad, who quickly took her hand. His dark eyes fixed on the officers, and he swallowed a few times, as if he wanted to speak but couldn't.

Mum took a deep breath and angled herself on the couch to look at all of us, then focused on me. "Heather, little Sarah Beth Garrity went missing during the storm."

"No!" I squeaked. We knew everyone in the village, but the Garritys were especially good friends. Jenna was less than a year younger than Lily, and usually came over to ride with us. Sarah Beth was two years younger than Rowan and would be starting lessons from Mum this summer. My stomach flip-flopped as I thought of what Monkey had said out in the stable.

"Heather, listen. That's not all." Her voice shook. Mum's voice never shook. She hated to cry as much as I did. "The other children, the missing ones…they…" She swallowed hard, and I knew what she was going to say. It felt like she was slowed down, freezing like a video that wasn't all downloaded. "They found their bodies on the banks of the loch."

"Sarah—"

"Not Sarah Beth, though." My dad's voice scraped. "Not Sarah Beth."

I couldn't stop myself from crying, so I buried my face in Dad's shirt. He hugged me tightly and kissed my head.

In a "just-for-kids" kind of tone, one of the officers said, "She could have just gotten lost with the storm. Perhaps she went to go hide somewhere, and then couldn't find her way back. The villagers have been searching since last night, but the area between the castle and the park is very big. Everyone's making search parties. We might still find her."

"Heather, if there's anything you can remember from when you were down by the loch or in the park, any detail…" Mum pushed softly. I could feel her hand rubbing my shoulder and back.

I wanted to scream. They weren't going to find her! Not alive! The kelpie didn't take prisoners. If it had gotten her, if she wasn't just lost, it was too late! I gritted my teeth so hard my jaw felt like it would shatter. I wrapped my arms around Dad and curled my legs up under me, not even thinking about my dirty feet and flip-flops on the antique furniture. Or the books that slipped down the cushion behind me. My dad seemed surprised at how tightly I squeezed, but he hugged me close, kissing my head over and over.

"Heather…" Mum began again.

"I told you…already…" I said into Dad's shirt. I'd told a bunch of lies, but it didn't matter anyway.

I could picture Mum looking from me to the officers, then heard her say to them, "She said she was thrown and all she remembers was shadows of horses fighting in the trees."

"Were there any people? A person?" asked Officer Salt-and-Pepper in that same voice.

"I didn't see anyone." I didn't look up from my Dad's chest. That was the truth.

"Did you hear…?"

"No." I didn't hear any people; that was the truth, too.

"Young Miss MacArthur, any detail you could remember…" It sounded like Officer Ginger now, and his tone sounded accusing.

"I don't remember!" That was a lie.

"If she did, she'd have said by now," my dad snapped.

Officer Salt-and-Pepper continued, "If there's anything that could help that little lass—"

"Heather would say," my dad growled. I felt him lean in the direction of my mum, so she must have put her hand on him.

"Have-have you gone out to the loch?" I tilted my head away from my dad a little, finally glancing at the officers out of the corner of my eye.

"Officers Stapleton and Miller were there this morning," Mum said. "And search parties have been going all over the park."

"The water level is really high, soaking or covering most of the trails and ground between the shore and the loch," said Officer Ginger. I wondered briefly if he were Miller or Stapleton. "So, even without…what's going on…it's awfully dangerous. In addition to the search parties, volunteers are covering all the public trail heads, keeping people out."

"If something happens to come to Heather," Mum said, "or if we see anything strange around our land, we'll call you right away. We promise." She stood up. "God help you find poor Sarah Beth." I heard a tear choke her voice. "Her poor family!"

Ginger stood up, too. "Thank you, ma'am." He shook her hand.

"Officer Miller," she nodded, then shook Salt-and-Pepper's hand. "Officer Stapleton."

Still keeping an arm around me, Dad stood up with me and shook the officers' hands. Mum was wrapping up sandwiches in napkins. "Please." She gave them to Miller. "I'm sure you must be hungry. I can ask Eliza to get some travel cups for the tea—it's a shame to waste the whole pot…"

"No, no, really," Stapleton answered. "Thank you for the sandwiches. That's kind enough, ma'am. Just give us a call if you think of or see anything."

"We will." Mum turned to me. "Heather, will you please take the service into the dining room, then get your brother from upstairs?"

I nodded, but couldn't quite make my feet move until Dad hugged me once more.

"Is Sarah Beth dead?" Rowan looked ready to cry as he asked.

"No—I don't know! Why are you asking me?" I snapped.

"'Cos you're crying, and you don't cry."

"I'm just…I don't know, but she's missing."

"Do you think she's dead?"

"I don't know!"

"You're lying."

"I'm not! I really don't *know* know. Now, just stop asking. Mum and Dad want a family meeting in the dining room."

Rowan gave me a furious look. "Not going till you tell me the truth! I know you know stuff."

"And how do you know that?!"

"I just do. You know I know."

I scowled, but he only glared back. If we got into a glaring contest, I'd lose.

"Can we talk later?" I caved, but strangely it made me feel better. "I promise, I'll tell you everything."

He considered and nodded. Accepting my conditions, he headed downstairs without another word.

I followed, and we took our usual places at the table. Miss Eliza, Anita, Ginny, and Mrs. McInnis joined us. Dad was sitting in his spot, but Mum was standing behind him, hands on his shoulders, instead of sitting at the other head of the long table.

She stared longest at the twins, and I imagined her struggling to think of how to phrase things for them. I'd taken the news terribly; who was to say how they'd react? Worse yet, Rowan. The dining room filled with oppressive, awkward silence.

Should I say something? I thought. If I just came clean, maybe we could do something. Mum *had* done the spell on Rowan… I studied my parents. Could I? Should I?

Dad looked up at Mum, then stood and pushed her into his seat. Moving a chair between the twins, who were fidgeting, he pulled them each onto his lap. They snuggled against him, hazel eyes big and wide with the anxiety they could feel but couldn't quite understand.

He was working so hard to be there for them. And he was hiding how bad he was. The image of him in the parlor—of not recognizing my own dad!—unsettled me more than I wanted. And Mum, Mum was trying to do everything else. I'd never seen her look so worried ever! Even when things were at their worst with Jess and Lily. Could my parents even take hearing the truth? Would it push Dad over the edge? How did faery things fit in with being the son of a minister…for someone who didn't have normal emotions? I never read anything about that in my Bible—and I had had to read the whole thing before I could take my first communion.

"Sarah Beth Garrity went missing in the storm last night," Mum finally said, interrupting my thoughts. The twins both grabbed Dad's arms, whimpering.

From behind me, I heard Anita whisper a soft prayer in Spanish and heard the movements of her and Mrs. McInnis crossing themselves.

Mum continued, "The police and everyone in the village are looking for her…and are hopeful they will find her soon." The assurance seemed to calm them some. On the far side of the dining room, I heard the other adults clucking and murmuring. From the corner of my eye, I saw Mrs. McInnis pressing a napkin to her mouth. Ginny pressed her lips to the edge of her shaking teacup, and her blue eyes looked at each one of us worriedly.

"That means I want every single one of you," Mum was looking at us kids, "inside unless you're with an adult. That means not even going down to the stables without one of us around. On top of that, if you see or hear ANYTHING, anything at all, that is even the slightest bit unusual, you MUST tell an adult. No exceptions. Period. And it will stay this way until we say otherwise! Is that understood?"

We all nodded.

"Tell me," she ordered.

"Yes, Mum," we all murmured. She didn't mention the deaths, but did glance at me. She wasn't going to; I knew she didn't want to share that.

Bringing up the kelpie would just make things worse, I decided. Add being terrified something evil and fey would eat your children and that would *definitely* push Dad over the edge, if not Mum, too, who might just go and break UK law and carry a gun like she could in the States.

"Aimee…you mean you're still staying here?" Ginny, though she was about the same age as Rose, gave Mum a disapproving look. "You've got the flat in London. Why not just pack up the kids and head back out there until this is all taken care of? There's no sense in—"

"I don't wanna go to London," Rowan cried, bouncing in his chair. "I wanna stay here!" I looked at my brother. "Here" was home for him; he probably didn't even remember living in London. Rowan hated change.

Ginny frowned at him.

"Rowan," Mum stated. "Don't shout at Ginny. Apologize for being rude."

"Sorry," he mumbled to her, then looked at Mum. "But I don't wanna go! I'll stay with the grown-ups and be good!"

"I need to talk to your dad before we make any decision, Rowan," she said, looking at my father. I did, too, and my heart dropped. He looked ready to pack and head to London today.

"I don't want to leave either!" I piped up. "And it's not fair for the McInnises to be left out here…and if they leave, what about all the animals?" I hoped that sounded like a mature argument. I couldn't exactly say that, between a ghost and a talking cat, it sounded like I had to be the one to fix things—and if I didn't, any of the other village kids could be next. Mum hadn't even brought those killed kids up in this discussion; she didn't need to. Those of us who needed to know, knew. Yeah, my parents and every other adult in this room would totally be against eleven-and-a-half year old me dealing with child-eating monsters.

"None of the adults have been attacked, love," Mrs. McInnis said in a voice that, I'm sure, was meant to sound soothing. "It's safer to have you children out of danger."

"School gives us lectures about how dangerous London is, so it's not really that much different." I pressed my case.

"Thank you." Mum's voice took on its "I'm in charge of this civilized discussion" tone as she looked around the room. I couldn't tell how she felt about the choice either, which worried me. "Michael and I will consider all what you said." She looked at the twins. "Ivy, Ash, what do you think? How do you feel about going to London for part of the summer?"

I tried not to scowl. They, like Rowan, just went to school in the village. It's not like they lived outside the castle for ten months of the year at boarding school, like Lily and I did!

The twins stayed snuggled against Dad, but looked at each other. Finally, Ivy spoke up, "Would we come right back when they find Sarah Beth?"

The question surprised both our parents. Neither answered right away.

Ash added, "Maybe we could go stay with Granddad, and pray that Sarah Beth is okay, and then we're closer to come back?"

Dad swallowed hard and hugged them tightly, looking like he wanted to cry again.

Mum smiled. "That's a very good idea, Ash." She looked at Dad. "Do you think your dad would mind a visit?"

"I'll ring him and ask."

"Well, we have more options now. Your dad and I will talk about them. For now, the new rules stand. You stay inside the castle, and any time you go out, even if it's just to the gardens, you HAVE to have an adult with you. Is that clear?"

"Yes, Mum."

"And when we go to bed at night, we should all say prayers for Sarah Beth and all the kids around to be safe. Okay?"

We all nodded again. There was no disagreement on that. In fact, I almost wanted to head back to my room and pray right then. If I was in trouble with the fey, who were definitely pagan, God would help with that, right?

"Any more questions?" Mum asked. The family meeting was almost over.

We shook our heads.

"All right, then. Remember, if any of you need to talk, you can come to us. You won't get in trouble. Promise."

I avoided her eyes on that one. I was already in trouble.

Mrs. McInnis and Miss Eliza stood up first, gathering the still-untouched food and tea. Dad started negotiating the freedom of his lap. I could tell he was struggling to not snap at the twins' stereo whining. Rowan gave me a look, and I announced we were heading to the library.

We started for the back stairs. "Wait," I said. Rowan gave me a dirty look, like he expected me to break my promise. "I just need to get the books I borrowed from Mum. I left them in the sitting room when the police were there. I'll be right up."

Chapter 8

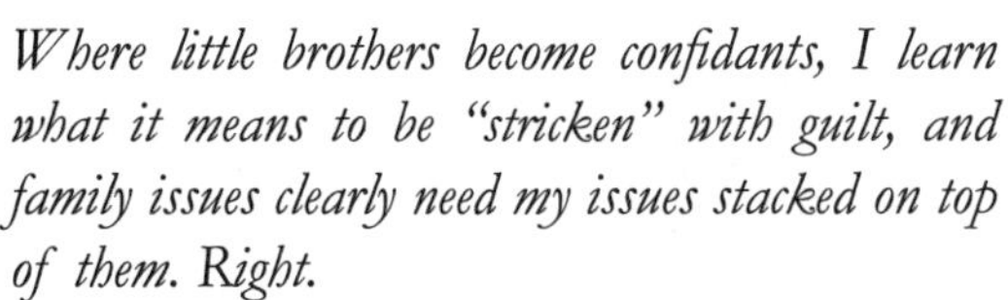

Where little brothers become confidants, I learn what it means to be "stricken" with guilt, and family issues clearly need my issues stacked on top of them. Right.

Anyone who says eight-year-olds or autistic children don't have a clear sense of power never met my brother. Rowan was in his corner and even turned off his computer as I approached, but he stayed in his taller computer chair, leaving me to pick one of the shorter chairs. I flopped into a beanbag chair, hugging the books to my chest.

"You know you're *not* Dad, right?" I asked with a frown, bristling against his stare.

His posture softened some, but his brow was still creased. "You promised to tell me everything."

"And I will." I put the books down carefully, still hiding the damage as best I could. Then, I recounted to him everything from the past few days, most of which he knew from our last discussion.

He nodded. "What else?"

I didn't answer right away and felt my stomach tie itself into about a hundred knots.

His small face grew even more concerned. "What? What's wrong? Are you going to be sick?"

I hadn't eaten anything since breakfast, so I doubted it. After a few deep breaths, I finally said, "And then there was the ghost…"

"Ghost?" His face grew pale. "Did it come after you?"

"I…I think she…meant to help with the kelpie." No matter how hard I tried, I couldn't bring my voice above a squeaky whisper as I thought of her. Dead kids, Sarah Beth missing, and a stupid *ghost* was getting me all worked up again?

Rowan appeared more confused now. "What happened? What did she do?"

"Nothing, really…just…she kinda looked like Lily… and…I…" I just about whispered, "was scared." I looked away, feeling my face burn with embarrassment.

I felt my brother staring at me for what felt like an hour. Finally, he asked, "When? Did she *say* anything?"

"When you were having your tantrum yesterday…and, I don't really…remember. Just that I had to fix things…" I was still mumbling and I still couldn't bring myself to look at Rowan.

"Huh? You don't remember?"

"I…kinda fainted…"

Rowan was quiet for a long time.

"I don't know why, and swear you'll never tell anyone ever!"

He simply nodded. "Did she say anything else?"

"Just…that I had to fix things. And that she didn't like or…trust faeries…I think. Something like that…I really don't remember." I squeezed my eyes closed so tightly it hurt.

"That was yesterday, what happened today?"

I took a deep breath and found I could open my eyes. Rowan's face was unreadable. I couldn't tell if he was just pushing to get the rest of the story or if he was trying to be nice and purposely was moving past my embarrassing confession.

"I went to get the books from Mum's study and…I *felt* the ghost again. She called my name, so I ran out to the stable and…decided to stay in Oppie's stall." Rowan just nodded. "As I was reading—" I stopped. I hadn't exactly told Monkey I wouldn't tell anyone about his being a faerie, but it still didn't seem right to just "out" him like that.

"What?"

"I don't know…if…"

He huffed angrily at me.

"No, really…I…" I thought his eyes were going to burn holes right through me. Then again, Monkey didn't actually *say* not to tell anyone. And he pretty much told me I should be careful about trusting faery…things. Just to be careful, I said, "You gotta swear you won't tell anyone—*anyone!*"

Pursing his lips, he stared at me a few minutes. "I swear I won't tell anyone."

I sighed. If there was anyone in the family who could keep secrets, it was Rowan. If only because he didn't talk a lot in general.

"Monkey talked to me about the kelpie."

My brother shook his head before asking, "Mickey's Monkey talks?"

"Yeah, he's some kind of faerie, too. He saw me going through the spell book and kept telling me what wouldn't work. But he said he would help…just, he didn't have anything for me then. He just, kinda explained more what the—the kelpie…does." I all but whispered the last word and felt tears coming back and couldn't stop them this time. I dug the heels of my palms into my eyes and then sat shaking in the beanbag chair, so I folded myself into a little ball and hugged my knees and buried my face entirely.

I jumped when I felt Rowan's breath on my cheek. I hadn't heard him move to the stuffed chair beside me. Moving my elbow a little, I looked at him. His face was a mix of anxiety, confusion and comfort, trying to figure out what he was supposed to do or say next. He put two fingers on the back of my hand, then snatched them back. "Thanks," I sniffled, recognizing he meant to comfort. "You won't…"

"Tell anyone you're crying because our friend might be dead?" he asked softly.

"Maybe she's not! Maybe, I don't know! If we could get back outside and talk to Monkey again!"

Rowan slid off the chair and sat across from me, moving aside the books.

"Heather!" he wailed in horror, picking up the faery spell book with its cover hanging by only a corner.

"Sssh!"

"Mum's going to be *angry!*"

"I *know!*" I sniffled in the last of my tears and rubbed my nose on my shoulder. "I don't need you to be, too!"

"Hmph!" He picked up the book and pressed it to his chest like a good friend. "Meet me in my room after Mum and Dad go to bed. I have an idea."

"What?" I asked, but he ignored me and started pulling out his art set. After a few minutes of him making sure all the pencils and charcoals and pastels were getting spread in exactly the right place, I got the hint and left him alone. He didn't mean to be rude or bossy; it was just how he communicated and functioned.

I had no desire to do anything else, so I flopped in front of the television where the twins were building and destroying Lego castles in front of some inane, brain-numbing cartoon. Brain-numbing… yeah, that was perfect right now.

When it came time to Skype with Lily, Dad had washed, shaved, and combed his hair. His eyes didn't look quite as hollow, but I sensed it was all rehearsed.

He'd had his mood swings since his teens. The public and most of the people he worked with never knew about his condition until Jess discovered it and blew it up in their first custody hearing for Lily. She wanted to prove Dad was an unfit father, even though Jess had let baby Lily go almost a full day without food or drink while she was cheating on Dad. (I knew this because I went through Dad's papers during the last custody battle; I wanted to know what was going on.)

I was pretty sure his depression hadn't passed, and he was on acting mode now. I wasn't sure how I felt about it. Mum once said he trusted us and needed us to be okay with things; that's why she put up with a lot. Family should be a safe place where you could have your worst days and still be loved. I didn't want Dad to not feel safe or like he had to be at work around us. On the other hand, my stomach still jumped around sick when I thought of how bad he looked in the sitting room, so bad I hadn't recognized him right away.

If I did bring up the kelpie, I'd only make things worse.

When he sat on the couch and let Mum set up the call, I beat the twins to him, threw my arms around his neck, and kissed his cheek.

"Love you, Daddy!" I whispered in his ear. Everything was horrible and awful and wrong, and if I was feeling like that, I knew he felt it a million times worse. At least I could try to help him not feel so bad.

"Love you, too, sweetie." He returned the kiss and pulled me into his lap. "No matter what. Promise." Lifting my chin with his fingers, he made me look him in the eye. He dropped his act, and I could see he was still very depressed. "I don't want you to worry about me, love, I don't," he said softly. "That's not your job, and I hate seeing you worry. I know I can't make you stop, you're just like your Mum like that, but…" He kissed my forehead and hugged me tightly. "I just want you to know I love you, no matter how I am, okay?"

"I know, Daddy." I hugged him back, resting my head on his shoulder.

Mum smiled and squeezed my thigh as she sat next to us. The twins started climbing her, and she adjusted to fit them both in her lap, then looked in the direction of Rowan's corner.

"Rowan, honey, come join us on the couch to talk to your sister."

"No!"

"Rowan!" My dad turned, ready to move me off his lap as anger filled his eyes.

Mum put a hand on Dad's shoulder.

"Rowan, that's not how you talk to me."

"Rrrrnnnh!"

"He's drawing a project," I said quickly.

"Rowan, I know you're concentrating, but if you don't want to be with us now, you know how to ask," Mum said.

"Rrrnnh!" His voice wasn't as adamant this time.

"Rowan."

"May I please stay over here and draw, Mum?"

Dad opened his mouth to protest, but Mum gave him a look. "Yes, you may, Rowan. Thank you for being polite about it."

"Wuhlcome," he muttered, without enunciating and just barely loud enough for us to hear.

The speakers did their bleepy ring for Lily's incoming call. As soon as I saw my sister, I knew something was up. She wasn't exactly the actor Dad was.

"Hey, everyone!" She waved cheerily. I felt Dad shift his weight so he leaned forward. Besides that tiny movement and his slightly faster breathing, his demeanor didn't give away that he'd noticed the same as me.

"Hey, Lily!" we all greeted in one form or another.

"How was shopping with your mother?" Dad asked.

"Shopping was great! Mum took me everywhere, including this amazing restaurant that you usually can't get into without, like, a month-ahead reservation. And she took me to these special boutiques, just her and me, and look! I got my first pair of Jimmy Choos!" She twisted around on the bed and held up her feet. She'd obviously gotten a pedicure, too. Perfectly shaped cherry red nails peeked through the tips of bronze strappy flat sandals.

"Those are cute!" I piped up before Mum could ask how much they cost.

"Thanks!" She smiled, flipping back around so she lay on her stomach and faced us. Her smile was a little more forced now. "So, uh, if I have to fly home, I've got to fly into Edinburgh… or will Ginny be back in London, like…tomorrow…and could she just pick me up?"

"Tomorrow?" Dad did move me off his lap, squeezing me next to Mum so he could lean forward more. "You just arrived…two days ago. Is something wrong? Are you all right?"

"I'm fine!" Her voice didn't totally hide a snap. "Mum just got offered a really good contract for a film, except that they're filming in South Africa, and she can't get me a visa in time."

"Wait, she *just* heard about this? When is she flying out?" Dad asked.

"She had a meeting with the director last night and the other actress that was going to do it didn't work out, so she's flying out tomorrow. It's an opportunity—a *lead role*—she can't pass up." Lily's voice was getting higher, and she looked like she was trying not to cry.

"What the—" my dad's face started to get red.

Mum gripped Dad's shoulder and interrupted him. "Ginny's up here for the night, but she is heading back tomorrow. She has four days off, though, so you'd either stay with Ginny for four days or one of us would have to come down and pick you up. It's just as easy to grab a transfer flight up to Edinburgh or take the fast train. What do you think would work best for you, honey?"

"Are we going to Granddad's?" Ivy asked. "And not London, then?"

"We haven't decided, yet, sweetie." Mum frowned.

"Why would you be going to London or Granddad's?" Lily asked. "Is something going on over there?"

"You know about the missing children…" Mum began, then glanced at Rowan and the twins. "Sarah Beth—"

"Went missing too?" Lily covered her mouth. "I saw Shari's Facebook post asking everyone to keep her in their prayers—and I did—but I didn't know! Oh, God! She didn't say—"

There was a knock at the door, and Lily wiped her arm across her face, scowling. "Hold on. It's Mum." I felt all of Dad's muscles tense.

The screen image bounced when my sister returned to the bed. We could only see her knees and shorts, then Jess's shorts and tanned legs until Lily adjusted the screen again.

Lily looked a lot like her mum. Jess was petite—probably no taller than I was now—with bright blonde hair and blue eyes. Her face was the picture of Hollywood perfection. On the other hand, she looked like she might be gaining weight. Glancing at Mum, who I could feel sucking in her stomach as she looked at Jess, I debated how I felt about Jess getting fat, because Mum was sensitive about using "fat" as an insult.

I hated Jess with every ounce of my being because of everything she'd done—even just in my lifetime—to Dad, Lily, and everyone in my family. Between Dad's clenched body and Mum rubbing his back while trying not to look chubby and the twins still trying to fit in Mum's lap, I was triply squished. It was all I could do to not glare daggers openly.

"Is there a problem with taking Lily?" she asked sweetly.

"No," my older sister answered quickly. "Just a family friend's daughter isn't doing so good. I saw it on Facebook and was getting the whole story. They were also planning a trip to see Granddad, who we haven't seen in a while…so, uh, it's better to fly into Edinburgh if possible, or book the train if I've gotta fly into London."

"Well, I'll see what Evan can arrange then. I'm sorry to hear about your friend's daughter. Is it something serious?"

"It's a private matter," Dad said. He had relaxed some, but his face was entirely unreadable to me. "You know we're always happy to have Lily back. Just remember, we don't have the extended summer vacation like the States."

"We can discuss the holidays, though." She flashed an exceptionally sweet smile. "I haven't had her for Christmas for a long time, and…" She blushed and patted her stomach. "It would be nice to celebrate with both my children."

"You're pregnant?" Dad's eyes widened, his voice sounding incredulous.

"Yes! Isn't that wonderful?"

No! I thought. *Not only is she not getting fat, but this is worse!*

"Of course." Mum said. It was probably better she answered. I glanced at Dad because it seemed he'd stopped even breathing. He nodded with a smile that was galaxies away from being real. Mum continued, "We can talk about Christmas later. Just let us know where and when to pick Lily up, and we're a go."

"Great, then." Jess didn't sound quite as happy as her smile said she was. "I'll have Evan fax the itinerary to you."

"Speaking of faxes, *Jessica*—" Dad seemed to have found his voice.

"Yes, *Michael*?"

The two were playing the "I can have the more ironic tone with your name" game.

"I still haven't gotten the contract for Lily's role."

"You're not going to make things difficult over her first role, are you?"

Lily looked between her mother and the screen in suppressed horror.

"I'm not making anything difficult. I'm the primary caregiver and custodian of her accounts. You're breaking the custody contract and guild regulations by not having me sign off on it."

The two glared a face-off.

"Evan can just fax it over when we're off the phone, right?" Lily asked, swallowing hard.

"I'll see if he can do it," Jess snipped. "I just think it's ridiculous to think I don't know a good career move for my daughter."

"It has nothing to do with your judgment, Jess. I just don't want Lily to get hit with fines or lose her pay because due diligence wasn't followed to the letter." It absolutely had to do with Jess's judgment, but I knew Dad always made a point to never outright insult Lily's mum, especially in front of Lily.

"Fine." With a breath, she switched back to her more bright and breezy attitude. "Well, I'll let you all finish up. Do hurry in getting the contract back so we *don't* have any snags. And let me know if you have any problem with the itinerary."

"Of course," Dad said.

"Ciao, dears," she waved in acknowledgement to the rest of us. Mum and the twins waved back. I didn't. Things were crazy enough where I might not catch hell for not playing nice.

Lily waited until after her mum left before talking to us again. "Well, that's that. I'm gonna start packing… Give Shari—Mrs. Garrity, I mean—and Jenna and all the family my love and prayers? Someone text me if you hear *anything?* Promise?!"

"Promise," I answered this time.

"See you soon, love," Dad said. His voice and posture softened. "Love you much, baby girl."

"Love you, too, Dad—and everyone! G'bye!"

As Mum closed down Skype, Dad collapsed back onto the couch again. I gave him a hug, snuggling.

He made a pained groan, and I looked up to see him try not to grimace.

"Did I hurt you?"

He shook his head, gently putting an arm around me. "No, love…just a little sore."

I rested myself more carefully on him, and he hugged me back. I could hear his heartbeat slowing down, but his breath still shook. He had explained once, a few years ago, that when he had the down cycles, it really, physically hurt. Like when you've got a flu that's settled into your bones. That's why, when it's bad and the medicine's not working, he just doesn't want to get out of bed. He probably wanted to go to bed now, but I knew he wouldn't until he'd gone over Lily's contract and itinerary himself. Twice, at least.

Mum leaned back on the couch too. She started quietly telling the twins her own version of Beauty and the Beast that I remembered reading in a comic book she wrote. I heard quiet snores from at least one of the twins by the time Mum finished. Mum poked me, and I looked over. She gestured to Dad with her chin and nodded down to the two sleeping twins.

With a sigh, I patted Dad's stomach. When he looked at me, I whispered. "Mum needs you to help her put the twins to bed."

"Mrm," he murmured, then bent down to kiss my head as he stood up. He picked up Ash and held him in one arm, lending his other hand to help Mum stand while she held Ivy. "Go make sure Rowan's okay, love?"

I nodded. "'Kay, Dad."

Rowan was adding more tufts of fur around the one torn cat ear in his drawing of Monkey. Isis and Osiris had curled up on his beanbag chair with each of their front halves sprawled on the floor. They half-opened their eyes and wagged greetings before slipping back into hound-doggy snores. Animals found the most awkward-looking positions comfortable.

"Wow!" I said. The boy couldn't string a sentence together in the presence of a stranger, but he could draw some amazing stuff.

Despite my exclamation, he didn't seem to notice I was there. I sighed and waited. I couldn't quite see the lines or smudges he was making, but I could see the picture getting clearer. I waited some more.

"Mind if I use your computer for a bit?"

I took his lack of response as permission and opened a new window. Facebook informed me that I had a friend request. With Joe grounded, it was either a spammer or some parting joke from one of the jerks at school. Mum had posted that the family was sending prayers to Shari about Sarah Beth, as had Lily. I clicked to see all the comments. About halfway down, I saw comments from people I didn't know telling Shari to delete the link above without looking at it. Shari had either ignored them or hadn't been back on Facebook yet. I didn't recognize the poster who had put the link, with only the note "Pray harder," but people were calling him or her (a "Pat Meirron") names that I hadn't even heard among the worst kids at school. Curious, I clicked the link.

"Jesus! God!" I shoved myself away from the computer, gagging. I couldn't blink the torn, bloated flesh from my mind. "God!"

That got Rowan's attention. "What? What's wrong?"

I scooted in front of the computer and turned off his monitor. "Don't look! Don't look!" My nightmares were going to be enough. Rowan didn't need them, too.

"What?"

"Just, just trust me, please? Please?"

He scowled and went back to his drawing.

I watched him out of the corner of my eye until I saw that hypnotized look creep back. Then, squinting my eyes so I couldn't see clearly, I clicked the mouse as fast as I could till I'd scrolled by the grisly pictures of dead kids younger than me. I would've just closed the window, but the headline caught my eye.

"Royal Family worried for horses while Scotland's children slaughtered, Borders Coast obliterated."

I wanted to be sick. I scanned the article, which said that Princess Maryan had been visiting about a foal while "young Sara-Beth Garrity" went missing and a storm destroyed nearly all the boats and more than half the coastal structures, which wasn't entirely correct. They had been here two days ago, and *then* the storm happened and Sarah Beth had only gone missing last night. I wondered how much of the damage part was true; the police hadn't said. Mum would have torn the article apart; she'd done that enough to papers of mine that were better written. Knowing it was a rubbish Internet tabloid didn't make me feel any better. Not only were they using Sarah Beth and the dead children to make a point about British royalty, those royal people were my friends! It was a bunch of lies with horrible, awful pictures of poor little kids!

Tears blurred my vision so I couldn't read, which was fine. I closed out the article. A Facebook message blinked from Lily.

"don't read the link on shari's post1!!1"

"too late," I wrote back.

"PROMISE ME YOU'LL BE SAFE???!!! TAKE CARE OF ROWAN AND IVY AND ASH AND MUM AND DAD?!!"

"Promise! I swear!"

"gtg. love you"

I bit my lip. Lily usually wasn't this affectionate, but obviously she'd seen those pictures, too, and was probably thinking every horrible, awful thing I wished I wasn't thinking.

"Love you too. Fly safe. Don't talk to strangers."

"Ha! K."

Facebook informed me she signed off. I sighed and saw a new message for me.

A "Jose Nietoreina" was asking me what was taking so long for me to answer his friend request. I couldn't help but smile as I recognized the Spanish. Joe had found a way to sneak past his grounding and create a new fake account. I quickly clicked on the friend request and accepted him. Within seconds, he was blinking a message at me.

"took u long enuf. Mum's on the phone to ur mum. guess who's coming back over tomorrow?"

"thought u were grounded. seriously? tomorrow?"

"yep. but not really a visit. press conference bout the storm damage and everything…u hear about the kids?"

"article with the pix?"

"u saw that!?"

Another chat screen blinked, then another. Livy and Sara-Not-Beth, from the horse camp Mum usually ran over the last two weeks of summer break, wanted to know details about "everything" and said their mums were pulling them from camp unless the police caught the killer, oh, and by the way, were we all right with the storm? I kept my chats with them short—they were more Lily's friends—and then asked Joe what time his family was coming, and weren't they afraid of bringing him?

"Rich and Annie not coming. Tourist kids were their age. I'm coming 'cos I'm older"

I thought about it and what Mrs. McInnis had said. All of the missing kids were six years old or younger. Yeah, it was a good idea his younger sister and brother, who were Rowan's and the twins' ages, weren't coming.

Lily blinked back on the screen and Livy and Sara-Not-Beth's screens stopped blinking at me. Lily sent me a note about her travel plans and could I make sure Dad didn't totally blow up over some detail or another. I told her Dad was in the office or still putting down the twins or something, and I was in the library. Mum was looking after him, though.

"Looking after?"

"Downswing, meds not working right."

"o_O that explains things. :(Poor Dad!" She proceeded to tell me to be careful again and to make sure I answer any text she sent me so she knew everyone was okay. I smiled at the screen and promised. As much of a pain as she could be, and as much of a spoiled brat as she acted, I knew she was worried. The whole first semester after she left me behind in primary, she checked in on me through her friends to make sure I didn't get into too much trouble in her absence.

Joe's name blinked twice before it turned grey to show he'd signed out. One of his parents or someone who'd snitch on him must have gone by. I was used to that by now. He'd gone through three different Facebook incarnations since we'd become friends. A few lines before he had to sign off, he'd posted some links. One of them was an article my mum had written a few years ago that talked about the "native Fey Folk" of Scotland, including kelpies, and how humans supposedly interacted with them. She'd noted that the only repeated story she found about dealing with kelpies included an enchanted bridle. The rest of the article discussed metaphors and histories of the different fae, and how the kelpie myth probably came from the wild or abandoned horses and the fears surrounding the equine fey may stem from the fear people had—and still have—of roaming gypsies and pikeys.

I wondered what she'd say if she'd actually seen the monster faerie. It made pikey ponies (a few of which had roamed through our land and had, indeed, had nasty attitudes) look positively cuddly.

The other link was more on that magickal bridle Mum had mentioned in her article. The most recent story stated that the Graham clan were the last "recorded" to have captured a kelpie. They used it around the farm and bred it because it did more work than any other horse, and its offspring also had supernatural strength and speed.

After seeing what it had done to those kids (I shivered again at just the thought of the photos), I couldn't imagine wanting to keep it! Would I be able to kill it? I'd never killed anything, not even bugs. Mickey wasn't allowed to keep the medicine they used to put horses down; we actually had to call Dr. Caroline for that because only vets could keep the stuff. Even if he had had it, he'd notice if it went missing.

Besides, I didn't even know if it would work on a faery horse beast.

Chris and Jared, two boys from the camp, Lily's friends again, blinked at me to say they were sorry they weren't coming and that it was their parents'/aunt's & uncle's fault. They certainly weren't scared of the killer and they'd probably do a better job than "the fuzz," anyway.

It was probably a good idea Mum was canceling camp.

"What are you two still doing up?!" Mum interrupted my thoughts, striding over to Rowan's corner. "And what do you think you're doing on Facebook, Heather? You're grounded!"

"We didn't specifically discuss computer privileges." I stifled a yawn. What was it about just being reminded of bedtime that triggered the stupid yawn response?

She didn't validate my argument with anything more than *that look*.

"Lily wanted me to make sure Dad knew she'd be fine traveling and asked me to keep my phone on. And the royal family 'cept Richard and Annie are coming up tomorrow for some press conference…" I tried to give good reason for being on the computer.

Mum closed her eyes tightly, took off her glasses, and rubbed the bridge of her nose. With a sigh, she said, "Your dad got Lily's itinerary…and yes, Princess Maryan told me they should be arriving in the afternoon. They must be taking a private jet or something to Edinburgh, since they've got a junket scheduled for noon there, and then they're taking cars out here—"

"Waitaminute, what?!"

We jerked our heads around (well, me and Mum; Rowan was still drawing) as Dad walked over, face a mix of anger and anxiety.

"Which I was going to tell your dad after he got off the phone with Jess."

"You're joking, right?" he asked.

Mum shook her head. "Not just Princess Maryan. Prince Christopher, and Prince Joseph…and the Queen…" Her voice grew softer as she listed.

Dad started shaking his head in time with hers. "No, no! Seriously? No! Couldn't you have done…said…*some*thing?" He turned around in dramatic anguish.

"Last I checked, dear, you wanted me to treat the sovereign royalty like I was a proper citizen, which means if the Queen and family state that they are staying at your castle home that gets government funding as a historical monument, you say, 'And what would you like for lunch, tea, dinner, breakfast, or anything else?'"

Dad groaned. "Brilliant time to not be an ugly American. We *can't* see them! We—we need to pack to visit my Dad."

"I guess that's on hold."

"You decided already?" Rowan gave us his attention. His drawing kit was already packed; he must've gotten the point about bedtime.

"Well, *obviously* that's now changed." Dad growled at no one in particular.

"If nothing else, we'll be safe," Mum said. "I can't imagine they'll stay here without this place crawling with royal guards. With actual guns, maybe."

Now the growl was half-directed at my mother.

"I already texted Eliza, Marie, Mary, Anita, and Ginny. Eliza and Marie will be here first thing in the morning to set up the guest rooms and clean and all that. Anita will keep the twins in her rooms in case they end up doing another conference here—"

"The *press* is coming, too?!"

"Probably not; they'll probably head out to Coldingham, Eyemouth, and St. Abbs so they can do whatever royals do to help with disaster stuff. They're *staying* here, though."

"And Ginny?"

"Ginny is okay with staying a few more days. She called her mum to check on her flat."

Dad slumped against the wall, looking quite sullen. Mum walked over to him, stood on her tiptoes, and kissed his cheeks until he gave in and kissed her back. I rolled my eyes and looked at my brother, who was carefully carrying the picture by its corner between his thumb and forefinger.

"Are you going to tuck us in?" he asked.

Keeping one hand on Dad's chest, Mum turned and smiled at us. "Of course." She looked specifically at me. "Heather, want us to go check on you tonight, too? Before you go to sleep?"

I'd been putting myself to bed with just a kiss to both of them for a few years now. Looking at the now-sleeping computer screen, I nodded slowly. "Could you brush my hair tonight?"

Dad's face softened. "Me or your mum?"

"Either." I just didn't want to go to bed alone, even though I knew I'd not sleep because I was supposed to meet Rowan for whatever plan he had with that picture.

"I want Daddy." Rowan surprised us. Usually, he preferred Mum.

"Well, then." Dad turned a smile onto him, looking touched. "Let's get you to bed." He reached for Rowan's free hand and the two walked to his room.

"I guess it's us girls." Mum put an arm around me and squeezed. "Go, put your jammies on while I make sure everything's off in here. I'll be right in, okay?"

Chapter 9

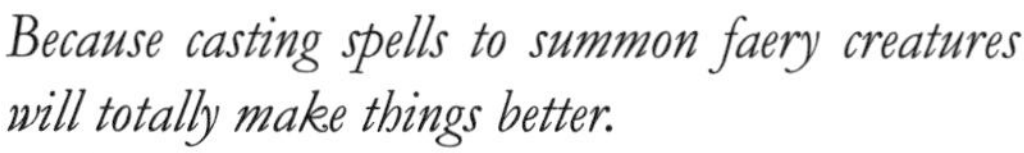

Because casting spells to summon faery creatures will totally make things better.

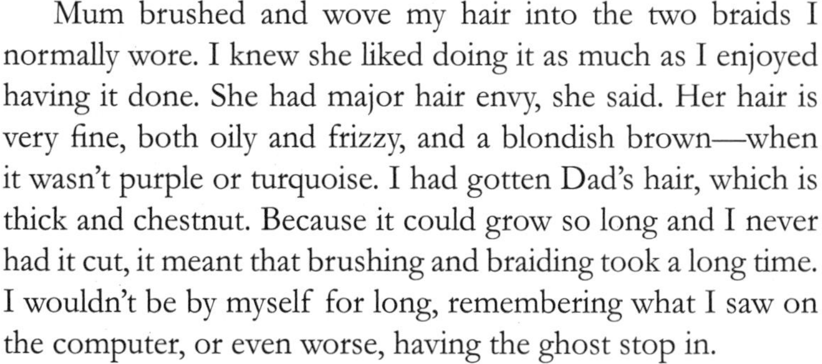

Mum brushed and wove my hair into the two braids I normally wore. I knew she liked doing it as much as I enjoyed having it done. She had major hair envy, she said. Her hair is very fine, both oily and frizzy, and a blondish brown—when it wasn't purple or turquoise. I had gotten Dad's hair, which is thick and chestnut. Because it could grow so long and I never had it cut, it meant that brushing and braiding took a long time. I wouldn't be by myself for long, remembering what I saw on the computer, or even worse, having the ghost stop in.

When she finished, I asked, "Are you going to bed now?"

"Probably not right away, but soon. You want me to stay till you fall asleep?"

"Mmmn…" If I wasn't supposed to sneak into Rowan's room once she and Dad were in bed, I would've said yes. I crawled under my sheet and comforter. "I think I'll be fine."

"You sure? I can read to you?" She rubbed the top of my head.

"Mmn-mmn." I shook my head and closed my eyes, trying to keep myself from falling into the oblivion of sleep that was already tugging at me.

"All right, then. Your dad and I will come check on you when we go to bed. Promise."

"Thanks, Mum. Love you." I made my voice sound extra mumbly and sleepy.

It wasn't more than a few minutes after she left my room that my heart began to pound. I wound myself in my covers because I was shivering. I almost wished the twins had wanted to sleep with me tonight, too. And I wished Lily were back home already in the other bed. I felt really alone.

What if the ghost came back? I pulled the covers tighter with every second, murmuring, "Please don't come. Please don't come. Please don't come."

I would cover my head, but with all the light blocked out, I saw the murdered children's torn faces and bodies, chunks bitten out of them, in my mind. That was even worse, but then I'd uncover my head, and the glow from my clock made me think the ghost would appear any moment.

Finally, I couldn't take it any more. I made myself move—all my joints ached—and I put on my slippers and robe. I dismissed the secret passages immediately. Checking over my shoulder with every other breath, I edged to my door. I opened it a little and looked around. No parents.

I crept over to Rowan's room. All of us had gotten good at opening the heavy wood doors without creaking them. (The discovery of where Mrs. McInnis kept the WD40 had helped).

"Rowan?" I whispered.

He sat up in the bed. I could only see a little of his face from his night-light, but he was glaring at me. "Mum and Dad are still awake."

"I know…I just thought we could still…I dunno, whatever it is you have planned?"

He shook his head at me. "They're gonna come check on us before they go to sleep. You want them to walk in on us summoning a faery cat?"

That was his plan? I felt stupid. I'd looked through the book and seen the summoning spells. I should've figured. His picture was so detailed it could have been a photo. He was right, of course.

"No, we don't." I sighed.

"They shouldn't be too much longer. Not even Mum. She'll be worried about Dad and go to bed with him."

I turned to go.

Behind me, I heard him readjust back into his covers. I snuck back out and back into my room. Leaning on my door, I caught sight of Old Benson, my teddy bear from when I was little. We'd put him in a cute little rocking chair by the windows. I bit my lip, made a mad dash to grab him, and then dove back into bed. I stared at the swishing curtains until they stopped moving, then realized my chest hurt from holding my breath. I blew it all out and hugged Benson closer, pulling the blankets into a cocoon, hoping it would protect me from… well…everything, right now.

By the time Mum and Dad came in to check on me, which was the longest forty-three minutes my bedroom clock had ever recorded in history, I managed to get my breathing under control so I could at least fake sleeping.

"She looks scared," I heard Dad whisper.

"They shouldn't have to go through this," came Mum's soft voice. I felt her hand brushing my forehead.

"Are you sure we can't just pack up and go to my dad's tomorrow?" Dad's voice was almost a whine.

"You know better. Besides, isn't it safer here with the royal guards?"

Dad grunted. I heard them move, then felt his face by mine. He kissed my cheek, rubbed the top of my head, kissed me again, and then sighed. It was all I could do to keep pretending to sleep and not throw my arms around him. Mum kissed me once more, and then I heard them both leave.

I waited for the clock to read exactly 11:06, fifteen more horrible minutes after the light went out in the hall, before I started making my clenched muscles move again. And I was still cold. Even my fluffy, winter robe didn't help. I did leave

Old Benson Bear in the bed and tucked in that pillow trick, which would work if Mum or Dad just peeked their head in. Not if they did a full check-in…which I thought and hoped they wouldn't do.

I hated how much I was shaking as I returned to Rowan's room. *I* was the big sister now, the oldest one here, and I was a coward.

"You're cold?" He eyed my fuzzy robe.

"Yes."

After a shrug, he handed me Mum's book, the cover and spine now covered in clear packing tape. It was opened to a spell for summoning one's faery guide.

"I don't know if Monkey's exactly a guide," I said.

"You said he said he'd help."

"Mmmm…" He had said he'd that he'd contact me when he had something. There was definitely a "Don't call me, I'll call you" vibe to our conversation.

"Heather?"

Why hadn't Monkey mentioned Sarah Beth in our conversation? She'd gone missing the night before! Had he known? Maybe he needed to know and would help more if he knew? What if he did know and hadn't told me? We were totally summoning him back here. I looked at the book. "Let's see what we've got to do."

"It said we needed a clear picture." Rowan carefully placed his drawing on the floor. "But I don't understand how it works with all the other stuff."

I read through and understood Rowan's confusion. It depended on an earlier spell, a meditation and visualization of one's faery guide. This one called for the caster to have a clear picture of the guide in her head before and while casting the spell. The suggestion for an actual drawing was just a reference, but Rowan took it literally. I had an idea to make it work.

"You've got the white candle and salt and honey, milk, and poppy seeds?"

He nodded and retrieved a cloth grocery bag from inside one of the beanbag chairs. When had he snuck around to get all the stuff? He pulled out the foodstuffs in zipper-lock bags, along with one of the white votives that decorated the different sconces throughout the house.

"It smells like lavender," he apologized. "It was the only one I could reach."

"Faeries like lavender, I think."

He nodded.

"Do you have like a little bowl or a dish for the candle?"

Rowan bit his lip. "The spell didn't say that!"

"'S'okay. You just always burn a candle on something safe. Let me see…"

I stood up and looked around his room, spying the water cup by his bed. I brought it over.

"Here, drink all this. It's thick enough to be okay with the flame, I think."

With a sigh, he slowly drank until it was empty and gave it back. I put the candle in the cup, then realized my whole idea was pointless. "You don't have anything to light it with, do you?"

Rowan looked like he was about to cry even though I'd only whispered the question.

"Just…let me think a second." Miss Eliza usually lit the candles for weekend and private tours. I had no idea where she kept the lighters and matches; candles and flames were pretty strictly monitored since we all knew that this wing had burned down to the ground years ago. No one even smoked in the house… Mum! Mum usually kept both a knife and lighter in her handbag "in case of emergencies." I looked at the door and frowned.

"What?"

"We can get Mum's from her handbag in the office. Will you come with me?"

He nodded and headed for his door, pausing to look both ways.

It took a moment for our eyes to adjust, but we were able to creep downstairs. We stayed on the edges of the rug where it was thicker. Once or twice, we stepped wrong. The small moan or squeak made us jump. About halfway down the stairs, Rowan moved his flashlight up, and I grabbed his arm, thinking of the ghost. He jumped two steps down, hand over his mouth, and glared at me.

"Sorry! Sorry!" I hissed. Bad enough he hated being touched on normal occasions.

I kept two stairs behind him the rest of the way, clutching my robe and trying to remember to breathe.

Please, no ghost! Please, no ghost! Please, no ghost!

There was a jingle and soft scratching coming towards us! I froze. Rowan bent a little, and the dim light revealed a smile. Upon seeing the lanky shadows of the greyhounds, I collapsed a little on the cold wall.

God, help me.

Rowan kept the dogs entertained and quiet while I rooted through Mum's purse once we got into her office. How many freaking pockets did she *need?* Receipts, keys, lip balm, about a hundred pens, a calculator, three different pads of paper, her wallet, her checkbook... *Really, Mum? Do you need all this crap?*

A noise from Rowan let me know he was getting antsy.

Finally, inside one of the inside-side pockets, I found two lighters, a Swiss Army knife, and a can of pepper spray. I grabbed one of the lighters and the knife and put them in my robe pocket. The excursion took less than fifteen minutes. No ghostly encounter. Things were going well.

Back in Rowan's room, I consulted the spell again.

"Okay, what we've gotta do is—" I began.

Scratch, scratch, pat, scratch.

Rowan and I both jumped and shoved hands to our mouths to stop from screaming. We looked at his window from where the noise came.

A muffled "meow" and the coppery-green rings of reflective eyes greeted us from the window.

"We didn't do the spell yet." Rowan sounded almost disappointed as he let Monkey in. The cat arched away from my brother's hand as he reached to pat him, and padded over to me. He sat down and regarded his portrait as Rowan put the screen back and quietly slid the window shut. (Mum and Dad had re-redone the windows in the part of the castle where we lived, so we had modern windows that boasted easy cleaning—and easy deconstruction for us.)

Not bad, Monkey commented about his picture, tail swishing as he stood and circled it. *My eyes are greener and my tail and mane aren't nearly that messy.*

"No, they aren't, and yes, they are," Rowan argued, taking the talking cat in better stride than I had. Well, he'd had advance warning.

Monkey sneezed in his direction.

So, you were trying to summon me? He sniffed the candle and puffed his tail, making a sour face. *I hate lavender. Try catnip next time. Or maybe just wait.*

"Is Sarah Beth all right?" Rowan demanded.

Monkey did one of those figure-eights around my legs, arching his back against the hem of my robe.

Yes. She's safe.

"So, the kelpie doesn't have her?" I asked.

Nope. He purred as he slipped through my legs and brushed my robe again.

"Where is she, then? What happened?" I pushed when it became apparent that his silence wasn't just a dramatic pause.

Do parents not teach their children manners any more?

"You just told me this afternoon that the kelpie kills its victims because it's like an animal, and our friend is missing, and you didn't bother to tell me that before, and you want me to mind my manners?!" I hissed my forced whisper between clenched teeth.

Monkey walked away from me and began grooming his mane.

"Will you please tell us what happened to Sarah Beth?" Rowan asked, sitting down beside Monkey, hands folded in his lap.

It was dusk, and she saw the kelpie glamoured like a pony just outside her yard, so she followed it. Fortunately, the Seelie Court has decided it was in their best interests to prevent further violence against children inasmuch as they could. One of the knights intercepted them before they reached the loch. The child is with the Court now. He paused, then added. *Obviously, the kelpie was infuriated with this. Thus the storm.*

"He can cause giant storms that destroy villages?" *What* was I going up against?!

You're by the ocean. Water...responds to it. And weather responds to water...something like that. Beyond my magick, anyway...

"And why didn't that faery knight just bring her home?" I pushed. "Do you know how worried her family is?"

Because its charm is still on her. She'd seek it out again and again. It would haunt her dreams. In the Court, they can weave protective dreams around her until the kelpie no longer influences her.

"You said earlier that the kelpie wasn't actively hunting! It just took people who crossed its territory. Now—"

It's expanding its territory. That's why the Seelie Court intervened; its actions were enough to warrant a response.

"Oh, well. Good to know exactly how much of an attack on humans it takes to warrant a response from other faeries."

Faerie, please. Or Fey Folk. Not "faeries." You make us sound like those ridiculous little pixies most humans think we are.

I continued glaring at the cat.

"Heather," Rowan said softly.

"What?!" I snapped. Was anyone else killed in the storm? It had to be really bad if Joe's family was dong a press conference about it.

"Sarah Beth is gonna be okay."

"I know. I'm just...angry." I realized I'd lied to him, too, and hadn't told him everything like I promised. Granted, it probably was for the better because knowing kids were dead might push him into a meltdown, but I still lied. I really wished I had Joe here, now, instead of waiting till tomorrow!

"It's like getting angry at a horse." How did Rowan have this much patience now? Was it because Monkey was a cat and not exactly a person?

"Monkey and the kelpie are both capable of human thought—"

Sentient thought, please. Such capabilities have belonged to beings long before humans were created. Oh, and I'm right here.

Rowan pursed his lips. "You and the kelpie think like animals, too."

Monkey turned around to face my brother, tail swishing as he stared unblinking.

You're right.

"I'm like Mickey," he told the cat. "I don't always get people either."

I know.

"So, why don't you like talking to me?"

Monkey stared at him for a long time before his eyes shifted to Mum's spell book. I grabbed it, which made the cat snap his eyes at me. It was my turn to ignore him and read the spell Mum had cast on Rowan.

"I have an idea," I finally said. "Dad helped Mum with the spell. Dad wouldn't want *any*thing from Faerie around you. Period." I paused, this time for effect, and added, "Unless, of course, you *really do* mean harm to us, too?"

Monkey's tail swish was angry this time, and he half-flattened his ears.

If that book is worth its salt, it will have a spell to determine my intention.

I flipped through the book, feeling the fanning of the cat's irritated tail. He *was* the one who told me never to give up my right to know a faerie's motivation.

"Give me the salt, Rowan," I said. He hesitated a moment, then complied. I looked at Monkey, who sat primly, tail wrapped around his legs, but twitching madly. I used the salt and circled a heavy line around him. Looking him right in the eyes, I put all my intention into knowing the truth, then I looked down at the book and recited the words on the page as if I were reading a prayer in church.

I looked him in the eye, and said…recited…no, it was something more. I *cast* the spell.

A warm wind tousled his fur and the belt of my robe and the air smelled like after a thunderstorm. The salt circling Monkey, however, didn't move. The room grew brighter and a bluish-white glow, what the spell said was a benevolent color, emanated from around the cat. Per everything I had read, I knew faerie could make illusions, glamour, but I felt this was real. It felt like church.

Satisfied? Monkey asked.

I nodded.

Will you let me out now? And did you really *have to make this circle so small?*

"You really can't get out?" The back of my mind itched at what else I should ask him, demand of him.

No.

"What happens if you try?" Rowan asked.

Monkey made a tight circle and growled. He looked between us, then twitched his tail. When it hit the perimeter, blue sparks appeared and he jumped, arching his back and puffing his fur. His tail twitched again, this time unintentionally, and he cried out. His body grew tighter and tighter, but he couldn't quite get his tail under control.

Please?!

Quickly, I brushed away the salt. He bolted from the circle, sat down, and started licking his tail. After a few moments, he laid down. *I appreciate your kind turn.*

"We don't want to hurt you," Rowan said.

Monkey looked at me. *You had me trapped in the circle. You could have demanded more.*

I nodded. Not really, I knew; I could also feel his fear and pain. "Like Rowan said, we don't *want* to hurt you."

The cat bobbed his head in a nod and stretched closer to me. *I know every animal who lives on the grounds and what you do for them. Your family leaves me and the other feral cats food, though you have seen nary a rat nor mouse in your stables. Every winter, there are blankets and shelter. I didn't believe you would harm me. I just didn't* know. I nodded, understanding, and reached to pet him and he rolled over, so I scratched around his ears and neck until he purred.

Then he rolled back. *We don't have much time. I came here for a reason.*

"What?" both Rowan and I asked.

You need to visit Sarah Beth. You need to give her a token to help her remember. Humans start to forget once they're in Faerie, and the kelpie had already charmed her.

"Oh! You mean…we've got to actually *go* to Faerie?"

You *have to.* Monkey looked at Rowan. You *can't. Unless you wanted to undo the spell that protects you.*

"No way! Rowan needs to stay safe," I said.

Then come on. He wove around my ankles and headed to Rowan's door. I looked at him in confusion. I wasn't exactly sure how we were going to get to Faerie, but I was thinking we'd open some portal or something. That's what happens in stories, anyway, I think.

Are you agile enough to go out the window?

I sighed and figured I'd just follow.

"Heather!" Rowan threw the rest of the salt, the candle, the lighter, and the poppy seeds into the canvas bag. His lower lip trembled as he handed it to me.

I took the bag and put my hand into my robe pocket and flexed my fingers around Mum's knife. "I'll be careful, promise."

He took my hand and squeezed it hard, cringing as he did so from the pressure. "Let me know when you get back?"

"Promise." I followed Monkey out of Rowan's room, out of the castle, out into the night—breaking every promise I'd made to my parents earlier that day.

I was really on a roll.

Chapter 10

Where I actually visit Faerie! Then make more fey "friends." Sort of.

We were passing by the main stable when I remembered. "Wait, you said I needed some sort of token to give Sarah Beth to help her remember. Give me a second to get something."

We must be quick.

I jogged into the tack room, hearing the shuffle of the family herd. Their warm, sweet smell slowed my racing heart just a little. I went to Clint Eastwood's bridle and dug my nail into the ring that held on his charm, a copper cowboy hat with his name engraved beneath the brim. East was my pony, a short, flashy Pony of the Americas. Sarah Beth especially loved him and all his spots. When I came from the tack room, shuffling in a pair of muck boots because my slippers were already soaked, East had finagled his way between the other horses and reached out his head. With a glance at Monkey, who seemed to nod, I went over to pet my baby's nose for just a second.

"Might I have your robe?"

"What, why?" I turned towards Monkey even as I realized I'd *heard* him speak with my ears as much as in my head. "Oh-Jeez!" I spun back around, hands over my eyes and face burning. Boy parts!

"Because humans are prudes and clothes don't materialize when I change," came his impatient response.

Squeezing my eyes closed, still, which did nothing to erase his naked body from my mind, I dropped the satchel and untied my robe. I paused for a second, hopefully slipping the knife into my hand without him noticing. He didn't say anything. I handed him my robe, quickly crossing my arms across my chest, acutely aware that my pink ruffled pyjamas didn't quite fit as well as they used to. How embarrassing! I had nowhere to hide the knife, either. It pressed in my palm against East's charm.

"All right, let's go."

"You're decent?"

He didn't respond, but I could still feel him in my mind and the unworded sarcasm resounded something to the effect that he wouldn't ask me to turn around if he wasn't.

I turned back around, hefting the bag over one shoulder, and looked at him. "You're just a kid!"

"I am not! I'm seventy-three years old!" He was quite offended.

I rubbed my head. "According to Mum's stories, anything under, like a hundred or two hundred, is basically a baby for faeries—I mean, faerie or fey, whatever—and can you stop talking in my head when you *talk*-talk, too?"

There was a release of pressure in my brain, and I could only *hear* the sulkiness in his tone when he said, "Animal fey mature faster, not that *you* know *that* much about faerie anyway."

"You *look* like you're Lily's age, though."

He glared at me, and his eyes still reflected the moonlight as we left the stable, which gave his now-mostly-human-looking face a really eerie appearance. He was also almost as short as Lily, which meant I was a good few inches taller, too.

"You still have a tail…and kitty ears." I jogged to catch up as he turned to stalk towards the preserve.

His tail swished angrily at my comment, lifting my robe so I had to look away quickly before I was exposed to his bare rear end, too.

"If I remember how your sister says it, 'Thank you, Captain Obvious.'"

"Can't you turn all-human?"

His ears flattened on his head. "I'm *not* human, and I don't *want* to lose my tail—humans walk funny! And trust me, you want me to hear with cat ears. The kelpie is still on the hunt."

I froze. "What if… " I felt myself start shaking.

Monkey's ears pointed at me, and his face softened. He held out his hand. "He won't find you if you're with me. I promise."

I thrust both my hands behind my back, glancing nervously at the hand of the teenaged-looking boy who I'd seen all the boy-parts of only a minute ago.

He sighed, not sounding as impatient as before. "That, and if you don't want to get lost in time when we cross back and forth into Faerie, you must hold my hand." He touched a wooden coin around his neck. "I've got a charm that will let us pass safely."

I took a deep breath, shifted the knife and charm, re-slung the satchel of stuff from Rowan over my shoulders, and took his hand. It was warm and very smooth. We started walking towards the preserve again.

We walked in strained silence for a while. His cat-ears told me he was getting more and more aggravated at my jumping at every sound, including stupid sheep *baas*.

"Mickey calls you Monkey." I tried to make myself relax with some normal conversation. "What's your real name?"

He looked at me, arching an eyebrow. "Real names have power. Fey folk don't give our real names."

"Oh…I didn't mean…"

"I know." He was still impatient, but as a not-entirely-cat, he seemed less annoying.

"Do you still want me to call you Monkey, then?"

His ears twitched in thought.

"Tom. Tom Cat."

It was my turn to arch an eyebrow at him. "Very original."

He sniffed. "Common names make it harder for people to pick us out and remember us. And Tom isn't as common as, say, Jack."

My mind flitted through the faery tales I knew well, and he had a point. Jacks definitely outnumbered the Toms… and the similar names did make one story blend into another, making it hard to tell if some of the adventures were just continuations with the same characters.

Still, Tom Cat? I sighed. Really, I had much more to be concerned about than what my faery guide wanted me to call him.

The few old trees and grassy sheep fields gave way to scrubby bushes and rocks, and I could hear and smell the pounding ocean waves. My eyes had adjusted to the light, and I recognized where we were.

Fear paralyzed me again, and I almost ripped my hand from Tom's.

"What?" Tom tightened his grip. "We don't have a lot of time."

"The only thing out here is the ruins of the castle before ours, and everyone tells the tourists to not even hike out here, it's so dangerous! If you wanted to, you could just push me over the cliffs and no one would find me and—"

"I am *not* going to push you off the cliffs. You did that spell—I don't *want* to hurt you!" His voice sounded as betrayed as it did angry.

"What-what if you used faery glamour stuff to make it look like you were a friend?" It wasn't really Tom that scared me, but something about seeing the ruins at this time at night, something about the air around here. During the day, it felt different enough…but tonight, it prickled my skin with goose bumps.

He stared at me, sizing me up, then spoke in a different tone. "I'm neither old enough nor powerful enough to mess with that spell. I promise, really." His voice sounded almost sweet, kind of like Joe, and I felt myself relax more. As if he couldn't maintain that level of nice-ness, he added, "Besides, if I wasn't here to help, I'd have just handed you over to the kelpie or someone else by now." A teasingly sharp smile glinted in a passing moment of clear starlight. "Or left you outside and found a way to alert your parents."

I stared at him for several minutes awash in more emotions than I wanted to deal with. Aggravation won out, which somehow got my feet and legs to move again. I don't know if it was the sound of his voice or the look in his eyes, but I did believe him. I squeezed his hand, and he squeezed back, like Joe would have. Taking a deep breath, I followed him through the narrow sheep paths between the bushes of heath and heather (I'd gotten sick of the jokes about my name shortly after we moved here). I was happy I'd changed into the boots, because the wet ground only made the sheep crap that was everywhere stick more—and it was too dark to see the stupid sheep crap. I could hardly even see the stupid sheep that still wandered around! And they were big and white.

It sounds dumb to think about, sure, but worrying about sheep crap was easier than worrying about dangerous cliffs in the dark. Or sneaking into a Faery Court.

We climbed down some wooden steps people had built along the steepest part of the trails and paused before the narrow strip of land that led to the piles of stones that were the old castle ruins. Monkey—Tom—slowed his pace, and kept shooting me questioning looks. After questioning look number ten where we'd stopped, several feet from the land bridge, I asked, "What?"

"Do you see it?"

"I see the old foundation of the old castle and old piles of rocks where there used to be old walls."

"So, you don't."

"What am I supposed to be seeing?"

Tom let out another of his impatient sighs. His tail twitched nervously and was extra-puffed. Something had him scared or nervous. Before I could ask further, he said, in a voice much softer and calmer than his body language would have me expect, "When the waves hit the rocks, look at the mist. And look at the mist that clings to the stones. Don't try to focus on it, though."

I did what he said and also added in the meditative breathing from karate. It didn't take long before I knew what he meant. The mist was a curtain. I could see it shimmering even without any moonlight or starlight. It rustled with each wave. And with each rustle, I could see it better. I don't know if Tom was in my head directing me, or if it was something I just knew, but I willed the curtains to part and reveal what they hid.

The castle glittered as if it were made of crystal and shimmered solid parts as if they were made of moonstone or cat's eye. It shouldn't have fit on the outcrop, but the outcrop seemed to have grown with it. Behind the castle, the clouds that had darkened our trails had parted and stars glowed brightly.

"Jesus!" I breathed, then pressed my fist over my mouth. "Sorry. I…didn't mean to offend…or anything. I…didn't hurt anything, did I?"

Tom smirked at me. "Why should it?"

"I—aren't—I mean…"

He was growing more amused the more flustered I got.

"*Some* people are bothered by others' religious beliefs," I finally spat and only barely kept myself from snatching my hand from him.

"Faerie are *not* demons or minions of Lucifer, in case that was what you're worried about. And the name 'Jesus' doesn't affect us one way or another." He was still smirking as he led me towards the land bridge. "Though, if I recall correctly, *your* family frowns upon saying that name in vain."

I ignored his chiding. A friggin' awesome faery castle had appeared from curtains of mist. If He were watching, He might have taken His own Name in vain. Maybe. And anyway, the fact Tom was *not* crossing the land bridge worried me more. "We're not going to the castle?"

The smugness disappeared from his face. "We are. Just… trust me. It's better if we don't get noticed."

"Am I not supposed to be helping Sarah Beth?"

"It's…complicated."

"Can't they tell we're here? I mean, they must have guards or a watch?"

"I've got my ways. Don't be so impatient."

"You're waaaaay more impatient than I have ever been in my whole life!"

"I'm a cat."

Being a cat, of course, explained everything. Whatever.

"Okay, this is where you're really going to have to trust me—"

I looked down alongside the narrow land bridge, into darkness and flashes of sea foam.

"You're kidding, right?" I really, really hoped he was kidding.

He put both his hands on mine. "I swear on my life, Heather MacArthur, that I *shall not* let you fall."

The solemnity of his voice surprised me, but didn't quite touch my panic. "You want me to climb down there?!" I'm pretty sure my voice was squeaking. I wondered if there was *any* promise or rule I wasn't breaking beyond death-by-grounding. "In the dark? And still hold your hand?"

"We're in Faerie now, you don't have to hold my hand. It's just when we go between the realms—"

I snatched my hand from him, angrily adjusting the bag over my shoulders and looking away. The castle wasn't as shiny and sparkly, and the cliffs looked way bigger behind us. I could see what he meant about having crossed realms.

"Heather, please, we don't have a lot of time. And I mean my oath, I do. I will not let you fall!"

I looked at him—this was almost a different Tom than the one who'd led me here. This was clearly something big. I closed my eyes and nodded.

"It's only a little ways down. I'll go first and guide your feet."

Taking a deep breath, I nodded again. Once he disappeared, I quickly rolled my knife and charm into my pyjama sleeve, hoping the elastic would hold. I wanted them close, and I didn't want to go rooting in the bag Rowan had given me if I needed…something. And I needed both hands to climb down. I was decently athletic, and tall, so the climb wasn't that hard. The bright stars made it easier to see handholds, and Tom caught my feet any time they slipped on wet rock. Having to focus made it easier not to panic.

Tom was right, too, it was only a little ways down. It was a ledge that you wouldn't easily see because it blended into the cliffs that may as well have been out of any mystery novel or movie or *Young Sherlock Holmes* episode. Another spray of heather grew from a crack, obscuring the entrance to a tunnel. If the cliché served us, the tunnel would probably lead to a not-so-secret dungeon or mad scientist's room or something like that.

I pulled off the bag I'd tied around my shoulders.

"What are you doing?" Tom whispered.

"Getting a torch."

"No, that'll mess with my vision! Just…" I felt his hand take mine again.

I sighed. Logically, I was pretty sure he could see better in the dark than I could with a torch, so it was safer. Sometimes, I really hated logic. My heart pounded as we moved deeper into the cliff. The sound of ocean waves echoed, making me a little dizzy, and my lips were dry from all the salt air. I wished I'd brought water.

We took a right and then a left, and I blinked when I saw flickers of light ahead. Tom slowed, and his tail was swishing so hard that it smacked my knees on more than one occasion, for which he half-mumbled apologies at my growls. A person-sized cat tail smarted no matter how much puffy fur was on it!

As we approached the outline of light, I looked at him and almost snatched my hand back. His face was changing! He turned to me, ears pinned in offense.

"I just—" I tried to explain that it was more the unexpectedness of watching skin and bones reform, but he "shushed" me before I could get that into words.

The slits on his nose twitched as he scented the air, and his whiskers pointed slightly at the door. I knew he was getting closer to one of the cracks that light came through, but he moved so slowly that I couldn't actually see the motion.

He placed a hand on the wall or door—a fully human-looking hand, at least, as was the hand that still held mine—and tucked his fingers into one of the slits. If I hadn't been listening for it, I would have missed the subtle *click*. The light grew a fraction then stopped. Tom turned his face, still more cat than human, and asked me, "You know the human rules for Faerie, right?"

Human rules? I paused, then, as if someone a button in my head, I recited from the memory of some poem or something. "Eat nothing. Drink nothing. Take nothing…but if something is hungry, feed it. If something is thirsty, give it a drink. If something is hurt, help it if you can…"

He furrowed his furry brow. "Close enough. Mainly, don't eat, drink, or take anything. Unless you're given a gift…but that gets complicated."

"More complicated?" I muttered. "I'd never have guessed."

He sighed once more and opened the door so we could enter.

Yep, a dungeon. "If there's an iron maiden on the other side of this…" I started.

"We wouldn't keep that much iron in Faerie."

I stuck my tongue out at him for spoiling my commentary on cliché. He ignored me, ears twitching, cat eyes watching everything.

It wasn't an iron maiden on the other side of the wall, but there was a set of what looked like copper manacles. The floor was laid out in a circle of stones that was stained brown and blue along the crevices and along copper grates on the floor. My stomach turned at the sight, an old story about faerie having blue blood coming to mind.

"They aren't keeping her down here, are they?" I asked.

"No, but it's the easiest place to sneak in."

My shoulders relaxed some. The thought of poor Sarah Beth in a dungeon gave me chills.

Tom led me through more dark hallways that he seemed to know very well and up a set of narrow stairs that might have supposed to have been hidden. We moved so quickly I could barely keep up with him, much less remember where we were going. I hoped to God (assuming He'd be listening while I was in Faerie) that I really could trust Tom to get me safely out of here.

At the top of the stairs, he stopped, nose twitching and tail puffed more. I waited silently until he nodded. He pushed against a door that, I could tell this time, was another hidden entry. We came out into a closet where Tom paused and sniffed again.

"We're good."

He slowly led me into the room. It was mostly dark, so it took my eyes a minute to adjust. To my left was one of those "princess" beds with sheer curtains around them. Lantern light filtered through it, revealing a silhouette that I recognized.

Tom nodded at me so I tiptoed over at a jog, whispering, "Sarah Beth!" When I pulled the curtains aside, she winced, gasped, and stared at me with bleary blue eyes. I knew the look:

you know you know someone, but don't remember who they are or how you know them.

I climbed on the bed, but she edged away. "Sarah Beth, it's me, Heather! My mum lets you ride our horses and Lily is my sister and Rowan is my brother, and there are the twins that you play with? I'm their big sister?"

Her lower lip trembled and tears glistened in her eyes, but she still looked confused. I could see the shadow of Tom through the silky curtains. I pulled East's name tag from my rolled sleeve without disturbing the knife and continued, "And I've got a pony named Clint Eastwood, East for short. You like him. He's pretty grey with white and brown spots all over." The girl started to nod a little. "Will you give me your hand? I have something that might help."

She held out her cute, pudgy hand, and I pressed the charm into it, wrapping her fingers around it.

After a few breaths, the tears came harder and she flung herself at me.

"Heather! Where's Mummy? Where am I? I wanna go home!"

From outside the curtain came Tom's loud "shush!"

"Sh, sh," I told her, much more gently than the cat fey.

"Who's that?" She whispered now, though she didn't sound any less terrified.

"That's Tom… He brought me here to help you."

"You'll take me home?"

When someone says, "that just broke my heart," you don't know what it means until you feel it. There might as well have been cracks spreading through my chest when I heard her beg and knew I couldn't do what she wanted.

"Not yet, love, not yet." I hugged her closer and let her bury her face on my arms. I could still feel her tight fist gripping the charm.

"Why?" she asked when her crying subsided enough for her to talk.

"Do you remember the horse you found last night?"

"He was pretty," she sniffled.

"He was going to hurt you, and we've gotta stop him so he can't."

"He wasn't going to hurt me. He was going to be my friend, my very own, who I could ride whenever I wanted."

"He was lying to you, sweetie." I smoothed her hair. "He's like a stranger. You know how your Mum would say that you can't trust strangers and they'll tell you nice things, like that they'll give you candy, and you shouldn't listen?" Sarah Beth nodded, sniffling even more. "The horse is one of those bad strangers."

"I wanted to be friends. I want my own pony, and he wouldn't cost Mum any money because he was magick."

"No, no… He lied to you. I'm sorry, but he did."

She started to cry again.

"I want a pony like you."

"You know, we can share Eastwood. I don't mind at all. And I wasn't going to bring him to school next year, so you could use him when I'm not around, and then your mum doesn't have to pay anything."

"Really?"

"Heather, we should go," hissed Tom through the curtain.

"One sec!" I returned my attention to the still-crying Sarah Beth. "Really, I promise. And I promise I'm coming back for you, okay? You just have to be brave and hold onto the charm and keep thinking about home and me and Eastwood. Can you do that for me?"

"Heather!" Tom sounded frightened, but Sarah Beth still clung to me, terrified. She needed me right now.

"You gotta be brave, Sarah Beth! Promise me you'll be brave and keep thinking about us?"

I felt her nod.

"Tell me. Say it."

"*Heather!*"

"I promise, Heather." Sarah Beth loosened her arms. She showed me the fist she still held the charm in. "I'll be brave."

"Good girl." I kissed the top of her head. "And I promise I'll be back for you."

"Thank you, Heather." My heart stuttered when I saw her fold herself back up and hug her knees again. She was all alone here! How could I leave her?

"Uh… Heather?" Tom's voice had changed, and I couldn't quite read it.

"I said I…" As I slipped out of the curtains, I saw Tom was not facing me, but two other faerie I'd never seen before—and a half-dozen of their armed guards. "Oh."

Tom glared at me out of the corner of his eye. I heard the softest shifting of cloth and saw that Sarah Beth now peeked through the curtains at us. I gave her a face that I hoped showed "Everything is okay," then decided that our best course of action would be to properly introduce ourselves.

"Hello, I'm Heather, and this is Tom. We stopped by to check on my friend, Sarah Beth. Than-thsst!" I sucked in my breath in pain as Tom stomped on my boot. Some half-shaped warning from him about "thank you" being bad cut into my brain. Right. That. I read that in one of Mum's books, too, but I didn't get it.

"She is pleased her friend is safe," Tom spoke for me.

The two Very Important Faerie stepped towards us. They looked like they'd walked right out of the *Lord of the Rings* or *The Hobbit* set. Well, all of them looked like that, actually, but the two who approached us had the fanciest clothes and looked the most like elves. I figured they were pureblood daoine síth, Folk of the Hills or faery nobility. The others—both male and female—either looked more animal or a little more human with not-as-pointy ears and eyes that didn't resemble anime or manga characters.

"So, you're going by Tom now?" asked the Very Important female, who was blonde like Galadriel in the movie, but had more like Liv Tyler's face and make-up, only with big, all-but-anime eyes. She wore a silver and blue dress.

"Um, aye."

"We wanted to make sure everything was all right with you keeping Sarah Beth until we take care of this whole…kelpie…situation." I hoped I sounded as official and important as I was aiming for.

Tom was still watching at me out of the corner of his eye, but I couldn't tell what he was thinking or feeling.

"For such a social visit, we have a lovely entry that doesn't go through the unpleasantness of the dungeon." The Very Important male approached me. He was dressed in a matching Renaissance-y suit and reminded me of a cross between Orlando Bloom and Hugo Weaving. I didn't exactly feel comfortable near either of them, but the way this guy looked at me totally squicked me out.

"We didn't want to disturb you, Lady Fana, Lord Cadmus." From the tone of his voice, I could tell who Tom preferred doing business with, and it wasn't Lord MacLooming-Over-My-Shoulder.

"Of course not." I wondered if Lady Fana always sounded like she was sharing some private joke with whoever she spoke to. "You've always conducted your business in your own way." She turned to look at me. I'd read enough of my mum's stories and research to know to avoid direct eye contact with daoine síth, so I focused my attention on her pouty lips that Lily would just *die* to have. The last thing I needed to do was leave myself open to one of *these* two charming me against my will. "So, is this the new liaison you've been working with for the MacArthur clan?"

"Yes…of course," Tom answered. In my head but barely a whisper, I felt him beg me to play along. From what I knew of daoine síth, I figured he had some idea of a plan but didn't want them to know what it was. Or that he was probably making most of it up as we went along. I nodded and stood straighter.

"She's young, even for a human."

"She's quite lovely, though." Lord Cadmus took a braid of my hair in his hand, and I reacted before I thought…which was probably why I was able to bat his hand away with a resounding smack. In that quick movement, Mum's Swiss Army knife fell out of my sleeve and clanked on the ground, out of my reach.

In my head and in Tom's "voice," I heard a word I didn't recognize but could tell was a serious, death-by-grounding-level curse.

The guards were on me, swords drawn. Lord Cadmus pulled his swatted hand to his chest and raised his other, as if he were about to backhand me. Lady Fana brushed her fingers on his arm and bored into me with a look even scarier than the thought of being beaten by a Very Important Faery Lord.

I stood up straight, like when I'd gotten into a fight on the schoolyard and was now outnumbered by the other students and teachers, and stated, "I don't like being touched without permission." I pretended the knife didn't exist and did my best to ignore the cold dread that was building in my stomach.

Lady Fana waved and the guards pulled back, just a little. Her glare was still painful. "You've entered our domain uninvited by us, child. You are lucky we have been so hospitable."

"My Lady." Eyes lowered, Tom took a step so he was beside me and a little in front. "She is here by my invitation. I had wished to bring her only to see her friend and support the good will between the families, as you wished of me. I had intended upon making this a quick visit without disturbing you or Lord Cadmus. I had not prepared her for a formal visit, so please, your mercy at her ignorance?"

It was a physical relief for Lady Fana's eyes to move from me to Tom, but now that he was sticking up for me, my stomach felt even worse that Tom was on the receiving end of that *look*. And Lord Cadmus was still smoldering in my direction, so there was that discomfort, too.

Lady Fana glided a circle around us. "This is the liaison you chose, Tom?"

"Aye, my lady."

Tom chose me? I glanced at him, but his face was still lowered and I couldn't read it.

"And you trust her?"

"Aye." He spoke without any hesitation. I bit my lip.

She stopped circling in front of my knife, took out what looked like a silk handkerchief and picked it up delicately. The movement hardly rustled her long skirts. "You will destroy the kelpie?" She was addressing me now.

"That's my plan, so far," I said.

"Not with this, I hope?" She handed me the knife.

"My lady," one of the guards began, but she gave him a look that ordered silence.

"No, m'lady." I took the knife from her, making sure not to touch anything but it.

"So, what *does* your plan entail?"

"A magick bridle-halter thing." I pulled from my memory what Joe had sent me.

"And that will destroy it, you believe?"

"No, but it's a step to allow that."

"And how will you use it?"

I really didn't have a good plan, but I had an answer. "American cowboys have been capturing wild horses for centuries, and I've had my training."

"Have you?"

"She has no idea what she's up against," scoffed Lord Cadmus. "We have no reason to trust her more than any of her kind." He cast a withering look at Tom, who was unable to stop an irritated tail flick, then looked at Lady Fana. "We should simply make a contract with the beast."

"He's not getting any contract," I said. "He doesn't deserve it!"

"Oh, and you are a proper judge of this, child?"

I have a temper; it runs in my family—both my parents admit it. So, occasionally, doing something really stupid based on that temper also runs in the family. And really, this was the second worst day in my entire life so far (you don't want to know about the worst one; that's a long story).

Squeezing the knife in my hand—it was mostly metal, so I figured it should give me some strength or defense—I *did* look

Lord Cadmus in the eye. I filled my head with all those photos of those kids the kelpie had eaten and hurt, and I crammed all my anger and all my fear and everything into one big long thought. I imagined throwing it right into his head. Then I imagined closing every wall around my mind so he couldn't get back in.

I felt a push in my brain, along with a sense of surprise—and sadness, a deep sadness—that wasn't my own. I squeezed my eyes closed, mentally squeezing anything out of my brain that wasn't *me*, praying to God that I wouldn't end up some kind of faery slave.

Lord Cadmus looked away from me, taking a step back. He pressed his fingertips to his lips. I didn't feel it in my head, but for half a second, I thought I saw a flash of that sadness—of something that hurt that was older than me—in his face before it grew stone cold once again.

Lady Fana put her arms around his shoulders and now turned a furious look on me. "What did you do?" The fierceness in her face sent chills up my spine and my skin began to prickle as if it were catching fire. I started to back away. From the bed, I heard Sarah Beth whimper. Tom sucked in his breath.

"No, love, no." Lord Cadmus squeezed her hands. The prickling abated and the heat faded. He looked down at my mouth. "If you need our help in this quest to destroy the monster, send our liaison and we will do all we can."

Lady Fana regarded him for several minutes before her face softened, and she nodded in agreement.

"You'll take good care of Sarah Beth? Let her keep the charm I brought her and make sure she's not scared?" While Lord Cadmus was conceding things, as ambiguous as he was, I might as well ask for something.

"We shall protect her, care for her, and let her keep her charm," he said. "Her fear is her own making; we've done nothing to warrant it."

Tom put a hand on my arm. I sensed that was the most agreement I'd get from the lord, and if I tried harder, I might lose even that. I nodded, returned to Sarah Beth and kissed her forehead once more. "I'll be back, I promise. Okay? You don't have to be scared."

"I'll be brave." She gave me a tiny smile. "Brave like you."

Well, at least I had someone fooled. I kissed her again, doing my best not to cry.

The two daoine síth and their entourage led us from the castle through the main entrance. I took Tom's hand once more, watched the misty curtain part, and walked back into my own realm.

The leftover storm clouds still hung in the sky, blocking out the stars and giving everything on the trails, including the sheep, a dimmer, almost grey tinge. As I took a moment to empathize with Dorothy coming back home from Oz, Tom spat out, "You could have gotten us killed, or worse!" He didn't sound all that angry, though, and as I was trying to think of an appropriate response, he added, "And yet, here we are."

He was smiling, like really smiling for the first time I'd seen, which made me smile, which made me feel a whole lot better and less terrified. "So, what is it with Lord MacCreepy-Pants?"

"Don't you ever think *that* in his presence!" Tom took a quick glance over his shoulder even though we'd left the reserve and were back on castle property.

"Well, then he shouldn't act so creepy."

Tom glanced away from me. "He has not interacted with humans for many, many years."

"Like, how many? Because there's something not right about him. How old is he?"

"Lord Cadmus is…" Tom paused in thought, "…about one thousand six hundred or so years old. Lady Fana is younger."

"But she's the one in charge?"

"It's her court. He has not been here very long, and he changed Major Courts."

"Major Courts?" I paused. "He...*used* to be Unseelie?" I thought back on our earlier conversations and wondered if I was way off in assuming I was dealing with Seelie...the ones who didn't hate-hate humans. I mean, Tom held no ill will... and he kept on helping me. But, if I knew anything from the abundance of bedtime stories Mum read to us, and all the books and comics I read, I knew that you couldn't assume anything when it came to faery things.

"Right."

"So, what's his story?"

"It's..."

"Complicated?" I asked.

"Hard to know, exactly, is what I was going to say," he said with a smirk. "Which is, I suppose, also complicated."

"Can you at least try and explain this time? We've got another fifteen minutes to walk."

"Lord Cadmus left his family under mysterious circumstances. It was after he'd met Fana a few times at Court Councils, so he might have already fallen in love and done it to please her and be with her."

I considered the tone of Tom's voice as he recited that. "But that's not what you think?"

"I don't think they fell in love until after he left. But, I don't know any of it for certain. It's just what I've heard and seen."

"Like what?"

"He wandered, courtless, for nearly a century. Had there been any type of a relationship, I believe Lady Fana would have taken him in. But I could be wrong. This all happened before I was born."

I didn't say anything. It sounded like he was still trying to talk in circles, as if someone he didn't want to would overhear us.

"So, how long has Lord Cadmus been...Seelie?"

Tom paused. "Long enough that you can trust him, despite his...personality flaws."

I raised my eyebrow at the cat fey, and he twitched his tail, ears half-pinned. He didn't want me to push, so I let it rest. Tom believed I could trust the Lord and Lady, and that did make me feel better—even though I'd only just met Tom today.

As we got to the door, he paused outside and let go of my hand. I hadn't realized he was still holding my hand. He gave me a sweet smile, then gestured that I turn around. I did. "Now, hold out your arm." I did, and felt the weight of my robe. Then, I felt a quick kiss on my knuckles as my head resounded with his psychic *Goodnight.* Feeling my cheeks burn from his kiss, I spun around without thinking. Fortunately, he'd disappeared or I'd likely have ended up embarrassing myself even worse if he'd been standing there in the buff.

Ugh! It *had* been a pretty good night. If I saw him tomorrow, he was getting cuffed!

With a growl, I snuck back into the house, hiding the spare key back in its hidey rock. The two greyhounds were sniffing me up and down before I had even re-locked the door and reset the alarm. After I calmed the dogs, I crept back upstairs, avoiding all the creaky steps and boards. I made my way into Rowan's room and felt really bad. My brother had fallen asleep sitting next to his bed, reading lamp still on. I put the bag down next to him, and he all but jumped up. He slapped his hands over his mouth, then made a big sigh behind his fingers.

"Sarah Beth is doing okay. They're taking good care of her, too."

Rowan nodded, then asked. "You okay?"

"Yeah…just exhausted. I'll tell you everything tomorrow."

He nodded again. "Glad you and Sarah Beth are okay."

"Me too, thanks. G'night."

"G'night." He climbed into bed as I turned out of his room. He flipped off his light, and I checked over my shoulder to see his shadow rolling up in the blankets. Despite the fact I probably still had dirt and salt and whatever else on me from this trip, I just crawled into bed and rolled into my own blankets, snuggling my teddy bear.

Chapter 11

Where we go from my nightmare to the "nightmare" of an official royal visit.

I couldn't breathe!

I wanted to scream and had lost my voice. Disembodied heads, little kids' heads, the ones the kelpie had killed, Sarah Beth's head all circled around me, horrible and bloated and bloody. And pieces of their chewed-up arms reached for me. Milky, empty eyes stared at me. The kelpie screamed at me, sharp hooves and teeth chasing me. Ghostly Lily laughed and called me slow and mental and useless.

My eyes snapped open so hard it hurt. I couldn't move and still couldn't breathe.

No ghost! No ghost! No ghost! I screamed in my head because I still couldn't talk or yell. Old stories at school about ghosts who held you down in bed and did awful things made my heart pound so hard it ached.

I wanted my parents!

Then, like magick, I could move. I didn't think; I couldn't think. I jumped out of bed, still clutching my bear, and ran right into my parents' bedroom. I didn't care I was eleven and really too old, but I crawled right between them over their covers, gasping for breath and coughing on my tears.

"Sweetie, sweetie, what is it?" Mum asked first.

"Heather, love…" Dad put his hand on my back and started stroking my braids. "What's wrong?"

I still couldn't make words, so I just flopped onto the pillows between them and cried. They both hugged me. Finally I murmured, "The kids…all the kids…"

I heard Mum suck in her breath. "Oh, honey, you didn't click on that link on Shari's wall, did you?"

I nodded and blubbered…something, I don't know what. In the back of my mind, I kept trying to assure myself that I'd just seen Sarah Beth, and she was okay, and that I'd just had a bad dream…but it was so real! I could still see them! And what happened to those other kids was *real.* They were all dead and in an awful way!

"Oh, God!" Mum wrapped her arms around me tightly. "Heather, I'm so sorry."

"What link?" my dad asked, even as he kissed the top of my head.

"Some…person…posted a link on Shari's page…of the crime scene photos. Of…the other children. Shari hasn't been online at all tonight, so she hasn't taken it down."

"God," my dad breathed, wrapping his arms around me, too, and kissing me again.

"Can I stay here? Please?" I whimpered. I didn't want to go back to my room alone.

"Of course, love." Dad moved the covers so I could crawl underneath. I still held Benson as I squished between them. Mum snuggled against me and Dad wrapped his arm around both of us. I was asleep instantly—even though it would only be for a few hours before the next day's chaos.

Mum got out of bed, muttering about ingredients for the rose geranium cake that Princess Maryan had enjoyed so much last visit and how horrible her hair looked. I looked down at myself as I crawled out of bed. I was a mess!

Water ran in my parents' bathroom sink, and I could see through the half-closed door that Mum was reaching for her contacts.

"I need to shower, too," I announced, heading for the door before she could catch sight of me with properly focused vision.

"Good idea," she said. "When you're done, one of us can help with your hair."

I supposed that plain braids wouldn't quite do it for Her Majesty. "I'll do it," murmured Dad, half-uncovering his face but gripping a pillow. He wasn't looking at me, which was also good because he didn't need glasses or contacts. As I headed out, I saw him sit up and narrow his eyes in the direction of the bathroom. "And yes, you have time to re-color your hair. Just a *normal* color, please?"

I shut the door at the beginning of Mum's growl, another good reason to leave quickly.

The hall was quiet, which meant that Rowan and the twins were still asleep. We—the kids—shared two bathrooms at the other end of the hall. Without Lily, we could rotate pretty quickly. After last night's excursion, though, and with the royal family arriving, I'd need extra time to wash my hair. With the others asleep, I wouldn't likely cause a bathroom battle royale.

I was toweling off by the time Rowan's knock started shaking the whole door. The twins must've taken over the second bathroom, and I knew it was Rowan because he was the only one in the family that knocked out song rhythms *all the time*. Even when he was aggravated. Like now.

"Just. One. Second!"

"I. Have. To pee!" He mimicked my tone.

Ew! I tied on my summer robe (the winter one, obviously, was in the wash), grabbed my shower caddy and an armload of wet, loose hair so it didn't weigh on my head, and beat a quick retreat past my dancing-in-place younger brother.

I opened the window. Outside was warm but still cloudy. I could smell the ozone and the ocean from the wind. I pulled over an armchair and knelt in front of the window as I brushed my hair. My hair was my favorite part of me. With it this long, I avoided people calling me a boy or a wannabe boy *some* of the time. When I looked at half my classmates and my sister, I knew being called a "boy" really didn't have much to do with hair. Whatever.

And, yes, I liked sports and knew all the football teams and who was playing whom. I played lots of sports and took martial arts. I also liked ruffles and dresses and sparkles.

But I pretty much hated most of the girls at my school. They all wanted to be like Danicia. Not all girls had to be like *them*. Joli and I couldn't be the only exceptions, right? Besides, it was an all-girls school. I couldn't exactly tell if I'd get along any better with boys that weren't Joe or Rowan. There'd probably be just as many nasty rumors if there *were* boys.

It took half the length of my hair to realize how hard I was clutching my brush. Why was I thinking about all this pointless crap? It didn't matter. Sarah Beth needed to get home safe, and I had to find a way to talk with Joe about the whole bridle thing and destroying the kelpie…while the castle and grounds were crawling with royal guards.

At least Sarah Beth wasn't in immediate danger and the kelpie couldn't get her. Would it go for someone else, though? Or would it have fixated on her and that would keep it from finding other prey? Or were the faery lady and lord still deploying guards to watch out for the village children? Why hadn't I thought to ask these things last night?

The wind brought a cooler breeze through the window and I shivered. Would the ghost know? I couldn't bring myself to *want* to ask her. I brushed the last few strokes from roots to ends and wound my hair into a pretty gold piece that my Dad had gotten for me when he was shooting a movie in Bali a few years ago.

Hair out of the way, I managed to not entirely run downstairs. In fact, I must have been rather quiet because I all but walked in on Mum and Mrs. McInnis arguing.

"Aimee, *ma'am,* this would not be the first time this house has hosted Her Majesty, the Queen nor is this the first time I have *run* the staff for such an occasion."

"I know, Marie, I do… It's just Maryan really liked the geranium cake I made, and I really want to make sure everything is perfect."

Okay, it wasn't much of an "argument" per se. Regardless, I didn't want to interrupt. I waited in the triangle-shaped hall that connected the stairs, the new addition, and the old part of the castle between the kitchen and dining room.

"It's a simple enough cake, and you haven't prepared anything ahead," Mrs. McInnis' voice softened. "You know Beezie and Ben are excellent bakers, who *do* have everything prepared, and they will get it here on time. Trust me on this, and let me take care of the kitchen and staff. You have your whole family to get ready. And didn't you say you wanted to retouch your hair?" That last question edged a little like Dad's and Mum narrowed her eyes.

It wasn't that Mum's hair was grey; it was a faded green. It had been turquoise for a while—on top of a blonde that was shades lighter than her normal color. Her roots had grown out, and with color faded, it wasn't particularly flattering.

While they "talked," I snuck from the stairwell hall that connected the addition to the castle into the dining room where the twins were "vroooooming" cars across the protective fake table top. It would be removed later to show off the real mahogany. In the meantime, it made for a good runway for spring-loaded cars.

"Has my dearest love not had her coffee yet?" My dad swooped into the kitchen from the back door. In half a second, he had one arm around Mum, kissed her lips, and thrust a coffee mug into her hand.

I stopped because I was as surprised with his mood as Mum was. Mum turned suspicious eyes on him.

"I haven't, no," was all she said, sucking a big sip from the cup.

"Nor has she eaten, nor will she let me cook," Mrs. McInnis added, folding her arms.

"Well, let's fix that." He kissed her again.

"You changed pyjamas," Mum commented.

"I got mud on the hem of my others when I went outside to check with Eliza on laundry for the upstairs rooms."

I ducked behind the hallway wall as they passed, rather happy my "skinny-boy" body could slip behind the decorative, arched partition.

"Eliza is on top of the guest beds then?" Mrs. McInnis had a slightly different edge to her voice that I didn't quite get.

There was some hidden meaning, I was sure, because Dad had an especially firm tone with his response of "she is".

"Aren't you going to have any coffee?" Mum asked, as he dropped her off by her chair. I walked into the dining room behind them. Rowan looked up from his eggs and toast and nodded at me, offering a little smile that warmed me.

"Morning, love." Dad gave me a huge smile that lightened my heart even more. "Feeling better?"

"Mmn-hmn." I nodded, grabbing a plate from the pile and an eggy-in-the-basket from where they were stacked.

"Hey." Dad gave each twin a look, reaching for their cars. They took their seats as he fumbled catching the tiny vehicles. His jaw tensed as one flipped into the breakfast plates. The twins giggled, and he forced a smile as he tucked the cars in his robe pocket.

"Your hands are shaking," Mum stated, giving him a *look*.

"Obviously, I've had enough coffee," he responded coolly, not meeting her eyes. He grabbed two of the eggies, stacked them with haggis, and even as he all but inhaled the sandwich he'd made, grabbed a scone as he paced up and down the dining room.

Mum's lips tightened to a fine white line. She scanned us, glared once more at Dad, who pointedly ignored her, and took a decisive bite of food. The rest of us grew quiet in the presence of whatever unspoken argument was going on.

"I'm done eating," Rowan announced, swallowing down the last crust. "May I be excused?"

"Of course," Mum said, as Dad also said, "Yes."

I wanted to follow, but my stomach was growling like crazy, though I was already on my second eggy. Being up all night made you *hungry*! I grabbed a third and debated if I'd call too much attention to myself if I asked for coffee, too.

I didn't. I'd make do, and I was pretty sure that there was a Diet Coke or Pepsi stashed somewhere on my sister's side of the room. She'd forgive me. In fact, she probably owed me one.

"Are you still gonna help me with my hair?" I asked in the general direction of my parents in a voice much smaller than I'd intended.

"Of course," Dad said. "I'll be up in about five, ten minutes?"

I nodded, grabbing my plate. "Thanks, Daddy." He smiled wider and returned to his third scone and a glass of milk he'd poured. Mrs. McInnis grabbed my plate and passed it to Mrs. Morris, from the village, who was doing dishes. My brother must have heard me coming upstairs because he was already sitting in my armchair.

On my dresser, my phone buzzed with a text message—eleven, actually, I saw after I disconnected it from my charger. As I scanned through, I told Rowan about Monkey/Tom, the ruins hiding the real faery castle, how Sarah Beth was doing, and the faery lord and lady.

"And Lily is on the plane now…wants to know if she should send the picture of the cute stewardess to Rose." I chuckled, showing the picture of the smiling flight attendant to Rowan, who, obviously, couldn't care less.

"Sarah Beth is okay? They won't hurt her?"

"No, I told you. They promised to take care of her."

My brother made a soft noise in his throat and wouldn't meet my eyes, which, for him, meant he wanted to ask something but didn't know how. Lines around his eyes grew tighter, and he started to rock. I put my phone down, but it buzzed another incoming message.

"Stoppit!" he shouted at me.

"What?" I asked softly, moving the phone even further from me. He stared into space, rocking more, frustration evident on his face. "Look, let me just tell Lily we're all okay because she's worried about us, and then tell her I need to be away from my phone, okay?" He stopped rocking, but still looked upset and wouldn't meet my eyes. "Sarah Beth really is okay. We talked and she remembered all of us. She was just really scared at first, but then she said she could be brave. She smiled at me before I left. That's the truth. And I believe Lord Cadmus and Lady Fana will take good care of her until we can get rid of the kelpie and she can go home."

I watched his lips silently count to five and then he looked me back in the eye and stared. It's not the most comfortable thing in the world to have him stare, but I let him, watching his breathing slow down.

The phone buzzed again, and he scrunched his eyes angrily. A soft, growling whined from his throat as he threw himself off the chair, stumbled a step, and then stalked to my door.

"Where are you going?" I asked.

"Gotta get dressed and ready. It's late."

His whole morning was off. If nothing else, his therapist had stressed to all of us that autistic kids like strict schedules and hate unexpected changes. Between last night and all the chaos today with the extra staff, Mum and Dad arguing while managing to be up early and running late, and knowing today would be full of visitors and rules he didn't know, we were really lucky he hadn't had a full meltdown.

I sighed and picked up my phone to see it was now up to thirteen text messages. I scanned through the next seven from Lily. She was glad to know we were okay and wanted to switch seats because of some drama (that she described in detail) with the old guy next to her and aforementioned cute stewardess. I rolled my eyes, then got to her note that the plane would be taking off, so please don't worry about her and "stay out of trouble," which would have been more humorous under almost any other circumstances.

The next five messages were from Joe. The first let me know that they had taken a private jet out to Edinburgh, the second that waking up early for press meetings sucked, the third that the press conference was delayed and he got to escape, the fourth was a picture that just reflected off some glass, and the fifth a note that said "Yes!"

I typed back, "What's the pic?"

He didn't respond, so I started unwrapping my hair. They were probably going into the press conference now. I heard Dad's footsteps on the stairs, so I got up and pulled out the whole right-hand top drawer of my dresser, which was filled with all my hair things.

"Hey, sweetheart." He leaned over to kiss me as I turned sideways, curling one leg under me on the bed so he could sit behind me. Taking my wide-toothed comb, he settled in and started combing. "Good job getting all the knots out." He used clips to pull my hair into sections, but had to re-do it a few times. I bit my lip; usually he did this part much faster.

"Your hands really are shaking badly, aren't they?" I asked softly, remembering what Mum had said at breakfast. I figured it must have something to do with his meds and the extra caffeine or something. I knew he had to watch how much caffeine or alcohol he drank all the time.

"Just a little. There's a lot going on today."

I tipped my head backwards and arched my back to try to look at him without messing up the chunks of hair. "Are you sure you're okay, Dad?"

"I'm fine, love. Really." He leaned over and kissed my forehead.

"What's Mum worried and angry about, then?"

He didn't say anything for a minute, but he stopped brushing. Finally, he said, "It's something I'd rather not talk about."

I paused and bit my lip for a few minutes of uncomfortable silence. "I'm sorry…I'm just worried. Is it about your medicine and stuff?"

"Heather." His voice was even, but hard as stone. "Have I not been respectful of the things you'd rather not discuss? Even when I'm worried sick about you?"

I closed my eyes, feeling embarrassed. "Sorry, Dad."

"I suppose, that said, it'd be unfair of me to ask about school? I know you were having a hard time with those girls."

"Mmmmnnn," I whined.

He got the point and just kissed the top of my head where he'd parted it.

"Has Alison sent you any new scripts?" His agent and job were easier things to talk about. We started in discussing the projects he would be filming or doing voice work for shortly. As he snapped an elastic around the first braid, he asked, "What are you wearing today?"

I smiled. "That dress you got me for Christmas should fit now! The blue and brown flowered one with the sparkly beads?"

"Excellent choice," he said. "So, blue ribbons." I patiently ignored that it took him a few tries to start the ribbon wrap when, normally, it took just one. As he started braiding again, we chatted about everything from the cute animals he'd narrated about for National Geographic to how badly Scotland was doing in football (really bad).

We didn't get too far in our lament before the twins, all squeals and giggles, flew into my room and jumped onto my bed. I let out a yelp because Dad hadn't let go of the braid fast enough, and it pulled when they bounced.

"Ash! Ivy!" he scolded. "This isn't your room. What do you think you're doing?"

"We want to play with Heather's hair, too!" Ash said, which I'm pretty sure meant Ivy wanted to play with my hair, but Ash simply couldn't survive if he didn't come with.

"Oooh! Silver ribbons!" my youngest sister exclaimed, pulling said ribbons from my drawer. "Are you using them? Can I? Pretty please?!"

"Ivy Hannah and Ash Bernard."

I watched Ash, then Ivy, wither from the look Dad was giving them.

"What?" Ivy's lower lip trembled.

"What did I just say?" he asked them.

Ash turned his hazel eyes to me. "I'm sorry, Heather," he tried, and Ivy quickly mimicked him. They looked back at Dad to see if that was the proper response to whatever wrong they'd done.

"Is. This. Your. Room?" he repeated. The twins shook their heads. "What do you do when you want to go into a room that isn't yours?"

They looked at each other. "Knock?" Ivy offered first, and Ash nodded. Then, she added, "But the door was open!"

"Doesn't matter."

Their heads dipped lower, and they filed out of my bedroom, turned around, and knocked on the doorframe.

Dad leaned around and looked at me. I tried not to smirk too much. "You may come in," I told them.

Like the greyhounds when they have to go out after being locked in all night, the twins raced in. Dad must've given them one more look because they nearly fell over each other as they stopped short of jumping back on the bed.

Since Dad was only just barely holding my hair this time, I nodded permission.

"Gently," Dad added. "Always, always, always remember your manners. It's *especially* important today and tomorrow. Do you two understand me?"

"Yes, Daddy," they dutifully said. Dad went back to the braid he'd been working on. Ivy started edging closer and closer, glancing between me and the package of silver fabric ribbons.

"You may use the silver ribbons," I granted. The resounding "Eeeeeeee!!" made both Dad and me cringe.

"Inside voice!" he growled.

Ivy repeated her squeal at a lower volume, then asked, "Will you do my hair, too, Daddy? All pretty like Heather's?"

"What about me?" Ash looked quite pitiful for being left out of hair festivities.

"You don't have long hair," Ivy stated, running her fingers through his short, blondish locks that, currently, fluffed out like goose down at strange angles from his face. He was the only one in the family to have gotten Mum's hair.

"I can do your hair, too, Ash. You can use some of my gel," Dad said. My baby brother all but glowed like the sun. Ivy scowled. "And we can braid your hair like Heather's," Dad promised.

"Can I use hair gel?"

"You and Heather don't need gel."

"But we have *your* hair, Mum says."

"It's longer, so we can braid it and it stays," I said.

Ivy took several moments to consider this inconsistency. As she did so, Dad asked softly, "What time is it, love?"

I grabbed my cell. He hissed through his teeth; it was already noon.

"I have an important mission for you two, if you so choose to accept it," he told the twins.

"What? What?!"

"Go and see what your mum is doing with her hair. In fact, you have my permission for this one and only time ever, to go directly into our room, and if you see her with any bright color that isn't blonde or brown or auburn, do *not* let her use it. Tell her I said so and I sent you, so if she wants to yell, she has to come see me. You may use any means but violence as necessary to carry out this mission. Do you accept?"

"Aye!" they agreed.

"Go forth and find your mum, little chicks. Go forth!" He dramatically waved them out of my room. I couldn't stop myself from giggling. I didn't hear any shouts or particularly loud whining in response to their mad laughter and footfalls. After a few seconds of listening, Dad returned to braiding.

Just as he finished the elastic, I saw Mum in one of his old tees and sweatpants at my door. She knocked on my frame.

"Auburn." She held up a box of hair color, looking past me and at him. "Happy?"

"Quite. It's a lovely color on you."

"I don't remember buying this one, so you must think so." She didn't look quite as aggravated as this morning, but her smirk was still harsh.

"I buy you lovely dresses, too," he added. "I haven't heard you complain about that."

Mum sighed and leaned her head on my frame. "Will you help so that all the green is covered, then? Please?"

"Of course. I'm almost done with Heather."

"Can you put some make-up on me, too, while you're waiting for the color to set?" I piped up.

"You're eleven." Dad disagreed from behind me.

"I'll be twelve in October!"

"Really? I was entirely unaware that you were born in October."

Mum gave Dad a sweet smile. "A little lip gloss and color won't hurt. It's for the royal family, after all." Yes! Mum was on my side for this one!

Dad sighed. "Nothing dramatic." He gathered the eight long braids he'd done and handed them over my shoulder. "Hold these, Miss I-Need-Make-Up-Because-I'm-Eleven-and-A-Half." I felt him brush and twist the rest before fastening everything at my neck.

"Eleven and eight months. Almost exactly. *And* because I get to meet the Queen!"

"Really?" He teased as he got up from the bed, taking my hand and spinning me around like we were dancing. "Will you remember *your* manners and not go and call Her Royal Majesty 'Maggie' or something ridiculous?"

"Da-ad!"

He caught me in a dip. "Do make sure you don't call her grandson 'Joe' in front of her, at least?"

"I promise, Dad." I bit my lip to try and stop an evil grin. "I'll call him Joey. Even he hates that!"

"Heather." He stood me back up.

"Prince Joseph. Prince Joseph. Prince Joseph. Prince Christopher, Princess Maryan, Prince Albert, your royal highness, his royal highness, her royal highness, your majesty…" He spun me around a few times as I chanted formalities. Despite all I knew I had to do, I couldn't help but smile and be Daddy's princess as he danced with me.

"Good girl!" He smiled and lightly tugged on the now-much-heavier rope of hair flowing down my back. "And the barrette holds all the braids, so good." He snatched the hand-held mirror from my dresser and turned my back to the dresser mirror so I could see behind me. "What do you think?"

My heart jumped with joy, and I made an "ooh!" with my lips and moved back and forth a few times. The smaller, ribboned braids were woven into two larger French braids on either side of my head. The rest of my hair was looped underneath and tucked into a silver clasp of tiger-eye and blue fire-opal roses that I didn't recognize. "Where…?!"

"It was going to be for good luck when you started at Saint Bridget's, but I thought you would appreciate it now."

"Thank you!" I whispered, tilting my head back and forth to catch the shimmering of all the petals.

Dad beamed at me. "You're welcome. I'm glad you like it."

"I *love* it!" I shook my head more, and it still felt secure.

"Good. Now…perhaps you could help me by seeing if Ivy will let *you* do her hair because you are the very cool big sister, and we are running out of time for me to make everyone in this family look gorgeous."

"Sure," I said, automatically, still admiring my new hair clasp. *I* felt like royalty wearing it! So handling my baby sister: Nooooo problem!

The dangers of the kelpie, ghosts, and even Sarah Beth were about as far from my mind as they'd ever been in the past couple of days. In that moment, I *was* Dad's princess and life was good!

Chapter 12

I knew I wasn't the only one with problems, but…
I never expected this.

My dress flared out on my bed as I brushed Ivy's hair. She was chattering on about the adventures she and Ash had in the garden with their imaginary friends who would get angry if Anita cut any flowers. I was still mushing my lips together to feel the silky gloss Mum had given me and flicking my eyelashes to feel the slight weight of mascara. I made proper listening sounds without paying much attention. Dad was still working on dressing Ash and Rowan. Ivy was definitely handling the separation better than her brother would, but then again, if Dad was lavishing him with attention, Ash probably wasn't angsting over his twin.

Ivy lowered her voice, which made me listen a little harder "…so Anita had to come in and get a Band-Aid because Ehranthal just stabbed her finger like that. And I said that she shouldn't have done that because we weren't ever supposed to hurt anyone, but she said that the flowers were special and that worse things would get angry at Anita…and that was dangerous. Do…do you think those missing kids might've picked flowers and that's what happened? We aren't ever supposed to pick flowers in the park, but we only know that 'cos Mum and Dad say so. I don't think there are signs or anything. I haven't talked to either Ehery or Melldad since Mum and Dad brought us all in. D'you think they would have told us?"

My baby sister's chatter chilled my bones. After everything I've been going through, their imaginary friends didn't sound so imaginary.

"I…" I tried to process all that Ivy had just said and remember whatever she might have said before that. "I don't think it's the flowers…but…do you only see them when you're outside? Ehery and Melldad?"

"Just by the flowers, and only the realllly old bushes over on the other side of the garden."

I tried to figure out what else I could ask or how to answer my little sister when my phone rang. I jumped off the bed, feeling my feet shake under me.

Ivy giggled. "Did you see a ghost?"

"No!"

She immediately frowned at me. "I was just teasing."

My phone continued to ring and it finally registered that it was the song I'd set for Joe. I grabbed it off the bed.

"Is my hair done?"

"Yes. Do you like it?" I asked. "Oi, J—um…Prince Joseph?"

I heard him snerk at me on the other line. "Pretty sure no one's listening in."

"It's pretty!" Ivy exclaimed, then threw herself at me in a bear hug.

"One sec," I told Joe and hugged her back, twirling her around the bedroom until she started laughing. I really did want to be the cool big sister. "Go show Daddy!"

With a squeal, she peeled out of my room, clopping in her shiny patent-leather shoes.

"Oi." I picked the phone back up. "What's up?"

"People rot. Media rots. Canary Fincher is a soulless cow who doesn't give a damn about what happened to the poor kids or their families or anyone on the shore who lost their houses or their businesses. And I have to be polite as can be while she all but insults my mum on television. We're on break, so I locked myself in the water closet before I punched someone."

"I'm sorry," I said softly. "So, it's probably not a good time to ask if sandals are too casual to wear whenever you get here?"

"Prolly," he said, but I heard him smile, which meant my plan to cheer him up worked. "Have you even turned on the telly?"

"No. Is it online?"

"Maybe on YouTube. Too early for anything else."

"You never answered me what that picture was that you sent me."

"Well, if it didn't come out, it's obviously meant to be a surprise." I could hear the smile in his voice. It was the smile that made his eyes light up with that "up to no good" look.

"You're a pain, you know that?"

"Oi, I might remember you said that in thirty years!"

"Thirty? How old's your dad now?"

"Well, forty or fifty if he holds the crown as long as my grandmother. But, still!"

"Uh-huh. Sure. Can you at least give me a hint?"

"Your mum wrote about it. And I found it! And my mum is likely going to kill me—rubbish!" I could hear knocking and muffled voices. "Gotta go."

His phone clicked off, and I was even more confused now than before he called me. It might be a good idea to turn on the telly, though, so I could inform my parents what happened during the press conference.

I grabbed a pair of tan flats (since sandals were out of the question), did a sparkling twirl in my dress in front of the mirror, and headed to the family room.

Actually, I didn't get very far from my room. Mum and Dad's door was open a crack, and I heard their "trying to be quiet while yelling" voices. I felt a sick sinking in my stomach.

The conversation with my dad rang in my head; he and Mum never eavesdropped. They made it clear that they trusted us. I checked the hall and, seeing none of my siblings, I edged closer to listen. I did trust them; they were good parents. Great parents, even. But…I don't know. Something in me was drawn to know. What if they were arguing about leaving for Grandfather's or London? I'd have to know that so I could plan accordingly with Joe!

"You're going to crash tomorrow, and they're still going to be here! You *know* better." That was my mum.

"I can do this for a couple of days, Aimee. I know what I'm doing!"

"Really? So, why don't you go apply for your own pharmacology degree!"

"Aimee, don't!"

"Don't 'don't' me, Michael. You *don't* know what you're doing. You don't know if your body can recover…and… and… You just don't know!"

I didn't really understand what they were saying. Regardless, my stomach clenched in an icy fist. This sounded important.

"You needed me today. I had to be—I *have* to be—alert. I have to be at least close to *me*."

"Michael—"

"Look me in the eyes and tell me that yesterday, the day before, tell me that was me. The *me* you know? Something… something else is wrong. After everyone's gone, when we go to my dad's, I promise, I *promise* I'll go see Dr. Snow. I swear to you. But right now, *right now*, just trust me! Please?"

Dr. Snow was Dad's psychologist. And he sensed something "else" wrong. Tom said the kelpie brought the storm…and I knew sometimes weather *did* mess with Dad's moods. What if it was the whole thing with the kelpie that was making Dad's moods worse?

"*Trust* you?" Mum asked.

"You've seen me all day, you've seen the kids. I'm doing *fine*. It's just a few shakes. I'm controlling things as best I can—"

"As best you can?" Mum was trying really hard to speak quietly; her voice was echoing like she was in their bathroom. "With caffeine pills and pot? How the *hell* do you know you're not going to have an interaction? So help me, God—"

My heart pounded in my chest. I leaned into the corner that separated our rooms, cupping my hand over my mouth to try to hide breathing sounds. This was *really*… I shivered.

"I'm not. I know I'm not. I've—I've done it before."

Dad did drugs before?!

"*What?!*"

I glanced down the hall to see if any of my siblings heard *that* shout, then gasped as I heard heavy footsteps heading towards the door. I squished harder into the corner. No way I'd get back to my room in the flats without getting seen. I didn't have to worry. The door just shut.

It was harder to hear now. I glanced at the door, slipped off my fancy shoes, ran to my room, grabbed my water glass, and dashed back, pressing the glass to the thinner part of the wood so I could hear. I had to know how bad Dad was. I had to know if…if this was my fault for making the kelpie angry.

"… when I was with Jess—"

"Oh, *that* makes me feel better!"

"Just listen! It was…was when she was pregnant with Lily. When I found the paperwork. I didn't want her to know, so I had to act normal, and I was shooting, so it was easy to say it was just the long hours giving me shakes. Aimee? Aimee—just hear me out!"

Mum said something too soft for me to hear. I hated Jessica more than ever if she had made Dad have to do drugs!

And I hated myself for making the kelpie angry at us.

I *had* to destroy the kelpie. It was destroying my dad!

Dad was speaking, but I could hardly hear him. "No, I didn't. Just now. I swear. I swear to God Himself, to whoever you want me to, this is the only time since Jess, *ever*. And it will be. Just…just let me get through these two days. I swear, you can hold my pills, you can have me check in with you every hour, whatever you want…just, please, please…I need you to not hate me right now, please?"

"I don't *hate* you. I'll never *hate* you." Mum's voice sounded dry, like she had a cold. "I love you."

"Forgive me, then?"

Once again, Mum was talking too soft for me to hear.

"I'll get Rowan ready. You go relax, see whatever they're saying at the press conference. It'll probably come up at tea, and they'll assume we watched. Okay?"

Mum didn't say anything. Very slowly, not taking my ear from the glass or the glass from the door, I picked up my shoes one at a time with my toes and tucked them under my free arm.

"I love you. More than anything, I love you." That was my dad. And my cue to leave.

I jogged on tip-toes to the library/family room, then, once inside, ran as fast as I could for the couch and threw myself on it, grabbing the remote and flipping to the news channels. From the hall I heard awkward clicking. Mum was in heels; she hated heels. That bought me enough time to rearrange my dress and feet, run a hand over my braids, and look like I'd been in the living room for at least a little bit of time.

"Oh!" she said when she saw me. "You're not downstairs eating lunch?"

"Wanted to see Joe." I scowled at the commercials. I turned to look at her. Her makeup didn't quite hide the redness in her eyes. "You okay, Mum?"

"Oh, well…got some stupid eyeliner in my contacts. Does it look bad?" She sat down beside me and gave a bright smile.

"Maybe touch up a little?" I suggested.

"Yeah, in a bit. So, what have we missed?" She fiddled with the forest green shoes that had three buckles up the front. I could tell she already wanted to kick them off.

"Canary Fincher is a stupid cow who doesn't care about any of the kids or the villages or anything and wants to make a name for herself by making Princess Maryan look bad," I paraphrased from Joe.

Mum muttered that cuss about female dogs, then slapped a hand to her mouth. I smirked at her, and she held her index finger over her lips. I gave her a smile and a wink, which seemed to relax her. Dad was not fond of how often Mum cussed, especially in front of us kids. "The woman hasn't got a shred of professional journalist in her. She should've been fired years ago."

"It's back," I said as the telly screen panned back to the podium where the royal family was…leaving.

One of the palace PR reps was at the mic saying that the royal family was not taking any more questions at this time (which, of course, meant that all the other reporters just screamed their questions louder).

"Crap," Mum said. "Gimme a quick recap?"

"Um…"

A reporter man behind a desk announced, "Next up is Captain Henry Anders, head of Scotland Yard, who will tell us where the police investigation is for this serial child killer."

"It's not 'serial', you idiots." Mum sneered at the television. "The two tourist kids disappeared just about on the same day. Stop sensationalizing this crap!"

"I wanna hear," I gestured back to the TV. "Maybe they have something on Sarah Beth?"

The Scotland Yard chief said a bunch of stuff about everyone looking, flashing a picture of Sarah Beth and asking that everyone be vigilant and possibly help this little girl get home safe, blah, blah, blah.

Mum growled again at the telly and got up from the couch. Opening an end table, she sat back down with a package of oat cakes, a jar of Nutella, and a plastic knife.

"Mm—thanks!"

"I don't want to deal with the lift or take the stairs more than I have to in these things." She banged the heels on the rug, sticking her legs straight out in a very unladylike fashion.

"You look really pretty, though," I said. And she did. She wore a silk suit-dress of green with a short jacket, both decorated with sparkly crystals. Her hair was in a French twist. Sparkling barrettes with dangling crystals trembled as my mum awkwardly leaned over so as not to drop any crumbs onto said dress.

"Thanks," she said around a swallow. "Another of your dad's finds that he snuck into my closet when I wasn't looking. And I have a jaunty little hat to go with as well." She added a more British accent, which made me giggle.

"The Queen and Princess Maryan were both wearing hats." I paused in buttering my oat cake with the hazelnut chocolate spread. "You think I need one?"

"I wouldn't be surprised if your dad pulls some out for you and Ivy, really." She chuckled and took the knife and another cake. "It's *such* a British thing."

"Look, they're doing a recap." I pointed to the telly.

"Your Highness, is there anything you've heard that might lead you to believe that these children's horrific murders are tied to any Islamic terrorist activity?" Canary Fincher, in a hideous hot pink suit and matching hat, called from the crowd.

Mum cast a sidelong glance at me, grumbling, "Yeah, effing terrorists are *really* interested in a tiny village, with more sheep than humans, that caters to hikers and divers."

The Queen herself had answered Fincher's question. "No, we have heard nothing of that ilk. It's a horrible, horrible crime, and our hearts go out to those families—as well as those who have lost their loved ones in the disastrous storm."

I looked at Mum. "People died in the storm?"

She pursed her lips. "Not that I heard. I think she's trying to suggest Sarah Beth was lost in the storm."

"What do you think?"

Before Mum could answer, I heard Dad's voice boom behind us. "My lady, the gentleman of Clan Arthur present themselves for your inspection and approval."

Mum shot me a look and stood up, walking around the couch.

"Oh, my *ladies.*" Dad gave me a big smile as I turned around to kneel on the couch so I could just look over the top. He was wearing proper MacArthur attire with his kilt in the green tartan (that Mum's dress just happened to match perfectly), formal tailed coat, gartered hose, and those lace-up shoes that I never remember the name of. He also had on his bonnet and pin. Mum was biting her lower lip to restrain a smile that would overtake her face, which, of course, made Dad smile more. It was no secret Mum was always looking for an excuse for Dad to wear his kilt. She said that men in kilts were a total American geek obsession.

"If I may," he continued, with a bow to Mum, "I present to you Young Masters Rowan Jacob and Ash Bernard of Clan Arthur."

My two younger brothers filed into the living room in matching attire.

Mum squealed in delight. It was all I could do to hold in the laughs that threatened to burst my belly. My brothers did look darned cute in formal kilts and all. Ash was beaming and Rowan seemed interested in the fur tassels on his sporran. He definitely looked calmer than before.

"Ooooh! You are so adorable," Mum said. "C'mere and let me see you two!" Ash dashed over and threw his arms around Mum's legs in a big hug, which she squatted to return (as best she could in the heels). "Rowan, come, let me see you!"

He glanced at me out of the corner of his eye as he went over to Mum.

"Turn around." She circled her finger in the air. "You look very dashing. Can I give you a kiss?" Rowan leaned forward and she kissed both his cheeks gently. Hugging Ash one more time, she stood up and looked at Dad.

He stared at her with a hopeful smile, as if asking, *Does this make you happy, at least?*

She sighed, went over to him, and kissed his cheek. He put one arm around her and the other hand on her chin to guide her into a bit more of a *kiss*-kiss, at which I rolled my eyes. "Eww! Hel-*lo*, children present. You're *traumatizing* us!"

"It's cute when Mummy and Daddy kiss," Ivy declared from the doorway. Of course she was here, too. I should've figured.

"Heather, love, have you gotten anything from Prince Joseph? How are they running?"

"They just got off the TV about twenty minutes ago," Mum offered.

I patted my dress, realizing I had completely forgotten my cell phone in my room. Stupid dresses with no pockets!

"One sec."

Joe, had, in fact, texted me. Three times.

"They had a post-conference meeting thingy with British Red Cross, Scotland Yard, and other important people," I read to my family as I walked back into the family room. "It took forever. They got in the cars about…five minutes ago. So, yeah, about an hour."

"So, we've got an hour to get everything in order," Dad said. "To the dining room for a meeting!"

He put an arm around Mum and waited for us to make our way downstairs. I grabbed my shoes from in front of the couch and fell in next to Rowan.

"Bunny fur." He sadly fiddled with his sporran again.

"I think so." I wasn't sure how to respond. I took a deep breath. Well, at least the fight was over for now. That was good. Dad's mood swings made things edgy enough sometimes, but if Mum ended up upset, then things really would fall to chaos.

I *really* had to find a way to destroy the kelpie. And it would have to be me and Joe. I looked at Rowan again, deciding it was probably better to keep him safe, too.

As my whole family and way more staff than I'd ever seen at once filled our dining room, it became clear that this wasn't the usual "royal visit" we were used to. During other visits, Dad and Prince Christopher would talk about movies and football or kick the ball around with the little kids while Mum and Princess Maryan would hang out with the horses. Joe (who asked me to call him Joe within an hour of the first time we met) and I would do our own thing. Of course, it was always just Joe, one or both of his parents, and sometimes his sibs. I mean I *knew* who Joe was, who his grandmother was. Her face is on our money, after all! But in my head, she was his grandmother.

I think Mum had the same problem as me, because Dad corrected her twice during the family-and-staff meeting. Once, she forgot "Princess" in front of Maryan, and another time she just referred to the Queen as Prince Christopher's "mum." Dad was patient; Mrs. McInnis gave Mum utterly horrified looks both times.

At the meeting, Dad was back to the head of the table running things, making everyone smile and feel important. Then he gave the floor to Mrs. McInnis who had, in fact (as she reminded us), hosted the Queen at this very castle twice before, once when the Queen was just a princess.

So, the meeting happened. And then both Ginny and I got texts. Ginny from Karina (Princess Maryan's personal assistant) and me from "Prince Joseph." The first car in the caravan (of five cars) had pulled up the long access road to our castle.

Mrs. McInnis herded the rest of us into a fancy receiving line outside. Mum joined us after a makeup rescue from Ginny, but looked somewhat terrified and quickly grabbed Dad's hand.

The rest of the staff did a line-up thing, too, based on Mrs. McInnis' clucking and pushing. Even Mr. McInnis was in his church suit (though he looked less than happy in it). Ginny shadowed Mrs. McInnis, helping tidy each person. Three of the five cars were security, and I watched them park and put themselves in what I'm sure were strategic places.

After that, I can tell you that I remember everything was nice, orderly, and in a very specific order of events and everything.

And I don't remember a thing about it.

Because, during the receiving line thing, Joe did that same stupid hand-kiss thing that Tom did. Except, unlike Tom, my first instinct wasn't to deck him upside the head; I wasn't quite sure what to do or how I felt. I vaguely remember him not being the only one of the guys to do something like that, and it was all formal and everything…but still! And, honestly, I am still rather upset at myself for being so silly about it. I didn't have time for that.

Especially since we had so little time to deal with a killer monster faery horse so Sarah Beth could go home…before our respective parents packed us up to leave.

After the receiving line thing, we then all walked into the castle in some fashion, herded by Mrs. McInnis and Ginny. Then the Queen announced that they needed to refresh themselves before tea and that it shouldn't be much of an issue, should it?

"Of course it wasn't" was the response, and high tea was reset to happen in an hour. Prince Christopher, Prince Albert, and Her Royal Majesty were led away. Joe must've gone with them, too, because I didn't see him…which was kind of a relief at the moment.

I did see Princess Maryan pull Mum aside into the ballroom and give her a proper hug and two kisses on the cheek. She held Mum's hands in her gloved hands and it looked like she was apologizing.

"Ahem." Dad appeared in front of me and crossed his arms.

"I wasn't trying to spy, really! Just…"

He nodded towards the stairs. I headed to the back stairs, but went all the way up to the third floor, where I knew Joe's family was staying. I didn't get too far out of the doorframe when one of the many suits in the hall came over to me and said, "The family wishes to rest. They'll see you at tea. Good day, young miss." (Or something like that. It might not have sounded quite so rude; remember, I was not entirely myself.)

I retreated to my room and flopped on my bed. Within a few minutes, I decided I was being stupid. Tom had kissed my hand last night, and it had ticked me off, yeah, but Joe was my best mate, so of course it wouldn't tick me off, so I was just being dumb and, besides, all of us were feeling weirded out by everything going on.

I settled things in my head, and my heart wasn't pounding like crazy anymore, which also made things a little clearer.

If we were leaving tomorrow, and with all the security people around, I might not get a chance to talk to Joe alone again! And if we didn't do something about the kelpie, no one would!

I looked at my closet. Upstairs, I had seen the most guards by the two tower rooms, most likely places for Her Majesty and Joe's parents; those were the two biggest suites. The other clump of guards was by the room just above where mine was.

Easy peasy. I'd use the secret passage.

Of course, there was the possibility of running into the ghost.

I scowled in the direction of the closet.

Then I had an idea. Lily wasn't home yet. I ran over to her side of the room and took the gold cross off the wall over her bed (I wasn't leaving *my* bed unprotected!). Then, after a deep breath, I entered the secret passage.

Chapter 13

Sometimes you just need your best friend to help you deal with life, monsters, bullies, and ghosts. Especially ghosts.

I don't speak Arabic, so I don't have any clue of what Joe said when I lightly knocked on the wall in his closet. I did hear him shout, "I'm fine. Just dropped stuff, thanks!" though. He must have been right at the closet when I arrived.

"It's Heather. Open the latch by the shelves."

It hadn't crossed my mind that the secret passage door would actually be locked on his side…even though I always kept mine locked.

"What. The. Hell," he hissed, glaring at me as I slid the door open.

"What? They wouldn't even let me in the hall."

He sighed, then narrowed his eyes again. "What's with the cross?"

"I…was worried about the ghost."

His face paled for a second. "My room is haunted?"

"Just the passages, I think, maybe downstairs. Can I please come in?"

He looked behind him. "They'll hear us talking. Go back around, and I'll make sure they let you in."

I gave him a pained face. He had *no* idea how terrified I was just coming up through the stupid passage.

"Go! They'll let you in."

I sighed and turned back down the stairs, holding Lily's cross in front of me. At least that seemed to be working.

When I came back upstairs, Joe—Prince Joseph—was talking sternly and quietly to the two men at his door. The stairs were closer to Her Majesty's quarters, so her four guards eyed me warily.

"Heather," Prince Joseph gestured me over, much to the clear disapproval of his door guards. The look he gave the men would have made me wince. One guard took a very tiny step out of the way as I approached the room. The other, who I recognized as Jonathan, Joe's regular bodyguard, now that I was up close, nodded more civilly. I curtsied to Joe, who gave me a brief nod, and then I followed his hand as he pointed me into his room. I turned around when I heard a soft thud like something grabbed the door. Jonathan's hand kept the door from closing all the way.

Joe narrowed his eyes. "Excuse me. What do you think you are doing?" I would never want to be on the receiving end of that tone. Joe sounded scarier than my mum or my dad!

I could have sworn Jonathan cracked the slightest smile as he spoke. "My deepest apologies, Your Highness, but it is protocol. You know you cannot be left unattended with someone outside your immediate family. You need to at least leave the door open if you insist upon entertaining a guest." Jonathan revealed even more of a smile, a mix of empathy and perhaps a little teasing, as if this wasn't the first conversation of this sort. "Even your dearest, best friend."

Joe narrowed his eyes fiercely and stood straighter, as if daring Jonathan to push the topic.

Jonathan was entirely unaffected. Bodyguards must get a lot of training or something, because I was flinching and Joe wasn't even looking at me. "I am simply required to ensure your safety. If you wish for an exception, I suppose we could ask your parents?"

Joe continued to glare and puff his chest for almost another whole minute before breaking into a semi-defeated scowl. "Must the door be *wide* open, or does protocol allow me some privacy with my best mate?"

"A crack like this should be sufficient, Your Highness."

"Fine." He spun angrily from the door, held up one finger, went to his suitcase, and pulled out a small set of speakers. He set his iPod in the stand and turned up the music right by the door. Folding his arms, he waited for a minute, glaring at the door's crack. There was no argument from the other side, so he turned on his heel again, and flopped on the bed, his shiny shoes just hanging off the edge. "Just…give me five minutes and we'll talk," he said softly, closing his eyes.

"Ok." I looked around the room to see what I could do for the next five minutes.

"Get comfy wherever, I don't care."

The room, while as big as mine and Lily's, only had the one king bed. During Christmas, all our aunts and uncles and grandparents came over. The kids would share rooms with us or use the bunks in the back of the castle, and the parents all got rooms up here. One of Joe's bags was on the computer chair and the suitcase was on another chair.

I walked over to the bed, kicked off my shoes, and flopped next to him. I hadn't exactly had the easiest day, either.

I heard a sharp rustle from him. "What are you doing?"

I couldn't quite read the expression on his face. "I'm doing something wrong?" I started to sit up.

"No…never mind." He shook his head and went back to closing his eyes as he faced the ceiling. I noticed color coming to his cheeks, though, which confused me. "Just, do you *normally* flop on other people's beds?"

"When...when I was in school...well, when I had friends, yeah. We just all piled on the bed. Should I move? I mean, we're not..." Why was Joe making a big deal about the bed? Was it some dumb boy thing that I was clueless about? Not that I was particularly clued in on girl things, but still...

"No. I didn't leave you anywhere to sit. I should've expected you'd want to come up anyway, especially with your friend... I'm sorry." He sighed. "I'm sorry. Just...just give me another second to get my head together?"

"Yeah, sure. You've had a worse day than me."

He turned to look at me again.

"What? You had all those people just...and that Canary cow woman..."

"You're being earnest?"

"Well, aye?"

"You've got a friend who—who could be dead because of some monster—waitaminute!" He sat up. Though he kept his voice very low, lower than the music. His green eyes were bright. "You learned something, didn't you? You found something out?"

"I...how can you tell?"

"Because you're not mental right now, and you should be. What happened? What did you find out?"

"I...well, aye." I bit my lip. "Last night. I... God, I haven't had a chance to tell you anything, have I? Um... Okay, there's a cat in the stable that's really fey, but a helpful one, I think. We did a spell, and he had good intentions. Anyway, he told me that the Seelie Court—the type of faerie that don't *hate*-hate humans—took Sarah Beth before the kelpie could take her, though he almost did take her, and she was still under his charm. So, I snuck out last night with the cat fey—he likes being called Tom when he looks human-ish, but with cat-ears and a tail. We snuck into the faery castle, which is in the same spot as the ruins overlooking the ocean, but in Faerie. And I saw Sarah Beth, and she's okay. Then the faery lord and lady caught us, but they said they'd keep Sarah Beth safe while we destroyed the kelpie, and they would help, except, besides Tom, I don't know how to contact them. But Sarah Beth *is* okay, and I do trust Tom and Lord Cadmus and Lady Fana to take good care of her. But my family's going to go stay with my granddad as soon as you leave, so we have to do it today or tomorrow."

It took me a few minutes to catch my breath after spilling all that to Joe, who, for his part, stared at me, mouth agape. He shook his head again and lay back on the pillow, covering his eyes with his arm.

"What?" I asked.

"I can't even begin to process what you just told me."

"Sarah Beth is okay. But we have to hurry and destroy the kelpie. What's the picture you sent me? Is that the bridle thing you sent me the article about last night?"

"Can we go back to you giving me a minute to think?"

"Mmmn-hmm," I agreed, but impatiently.

I didn't have to wait too long. After he took a few breaths, he peeked out from under his arm. "Are you sure it wasn't just a dream? The whole trip to Faerie?"

"Yes, I'm sure. I had to sneak my robe and pyjamas into the wash because they were filthy from walking out there."

He let out a soft groan and covered his eyes again. I sighed once more and flopped back onto the pillow.

After a minute, he sat back up. I winced from his angry frown as he scolded, "You snuck out last night, by yourself, with a strange faerie that you *think* you can trust when there's a killer monster running around your property?"

"You're not my dad!" I glared at him.

"I'm best mate, though. I think that gives me the right to *not want you to kill yourself!*" I saw more pink rise to his cheeks. God, I didn't need Joe to start worrying about me like my parents!

"I'm fine, really!"

"You're lucky. You could've gotten yourself killed! Heather, listen to me, promise me you won't do something that stupid and mental again. Promise me!"

"Now you *really* sound like my dad."

"Well, he'd be a pretty rubbish dad if he didn't *not* want you to die! Heather, promise!" He grabbed my hand and held it.

For a second, I felt that fuzzy, floppy feeling that I did when he kissed my hand, but I squelched it. We had to talk business, and I knew he wouldn't tell me anything more unless I promised.

"Fine, I promise. We'll do this together."

He sighed, looking relieved, and let go of my hand. "We'll have to do it tomorrow. The bridle won't be here till then. Hopefully first thing in the morning."

"That *is* what it is? How did you find it? How did you know?" It was my turn to sit up really fast and squeeze his hand.

"It's really mad, actually. When the conference was delayed, Mum and I went for a walk. The museum was having a special equine history show thing, and today was the last day. It was a private collection that, we—my family—technically own. Don't ask, it's complicated, but the point is, they had this bridle, except it looked more like a halter—no iron, no bit, nothing, and it came to the Crown when the last Graham of Morphie died. It was part of their estate."

"In Mum's article, Graham was the last one who ever caught a kelpie and they made it do a whole bunch of work, then let it go, and it cursed him. Right?"

"Right, and you remember there was also a MacGregor who supposedly *took* a bridle from a kelpie?"

"Sorta." I didn't want to admit I'd only skimmed the article. I'd been too busy thinking about Sarah Beth and my brother's plan for summoning Tom.

"Well, since those two were the only families named in any of the other lore I found, I thought I could look up any business transactions between the two. I found that a MacGregor owed a debt to Graham, and the payment included, among a bunch of other stuff, a supposedly 'magickal bridle.'"

"They actually wrote 'magickal bridle' in the list of stuff transferred?" I asked.

"At least half of all the lists I read had something 'magick' or sacred or blessed. Seriously," Joe said.

"So, you've got access to lists of everything ever people traded and owed to each other?"

"More or less," Joe smirked. "Big ticket items, because it affected taxes. Any major estate transaction has to be reported to the Crown for taxes. We've got piles of those records. We even have staff whose job it is to catalogue all of these old papers and make electronic copies." He paused. "My mate Peter, from school, I told you about him, in the wheelchair? He helped me hack into the electronic stuff last night. And that's what I did while you were off risking your life to gallivant in Faerie."

"I wasn't gallivanting." I gave him a half smile. "But, anyway, how are you getting the bridle *here*?"

"Pete helped again, doing something on the computer to get it shipped here. It technically belongs to my family." He smiled proudly. "It should be here in the morning."

"Oh." I was stunned. "Wicked!"

He glanced at his watch and his smile dissolved. Quickly rolling off the bed, he told me, "Toss that bag on the bed." He grabbed his suitcase and hefted it on top of the bureau.

He sat in the big chair the suitcase had been in and pointed between me and the computer chair. I sat, confused at the change. I slipped my shoes back on and asked, "So, we've got to get the bridle on the kelpie…and then…"

"Kill it."

I shivered. "Kill it" felt very different from "destroy it," though I don't know how.

Joe continued, "I have a plan. We can talk about it tonight, though."

"Why—"

There was a knock. "Your Highness, Her Royal Majesty will be ready to head down for tea within the next ten minutes," Jonathan shouted over the music. "Perhaps Heather might like to freshen up, herself, before then? I believe you will be eating in the dining room."

"Yes, thank you for informing us." Joe turned to me and explained in a softer voice, "That's why. They work like clockwork. You should go."

"Ok." I stood up and so did he. We headed toward the door; before we got to it, I grabbed his hand. "I'm really glad you're here."

He smiled back and squeezed my hand. "Me, too. By the way, you look really beautiful. I said that earlier, but you looked a little overwhelmed with everything."

"Thank you." I felt myself blush. "You clean up pretty nice, yourself, Your Highness." I may have imagined it, but he seemed to be trying to hide more of his smile as his cheeks got pink again.

As I headed back to my room, I let just a little bit of that nice fuzziness come back. Just enough to make me smile.

Tea was…interesting. We were all shuffled around so that Her Majesty was at one head and Prince Christopher at the other, with Maryan to his left. While Prince Christopher didn't visit as often as Joe or his mum, he still was friends with my dad, so it was weird seeing him all formal. And unnerving. He was almost a different person.

I did end up sitting next to Joe, which made me happy, but it definitely would have been better if we actually could have talked. I remember being about to ask something when he gently kicked my foot and hissed, "We don't say anything." Dad or Mum must have imposed that on the twins, too, because they were not chattering and looked just a little nervous. Rowan, fortunately, was perfectly fine saying absolutely nothing and being ignored.

After a bunch of "if it please her Majesty" stuff, they started discussing the earlier press conference, and then Prince

Christopher started asking Mum and Dad how bad things were in the villages so they were prepared for the evening press conference. I hadn't heard much about this, so I paid attention. No one else had been killed, but several were injured and in the hospital at Eyemouth, two fishermen in intensive care because they had not come in before the worst of the storm. More than half the boats that were on the water and couldn't be pulled in were utterly destroyed. There was severe flooding on the roads, and several businesses would be closed for weeks, if not for the whole season, due to the water damage. As Mum and Dad described things, I noticed one assistant I hadn't met before who stood taking notes.

Then, as if some magick moment had occurred, Her Majesty asked if our parlor was ready. It was, so everyone stood and the adults left, including about three quarters of the guards, the note-taker guy, and half the food. The rest of us sat down with Anita and Ginny while three guards remained at the door.

Once most of the adults were gone, the twins started talking and asking Joe about his siblings. He sat back in the chair for the first time. "They're both good. My parents found a school for Annie, finally. Richard picked out his first colt that he's going to learn how to train, so he's pretty excited."

They wanted to know all about the colt. After he gave them a detailed explanation, Joe gave me a questioning smile. I looked at Anita and Ginny and asked, "May Prince Joseph and I go out to the stables?"

"The guards will be with us," Joe added.

Rowan wanted to go out too, if Joe and I could go outside, but he wanted to ride. The twins then wanted to go out, but not change out of their clothes. After negotiating that no kid would be without adult/royal guard supervision, Joe and I were finally walking down to the main stable, as much "by ourselves" as Jonathan and the other guard's presence would allow.

We were about halfway there when Joe turned around and gave the two guards a look. "Could we have a *little* privacy, please?"

"Of course, your highness," said Jonathan. They fell back several more steps.

Joe sighed a little and then, asked—I think asked from his tone—something I didn't understand.

I gave him a blank look. "Um…my school doesn't teach Arabic?"

"You're not studying it on your own so we can talk?" He gave me a half-smile.

"I didn't know I was supposed to?"

"It's all right. I think Jonathan speaks both Arabic and Farsi, so it doesn't matter."

"*¿Hablo español?*" I offered.

"*Los dos lo hablan*," he replied.

"*Et français?*"

"*Ils les deux opulent que, aussí. Et jár pensé que tu viens de passex en français?*"

"You suck. How many flipping languages do you speak?"

"I don't think you're allowed to say that to me." He gave me a wicked grin.

"What, ask how many languages you speak? Is that secret information?" I asked sweetly.

He laughed, eyes twinkling. "I knew there was a reason I liked hanging out with you."

As we went into the big stable, I walked to Eastwood's stall. All the doors were open to the paddock so the horses could come in and out as they pleased. The two guards settled by the main door, still giving us space.

"We still can't really talk about…things, can we?" I leaned on the door, whistling. Eastwood trotted in.

"We'll talk later about that. I can take that passage down to your room, right?" he whispered back.

"Yeah."

"That'll be better." He started to lean next to me then stopped. "One sec..." He took off his coat and jogged over to the guards, handing it to not-Jonathan. As he walked back, he rolled up his sleeves past his elbows. He leaned on the stall beside me. Dream followed Eastwood and the two wrestled for our attention. Chixie and Artemis were outside the stall, ears pinned at each other as each tried to come in.

"Artemis," Joe called, whistling softly.

His call seemed to give the black Arabian mare enough of an edge that she decided to plough in, throwing a cow kick at the chestnut thoroughbred. He smiled as she pressed her nose into his hands and chuffed on them.

"So, we'll deal with the kelpie issue later." His voice softened, as he gave me a really sweet look. "You never got to tell me what happened to you at school. With that Danicia girl and her friends. When Joli's dads took her out and you were by yourself that last month..."

I groaned. "That's even worse." At the same time, I felt a warmth spreading in my chest that he even remembered that many details from the almost-conversations we'd had.

"Worse than a murderous monster horse?" He raised an eyebrow at me. "Anyone ever tell you that you've got some messed-up priorities?"

I pressed my face on Eastwood's nose and growled again. The pony aggressively licked my hands.

"Well?" he asked. He leaned closer to me so that his shoulder brushed mine for a second.

I purposely repressed the kinda-nice shiver I got from that. "Um...after Joli and I got into that really big fight with Danicia about Joli and my sister being gay, Joli's dads took her out of the school. But because I was the one who actually broke Danicia's nose and Mali's wrist and then Amber said it was my fault, I was gonna get expelled. Which would've messed with me getting into Saint Bridget's. But, Mum and Dad talked to the school, so I didn't, but there was still almost a month left. And you can probably imagine how well that went."

Joe leaned on my shoulder again and took my hand. "I'm sorry."

"It's not *your* fault."

"Yeah, but you called me a bunch of times."

"I figured you probably had important family stuff."

"I did have family stuff. But you're important, too. I'm sorry. I could've found time to call."

I leaned my shoulder on his and he put an arm around me, leaning his head on mine…which kind of surprised me, but felt nice. I heard a soft throat clearing behind us. Joe growled, but let go and took half a step away from me.

"Thanks," I said.

"For what?"

"Asking anyway."

"We're mates," he said. "Of course."

I sighed and gave him a smile.

"If you ever need to talk again, text me…I dunno, text me 'chips and curry'. I'll make sure to call you back."

"'Chips and curry'?"

"I like chips and curry! That's what I eat when I'm angry."

"You're such a boy."

"What's that mean?"

"Chocolate, cookies, cookie dough, brownies…but chips and curry?"

"You girls are weird. Chips and curry tastes great. The spicier the better."

I laughed. "'Chips and curry.' I'll remember."

"So, you broke someone's nose *and* someone's wrist? What about you?"

"A bloody lip, a black eye, and a few bruises. They all have no clue how to fight. They're really girly girls."

Joe laughed again. "How many were you up against?"

"I dunno, four or five," I shrugged. "But it wasn't as if my parents and Joli's parents hadn't already made complaints to the school earlier in the year, so that's why I didn't get expelled."

Joe paused. "Have you talked to Joli?"

"Why?"

"Why not?"

"She probably hates me, too, because she had to leave and I don't know if that messed up *her* chance to get into Saint Bridget's."

"But you haven't talked to her, so you don't know?"

"Why does it matter?"

"What if she's scared you hate her because she left you alone?"

I stared at Joe for a few moments, then turned back to the horses. Chixie had pushed Dream out of the way, but Eastwood wasn't letting her push him. I yanked my hands back so they wouldn't get accidentally nipped.

"You should call her. Or at least text her or something."

"What if she does hate me?"

"Then you ignore whatever she says and go on with your life. But you'll know."

I sighed. "Maybe."

I saw my brother, now in riding clothes, head into the paddock. Having been ousted by Chixie, Dream went right to him. Rowan gave him a little smile and threw on the halter. The guard who had offered to stay with Rowan came through the doors, letting the other two know that my brother would be bringing a horse in.

"So, how's school for you?"

Joe laughed again, but mirthlessly. "I'm not getting into fights because people think I'm gay, but that's about the only thing better than you've got it."

"You're a flipping prince of England. People ought to be falling each other over to be friends with you."

"Yeah, and that's *exactly* the kind of friends I want. Pretty much you and Peter are the only two people who treat me like, you know, a *person.*" He nodded at my brother as he hooked Dream up to the nearby cross-ties. "Need a hand?"

"No, I got it." Rowan kept his eyes lowered and got the stepstool so he could reach better to groom and tack Dream.

Joe shrugged and turned back to Artemis.

"What kind of fights *are* you getting in, then?"

"Not really fights. People just pick on Peter because he's in the chair…and I *want* to deck them, but…God, that would be a mess! You have no idea." He frowned and shook a fist.

"Sorry." I leaned towards him until our shoulders bumped again. He rested on me for a second until we heard another "ahem" from one of the guards. Joe rolled his eyes and we leaned away from each other. "Cookie dough."

"What?" He chuckled and gave me a look.

"Text me 'cookie dough,' and I'll call you."

He laughed softly. "Deal."

With Dream tacked, my brother turned him around.

"Hey, Rowan, why not use the indoor ring?" Joe asked.

"Because it's nice out."

"Will you please use the indoor ring?" I rephrased.

"Why?"

"Because…it's inside." I gave him a look. He stared at me for a minute.

"Why? Is it easier for you to talk inside?" He scowled.

"No…*you* know." I gave him a look. "It's inside. Safe."

Joe looked at me. "He knows?"

"He helped me last night," I said softly.

Joe frowned.

Rowan blinked again, still totally avoiding looking anywhere near Joe. "I'll stay inside." He turned back around and headed to the indoor ring. His guard still shadowed him, but that wasn't too surprising. Our parents had insisted no kid be without an adult anywhere, ever, until further notice. The other two guards waited by the doors to see what we would do.

"Why does he know?" Joe hissed. "It's not safe."

"That's exactly why he knows."

Joe sighed and turned back to the other horses. "And the twins?"

"No… but…"

"But what?"

"I think…they might have their own thing." I lowered my voice as I saw Jonathan's and the other guard's eyes on us. "I'll tell ya later."

Chapter 14

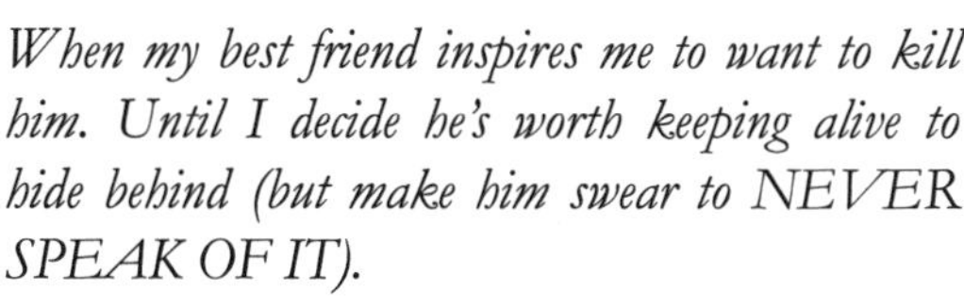

When my best friend inspires me to want to kill him. Until I decide he's worth keeping alive to hide behind (but make him swear to NEVER SPEAK OF IT*).*

It wasn't as if Joe hadn't told me he'd be sneaking into my room via the secret passage. I *was* expecting him. I'd even made sure to leave it unlocked.

I was *not* expecting: "Oooooohh! Heeeeaaaatherrrrr! Hhhhheee*eeaaaa*ther!" followed by the secret door rattling.

"EEEEEEEeeeeeemmmppphhh!!!" I yanked all the covers around me and pressed my face into my comforter.

"Really?! That really scared you?" Joe poked his head out of my closet, pressing a hand to his mouth and doubling over in suppressed guffaws.

"You *suck!* I *hate* you!" I hissed and flung pillows at him. He dodged one, then caught the other and threw it back at me.

"*Really?*" He was still snickering as he picked up the first pillow I threw.

"I don't care if you're the flipping prince of the *world,* that was *not* funny!"

"That was hilarious." As if to prove his point, he pressed his hands over his mouth to keep from laughing out loud.

I threw another pillow, which he caught again. Stupid athletic prince! Regardless, I scooted over on the bed. He handed the pillows back to me, but hesitated.

"I promise I won't actually hit you and commit treason or whatever. Even if you deserve it for scaring me like that."

The soft green glow of my alarm clock and the remaining late sunset lit up the room enough for me to see him raise an eyebrow at me.

"What?" I asked.

"Not that I generally hang out with girls, but really, you're strange even for a girl."

"I have no idea what you mean by that."

He shook his head and climbed onto the foot of my bed, kicked off his slippers, and sat cross-legged.

"Maybe that's why the rest of your school doesn't get you." He looked at me curiously.

I scowled at him, feeling like I may as well be some "weird" specimen he was studying. "Whatever. They're all stupid."

"Well, both your parents are, like, in MENSA. They probably *are* dumber than you."

"How do you *know* these things? Like about my parents?"

"Hello…prince? I know everything about everything."

I gave him a look to tell him I wasn't buying it.

He gave me a half-smile. "And I listen in on my parents' conversations."

That made more sense, at least. My dad was rather proud of the MENSA thing, though Mum hardly mentioned it. Prince Christopher probably had heard it from Dad.

"Whatever," I said again, sitting up like Joe was. "We have business to discuss."

"Yes, ma'am." He grinned at me again, then grew more serious. "So, the bridle should arrive here first thing in the morning. Once it's on, though, the kelpie can't attack us—or, shouldn't, in theory. So, we kill it."

Again with the "kill." I knew it had killed those kids, and it would have killed Sarah Beth, but…us actually *doing* the killing?

He hunched his back and lifted his pyjama shirt. I could see his waistband was thick, concealing something. As he unrolled the waist, he produced a thin knife of dark metal. It looked really old.

"It's iron. Faerie don't like iron," he stated.

I nodded. I knew this. He put it on the bed between us. I leaned over and picked it up.

"It's sharp. Don't touch the blade."

"Really?" I asked sarcastically, rubbing the edge over the sleeve of my nightgown and watching it thin below the blade. Iron. I wondered how much Joe's family knew or believed in faerie. "Where'd you get this?"

"I borrowed it."

I lifted my eyes and frowned.

"My dad won't miss it, I swear. It's just a decoration in his upstairs office." When I didn't say anything else, Joe added, "I sharpened it myself! I snuck into the kitchen after breakfast."

I looked at him for half a second. His eyes were so intense, they held me. "Cool," I said. "Really cool! Thanks."

He seemed to relax. "It was nothin'."

Had he really wanted *my* approval?

"Anyway…" He was back to business. "The hard part is actually going to be getting the bridle on the thing. But I've got an idea for that, too!"

"What?"

"Me!"

"You…what?" I had a feeling I knew where he was going with this, and I didn't like it one bit.

"For bait. Remember when at the loch I cut—"

"Aye, I remember, and no! No way, not at all, no. That has to be the stupidest idea you have ever come up with in your life!"

"Wait—just listen—"

"No! You gave me a guilt trip about sneaking out last night, and now you want to be bait and really, really get yourself hurt or-or—" I couldn't say it. "*You* know!"

"No, just listen. Not really me. Look!" From the pocket of his pyjamas—how much stuff had he smuggled in?!—he produced a pale blue handkerchief and began to unwrap what sounded like clicking plastic. In his hand were three medical phials of dark red fluid. His blood?

"Okay. Explain." I wrinkled my nose. "You didn't just nick that from somewhere in the palace or your parents are way creepier than anything."

"My parents are not at all creepy!" He snatched his hand back.

I looked up at his face, surprised at the actual offense. "I was *teasing*, yeesh! So, what? I'm assuming…that's yours?"

"Yes. My uncle…he's got diabetes, or so he and his personal physician says, so he keeps a needle on him at all times."

"Wait, don't they have, like single applicator needles for insulin, now?"

Joe raised an eyebrow. "This is what my uncle says he has to use, and his personal physician—not anyone else—agrees."

"Oh." I didn't know a lot about Joe's uncle, Prince Albert, but Joe had given me enough hints that there was an awful lot that just "wasn't said" about his dad's younger brother.

"So, obviously, I don't feel bad borrowing his stuff. And, yes, I know he keeps it sterilized. He's not stupid." Joe laughed mirthlessly. "Anyway, we use this," he held up the blood phials, "for bait. And then, maybe…you said your Mum taught you a few Western rope tricks, right? We rope the thing and get the halter on like that? Then, either you or I…" He reached for the knife with his other hand and fiddled with it, but only looked at me.

His eyes were more uncomfortable, and it made me feel a little better that he wasn't quite as gung-ho about killing the kelpie as he'd sounded. I nodded.

"I guess—" I gasped as the room chilled. Joe must have felt it, too, because he turned around, looking anxious. Goose bumps prickled every inch of my arms and legs, and I started to shiver. Without thinking, I jumped across the bed and wrapped my arms around my best friend's back. Breath rasped my throat as I felt I couldn't get enough air.

Joe stiffened a moment, then I felt him squeeze my arm. He slipped the blood phials back into his pocket and took my other hand.

"It's all right." He sat up on his knees as the room grew even colder.

I looked up from his shoulder, where I'd buried my face, and noticed he was blushing, definitely blushing, but I couldn't make myself loosen my arms. Up till the silly kiss on the hand, about as close as we got was like a nudge or holding hands. Hugging seemed definitely non-royal-protocol or whatever. I really didn't care. My knees felt like jelly and I was shaking as the scent of dirt and ozone filled the room. In front of us, at the foot of the bed, a pale light coalesced into the form of the ghost who, this close, wasn't quite as similar to my sister as I thought, but was still terrifying.

"You really do have an issue with ghosts," he whispered to me. I could tell he was trying to be reassuring because he was rubbing my arm and holding my hand, but all his muscles were tense, too.

"Ye have no idea!" said the ghost. "Ye're lucky she does nae—"

"Shut it!" I almost shouted, though my voice (fortunately) was muffled by how hard I was still pressing against Joe's shoulder. Impending horrible embarrassment beats down ghost terror. He *so* didn't need to know how I reacted last time I saw her.

"Who are you? What do you want?" Joe asked.

"Abigail MacArthur. And I've been *trying* to help."

"Hmph," I muttered softly. She didn't have to be so *scary* about it!

"How?"

"Well, at least ye're capable of communicating, but really, I figured *you* would have more manners." Her eye sockets looked hollow, but tiny flecks of light within them pointed at Joe.

"Do you *know* who I am?"

Really, I wanted to ask him, was this the time to pull rank? However, my speaking abilities had further diminished. Especially with how good a look I was getting (when I could open my eyes) at Abigail's phantom form.

"Of course I know, Yer Highness…" Okay, even I didn't like her tone on that. "How could any thing, living or otherwise, miss the grand entrance? But it's a little late to have me hanged for disrespect, eh?"

"From what I know, it takes a lot of energy for a spirit to manifest, so I figured we should get to the point," Joe said coolly. "I thought you were skipping formalities; I apologize if I misread, and you want to take longer." As he spoke with her, I felt him relaxing more, breathing deeper, which helped me relax a little, too.

"Aye, well, since your intent was respect of my time and energy, we can be direct, Joe."

"Prince Joseph. *Some* courtesy."

"Really?" I hissed at him. I just wanted to get this over. He ignored me and stared pointedly at the ghost, who narrowed her eyes—another especially creepy trait because her face hardly changed shape.

"Prince Joseph, Miss MacArthur…if ye'll follow me." She drifted towards the closet, her form becoming fuzzier.

"Heather." I said softly, loosening my arms around Joe, so he could move.

Even as her figure faded, I could make out her turning her head to look at me. "Abigail."

I nodded. Joe hastily grabbed the knife, folding it back into his waistband. Abigail became nothing more than a moving glow that lit up my closet. The secret passage door swung open and her light appeared to move down. Joe slipped a small LED torch from his other pocket and followed—talk about coming prepared! He put the torch in his mouth and we negotiated our way down the spiral stone stairs, him keeping at least a hand on me the whole way. Which I really appreciated.

Chapter 15

Doesn't every castle need a secret alchemy room down the secret, secret staircase?

The modernized addition to the castle was built, originally, in the late 19th century, but it burned down sometime in the 40s. It was ignored like that for almost twenty years The main castle had a cellar that housed the furnaces, leftover bits of dungeon—yes, actual dungeon—and a hidden library room that Dad had discovered and made into his own little history project.

As far as we knew, there wasn't a basement or cellar under the addition. But once we got to the level between my parents' offices and Ginny's, Abigail's glow turned and appeared to duck right through the far back corner that adjoined with the original castle wall. Moving closer, shadows betrayed the illusion of the wall's end and the narrow passage that led to another tight, spiral staircase of old stone.

"I've been down here before," I told Joe softly, gripping his hand. "I didn't know that was there."

"Secret passages off the secret passages, who knew?" Joe smirked, then paused, pulling his hand from mine for a moment. "Do you have any idea how strong you are?" He flexed a few times. Not having something to grip, and still seeing the slight glow from the secret, secret passage, I wrapped my arms around myself. He looked at me, pursing his lips in concern. "C'mere." I edged closer. He took one of my hands and wrapped it around his upper arm. "That way, you don't accidentally break my hand." He gave me a wink that definitely did more for making me less scared than anything else had yet.

I held his arm, and we continued our downward trek.

I wrinkled my nose about halfway down the stairs.

"It smells like wet campfire down here," Joe said.

"I don't think anyone knew to rebuild this part of the house."

"They didnae want to." Abigail's voice made me freeze. Joe squeezed my arm, nodding for us to keep moving.

"Why not?" he asked.

Abigail didn't answer.

"All right, be secretive in the secret, secret passage."

More silence as we descended told us that she was good with being secretive, all right.

The further down we got, the smokier it smelled. I stifled a cough and pressed my face back to Joe's shoulder so that I wasn't breathing so much soot. And he smelled pretty nice, too. It wasn't a cologne smell, but definitely stronger than just soap. I didn't recognize it, though. Still holding the mini torch, he lifted his own arm to cover his mouth and nose, coughing softly.

Around the corner from the last stair, we entered a hallway that was entirely blackened and full of debris. Abigail glowed brighter here, but that didn't make it less shudder-inducing. Even Joe, who seemed especially calm so far, shivered.

Chunks of wood and metal lay around the floor. Fortunately, we'd both grabbed slippers before coming down here; there were a lot of tiny rusted bits and charred wood that would have been a nightmare to step on (and explain to our parents in the morning). The blackened stone wall was pockmarked with holes almost as big as my fist.

Directly in front of us was a doorway. A few bits of burned door clung to hinges and around what looked like a lock.

Abigail seemed to hesitate, her light wavering. We couldn't see into the room beyond the door, but a distinct chemical odor added to the assault on our noses, mouths, and lungs.

"Is this where…" Joe began.

Abigail's disembodied face seemed to materialize and glare at us. "If ye're about to ask what I think ye are, don't! That's a terribly rude question to outright ask a spirit."

"Oh…" He seemed taken aback. "Sorry."

"This is where the fire started. As I'm sure yer keen perception had already picked up on."

My keen perception detected a soft growl from Joe at her veiled insult.

She entirely dissipated again, floating her glowiness into the room. "This is the alchemy lab. That's what my uncle called it," said her voice.

"Alchemy?"

"Aye."

In the faint light, I saw Joe frown sharply. "You're wearing a pretty modern dress for someone whose uncle believes in alchemy."

How did he notice these things? I was turning out to be a pretty crummy detective.

"Believed," was all she said.

"It's from what, the 30s or 40s? The records said the castle had gotten hit in World War II, and that's what destroyed the living quarters."

"Records can be altered." The tone in her voice was soft, pleading. She didn't want to talk about it. I bit my lip, feeling bad for our terrifying hostess.

Joe simply nodded and shone his light around the room.

Tiny bits of glass and debris littered the floor like scattered sand. Several tables lay smashed against the walls.

"The explosion started right in the middle of the room," he observed. "But people have been in here since." He lit up very faded footprints and trails through the debris.

"Not for many, many years," Abigail said.

"Mmn-hmn." Joe agreed. He moved his light along a few of the paths until it landed on a wooden chest. A completely intact, albeit dust-covered, wooden chest.

"That's what you brought us down for?" He walked over to it.

Dust-covered, but not soot or debris-covered.

"Aye." Her glow seemed to be fading with her voice.

He handed me the torch and pulled from my grasp, reaching for the lip to open it. A loud "click-clack" reverberated twice and he jumped back, barely keeping his feet. I recognized some of the curse words he'd spouted at me earlier, when I'd snuck up to his room, and got a whole bunch more I'd never heard before. He alternately stuck his fingers in his mouth and shook them. Blood colored his lips and grew darker with each time he sucked on his obviously injured fingers.

"A MacArthur needs to open it."

"A warning would have been nice, thanks," he growled.

I'd started trembling again, separated from him, but I bit my lip and stared at the chest. I handed him back the torch. "You okay?"

"Yeah," he muttered, showing me his fingers. "Just stupid pinpricks."

I approached the thing, slipping my hand into my sleeve to dust off the cover better.

"Anything else I should know before trying to open it?"

"It will sting a bit. Find the finger grooves first, and it will prick smoother." Her voice and light were fading. I remembered what Joe had said about ghosts only having so much energy.

The cover, which shone almost metallic in the torch's and Abigail's light, bore carved and darkened lines that served as a diagram for where I should put my fingers.

Significantly bigger than my hands, the holes spread my fingers widely. There was a *sh-click,* and I felt pricks on my two index fingers. It stung, but it definitely didn't hurt enough for Joe's reaction. A much softer click and the holes widened. I retrieved my fingers, seeing dots of blood swelling, then just lifted the lid.

"That's crazy. I mean…it's not like they had DNA detection back then," Joe breathed.

"Alchemy." Abigail's voice was barely a whisper now. "Combining science and magick."

"I see." Joe shined the torch, which was now brighter than the ghost's glow, into the chest while I pressed my fingers into my sleeves until they clotted. I'd definitely have to wash them out when we got back upstairs. In the chest were more books, some tools, an old canvas bag, canisters of some sort, and something sinuous that glinted silver.

"I heard ye mention ye knew rope tricks. I believe this will help. I wish ye both luck with the beast." Abigail seemed to pull herself tighter, making a very tiny ball of light that alit on the silver rope before she popped out of existence. Joe grabbed the rope, looping it across his shoulder and neck. It was pretty long, a good twenty meters, maybe, but was only slightly thicker than a clothesline.

"It's heavy." He handed me a coil. It was about the weight of a regular horse lead rope despite its fine diameter.

"I guess we rope the kelpie with this, then." I paused and coughed on a swallow. Joe had mentioned me knowing rope tricks well before Abigail had shown up. Could ghosts just *listen in* like that? I shivered.

"You all right, Heather?" Joe stood up.

I nodded and closed the chest, hearing it lock again. The room was so much darker without Abigail's soft glow; I almost missed the ghost…who could totally listen in on me. I felt Joe's hand reach for mine and I took it, feeling the frown melt from my face and not feeling nearly as scared as I had before. On the other hand, he squeezed my hand tightly and pulled me close, seeming even more anxious now. "Let's get out of here."

"Okay."

He all but jogged out of the room, pulling me with him. He moved just as quickly and carefully through the passage and up the secret, secret stairs. Once we were back on the ground floor, he slowed down, and I heard him take a deep breath.

"What?" I asked.

"You don't do ghosts; I don't do pitch black and underground." His whisper was hoarse. "Or really old smoke." He stifled another cough as he took one more deep breath. I squeezed his hand, and he squeezed back as we climbed back up to my room.

He didn't follow me in. "I should get some sleep tonight," he said. "You too. Abigail ran out of energy, so she won't come back tonight."

I nodded, but didn't let go of his hand. "Thanks…" He cocked his head as if to ask what I was thanking him for. "Just…you know. Thanks."

He gave me a half-smile and lifted my hand to his lips and kissed it again. Fortunately, the torch was aimed at our feet, not my face, which I felt turn bright red. In that moment of my inability to speak, he tossed the rope over my neck. I "uffed" at the unexpected weight and threw one arm through the loop. "You, too," he said. "Thanks. G'night."

"G'night," I said, proud that my voice sounded somewhat normal.

He let go of my hand and headed up the windy stairs. I closed my door when I saw the light of his torch disappear, but I didn't lock it.

It wasn't until I had hidden the rope, cleaned up, and was snuggled back under all my covers that it occurred to me that I hadn't thought to talk about the twins' "imaginary" but potentially faery friends.

Tomorrow. After all, we were going to have to figure out how to ditch the guards again. I figured Joe could cover that one; he was already used to doing that.

In the meantime, the really stupid grin wouldn't leave my face. Especially because one of my pillows now kind of smelled like the spicy cologne or whatever made Joe smell like himself.

Chapter 16

When another complicated family complicates my already complicated family—while I'm planning a stand-off against a monster faery horse.

Breakfast, like yesterday's tea and dinner after the press conference, was interesting. Except…well, even more so. Not only was there a second royal trip to the villages this morning to follow up on the press conference, they'd also gotten an invitation from one of the Earls further north for a dinner. So now there were *two* guys standing by the table taking notes and checking their Blackberries.

While the adults hashed out details, Joe and I kept giving each other anxious looks. Our time to pull off any kelpie plan was getting tighter and tighter.

Just as it looked like Her Majesty was going to do one of those "Let us adults retire" things, yet another suit appeared in the door, looking as if he had something important to say. When the Queen acknowledged his presence, he bowed and said, "Your Majesty, Your Highnesses, a package has arrived." He looked at Prince Christopher. "It is signed both to and from His Royal Highness Prince Christopher. I felt that was suspicious."

"I sent no package."

"Your Highness, Father," Joe said meekly. It was so weird to hear him address his dad that way! "That's mine. I miswrote. It's…for Heather. And I apologize for interrupting, Your Majesty." He lowered his eyes to his plate.

"For Heather?" Princess Maryan gave a small smile to my mother and me. Oh, great! The last thing we needed was our parents thinking we were sweet on each other or something (despite my own silliness about this whole hand-kissing thing, which was probably normal for royal people).

"You miswrote your father's name instead of your own, Joseph?" his grandmother asked in a voice that, if it were a knife, would cut skin without you feeling it.

"Yes, Your Majesty." His eyes were still humbly on his lap. "I meant to just address it to him here, so that it would be expedited and we'd get it today, but I wrote it in both places because I was in a hurry."

"Using your father's name, for whatever reason, is impersonation and unacceptable behavior."

"I'm very sorry, Your Majesty. It won't happen again." While he appeared still and meek from the chair up, I felt him digging his shoe toes into the rug.

"What is it that you found so important that you needed to borrow your father's identity?" she pressed.

"It's…a gift." Dig, dig, dig, went his toes, and I noticed his neatly folded hands all but clenching.

"A gift?" Despite her phrasing, it was *not* a yes or no question.

"If I may, if it may please…Your Majesty, Highnesses?" I squeaked, hoping I got everything right as I matched Joe's posture and demeanor.

"Yes?" Ack! It was the Queen talking—to *me!*

"It's actually a favor for me… My sister is coming home later today unexpectedly, and not under the best circumstances, and I wanted a surprise gift for her." I consciously glanced at my parents because that seemed the right thing to do for my story. "I asked His Highness, Prince Joseph, if he would pick it up for me as a favor. I paid him back for it when we visited yesterday." I strategically glanced at the appropriate guards. "I…was just hoping it would be a surprise, if that is okay? Please? Sorry. I didn't mean to upset anything. Sorry!" I bit my lip. I'd just lied to the Queen of England!

Since I was staring at my plate and lap, as Joe had been, I didn't see anyone's expressions, but I heard a few sighs.

"I see," was all the Queen said. "Thank you for your honesty on my grandson's behalf." Ugh! She may as well have plunged a knife into my stomach. Not only was it a lie, now I'd gotten Joe into more trouble. "Joseph, we can speak about your own behavior later."

"Of course, Your Majesty. At your will." He sounded a little more relieved than I expected. "May…may Heather and I be excused?"

There was another long silence that I'm pretty sure was more for effect than actual consideration.

"I was planning to suggest we adjourn," the Queen stated, standing, cueing all of us to also stand. "You children may do as you will per your respective parents." Joe and I glanced at our respective parents. My parents, Dad especially, looked particularly happy. Ugh! Out of the corner of my eye, I caught Prince Christopher giving Joe a particularly scathing look, but nodding permission to leave. Double ugh!

Once the adults had gone, Joe and I headed to where several guards were standing around our rather large box, nodding as they heard in their earpieces that it was okay to give it to us.

Joe hefted the box and, before anyone could offer to carry it for us, we ran up the main staircase. "Brilliant," he breathed. "Sometimes, you are just brilliant!" He gave me a big smile.

"I, uh… aren't you going to get in trouble now, though?"

"I'm going to get a nasty lecture." He shrugged. "And it's my own stupid fault. We get suspicious packages all the time. I hadn't thought of anything but getting it here." He gave me another smile. "We make a sweet team. I hate improv. Give me a good plan any day, and I'll make it work, but you can sell it like anything! And on your toes!"

"I guess." I shrugged, though I appreciated the compliment.

We got to my room where, surprise of surprises, Joe's usual two guards were already posted outside my door. As we approached, Jonathan reached out his hand. "Your Highness, shall I open the box for you?" He pulled a multi-tool from the belt under his suit coat.

"I've got—" I began.

"After all," Jonathan interrupted, giving me a firm, but not unkind look, "we couldn't, in good conscience, let His Royal Highness enter a room without us in his immediate presence if we were aware the room contained weapons or blades of any kind."

"Oh." I handed over the box. "Thank you, yes. I thought we just might tear it…but it is a pretty heavy box." Yes, the great Craft Scissor Assassination Attempt of 2011. I did have my camping and boot knives in my room, but I'd really just been thinking scissors. Jonathan opened the box and handed it back without looking inside, though I swear he smiled just a little.

"Thank you," Joe echoed and we went into my room. He swung the door closed behind us, and I heard the thud of Jonathan catching it and glancing in. Joe gave him a look and gestured with his thumb and forefinger if we could close it just a *little more*. Jonathan did, *just a little*. Joe turned around, scowled, grabbed my clock-MP3 player and set it up by the door, as he'd done yesterday before tea.

We sat down on the other side of the curtain from the door and dumped the box on end. White, pink, and blue packing peanuts skittered across the floor, and another box came out covered with warnings of being sealed and the danger of air getting to the artifact and blah, blah, blah. Joe pulled out the iron knife.

"Wait, don't want them to interfere with each other…in case it's faery magick that makes the bridle work."

"Good point."

I went over to my bureau, glancing at the door, but neither guard was looking in, so I grabbed my boot knife from the sock drawer.

Very carefully, I cut the seals and opened the box to reveal...another box. We both groaned. This one was opaque plastic, though, so we had to find those seals, break them, and then—then!—we got inside.

The brown leather bridle was on a foam horse head. All of the buckles and metal were copper with a green patina.

"This is it?" I asked.

"Mmn-hmn," he nodded. "Not much to look at. But isn't that how it goes in the stories? I don't quite get how it works, though. No bit."

"It's bitless." I pointed at the copper rings on either side of the noseband and mannequin muzzle. "It uses poll pressure. Where the neck connects to the head is sensitive on horses." I pulled braids on either side of my head to demonstrate.

"Oookay." He still sounded confused.

"If I remember the story right, it wasn't ever supposed to come off, so the kelpie has to eat somehow. You can't keep a bit in all the time." I moved the head around, not quite ready to touch the bridle. Just getting close made the air fuzzy—like when you put your fingers near one of those static electricity globes. "Funny, all the equestrian games say they don't want crazy new things like bitless bridles messing up tradition or whatever, and here's one that's hundreds of years old."

"The leather looks pretty good for a few hundred years old." Joe reached to touch it, pausing, probably feeling that static charge I had felt.

"Magick." I bit my lip as it dawned on me that I had said it as a fact.

Joe recoiled his hand. "Grab the rope... I don't remember it *feeling* like this does."

I nodded, stepping to my closet. Because I was buried behind clothes, it took me a second to respond when I heard the angry stomping and the "Get out of my way!" as Prince Albert burst into my room.

"You little sod! You think you're smart? You think you're smooth? You think I wouldn't have noticed?"

Price Albert's dark-blond hair hung half in his very red face as he all but spat upon the now-standing Joe. He looked almost ill.

"I don't know what you're talking about," Joe replied calmly, though his hands were in fists by his sides.

"Your Highness!" Jonathan was moving between them, looking worriedly at Prince Albert.

"You know damned well what I'm talking about, boy!" Prince Albert shoved Jonathan aside with a hand to the chest. "I need my medicine and my supplies, and I open my box and see three vials missing? You've always been trouble, just like your mother—"

"Don't you *dare* speak ill of my mother." The evenness of Joe's voice chilled me even more than his uncle's rage.

"Your Highness." Jonathan stepped in front of Prince Albert again, face dark. What were bodyguards supposed to do when they're supposed to protect both people about to get into the fight? Joe's second guard was coming into the room, slipping a phone into his pocket.

"Stand down! This is family business," Prince Albert sneered at Jonathan, stepping around him to stare Joe in the eye. "What? You have no say. You're nothing right now, boy, you hear? Don't *you* dare give me any of your lip!"

"I am not giving you any lip, Uncle. You came in here, yelling—"

"Uncle?!" Prince Albert rebuked Joe, though he looked at me, and I winced. His blue eyes were bloodshot and sweat dripped down his face, soaking the neck and armpits of his dress shirt. Then, his arm coiled up for a backhand. Behind him, Jonathan jerked his head and moved.

Dropping the rope, I launched across the room without thinking.

Joe moved quicker and caught me as I heard a *smack* and saw Jonathan stagger back a step. I'm not quite sure how he maneuvered it, but Joe placed me, more or less, on the rug. Facing his uncle, Joe's face shattered into fury, as he raised his own fists. Prince Albert threw off his coat *and* the other bodyguard with a strength I didn't expect him to have. As floored as I was, I kipped back up, trying to get between them, seeing the horse mannequin and bridle skid under Lily's bed.

Moving almost like water, Joe was between me and his uncle again, and the resounding smack shoved him into me, and both of us onto the ground.

"Your Highness, please!" Jonathan, a red welt on his jaw, grabbed one of Albert's arms; his partner grabbed the other.

"Don't you touch me! You have no right to lay hands on me. You're hired to *protect* me!" snarled Prince Albert.

Jonathan, his glasses on the floor somewhere, ignored Prince Albert and looked at Joe with horror. "Prince Joseph? Heather?" I don't think I'd ever heard that much emotion in any of the guards' voices.

"Fine. We're fine, really." Joe turned away from them. As he helped me up, I saw a welt over his right cheek. "Are you okay?" he asked me in a whisper.

I nodded. "Joe—" I started in a whisper.

He shook his head, herding me from the guards and his uncle. "I know you meant well, Heather, but promise me, *promise* me you'll never do that again!" he hissed at me.

"I—" Behind Joe, I saw Prince Albert trying to yank free from the guards, growling curses and orders.

"I know, like I said, but you have no idea how much worse it'll be if he...you..." Joe shook his head and, for a moment, looked almost ready to cry. "Please, just promise me you won't ever get between us again?"

"I promise," I said.

Then, the real storm descended. More guards, Joe's parents, and my parents all shoved into my room.

When I saw the look my dad gave to Prince Albert, I knew what Joe meant about things being a whole lot worse. Prince Christopher, upon seeing Joe's face, found a guard pressing one hand on his chest, looking quite uneasy as he kept himself between the brothers. I could only imagine Dad or Mum losing it if I had gotten the business end of the blow, and to hell with royalty.

"Her Majesty approaches," said one of the guards. He spoke at regular volume, but we all shut up.

Prince Christopher relaxed, straightening his coat. Even Prince Albert, who now had four guards holding him, stopped struggling. Princess Maryan wrapped her arms around Joe's shoulders and Mum did the same to me.

The people parted like the Red Sea to let the queen enter my bedroom. Beside her was the better-dressed and older-looking of the note-takers I'd seen, the one who I'd figured was her personal assistant or secretary. Eyes narrowed in disapproval that could only be described as "queenly," she looked down her nose and we collectively shrank under her gaze.

"We should be leaving for the second tour of the villages. I trust this nonsense will be taken care of and we will be ready to leave in an hour?"

Prince Christopher led us in polite, properly addressed murmurs. The queen nodded to all of us and, even though I dared not look directly at her, I think I saw a hint of compassion when she looked at Joe's face…or maybe I just wanted to see that.

Her voice was like winter when she said, "Albert, walk with me to my quarters."

"Yes, Your Majesty, Mum."

As she took his arm, she added in a slightly less icy tone "Christopher, you can get your family together on your own."

"Of course, Your Majesty, Mum."

"Lawrence, see to any details that need attention."

"Of course, Your Majesty." Mr. Personal Assistant or Important Secretary Lawrence turned sharp brown eyes on me.

"Young miss," his tone softened, but it didn't seem genuine, "this is your bedroom, is it not?"

"It is, sir," I murmured, feeling less shaky as Mum still held me. I felt Dad right behind her.

"Will you tell us what *you* saw happen?"

I glanced at Joe, whose face was tight, green eyes bright, like he wanted to send me some telepathic message I wasn't getting. I took a deep breath and made my best guess at the answer. After all, I was sure they'd get the story from Jonathan and the other guards. It wasn't an information-collecting question.

"I really didn't see much. I was in my closet when Prince Albert came in. I didn't really hear what anyone said…and I… it was just a lot. I couldn't remember any details if anyone asked me."

A shade of relief washed over Joe's face, even as more purple crept into the bruise. I was on the right track.

"And should anyone ask?"

"Well…they shouldn't, but, really, I can't say what all happened. It was just such a blur. It's not something I'd want to talk about."

Lawrence scrutinized me for probably a full minute. I felt my parents shift behind me and wanted to look at them, but I worried it'd be rude to look away. Finally, he relaxed and turned towards Prince Christopher, Princess Maryan, and Prince Joseph. "At your leave, Highness."

"Go ahead, Lawrence." Christopher nodded at the door.

"Your Highness." He bowed, and left the room.

Prince Christopher and my father looked at each other, then the prince squatted and looked me in the face. "Heather, honestly, are you all right? You're not hurt?" He sounded more like Joe's dad than His Royal Highness.

"No, really. I'm okay." I stepped away from Mum to show I was uninjured.

"I'm sorry. Truly, I am. I will *not* let such an occurrence happen again. You have my word."

I nodded again. "Th-thank you, Prince Christopher." I wasn't exactly sure what else to say, but that seemed right.

He led Princess Maryan and Joe to the door, but Joe pulled from his mum and came to me, taking both my hands. We didn't say anything to each other. That was enough.

When they left the room, my dad was down on one knee. "Heather—" he began.

I leaned over and kissed his cheek and hugged him. "I'm really, really okay, Daddy. I promise."

He frowned, not looking particularly convinced.

I kissed his other cheek. "Really."

Still not reassured, he pulled me into a hug and kissed both my cheeks. "We'll talk later." He stood, smoothing his kilt. From behind me, Mum pulled me into a tight hug and kissed my face.

I sighed as they left me, and started cleaning up all the packing peanuts and cardboard; Lily was as much of a neat freak as Dad. I pulled the mannequin and bridle from under the bed and put it in the corner, touching only the form, not the actual bridle, and then wound the rope beside it. Biting my lip, I snuck back into the secret staircase and tiptoed up to Joe's room.

His secret passage door was unlocked, but I heard a lot of noise. The door creaked open just a little, then hit a soft thud.

"Let me grab what I have in the closet," I heard Joe say.

He flipped on the closet light, blinding me. When I could focus, I saw him looking right at me, shaking his head as he crouched over his suitcase.

"Not a good time," he whispered, shaking his head.

"I'm sorry!" I whispered back.

"No, I am. Really…just…one sec." He glanced over his shoulder. "Would one of you please bring my other bag down? I need to rearrange this a bit."

I heard shuffling around his room.

"Lily's arriving soon, right?"

"Aye."

He reached through the crack in the passage and slipped me the blue handkerchief of phials and the iron knife. "Swear to me, swear to me on our friendship, that you'll make her help? You won't try and do this on your own?"

In the closet light, I saw moisture in his eyes. The welt on the side of his face made an awful shadow.

"I swear. I'll ask Lily for help."

"Don't just ask; *make* her. You can't do this alone!"

"I won't; I swear."

"On our friendship? On us?"

I swallowed hard, but if things were switched up, I wouldn't want him to do this alone, either. "On our friendship."

He nodded. "You better go. We'll say goodbye later."

The goodbyes were not nearly as awkward as I'd expected, but they were surprising.

Despite his grandmother's and father's glares, Joe broke royal protocol (or something) and gave me a big hug. I hugged him back tightly.

"Remember, you swore!" he hissed in my ear.

"I did, and I do," I whispered back. I felt him nod against me.

It seemed like the only one on the queen's blacklist was Prince Albert. Her goodbyes and thank-yous to my family were kind, even in her reserved, royal manner. She even suggested they return to visit under "less tragic circumstances." From the look on my dad's face, I gathered that was a compliment to our hospitality. Mum, for her part, looked like she was hiding as much confusion with this whole visiting royal thing as I was.

We stood in front of our castle until the last of the cars drove out of sight. Once they did, my dad, looking exhausted—I wondered how he'd managed to "enhance" his medicine with all the guards around—told us to go change into casual clothes and pack for Granddad's. Then, he asked me, "Are you good with your hair still braided? No headaches?"

"No, I'm good. When's Lily getting here?" Even as I asked, I heard the crunch of gravel as Ginny's Audi came up the driveway.

"Looks like now, love. You'll give her an update and help with her things?"

"Yeah…um…should I mention…you know?"

Dad paused and sighed. "You cleaned your room up?"

"Aye."

Ginny parked near the entrance and got out of the car. "They all left already?"

If Ginny looked disappointed, my sister looked downright crushed as she got out of the car. "You mean I *missed* seeing the Queen?"

"May as well," Dad conceded. "I'll explain things to Ginny. Just…" He made a pained face.

"Not for public knowledge. I know…and she'll understand."

"Good girl." He kissed the top of my head. Turning to Ginny, he said, "It's bit of a long story."

"Whatcha got for luggage?" I asked my sister.

"Two suitcases and my carry-on," Lily said. "Why did they leave so soon?! Ginny and I totally took over the family water closet at Edinburgh so we could get all dolled up." She spun around in a pretty white and blue sundress with a lacy, crocheted sweater that I didn't recognize. "I picked this up special at this boutique dress shop inside JFK." She glanced at Dad. "I figured it was important, so I used the card."

"That's fine, sweetheart. It looks lovely on you." Behind us, my dad hefted one of Lily's suitcases. "I'm sorry you didn't get to meet the Queen. I'll get Ginny up to speed; Heather can tell you everything. We're going to your grandfather's as soon as we're all packed up."

"What? What happened?! Have you heard anything about Sarah Beth?"

"No, we haven't, but we decided we don't want any of you in danger. The police will figure this out."

My heart hammered in my chest. We didn't have a lot of time.

"I want to bring some of my clothes from here, can we grab them?"

"I'll help." I grabbed her other suitcase. "C'mon."

My sister looked at me funny, and even more so when I decided to use the lift. The latter bit shouldn't have been a shocker. Lily has no concept of packing light. I could have filled her suitcase with grain bags and it would have weighed less!

"Sarah Beth is okay," I said as soon as we started moving. "I saw her last night, but I need your help to save her."

"What?! I… Seriously, *what?!*" Her mouth gaped at me. "You didn't tell Mum and Dad?!"

"I…" I thought of my earlier considerations regarding my parents and how bad things were with them. "It's complicated. You just gotta listen to me."

"Um…okay?" She opened the lift door as soon as the lift stopped. "Is this related to why the Queen and everyone left in such a rush?"

"No, that's totally different," I said. "Prince Albert and Joe had a bit of a row in my room and he slapped Joe right in front of me and then was about to smack me." Lily's jaw almost hit the floor at that. "But he didn't before the guards came in, so they all rushed out for a second tour of the villages."

"Ho-ly crud! Seriously? Is-is Joseph all right? And you?" I don't think my sister had ever stared at me in such awe. I rolled my eyes, not feeling particularly "cool" about having been in the middle of Joe's family fight.

"Yeah, we're fine, but that's not important now, and we can't say anything—"

"Well, duh!" my sister added, shutting our bedroom door behind us. "So, what's up with Sarah Beth? How the hell did you see her last night?"

I paused. "I swear to *God* every word I'm about to say to you is the absolute truth, no matter how crazy it sounds—"

"That's not particularly reassuring."

"Just…just be quiet and listen!" I growled. "We don't have a lot of time, and a whole lot of major, major crap has gone down this week, and I really need your help!"

"All right, all right. I'm listening." Lily bit her lip, looking especially worried.

I jammed as much as I could about the kelpie, Tom, Sarah Beth, Abigail, and my promise to Joe in the time span of two minutes. As I was talking, I stripped off my dress and changed into a pair of riding jeans and a hiking blouse.

"Jesus!" my sister breathed. I glared. "Don't look at me like that, if there was ever any time to say His name, it's now. And *you* swore to God!"

I shook my head. "So, Joe gave us a good plan. And, with him not here, it's probably even safer—"

"You and Joe were going to take on a killer horse monster by yourselves?"

"Yes—"

"We should really tell Mum and Dad. This is big, Heather!"

"We don't have time, and they're beyond stressed right now. We can do this, Lily."

"Heather—" Lily started changing her clothes.

"Lily, please, please do this with me! Have I ever *not* done a favor for you? Have I ever *not* kept any of your secrets? Like going off with—"

My sister sighed. "What's the plan?"

"I'll tell you on the way to the stable." I pulled out the mannequin horse head and took the bridle off. As I touched it, I felt a shiver overtake me.

"You okay?" Lily asked.

"Yeah…just. This thing is…powerful."

"I still think we should get Mum and Dad," she said. "They'll believe us. I mean, you could show them that... thing...and the rope."

"At this point, if they do believe there's a monster killer faery horse, Dad will *duct tape* us into the car and make it fly to Granddad's. And Mum will just help him, she's so worried about him."

"For the record, I'm saying we should."

"Record noted. Ready?"

"To face down a killer magick monster horse? Sure!" She snapped an elastic around a ponytail. "Let's add achieving world peace before sunset to our to-do list, too."

"Lil—"

"Just give me the damned rope. I'm better at that than you are."

"Thanks, Lily."

"Thank me when we're back home and not dead or grounded."

Chapter 17

The kelpie showdown.

The loch was high and choppy. Though the sun shone brightly, it *felt* like another storm was coming in.

The day had finally gotten to Rowan, who was having a meltdown; between him and the twins, all of the adults were preoccupied, which worked in favor of our sneaking out. I told Lily to take East because he was smaller and I felt bad for him having to carry now-super-tall me. I remember one of the judges saying mismatched riders hurt horses' backs. But as we broke through the trees beside the loch, I regretted that choice. Chixie fought me hard. East was also antsy, but Lily kept him under control; she was always the better horsewoman. Besides, we didn't have time to change horses now. What if the kelpie came out of the water while both of us were dismounted?

Doing my best to neck rein the thoroughbred with one hand, I pulled out one of the phials of Joe's blood. I moved farther from the water and dumped it.

"You sure this'll work?" Lily asked.

"No."

"Brilliant."

The waves grew higher and my heavy braids slapped at me from a gust of wind. Chixie screeched. She lunged for the tree line. I yanked the reins and kicked her into a disengage, crossing her back legs so deep I thought she might fall over. Lily pushed East into a circle to control him, too.

Nothing more happened.

"Maybe try closer to the water." Lily jerked one rein to keep East from dropping his head and bucking.

"That's where it gets its power."

"We can make it move. This won't work if it doesn't come."

"Fine."

I fought Chixie till we were almost at the water's edge. As I pulled the cover off the second phial, the mare jerked her head from my grasp and started to buck. The phial went flying into the water as I grabbed the reins in both hands.

"Heather!" I could hear Lily forcing her "coach" voice even as her pitch heightened with fear. "Stick with her. Find your center, heels down. Keep your seat… Let her get away from the water."

I let her get away from the water, but she was seriously done with me. As I tried to steer her from the woods, she threw me. I landed not far from the rock-wedged branch that had trapped Oppie just days ago. Chixie disappeared towards home.

I stood. Lily rode over to me. Froth dripped from around East's bit, and his eyes bulged white with terror.

Then, everything grew calm.

Swallowing hard, I looked to the water. The remaining waves radiated from something moving towards the shore. The smell of briny weed and ozone and dead things lapped over us.

From the water, the kelpie rose, looking even more nightmarish than I remembered. Slimy plants clumped down as its mane and tail. It spread its lips and sucked in air, revealing its sharp, wolfy-sharky teeth. Fiery eyes looked right at us.

"Bloody hell," my sister breathed.

East gave a squeal at the horse that was much bigger than him, almost as big as the massive Oppie. My champion-rider sister barely kept him from bolting.

"Priiiiinnce!" Its hissing voice sent shivers up my back. Its green-black nostrils flared as it walked to where I had spilled the first phial. Lowering its head, it licked the ground, hell-red eyes never leaving us.

"Lily!"

"On it." She started swinging the rope into a lasso. The kelpie stopped lapping and charged.

"Hee-yah!" She kicked her heels into East, lasso twirling over her head.

The kelpie reared. East panicked, turning away as my sister threw the rope. And missed.

"Goddamnit, East!" She yanked the reins, trying to gather the rope one-handed.

The kelpie charged me.

"Hell, no!" Lily snapped the rope at the kelpie's face. "Hee-yah! Hee-yah! Move it!"

As she circled sharply, East's back legs kicked dirt and mud at me. Lily re-collected the rope as the kelpie did a roll back and came at us once more, snorting.

East screamed again, trying to flee. Lily kicked his side and drove him back towards us, swinging the rope. I undid enough buttons on my blouse so the bridle was easy to access. I didn't know what else to do.

After another unsuccessful circle for each, the kelpie halted and glared at us. Lily stopped a shaking, panting Eastwood by my side.

"Remember when I lost the dare that you couldn't hop on Oppie while he was running?" Lily asked.

"Yeah."

"Wanna make double good on it?"

No—really, no!—but what choice did we have? "Sure."

Lily charged first. I crouched, ready to run wherever she drove the thing.

It came from my left, so I sprinted in the same direction. Except, instead of trying to avoid me, like Oppie—or any *normal* horse—it was ready to attack. Lily's whip snap of the magick rope pushed it from me.

I had not even half a second. I didn't think. I just launched, grabbing the slimy mane.

When I touched it, I expected to slip. I didn't think I'd find any purchase on the water-slick sides. I didn't expect *it* to grab *me*!

I squealed. Its coat was like tiny moving tentacles. I didn't climb onto its back; I was *moved* there. The black hairs tangled around my fingers. Like Velcro, they stuck to my clothes.

Lily couldn't see my predicament. "Nice job! Now, catch the rope!"

"I can't!" I choked out in a scream.

The kelpie released a laugh even creepier than its voice.

"No! No!!" I struggled, trying to free myself, but that seemed to only tangle me more. "Let me go! Lily! Help me! Oh, God! Oh, God!" I prayed.

We were heading right for the water.

A screeching, growling, feline yowl punctuated the gallop. The kelpie reared again, and I saw tortoiseshell fluff scampering below the kelpie's head.

The kelpie cried in pain and blood splattered onto my arms and hands. I caught a glimpse of Tom's amber-green eyes as he clung, clawed, and bit at the beast's neck. Tom curled his back legs, gouging down the throat.

Then came barking and howling.

"Hee-yah!" That was not my sister's voice. A regular rope lassoed the kelpie's head. It tipped backwards and to the side, rolling over, knocking the wind out of me. The buckles on the bridle pinched, bruised, and scraped my skin. The iron knife bruised through my pockets, but I could barely squeak in pain. Worse, the last phial of blood cracked. The smell made me sick and its stickiness soaked through my shirt. My helmet smacked against rocks. I was no longer attached to the kelpie. But I couldn't move.

I saw a blur of two black and two white legs driving the kelpie away, its hooves *just* missing my prone body.

"Stay down, you sonofabitch!"

Mum?

"Heather! Baby!"

Dad?

"Bloody hell, Chixie!"

What?! Dad was here?!

"Just let Chixie go!" Mum called.

I heard the receding sounds of Chixie's hooves, then Dad knelt beside me. "Baby, can you move?"

"I dunno." As much as I hated seeing the fear in his face, I was so happy to see him!

Snap! broke Mum's rope. More dogs howling and horses screaming. They must've brought Isis and Osiris.

"Michael, get her out of there now!" My mum called, then howled at the kelpie. "Move it! Get away from her, you monster!"

My dad scooped me in his arms and ran.

"Lily! What are you doing? Let it go!" Mum shouted.

"We gotta kill it, Mum," she said. "That's how we save Sarah Beth."

"What?!" My dad stopped for a moment and looked back.

"We gotta." I caught my breath, starting to feel the rest of my limbs—pained as they were. I squirmed in his arms. "Let me down."

He let me stand. "What are you talking about?! We need to—Watch it!" He pulled me as the kelpie charged us. A sickening yelp came from Osiris. The dog went flying and fell into a limp pile. Mum ran Dream in a circle, driving the beast back towards the water. Isis was clinging to its throat. Behind them, Lily paced Eastwood just at the water's edge.

"Sarah Beth can't go home while-while it's still alive, I think. Where-where's Tom?"

"What are you talking about, love—"

I'm here!

"Holy—What?!" My dad jumped, pulling me away from the now-matted cat that he'd obviously just "heard."

"Good, you're okay," I said to Tom.

"Heather, what the hell?" Dad's face was red.

"I'm sorry, Dad, I am! It's just...we gotta do this." I turned back to where Mum and Lily double-teamed the monster.

"Do *what*, exactly?"

"I gotta get this on...*that*." I showed him the edge of the bridle tucked under my blouse. Another yelp grabbed our attention as we saw Isis fly towards the water.

"No. No!" Dad shook his head hard. "We're getting out of here, now! Let the police or-or animal control...deal with-with *that!*"

"They can't. This won't work for them."

"What do you mean it won't work for them?"

I didn't know what I meant, exactly, I just knew it was the truth when I spoke it.

"Please, Daddy, I know—I know you've got no reason to believe me or trust me right now, but please, I've gotta do this!"

No human police or animal control can do a damned thing about a kelpie, Tom added with a hiss at my Dad.

Dad gave the cat an especially withering glare.

"Mum, take this!" I looked to where Lily and Mum now circled the kelpie in alternate directions. She threw Mum the silver rope as they approached each other.

The weight of the rope threw my sister off-balance for a fraction of a second. The kelpie noticed. It changed direction towards her and East.

East, for the first time I'd ever seen, broke into a series of bucks, throwing Lily.

"Lily!" My dad took a step towards her, looking in terror from her to me.

She landed better than I had. It looked like right out of a movie. She shoulder-rolled and was back on her feet.

The kelpie ran at her.

Tom flew from beside my dad and me. He pounced, digging his claws and teeth into the kelpie's rear right leg. Osiris was back up, too. Though he looked groggy, he joined Tom, tearing into the same leg. The kelpie started bucking. Osiris hit the ground once more with only half a yelp and didn't move again.

Mum spun Dream around, his hocks nearly touching the ground, and galloped for Lily. Leaning almost sideways, Mum grabbed Lily and swung her onto Dream's back with her.

The kelpie finally kicked off Tom, who hit the ground beside the water. He twitched but didn't get up.

"Tom!" I called.

Brilliant. The kelpie now ran at me and Dad!

"Move, baby, move." He grabbed my arm. No way we could outrun the kelpie, but no way my dad would give up, either.

A shimmer of silver shot from Mum and right around the kelpie's neck. A quick jerk from her hand and it stumbled.

"Hold this," she told my sister, then whipped out the remainder of her own rope. Another flick of her wrist managed to loop it around one of its rear legs. It fell onto its haunch.

"Heather, now!" Lily called, but I had already broken Dad's grasp and was running towards the monster. I pulled out the bridle, ignoring the scraping copper buckles. The kelpie screamed upon seeing me, seeing the bridle. Strangely, I felt calm as I approached.

I stopped and looked into its glowing red eyes. It sneered at me, hissing, showing off its monster teeth.

"Hurry up!" Mum called.

I didn't hurry. I was careful, avoiding the chomps of its mouth, bracing my arm around its muzzle. If I hadn't grown those extra inches this spring, it probably would have lifted me off the ground. I flung the reins over the neck and dragged the bridle on over its face. It fought my every move. My feet slipped on the water and blood and sweat dripping from both of us, but I held on.

No! No! No! No! It was speaking like Tom, in my head. Time seemed to slow, and it occurred to me regular speaking was difficult for it. It knew its voice was scary; it was a tool. Now, it just wanted to communicate.

A shiver crept from the top of my head and down my whole body. As if I were breathing in a weird scent, I felt myself inhaling…*something.* I recognized a terror in my head, a…*presence*…that wasn't me. Not just the talking thing, like Tom in my head. *More.*

And I felt something in me break off, sending my stomach into a downward sick spiral. Then something sucked my breath right out of me.

A jerk dragged me into the moment and I gasped for air, aware of every ache and pain in my body—but with a feeling of being *outside* my body. The jolt nearly threw me from the kelpie. I realized, in a weird time displacement, that Mum's rope had broken again. Then, Lily lost her grip on the silver one. The kelpie turned, ready to run. I swung back on its back. I don't know why; it seemed the right thing to do.

The tentacle fur didn't *bind* me, but it did hold me on for two bucks. There was one more buckle to latch. I pulled on the attached rein, trying to get him to turn his head so I could reach. He—I had known it was a "he" before, but now he *felt* like a "he"—fought for just a second, then moved into the turn.

I felt comfortable, *safe* almost. There was a connection between us now, and it made me shiver. I…I *knew* him, and I knew he *knew* me. He stopped and stood stock-still, bending his neck, head lowered to his shoulder level. I reached for the loose buckle. Once my hand touched it, he turned closer. I buckled it easily. The kelpie snorted several times, not in anger, but release. Swallowing, still holding the reins, I dismounted. The second I decided to do that, the sticky fur released me.

Mum and Lily rode over. Dad ran to me. The kelpie spooked, backing away. He was scared—no, *terrified.* I looked at his face and gasped. His eyes bugged out, but instead of fiery red, they glowed blue-green. The color of the ocean. The color of my eyes.

"Hold up, hold up! Stop!" I told them all, holding up my hands.

Kill it! You've got iron on you; I heard your plan. Tom limped over to us from the shoreline. *Just kill it; it won't fight you.*

"Heather…?" Mum asked, glancing between me and Tom. Obviously, the cat fey was projecting beyond my mind.

Please, don't kill me. Please! I beg you!

I turned and looked at the kelpie. "After all you've done? You *killed* two kids! You *destroyed* the villages, and people's houses, and sent people to the hospital! You would've *killed* Sarah Beth." My hand was on the sheathed iron knife still in my pocket. I pulled it out and shuffled it in my hand.

The kelpie lowered his head and licked his lips. *You have no reason to spare me. But I beg you, please.*

The connection I felt when I put the bridle on him felt even stronger. He was in my head! No, more than in my head, but I couldn't explain how. I'd never felt this much fear, not even from the ghost—I couldn't even imagine this much terror.

"Heather, baby, if you can't do it, let me," my dad was saying, though he sounded far away. He reached for my knife. There was *something* between me and the kelpie, something I felt that I should know, but couldn't grasp.

"No—no!" I backed towards the kelpie. "Give me a second. Please. He's not going to do anything now. He can't. Let me think!"

What's there to think *about?* Tom demanded. *It's a monster, a killer!*

"I *know* that!" I said. "But *I'm* not! And—and just letting—letting someone else do it is just as bad! It's still murder."

"Heather, it's not a person; it's not murder," Dad said. "It doesn't have a soul!"

"No!" That was it. "He does—he does now!" I looked at the kelpie's face, his eyes—*my* eyes—and I saw he felt the shame and weight of his actions. Like I would feel—and it was sickening. "He's got a piece of mine."

"Heather, no." Dad shook his head.

"Michael," Mum said softly.

"What?" He gave Mum a look harsher than any I'd ever seen him give, and it made me shiver.

She winced, but continued. "What Heather says…makes sense."

"*How* the *hell* does it make sense?" my father demanded. "If that *thing* is what killed those children—"

It is, said Tom, who was not helping my case at all. *And if that bridle ever comes off it, it will return to being a murderous monster. More children. And it will be especially vindictive against all of* you.

I looked at the kelpie.

"Is that true?"

I cannot take the bridle off; only another can. He backed away more, not meeting my eyes.

"That's not what I asked." I put the bridle on, he had to do as I commanded, so I ordered, "Tell me the truth. If that bridle comes off of you, will you be a killer again? Would you kill us?"

Yes. I would return…to what I was before. And I would likely come after you first.

"Heather, it has to be destroyed!" my father said.

"No!" I shouted back. It wasn't that easy!

You can't listen to it, Heather, Tom said. *Faerie will try and manipulate you by talking—*

"Well, what does that say about you?!"

The cat flinched. *I've never lied to you.*

"No, but you hide stuff. You didn't tell me about Sarah Beth, you used me to fix this whole faery mess. *He,*" I nodded at the kelpie, "has to tell me the truth and the whole truth if I ask him. He has to listen to me."

So, you'll keep him as a slave? Tom's stare was so hard I could literally *feel* it.

I swallowed hard. That didn't sound much less worse than murder. How many people say they'd rather die than be enslaved?

I would rather be a slave than die. Please? The kelpie must have heard my thought; I was surprised at how *not* surprised I felt at that realization. He moved one hoof closer to me.

"Heather, please—" My dad's eyes locked on the kelpie.

"*Dad*, please!"

"We can't take the chance it will kill again! I understand you don't want to kill, that's fine, that's *good*! Just give me the knife—"

"You're okay with killing a piece of my soul, Dad?"

The color drained from his face as he stared at me.

"We don't have to decide this now," Mum said. "Let's get home. Heather, you're bleeding."

"It's not my blood." I touched the stain from Joe's blood.

"That's some relief," she said. "But standing here is not a good way to make a decision like this."

"And what are we going to do with *that*?" my father scoffed, returning his glare to the kelpie.

Mum handed the reins to Lily, who was thankfully and uncharacteristically silent, and dismounted Dream. "You…." She looked at Dad. "You check on the dogs."

The kelpie lowered his head and chewed, eyes—*my* eyes—looking at me.

Dad headed to Osiris first, but didn't even reach the body before he clasped his hand to his face, gasped, and backed away, shaking his head. He turned towards the water, where we'd seen Isis fall. She wasn't there. "Isis? Isis! Come here, girl!" No response. He looked at Mum.

"Maybe she's heading to the house. You and Lily ride Dream back and look for her. See if Jack will let us put the Shires in with his Belgians, at least for tonight—"

"Jack is not going to accept *this* on our property!" He gestured at the kelpie even more hatefully. Isis and Osiris were Dad's dogs.

"As I understand it, Jack has to accept *our* decisions about *our* property," Mum said. "And if he won't let the Shires stay with him, the mares can go in the big stable with the main herd, and Oppie can spend the night in one of the round pens. We'll set up a tarp if it looks like rain."

Mum and Dad stared each other for a good long time. Lily and I glanced at each other nervously.

"This is major." Mum spoke softly. "We should not rush this decision. You *know* this."

More silence. With a huff, Dad turned from Mum and mounted Dream behind Lily. They trotted towards the woods and our castle.

"Mum…"

"It's not fair to talk about this without your dad here." She sighed. "I'm not even sure how much of this has even registered beyond 'My little girls are in danger, I must do something.'"

"I'm sorry…and thank you."

"Don't thank me for anything right now."

What she said about how much of this registered for Dad sat with me for a beat. "Mum…?"

"Yes?"

"So…you're…okay with this whole 'faery beings exist' thing?"

She paused. "Yeah, I am." Without explaining further, she looked at Tom. "Is that Mickey's Monkey?"

"He prefers Tom."

"Tom?" She raised an eyebrow before approaching him. He backed up, puffing his fur and tail, growling. Crouching on the ground, she held out both hands, palm up. "Tom, you look hurt. Would you like us to bring you back to the stable?"

On that? He glowered at the kelpie.

"He can't hurt you. Heather won't let him."

Tom swished his tail, growling, but each wag drew a pained mew. After a moment of consideration, he limped to Mum.

"Would you like me to carry you?"

Not really, no. Despite his words, he moved between Mum's arms and let her pick him up. He didn't stop growling, though.

"You should ask him his name." Mum nodded towards the kelpie.

"Names bind—"

"Exactly." She gave me a firm look.

"Oh. Um…" I turned to the kelpie. "What's your name?"

What name are you asking for? He flicked his eyes distrustfully at Tom.

"Your real name, but you can tell just me, if you want." Mum cleared her throat. "And Mum gets to know."

I would prefer that, aye.

"Um, okay."

Come nearer.

I balked. "You can't hurt me at all, ever, while you've got that bridle on, right? Under any circumstances?"

Correct. I cannot and will not hurt you under any circumstances, ever, whilst I wear this bridle.

I came closer to the kelpie. He put his muzzle to my ear and whispered it to me. His breath was hot and horrid, like rotting meat and fish. Once I'd heard his name and whispered it back, I wondered if he'd be offended if I offered him peppermint treats.

I backed away and asked, "Okay…what would you like us to call you?"

"Ehrwnmyr." It sounded more like a whicker than a name.

"Err-win-murr?" I repeated back.

Close enough. The kelpie nodded.

"So, you can carry me, my mum, and Tom back to our castle safely?"

If that is what you wish.

"Yes, it is. Please."

I will bring you all safely to your castle.

"Cool."

Ehrwnmyr nodded, and we rode back in silence.

Chapter 18

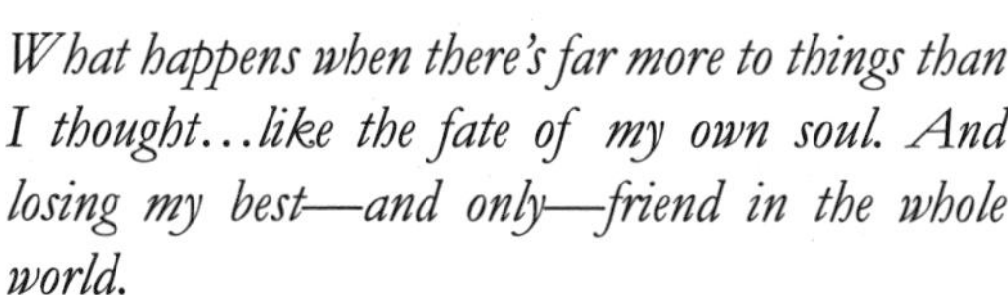

What happens when there's far more to things than I thought…like the fate of my own soul. And losing my best—and only—friend in the whole world.

Dad looked at the couch, silently ordering Lily and me to sit down and shut it. Neither he nor Mum sat. After a lot of strained waiting, he finally said, "Heather…I don't even know *what* to say right now."

"I'm sorry, Dad, I really am!"

"Don't!" He gave me a look. "You've told me that before, and it obviously doesn't mean anything to you."

I felt like I'd been stabbed in the stomach. I couldn't breathe.

"And the worst of it, the worst of it: you got Rowan and Lily involved. You put your own brother and sister in danger—*real* danger. You could have—you almost died!" His face was bright red. "If your mother and I hadn't arrived when we did!"

"Daddy, I—"

"I already said, 'don't'!"

I burrowed into the couch, wishing I could sink through the seat and the floor and even all the way down to the secret alchemy room. The only time I'd ever seen my dad this furious was at Jessica; nothing was worse than that.

"If Rowan hadn't told us..." Dad growled.

I flinched. I didn't even know Rowan had seen us leave. He'd been having a meltdown or something. He told on us!

How dare I feel betrayed when he had probably saved our lives?

"Heather," Mum was talking now, pulling me from my thoughts. She folded her arms across her chest. Dad paced by the window, looking like he was fighting a whole troop of demons in his head. "Why didn't you tell us? Something this big? When people's lives were at stake?"

Lily was sitting next to me, shoulder to shoulder. I felt her sharp poke under my arm. For the record, she'd been right.

"I dunno...murderous faery horse? Sounds...mental?"

"Even after you knew that my spell on Rowan was real? And Rowan said you used *my* research?"

My dad stopped pacing and was now staring at my mum, eyes wide with his jaw hanging open a little.

"Okay...I didn't say anything because...because..." In my head, I ran through all the things that had quashed any thought of possibly talking to my parents. They—well, Mum, at least—wasn't going to think I was mental, okay. But Dad was already a huge wreck with his pills not working, using other drugs, and the issues with Jess and Lily (only worsened by my running off with Joe to try and be a hero the first time). And Mum was worried about Dad. Then Joe's whole family came and everyone was nuts over that. Abigail and Tom and Lord Cadmus and Lady Fana certainly weren't big on getting my parents involved...but they all had their own agendas. After facing down the kelpie, all of those excuses sounded weak and pitiful. "Because...I'm an idiot and thought I could handle it."

Dad gave me a look, but didn't say anything. He was biting his tongue, possibly literally, but I couldn't see behind the white line of his lips.

"Lily?" Mum asked her.

"She wanted to," I said quickly, so my sister wouldn't have to feel guilty for either lying or spilling. "I wouldn't listen to her. It's my fault."

"Your honesty is appreciated," Mum said. Dad *hmphed* behind her. "But I asked Lily."

"I didn't want her to go by herself…and…I wasn't even sure I believed her until, y'know, I actually saw it come out of the water." Lily shivered beside me. "I just got home, and she told me everything."

"Well, in the short time you've been home, you've been more informed than we were," Dad said sharply.

"I'm really sorry," I whimpered, only to cringe from his cutting look.

"Would you be so kind, then, Heather," is what he said, "as to tell us everything we don't know, and I mean *everything*. From the beginning, the very beginning. No more lies, no more secrets. Just talk."

So, I did. Everything. I puked out the whole story until my ribs hurt and I could barely dry-heave the end where Mum and I came home, making sure that Ehrwnmyr stayed in Oppie's vacated paddock.

Dad stared at me for an uncomfortably long time. He ground his jaw. Then, he closed his eyes, pressed his thumb and middle finger over the bridge of his nose like he had a headache, and began to pace. He repeated, "I…I don't even know what to say."

Potentially bending the laws of physics, I shoved myself even further into the couch cushions.

Mum's lips were tight. Her fingertips dug into her arms. With a puff of breath, she eased her feet out of her barely-tied hiking boots; she still had pantyhose on under the jeans. Dad still had on his blousy dress shirt; it was tucked into a pair of jeans that looked crumpled from the hamper. Imagining their rush to come and find us, I felt even worse.

Dad stopped pacing and fixed his eyes on my sister. They didn't look quite as harsh. "Lily," he said, "you should have come to us anyway. No matter what. Do you understand?"

"Yes, Dad." Her eyes were on her lap.

"Let your friends know that you're grounded for the rest of summer, and then give me your phone, laptop, and tablet."

"What about Mum?"

"I'll keep your phone and answer."

"What are we going to tell her?"

Dad bit his lip, but it didn't entirely hide the potent curse he mouthed as he turned away from us.

"You can discuss that later, you and Lily, no?" Mum asked.

"You're right, we can." Dad nodded, looking a little relieved, then turned his attention back to Lily. "You have an hour, then I want all of your stuff turned in to me down here. And no using the library computers, either."

She nodded, not arguing. She was getting off easy, and she knew it.

"Now, off with you."

She gave me a look that was entirely sympathetic and squeezed my hand before she got up.

"Close the door behind—wait!" Dad looked furiously between us. "Did you know about the passage in your closet?"

"I…" She lowered her eyes and nodded slowly. "Do…do you want me to show you?"

"Aye. Yes, actually."

She mouthed the same curse Dad had, but I don't think he saw it through her hair. I knew she'd used the passage to listen in whenever Dad was on the phone with Jess. Lily walked along the built in shelves, and pulled out one of Mum's reference books to show them the switch that opened the shelf into the narrow hall behind.

"I always thought those shelves were too shallow." Mum shook her head.

Dad was biting his lip again, only he looked more curious than angry at the moment. Mum put a hand on his shoulder.

He nodded. "We'll look at that lab and everything later," he said as though he was answering some unspoken suggestion. He nodded back to the hall door. "And I don't expect you to come down and listen in, either," he added as Lily shuffled out the door. He gave the two of us a hurt and angry look. "Your mother and I have *never* eavesdropped on any of your conversations. We expect the same courtesy from you."

Both Lily and I hunched even further. "Yes, Dad," she said before slinking out the door.

It was just my parents and me.

Mum sat in her chair, and Dad started pacing again.

"I don't know what we're going to do with you, Heather," he said.

"We need to tell Mar—Princess Maryan and Prince Christopher," Mum said. "I believe Heather should be the one to explain what she did, and apologize for putting their son in danger. What do you think?"

Dad turned and faced me again. "You lied to the queen, the royal family!"

"So did Prince Joseph," Mum said. "I'm sure his parents will have a few things to say about that."

I had kept from crying until then, but the thought of telling Joe's parents—and the chance they'd never let us see each other again—that was my breaking point. I took in a deep breath that was all sniffle, and tears flooded down my cheeks. I couldn't look at my parents, but I heard Dad stop pacing.

The phone rang.

I jumped and wrapped my arms around me. Was that Prince Christopher or Princess Maryan?

"It's Shari," Mum said.

Sarah Beth! I thought. *I didn't go get her!*

Dad nodded, and she opened her phone.

"Shari, hey… Oh, thank God! What happened?"

The faery court must have returned Sarah Beth home themselves.

"Really? My God!" Mum's brow furrowed.

"What?" Dad asked, but she held up one finger impatiently and waved him away.

"So…the police have the body—"

"What body?!" Dad practically shouted.

"Sh! The guy who was taking the kids." Mum frowned at him.

"What 'guy'—"

"Give me a sec, dear! Sorry, Shari, Michael's here. He wants to know, too. We've all been so worried, and praying… Yes, yes, God was obviously listening. How is Sarah Beth? What… what did she say? No, no…of course I wouldn't want you to push. I understand she wouldn't want to talk… Yeah, sounds like a good idea; we like the psychologist Lily uses. Dr. Snow, Michael's doc, recommended her. Yeah, yeah…you got a pen? Dr. Karin Johnson." Mum rattled off the rest of her contact info. "Tell her we sent you, sure." She nodded and gave a few more mn-hmns. Dad continued grinding his teeth, arms folded, and casting looks at me. "So…did the police ID the body of that bastard? … Got it. Yeah, keep us posted. Yes, y'all can definitely come over tomorrow…"

Dad rolled his eyes, and threw his hands in the air. "Yeah, sure, thanks for asking me."

"Michael had called his dad, too. He'll be happy to know Sarah Beth's safe." At Mum's sharp look, Dad looked somewhat shamed. "Oh, yes, definitely. Thank you for letting us know you're all safe now… We love y'all, too, honey. Take care."

Mum hung up the phone, tapped the screen a few times. Dad tapped his arms impatiently, but he waited until she put the phone down before asking, "There's a body? A person?" He turned to me. "Where did the body come from?"

"I have no idea, I swear!" Panic made my voice almost squeak.

"It could be a changeling." Mum tapped the nail of her index finger on her desk.

"A changeling? What—how do you even *know* this?" Dad asked.

"Research."

"For fiction!"

"Some people think the Bible's fiction."

Dad opened his mouth, closed it, and glared again. "So, some poor bloke didn't just get offed thanks to…to this mess?" He didn't look at me this time, and that chilled me. Did he think that the faerie had just killed some guy? And that it was my fault for not killing the kelpie?

It was bad enough I was thinking that. I couldn't bear imagining Dad would think that about me, that it was *my* fault some other innocent person died!

"That would just make more questions and cause more problems. They probably created a body. If they're as old as Heather said, they could do that. They can even make it look alive for a short time. Faerie would replace stolen children with it. It's…kind of like a human golem. No soul, just a semi-alive body—"

"Enough! Enough." Dad shook his head, now more focused on Mum than me. "You…just *know* all this? You knew this would all be real?"

"Not exactly." Mum shrugged, looking away from Dad. "I mean…I mean, it's not like you or your dad *know* everything in the Bible was real. And I don't mean it the way that sounds, either, so don't give me that look. You know what I believe!"

Dad *pfft*ed. "More or less." Well, at least I wasn't the only one confused about that, either.

"You *knew* about the ghosts," she said.

"You did?" I sat up. Mum's whole whatever-belief and knowing stuff about faerie, I could deal with, but Dad knowing about the ghosts? What?!

He looked at me, face softening. "It's how I found the first secret passage. The one where we found the records. That was Annabelle, though. I never met Abigail—"

"There's more than one?!"

"They're family. They aren't going to hurt you," he dismissed. "Annabelle said they were here to protect the family.

She promised she'd scare none of the children." He looked away and went back to pacing.

"Right, that worked well." Mum leaned back in her chair. "Abigail *did* lead her and Prince Joseph down to…what did you call it?" She looked at me. "The alchemy room?"

"Aye."

Dad massaged his temples.

"And she didn't seem particularly keen on letting us know what was going on," Mum added. "Or do ghosts not talk to each other? Would she know that Annabelle talked to you?"

"I. Don't. Know. But is that really important, now?"

"No, you're right. We should have Heather call Prince Joseph, let him know what happened, and have him hand his phone to his mother, so she can tell Princess Maryan the same. And then, we need to decide what to do with the kelpie. At least, that's my thought on the matter. What do you think?"

Icy stones settled in my stomach. God, no! I knew that I had done the worst imaginable thing ever, putting people I love in danger. Ground me forever, I'll never leave the house or anything! I couldn't call Joe. I couldn't talk to his parents!

"I agree," Dad said.

I started shaking my head and couldn't stop the blubber that burst from my lips. Neither Mum nor Dad said anything. Between my fingers, I glanced at them. Both looked uncomfortable, but they weren't going to back down. Not that I really expected them to. Still…I felt totally alone on this, now. After a few gasps and chokes, I wiped my nose on my sleeve.

"Heather." My dad's voice was soft, hardly angry now, and he handed me a tissue, but there was no arguing.

My hands shook, worse than his yesterday, but I fumbled my phone out from my pocket. I touched each digit of his phone number to dial.

"Heather!" Joe's voice on the other line sounded relieved. "Thank God. You're okay. What happened?"

I choked again and even more tears came that I couldn't stop.

"God, Heather, no, no! What happened? What?" I could picture his face pale as he gripped the phone, scared for the worst. "Lily—is she?"

"Lily's fine," I gasped into the phone. "We're all…okay. Barely."

"What happened, then?" Relief again, confusion, and still a lot of worry were in his voice, but it made me feel better just to hear him.

"My parents…they—they…it almost did get me…but Rowan said…and they came and—and saved us." I was still sobbing a little as I spoke.

"Oh…" A long moment of silence. "But, you're all okay, though? And Sarah Beth…? Is it over? Is the thing…dead?"

"Yeah—no, I mean… Yes, we're all okay. Sarah Beth is home. But…it's…still alive."

"What? Why? What happened?"

"I…"

My dad cleared his throat.

"I… My parents…my parents say that I need to talk to your mum. Um…now."

"They're right there?"

"Mmn-hmn." I felt even more shakes in my hands and chest.

"I see… Will you, will you ask your dad if I can talk to my parents first, and…and then have them call you right away? Please?"

"One—one sec." I looked between Mum and Dad. "Joe—Prince Joseph…wants to talk to his parents, himself, first. Can he do that, please? He—he'll have them call you, so you know."

My parents looked at each other. Mum gave a slight nod first, then Dad agreed.

"They said okay."

"Thank you… And tell them thank you, too."

"He says 'thank you,'" I repeated. Dad nodded again and held out his hand for the phone. "I gotta go."

"Yeah, me too. Heather, whatever happens, you're still my best mate and—and whatever, it's worth you still being alive. Remember that, okay?"

"You, too." More tears. "You're the best. Bye." I slid my phone shut and handed it to my dad.

He put it into his pocket. "As of now, your tablet, your laptop, your iPod, all here on my desk. No computer, no telly, nothing. Outside only for chores, and only by our permission. Send Lily back down if she's not already on her way, and you're to stay in your room until dinner. Do you understand me?"

"Yes, Dad." I stood up slowly.

"And this isn't the end of it. We need to figure out what to do with that…*thing*."

"Ehrwnmyr." The last thing I needed was to talk back, but I couldn't stop myself.

"What?" He narrowed his eyes at me.

"His name's Ehrwnmyr," I whispered, staring at my shoes. "He's not…not just a thing. He's…like, a person."

"We'll discuss Ehrwnmyr later," Mum said quickly. "Now, go and do what your father said. Got it?"

"Yes, Mum."

"Go on, then." Dad's voice had a low growl to it, and I pictured him giving Mum a *look* for sort-of siding with me about "the *thing*." For the moment, I didn't care. I was probably going to lose my best friend from all this, but I wasn't going to let anyone else die! Not even the kelpie.

I turned slowly and left the room. Every part of my body hurt, and I gasped with each step I took to my room. My eyes and nose dripped all over my already filthy and bloody blouse. I couldn't even imagine what my hair looked like. It felt like it was being pulled in a hundred different directions.

Rowan, face red and tearstained, was leaning on the wall between our rooms. His lower lip trembled, and he was staring at my feet. My first impulse was to ignore him, just go right into my room, slamming my door. I stopped. "You ratted on us."

"Ivy and Ash told me. They have, like, *faeries*, little pixie things, too. But they don't like me. They said you were going to get killed. So I told them I'd tell Dad, but they should be quiet. And they were." He made a little hiccup that sounded like he was about to cry. "Heather…"

I nodded. "You probably saved me and Lily." I swallowed. "Thanks."

"Mmmn." He nodded, too, and turned and walked away.

The curtain between my and Lily's sides of the room was shoved all the way open. Lily sat on her bed.

"Heather…"

"Dad said he wants you downstairs. You may as well bring all my stuff, too."

"Sorry, Heather." She didn't need to say anything else. I piled my laptop, tablet, and iPod on top of hers and just nodded.

So, Ivy and Ash really did have faery friends—friends?—too. I should have talked more to Ivy yesterday. I stopped myself before diving onto my freshly-made bed. I was beyond gross, and although I was at the bottom of the rubbish list, I was pretty sure my parents wouldn't begrudge me a shower.

Slowly, I took all the barrettes, pins, and ribbons from my hair, looking forward to the spray that would camouflage my crying—even from me.

Chapter 19

Where I learn a little more about the fey folk and soul magick...for better or worse.

I don't know how much time passed before Anita brought dinner to my room. I wasn't even in good enough standing to eat with my family.

"Your parents say, when you are done, to get your boots and meet them in their office." She kissed the top of my head. Nannies get to do a little spoiling once in a while, even when their charges have insisted they were too old to need a nanny for almost a year, like I had. I also noticed she'd snuck a small piece of chocolate under my napkin.

"*Gracias*," I answered back, hoping that speaking her native language showed more of my gratitude.

"*De nada.*" She closed my door carefully.

I ate slowly, slipping the chocolate under my pillow. My stomach was too sick to waste the chocolate on it. Around midnight, when I knew I wouldn't be able to sleep, it might be some comfort.

I tied my boots on tightly and straightened my jeans. More little favors: Miss Eliza had delivered freshly cleaned laundry. I'd spent most of my exile re-folding it the way I liked and hanging the items I liked hung. It took a few deep breaths before I had the courage to take my tray of dishes downstairs.

Miss Eliza took them without a word. I paused in the doorway, staring at the hallway to everyone's offices. Like in one of those nightmares with that hall of doors that goes forever, fear squeezed my stomach. But you can never just stand there in the dreams, either, and I heard Miss Eliza clear her throat behind me.

Unlike that hallway dream, my mum and dad's study door didn't get any further away, and I was in front of it in no time. It was open a crack. I didn't hear any talking. I knocked.

"Heather?" Mum's voice.

"Mmn-hmn."

"Come in."

I did. They were both sitting at their desks. I felt like I was back on trial after a rest for the judge and jury. I was guilty, of course, but Ehrwnmyr added another dimension. It would be his execution, not mine.

Mum stood. "Let's go out to the barn."

Outside, the gravel crunched under my feet. Stiffness and soreness from being thrown and fighting Ehrwnmyr hadn't let up much, even after the double dose of children's Tylenol I'd taken after I ate. Even my feet hurt; the stones' edges bit into my boot soles painfully.

"Um, did Princess Maryan call?" I asked, trying not to grunt with each step.

"Yes," Mum said. "We had a long talk."

"What…what did she say?"

"She, Prince Christopher, and Prince Joseph are coming back in a few days. Considering we have some of their property keeping a murderous fey beast in check, they have some say in the matter."

I'd left the iron knife in my room. On purpose. The thought of at least seeing Joe again lifted my step. I didn't notice my body's pain quite so much after that.

"She also says that Prince Joseph insists that the secrecy was all his idea and he had convinced you not to say anything."

I bit my lip and felt a bit of warmth spread in my chest, and I blinked away some threatening tears. It was one thing to know someone was your best mate, another when they willingly took the brunt of blame—even lied!—for perhaps the worst thing either of you had ever done in your whole lives. What could I say to that?

The family horses were running circles, stomping, and whinnying nervously in their paddock. We left the path to go to the back of the Shire stable, where we normally kept Oppie separated because he was a stallion. That's where we'd put Ehrwnmyr.

He approached the fence as we did, whickering. I paused. He looked more like a horse now and less like the loch monster that had haunted my nightmares.

It is what you want, right?

I looked at my parents. Mum's face was unreadable. Dad's…was unreadable but in a different way. Where Mum was focused, Dad's face kept changing. One second he looked terrified, the next I feared he might try and throttle the kelpie bare-handed. It was frightening, like watching the ocean from the cliffs as a storm rolled in.

Neither, however, appeared to have heard Ehrwnmyr.

I was just talking to you. I can direct my thoughts.

Oh. I responded.

You do want me to look…more like this?

Yeah. I nodded before I realized.

"What?" my mum asked.

"Um, he knows that looking more like a horse is…um, better."

He chuffed. Mum's eyes darted to him. He took a step back, lowering his head, swishing his tail.

"You don't communicate much like a horse at all, do you?" Mum asked.

I have not spent my life among horses. Kelpie are solitary beings.

"Are you not born? Do you just come into being?"

Ehrwnmyr chewed in thought again. I could sense he didn't know what to make of my mother. That made two of us.

I was born.

"What happened to your family?"

More confusion from the kelpie. Behind me, Dad shifted impatiently. In my peripheral vision, I saw Mum shoot him a "give me a minute" look.

My father was captured and murdered. On this land. I know nothing of my mother but that she is dead.

"I'm sorry your father was murdered," Mum said softly.

The kelpie's snort sounded more like a growl, and he reared in a tight circle. When he stopped, his eyes were focused behind me, glaring at my father.

"How many children did your father kill?" Dad asked coldly. He glared back at the kelpie with no remorse.

Ehrwnmyr circled angrily again. Now, he looked between me and my father. I sensed he wanted to say something, but was holding back.

"So, you came back for vengeance?" Mum asked.

No. I came back because I belong here. On this land.

"*Why* are we having this conversation?" My father finally exploded. "If that thing comes off your head, you'll kill us all and anyone else getting in your way, won't you?"

Ehrwnmyr stopped pacing and grunted his anger. He pulled his gaze from my dad and looked back at me, then at Mum.

That would be my thought, yes.

I shivered.

"Then that's all we need to know." Dad looked at me. "Do you want to take the chance that this thing will get loose and kill everyone in this family, in the village? You *know* what it's done!" His lips were tight, and I saw a flash of guilt in his eyes. He didn't want to remind me of the horrors I'd seen, but he wanted to prove his point. The kelpie should die.

"You're not making a good case for yourself," I told Ehrwnmyr.

You *do not like lying.* He dipped his head and rubbed the bridle on his leg. *I am compelled to act as you would while I wear this.*

"How does it work?" Mum asked. "Does it really have a piece of Heather's soul in it?"

Not in it. *In me. We are connected.*

Dad edged closer to me as Mum continued questioning. "But you hold a piece of her soul, regardless? How?"

I do not know why or how. I just know that we are connected.

Mum looked back at Dad and me. "So, what would happen to Heather if we were to kill you?"

I do not know.

"What's your best guess?"

Ehrwnmyr didn't give a specific answer, but merely projected his confusion. This was a new experience for him.

Mum frowned. "What is the chance that Heather's soul is tied to your life force?"

"What does that mean?" my dad demanded. Mum just held up a single finger, eyes fixed on the kelpie.

It feels so to me.

"And what happens to your essence when you die?"

I don't know. None know this.

"What are you getting at, Aimee?" Dad snapped. He was behind me now, hands tight around my shoulders. I had a feeling I knew where she was going, and it seemed Dad did, too. In my head, all the way to my stomach, I felt Ehrwnmyr's fear spreading cold through my very being.

Mum looked at us, face very serious, "If the soul's now part of you, as it sounds like you're saying…" Ehrwnmyr tossed his head up and down; Mum understood correctly. "Then, if you die, might that piece die also? And would…would it be treated as if it were your soul?"

The curse of the bridle is that I do feel the weight of a soul as if it were mine. Yes.

"That doesn't answer my question."

Ehrwnmyr looked at me.

"Answer my mum plainly," I ordered him. "And completely."

For a half-second, his glamour fell away, and I saw the monster bare jagged-spike teeth at me. *The question is not phrased plainly.*

"He's got a point there," Dad grumbled.

"Mum doesn't want to say what she's thinking." I shivered, and my teeth started to chatter. Ehrwnmyr's terror in my mind was not for just death. And Mum seemed to know a thing or two about faerie and souls that had never gotten into anything I'd read.

Mum took a deep breath. Her face paled. "Fine. Now that you've got a soul, when you die, could you go to Hell for all you've done, and since it's Heather's soul you're sharing, what does that mean for her?"

"No." Dad clenched his hands around my shoulders.

Ehrwnmyr stood completely still, eyes flicking to each one of us, finally landing on me. Yes, that was exactly what he was afraid of. Not necessarily what it would do to me, but the fact that he might end up in Hell now.

That is still not a plain question, and I do not have a plain answer. But I know I have never felt this terrified of death in all my existence. And I know the soul I feel is now both mine and hers.

"No!" My dad started pacing behind me. He tried moving towards the kelpie, but he couldn't seem to make himself get any nearer. "No! Christ would not permit a child to be punished for your crimes! I don't believe that."

It was her choice to put the bridle on me. Humans are responsible for their choices.

"No! This wouldn't be what she chose!" He looked at me, his eyes wide. "Did you know this would happen? About your soul?"

"No." I shook my head, shaking all the way to my bones.

Ignorance of consequences has never been a release from any contract or action.

"Then we bind you, tie you up, use that-that magick rope, take off that bridle, and then bloody well kill you!"

"Dad—"

"Hush!" he snapped at me. "If we take it off, does she get her whole soul back? Is that how it works?"

That would return her soul, but do you have enough of that rope or iron chains to keep me from tearing out your throat and devouring you the instant it comes off? Are you so sure you can slit my throat before I kill you and escape?

Ehrwnmyr dropped his glamour once more and sneered with his monstrous teeth. In my head, I felt his joy at his vision of killing and eating my father.

"No!" I yelled at him. "You said you were compelled to—to be like me! Don't even think that!"

The kelpie took a step back, lowered his head, and resumed his glamour so he looked more like a horse again. Except for a brief, wolfish sneer that was more of a "You're no fun" than any actual threat.

I don't know why, but his tease, like we were sharing some sick, private joke, bothered me more than if he'd meant to hurt me.

Dad came back to me, pulling me into his arms protectively.

I rested my forehead on his chest, feeling new tears. This was a huge mess. No, huge mess didn't even begin to describe this situation. It was a million times worse than "a huge mess." Dad kissed the top of my head. "We'll figure this out, love."

I heard Mum walk over, and then I felt her arms around both of us. She kissed Dad, then me. After a hug, she turned back to Ehrwnmyr. "So, now what?"

I pulled from Dad with a sniffle and looked at Mum and the kelpie. *Last I checked, I have no say in what happens next.*

Even how he spoke was changing. His response sounded like something I would have said. Would he *become* more like me? Maybe he'd change into something that wasn't a monster?

Your soul does have an effect on me, yes.

I thought back, *Please, can you* not *just hop in my head and read my thoughts?*

Keep your private thoughts closed, then.

I resisted glaring at him. I had a feeling my parents weren't "in" on this conversation. Instead, I imagined myself glaring at him in my head.

Clever.

I imagined a rude gesture in his direction, too. Mum and Dad were staring at each other, having their own silent conversation.

Mum spoke first. "I'm not willing to take the chance either way of killing him."

Dad scowled and paced. Pausing, he looked from me to Mum, avoiding Ehrwnmyr. "There must be some loophole, some way to do it…without risking Heather's soul. The Christ I know would not send a child's soul to Hell!"

Mum took a deep breath, leveling her eyes at Dad. "Unless there's some hundred-per-cent celestial, delivered-from-God-Himself guarantee, I refuse to take the risk."

"So, what? You're saying you want to keep that *thing* here?"

"'Want' isn't exactly the word I'd choose, but I don't see any better choice." She sighed. "Besides, we should still probably consult with Prince Christopher and Princess Maryan."

Dad scoffed. "Do you even know how to…I don't know… take *care* of it?"

Mum rolled her eyes and turned to Ehrwnmyr. "What must you eat and drink? And don't be smart or disgusting with your answer. It has to be something we're willing to do."

The kelpie looked at me.

"You have to take my parents' orders, too." Even as I said that, I hoped my dad wouldn't try to order him to just die or something.

He sighed. *I cannot stay away from salt water indefinitely. I can survive on fish and water plants. I do not need to eat until tomorrow, but the trough needs to be full.* He gestured his head to the large water bucket we kept for Oppie. We normally just kept it half full so we could easily dump and wash it every few days.

"We can do that," Mum agreed. "You will stay here?"

He looked at me, again. *I have been ordered to stay here until otherwise commanded. I will not leave.*

Mum nodded, then looked at me. "Go fill his water the rest of the way and then meet us back in the office."

"You're leaving her out here *alone* with that thing?" Dad asked.

"He can't hurt her—"

"So glad you trust it."

"It's the spell." Mum frowned. "And I know a thing or two about spells like this."

Dad frowned even more deeply. "We can wait for Heather."

Mum gave Dad a look. Obviously, to me, anyway, she wanted a few words with him out of my hearing. With an exasperated sigh, she handed me her phone. "Speed-dial one is your dad if anything, *anything* at all, even hints at going wrong."

I took a deep breath and headed for the hose in the stable. The kelpie followed along the fence line and into the run-in stall, watching me. He said nothing, either in my head or otherwise.

I dragged the hose, dropped it into the large bucket, then trod back to the pump.

"Meow."

I jumped. Ehrwnmyr chuffed and grunted. We both looked at the fluffy cat walking towards us.

Your friend's home safe.

"I know. Her mum called. Is she lying, or did the faerie mess with her head?"

Tom sat down and averted his eyes.

She's not lying. But erasing her memory was for her own good.

"Umn-hmn. Yeah, I'll ask Lily about that between her therapy appointments." I scowled at him.

What?

I didn't feel like explaining to him. When Lily was my age, Jessica kidnapped her, and then Jessica's then-boyfriend kidnapped Lily from her. Lily still can't remember what happened, except waking up and running away in her pyjamas.

She still has nightmares, but she says not remembering, not really knowing, is the worst part.

Sarah Beth will be fine. She'll suffer and heal as any kidnapped child.

"Whatever."

I thought you would be happier knowing that she's safe.

"I *am* happy she's safe. But now we have a kelpie. Who has a soul. *My* soul."

I didn't know that was how the bridle worked. It makes sense…but I did not expect that. I wouldn't have suggested you kill it if I'd known.

"It 'makes sense'?" I asked. "Could you share what you think 'makes sense' about this whole mess?"

I believe your mother may actually know more than I do.

"That's helpful."

I'm sorry, Heather. Tom rubbed against my legs.

"Why didn't you have me talk to my parents?"

Tom didn't answer, but continued to weave.

"To-om!" I may have sounded a bit whiny, but I was seriously exhausted, in pain, and impatient.

You never brought it up, so why would I?

"Because I'm eleven, and this was pretty foolish of me to try on my own."

I didn't think it was that foolish.

I sighed. In my head, I could sense he was hiding something from me, but I just didn't have the energy to push. Carefully stepping around Tom, I went back outside. Ehrwnmyr whickered softly and stepped slowly towards the fence.

I looked at him warily. "What do you want?"

He didn't form his thoughts into words, but I could feel his emotions. He didn't want to be terrified. He didn't want to fear for his life. He didn't want me to mistreat him. Almost hidden in the fear, I picked up that he didn't want me to *hate* him.

"You hate my dad."

He wants to kill me. He would take pleasure *in killing me.*

"Kinda rots to be on the receiving end of that, huh?" I asked.

He lowered his head and rubbed his nose on his knee. *Aye. It does.*

"And he wouldn't 'take pleasure' in killing anything. He's just..." I paused, doing my best to analyze Dad, who required regular visits to a professional for analyzing. "He's scared, like you are, maybe even more 'cos he feels, like, moods and emotions more than most humans...but he's afraid you're going to kill us or another kid or something."

The kelpie chewed his mouth for a few minutes, then his eyes darted behind me and he pinned his ears. Tom was sitting on the railing.

"I don't think taunting him's a good idea," I told the cat.

He gracefully jumped down from the fence. *Would you let him hurt me again?*

"No, but..." My keen powers of observation decided to hit at that point. "You were hurt pretty bad, I thought. You seem better?"

Lady Fana and Lord Cadmus healed me, the cat fey answered.

"Oh. That's good."

Ehrwnmyr's water was beginning to trickle over, so I went back inside to turn off the hose. Even though I was out of eyeshot, I could hear the kelpie in my head as he asked Tom, *And what do they say of my survival?*

About that... I looked at the cat who, despite my untrusting glare, rubbed another figure-eight around my legs. *As your parents are now involved, and it seems you'll be keeping it that way, they wish to meet with them.* Still wrapped around my legs, he paused and looked at the kelpie. *They want to talk about his "survival."*

I stopped walking, and while I didn't kick Tom, I pushed him away, *hard*, with my booted foot. He looked more miffed than hurt, confirming my suspicion that feral faery stable cats used affection as a means to get humans to serve their whims like any other cat.

I'm sure *the fate of Heather's soul will have as much impact on the lord and lady as it does on her parents.* Ehrwnmyr hung his head over the edge of the fence, looking into the stable at the two of us. I swear he even batted his eyes.

Manipulative sods. The *both* of them!

"I'll let my parents know," I said primly, deciding I didn't want to get any further in the middle of this pissing match. Tom's tail fluffed as he eyed the kelpie. Ehrwnmyr snorted angrily, glamour dropping enough to reveal his nasty teeth. Tom proceeded to clean himself, showing the kelpie exactly how intimidated he was.

Flipping cats. And kelpies.

I turned my back on both of them and returned to the house.

Chapter 20

Where I learn a lot *more about my mum… I think.*

"It's like the Tarot reading, Michael. As far as I'm concerned, it all works together."

The door to my parents' study was only half-shut, and Mum was talking pretty loudly. I knocked a little and there was a moment of silence.

"Heather?" Mum asked.

"Aye."

"Come in."

Even if I hadn't heard anything, it was pretty clear from their posture and eyes that they were arguing. "Um…not that I was eavesdropping, I promise, but what Tarot reading? About the kelpie?"

"No, in general." Mum shook her head, then reached for one of her drawers. "Though, maybe—"

"No!" My dad spoke so sharply, I backed up a step.

"Right, because you know, consulting a higher power wouldn't be *any* help at all." Mum's sarcasm was equally as harsh, but she folded her hands on the desk.

I swallowed. I hardly ever saw my parents fight. Occasionally, there'd be the hint of it. A strained voice, an especially harsh look, or a cryptic comment obviously meant to hurt. Then yesterday was the stupid pot row, and now this.

My parents were now having marriage problems because of me. Could I feel any worse?

I must have looked at least close to how awful and guilty I felt, because Mum immediately softened her voice and said, "Oh, honey, I'm sorry. This," she gestured between her and Dad, "this isn't you. It's an ongoing thing that's just us. Promise."

"Your mum's right," Dad added. "I'm sorry you had to hear us like that."

I bit my lip and shifted my weight. What was I supposed to say to that?

"Go ahead and sit," Mum said.

Dad looked at the clock. "You were out there a while. Is everything okay?"

I looked up at him. "'Cos of me, we've got a killer horse monster in our Shire stable that has a piece of my soul and… and everything…" I took a deep breath that shook as it came out. "Well, *nothing* is okay."

Dad looked down at his desk. His face looked much older and even more shadowed. He was exhausted and probably using all his energy to, I don't know, not explode or implode or whatever he really felt like.

"Did anything happen at the stable?" Mum asked. "Did Ehrwnmyr say anything after we left?"

"Sort of," I answered. "Mostly it was Tom, who came over to talk. He and Erwnmyr hate each other, so there was that, but he said that he wouldn't have said to kill him if he'd known about the soul thing. Then he said that Lord Cadmus and Lady Fana wanted to meet with you."

Dad made a skeptical glare that gave me shivers. Mum made a face at him, and he bit his lip, softening his features and closing his eyes.

"Where and when?" she asked.

"He didn't say. Just that you—or I—could meet in the stable and talk about it."

"That's convenient." Dad made his sour face again, eyes still closed.

"I'm just saying what he told me," I said defensively.

He opened his eyes and looked at me in surprise. "I'm sorry. That wasn't directed at you, love."

I shrugged. Did it really matter?

"Listen to me." He leaned forward in his chair and staring at me more intensely than even Rowan could. "I'm not saying your mum and I aren't furious at you for hiding this from us, but we're also upset with the whole situation. With the fact that *they* called on you and put your life in danger. We're even more angry at that. And we don't know what to do, and that scares us."

"I guess." I looked away, not quite sure why, except that being stared at like Dad and Rowan could do was just plain uncomfortable.

"No, no, love, don't 'guess.'" I heard him stand, which made me look at him. He came over and sat beside me, putting an arm around my shoulders. "We love you, baby. No matter how angry we are, you must know we love you and always will."

I let him pull me into his arms and leaned on him. "I know you love me." That was the truth, but it still felt better that he said it and was holding me.

"We'll meet them. In the morning, before Shari gets here," Mum said.

Dad groaned slightly. I didn't know if "we" meant just them, or them and me, but part of me didn't care and was perfectly fine letting them figure it out. I didn't have to think about it or plan it all out. I didn't want to anymore.

"Tom also said that he thought Mum knew more about the whole soul thing than he did when I asked him." I didn't lift my head from where Dad held me.

"I wouldn't say 'know,'" she said. I had a feeling Dad was making some sort of face at her from the tone of her voice. "Just…there are different theories…"

"About bridles that take pieces of souls?" he asked.

"About faerie, souls, and soul magick, in general." She took a deep breath. "Whether you're going with the theory that they are spirits of nature that predate Judeo-Christianity—" Dad drew a breath, but Mum ignored him. "Or if you believe that they're the angels that didn't pick a side in Heaven's War—"

"Wait, what?" Dad sat up straighter, and so did I.

"Wait, what, what?" Mum asked.

"What's that about angels?" he asked.

"You don't know that?"

Dad shook his head and looked at me. I shrugged. I certainly didn't know anything about angels.

Mum sighed again. "It's a legend *from* the British Isles. Granted, more Catholic Ireland than the Protestant ideas of fae, but Milton—"

"Love you dearly, Aims, get to the point."

Mum growled softly. "One of the origin stories for fey folk was that they were angels who didn't pick a side in Heaven's War, so they weren't condemned to Hell, but they were still cast from Heaven and forced to walk among the humans, soulless and immortal."

"I did not know that story," my dad reiterated. I nodded in agreement.

Mum rolled her eyes. "Well, whichever story you go with, faerie are an entirely different sort of being than human. They don't have souls, but they have a sentience or sapience, and their own kind of spirit. They don't have an afterlife unless, by choice or curse or spell, they get a soul. Having a soul means sharing the fate of humans, a species they look down upon as playthings, at best. Or, at worst, a species they despise and actively seek to destroy."

"What does that mean for Heather?" Dad was barely staying patient.

Mum didn't say anything for a few minutes. Her lips were tight and she tapped a nail on her desk.

"Aimee—"

"I don't know! I'm thinking. I make up most of the sh—stuff I write about magick." She looked at the clock, eyes brightening. "Maybe Hunter would know! It's the middle of the day in Cali. Heather, give me back my phone."

"You think she really knows this sort of stuff?" Dad was frowning.

"I'm going to ignore the implications of that statement, dear, and just call and find out."

"What implications? My dad's a minister, and I've never heard that fallen angel story!"

Mum raised a brow at him, holding the phone to her ear. I had a feeling there had been a prior conversation about this somewhere. I did know Dad was more unsettled that Hunter was Wiccan than the fact she and Rose were dating—now engaged. He could deal with gay, not outright pagan.

"Hi, Hunter, it's Aimee. When you get a chance, could you give me a call back? Thanks." She scowled at the phone as she hung it up, sliding it open and closed three times before tapping the edge on her desk. "I'll try Rose." Dad sighed next to me, leaning back on the couch. "Hey, Rose, is Hunter around? Oh… When's she coming back? Oh…no, no…just a question on magick." Mum gave a slight laugh that her eyes said was fake. It disappeared quickly, and she glanced at Dad. "No… no, he hasn't heard from his dad yet… No, no, honey, don't feel that way. He's just busy."

Dad buried his face in his hands and groaned, rubbing his temples with his index fingers. Only because I was right next to him, I could hear the soft *f* and *ck* sounds he breathed into his hands.

Granddad, like Dad, would never be "too busy" to return a call after a few days. Either he didn't give Dad an answer when he'd called during the storm or he had, and Dad didn't want to admit it.

I wondered what Granddad would say about a killer pagan faery horse that may or may not be descended from a partly fallen angel was now the proud (or not so proud) owner of a piece of my soul. Would that make the prospect of a lesbian wedding any less daunting?

With a "love you," Mum hung up.

"So, if you were writing this in one of your stories, Aims, what would it be? How'd it play out?" he asked. "'Cos I got nothing."

Mum scowled and blew air out of her partially pursed lips. "The scene would end with a character saying, 'Screw this. The goddamned horse will be there in the morning.' And then I'd leave it till I figured out what the hell I was doing with the plot."

Dad glared.

"Don't give me that look. That was a stupid question. And 'goddamned' might be some appropriate." Now, a bit more of Texas or somewhere was coming through in Mum's accent. We'd visited those American cousins a couple of years ago. Why I noticed this, I don't know. Then, something else struck me.

"Can I ask a question?" My voice squeaked like in one of those dreams where you want to cry for help but can't.

"Of course, love," Dad said. Mum nodded.

"Ehrwnmyr said that he was compelled to tell the truth because I don't like to lie—and I don't!" I felt I had to clear that up. "So, if he's got a piece of my soul…could he, like, become good? Like…you know, people can?" I was pretty sure I was reasonably good. Granted, this whole mess was my fault, but now I was doing everything I could to make up for it. That had to mean something, right?

"He killed two children…" said Dad. "And God knows how many more before he even got here!"

"I know, I know…but—but… I thought…" I didn't want to make less of the horrible things he'd done. It was awful—I saw it! But…

"Even murderers can be forgiven," Mum said. I looked at her hopefully. She was staring intently at Dad. "If they are truly repentant."

Dad clenched his jaw and said nothing.

"Of course, the chance at redemption comes with the whole package, free will and all. He has to *want* to be good. To…"

"Be 'saved,' Aims?" Dad raised an eyebrow. "He has to want to be Saved. That's what you're talking about."

More *looks* passed between them.

"What if he decides he does?" I pushed. "We have to help him, right?"

"If he wants to choose the life of a *good soul*," Mum said evenly, though her eyes never left Dad's and looked almost electric despite her tone, "then it would be our responsibility as *good people* to support that."

"So, we should ask him if he wants to be good!" Whatever they were not-arguing about in that psychic parent talk of theirs was something I didn't get, but at least now I could focus on something useful. If the only way to keep from killing anything else meant he had to have a piece of my soul, then I could convince Ehrwnmyr to be good. Maybe I could go into police or detective work, and the two of us could save other people. If we could keep other people from getting killed by other evil things, that would make things right, right?

I thought of the other kids, tourist kids I didn't know. As awful as those pictures had been…it seemed far away now. If Ehrwnmyr *had* killed Sarah Beth, would I feel more like Dad?

Dad looked away from Mum first and scrunched his face, rubbing his temples.

"You know what? The *thing* will be here in the morning if it really has to do what Heather says, and we've got to meet with the damned faeries that got Heather into this. This is *not* something we can resolve tonight." He didn't say it, but I sensed he *wanted* it to be resolved tonight; he'd hoped it would be. I also had a feeling that "this" was more than just Ehrwnmyr. He stood up and stretched.

Mum sighed, but looked a little more relaxed as she leaned back in her chair. "You're absolutely right on that, dear. Let me lock up down here, and I'll be right up."

"Heather?" Dad looked at me. I glanced between him and Mum, my mind whirling with more thoughts than I could count. They had every right to be furious that I'd hidden this mess from them, but their secret conversations only confused me and made me feel even worse because I didn't know how I had messed things up between *them*.

"Sweetie, let me see what you did to that shirt," Mum interjected with a frown, then turned to Dad. "I'll send her right up and make sure she's in her bed." She looked at me. "Where you will stay put, right?"

I nodded, standing up and going over to her, looking down at my shirt.

Dad narrowed his eyes for a minute, as if he suspected conspiracy, but then shrugged and left.

"Did you spill something on that?" she asked, though she obviously cocked her head in the direction of the stairs.

"I dunno." I bit my lip, wondering if she was conspiring or if I really had just somehow ruined even more clothes.

After Dad's steps disappeared up the stairs. Mum pursed her lips. "You wanted to ask me something?"

"I'm sorry I made things…bad between you and Dad." I stared at my stainless shirt.

"It's not you, I promise you that," she said. "Your dad and I…there've always been a few issues that we agree to disagree on. Except when we can't. But you looked like you wanted to ask me something when your father was sending you to bed. Was that it?"

"I…uh." There were actually a million questions I wanted to ask Mum. The stupidest came out of my mouth first. "It was that obvious?"

"Don't ever try poker, honey. Now, what was it you really wanted to ask me?"

There was one thing I needed immediate help with. "Can…can you send Mrs. McInnis and Miss Eliza and Anita a note to not make breakfast tomorrow? I need to make an Apology Breakfast." Apology Breakfast was something one of my parents, usually Dad, would do after one of their few fights. I'd never made breakfast by myself, but I figured, if I thought I could try and take down a killer faery horse monster, I might as well try my hand at breakfast. I certainly owed it to everyone.

Mum smiled one of those smiles that make you feel better just by looking at it. Dad always called her his angel, and at that moment, I knew exactly what he meant. She gave me a hug. "Yes, I can do that. Just promise me something?"

"Anything." At this point, I meant anything.

"Make something a key or two less complicated than your dad or I would? He'll never let us live it down if you start a kitchen fire. Okay?"

I couldn't help but giggle, which, after everything, turned into really big belly laughs. I don't know why, but tears spilled down my cheeks again as I laughed. Mum pulled me into a hug, kissing the top of my head.

"I'll keep it simple. Promise. And I know how to use a fire extinguisher." I laughed a little more as Mum herded me out of the office.

"You'll have to set your alarm early. Your dad's the worst early bird sometimes. Especially if he's anxious."

"Will do."

We kissed each other good night, and I headed to bed. Lily was on her bed, scribbling in her journal.

"Sorry I dragged you into this."

"Last thing I want is your crazy arse killed." Her eyes never left her journal.

I bit my lip, then jogged to her side of the room and dove beside her and hugged her tightly.

"You're just trying to see what I'm writing." She tucked the pastel book under the mattress with one hand while she proceeded to tickle me with her other. "Seriously, you know how much crap I'd be in if I didn't have you to blame things on?"

I giggled and hugged her again. "I'm making Apology Breakfast in the morning."

"Want a hand?"

I shook my head. "I owe you the apology, too."

"Whatever." She shrugged, looking like she didn't care as she fished her journal back out. I saw her watching me out of the corner of her eye. I closed the curtain between the two sides of our room and changed into pyjamas.

Finding Anita's chocolate under my pillow gave me one last smile before I did, indeed, fall asleep.

Chapter 21

I just bridled a monster with my soul. Now what? Apology Breakfast should be no problem…

The sky was still more pink and grey when I woke up. I lay just thinking for a few minutes, then did some stretches that didn't require leaving my bed. I was *hurting*! Peeking under my pyjama shirt, I saw more than a few bruises across my ribs and groaned.

From the other side of the curtain, Lily muttered, "Sure you donwan 'elp?"

"I'm fine," I said back, though my mouth was dry. Bleh, morning. Morning with a whole bunch of rubbish that needed to happen today.

Taking one more deep breath, I rolled out of bed. Stifling another pained groan, I did a few more stretches and got myself dressed, finding more bruises on my hip and thigh where I'd fallen.

The children's Tylenol on the top shelf of the medicine closet in our washroom was my first stop. I took the highest dose the directions allowed for my height and weight.

As I waited for the medicine to take effect, I poked around the kitchen to see what we had for ingredients. There were fresh melons in the fridge; I could probably manage to slice those with reasonable safety. I could definitely do eggs, so I put those on the counter, too. There was a slab of American-style bacon in the meat drawer, which I considered and decided against per Mum's comment about not burning the house down. Cooking bacon usually caused at least one or two curses or yelps from her or Dad.

Eggs and melon certainly wasn't sufficient for an Apology Breakfast at the level I needed. I grabbed the cookbook Mum and Dad used most frequently. A trick I knew was to flip through and see what pages it opened to. That led me to all of Mum's Christmas cookies, a scone recipe, a pancake recipe, and a waffle recipe. All of them were annotated in my parents' and Mrs. McInnis' handwriting.

I went for the waffles. Not only were the notes all in Dad's writing, which was easier to read than Mum's, but it was mostly automated with the waffle maker.

Also in the fridge were some leftover haggis and paté from the royal visit, as well as some cooked sausages. I could nuke those and set them prettily on a platter.

I could do this.

First, I had to set the table.

No, first I had to put the waffle batter together so it could sit. That's what Dad's notes said: "Let batter sit for twenty minutes."

For the record, I would like to confess that my unsupervised cooking experience to this point was limited to cooking eggs, toast, and mac and cheese. And reheating things in the microwave. All my other kitchen experience included at least one adult who was, by all accounts, an excellent cook. I can only imagine what my mother was thinking when she said I could do this myself. Maybe she assumed I wouldn't be up earlier than Dad, and he'd rescue me from the monstrous mess I would make.

Which he did. In one fell swoop, he flew in from the back door (which I hadn't seen him go out of), grabbed my smoking frying pan of eggs, deposited it on the butcher's block, then snatched the bowl of too-thick waffle batter before I dumped it down the sink.

"Heather, what—"

"I'm trying to make Apology Breakfast!" Tears stung my eyes as I looked away. "And I can't even do that right!"

He sighed, put the batter bowl down, and pulled me into a hug. "Oh, love." He kissed the top of my head. "After all this, haven't you learned to just ask for help?"

I sniffled. "But it's all my fault." After I said that, I clenched my teeth because under the fresh laundry smell of his clothes, I recognized the herby smoke scent.

"Not all, but I suppose we can't demand the prince and princess send their eldest son to cook for us, can we?" He let go of me and offered a smile. "What about Lily?"

"I owe her an apology for dragging her into this."

He kissed my cheek, then took over the waffle batter. His brow furrowed as he stood the spoon up in the batter.

"If you just tell me what to do, I'll do it."

He tasted the batter and stared at it in thought. "No, I'll help. I have my own apologies to make."

"For doing pot again?" I slapped my hands over my mouth, horrified I'd even said that out loud.

Dad froze. His lips tightened, and he looked at me out of the corner of his eye.

"Sorry! I heard you and Mum arguing the other day and I just smelled it and I…well, I—sorry!"

Dad sighed and squeezed his eyes closed, color flushing his cheeks. He clenched his teeth, and there was a good two minutes or more of silence between us.

"Dad…"

He held up one finger, eyes still clenched shut. After taking a deep breath, he spoke in a soft, firm voice. "One. No more eavesdropping on any, and I mean *any* conversations of anyone in this house. That is not up for discussion. Your mother and I specifically choose to respect all of you, and we expect the same back.

"Two." He took another deep breath. "Exactly how does my eleven-year-old know the smell of pot?"

"Older kids at the horse shows," I said, barely above a whisper. "They do it behind the trailers. One of them offered. I said, 'no,' I swear! And I won't say anything to Mum, promise!"

Dad put the bowl of batter down and stared at me with a very serious, but not angry, look on his face. "Heather, listen to me, and listen well. If you ever see me, or any other adult doing something harmful like that, you better damned well tell your mother."

"I…" God, could I do anything right?

"C'mere, love."

I inched in front of him.

He put his hands on my shoulders and rubbed them. "I know you don't want to see us fight, and I know you don't want to get anyone in trouble, but if you know it's bad, you're *letting* someone hurt themself. Your mum has every right to be furious at me. And you, too. I'm messing with my drugs, and while it makes things…bearable…for now, you all will have to…" He paused, closing his eyes and clenching his teeth. "Suffer with me later."

I didn't know what to say back to him.

"I'll tell your mum. And you ask her later to make sure of it. You'll do that, for me?"

I nodded.

"Good girl." He kissed the top of my head, then paused again, still with that very serious look on his face. I waited. "Heather…your mum and I were talking last night…" He paused for another long moment. "I…we…we wish you hadn't put yourself and Lily and Rowan in that kind of danger. You could've… God, you have no idea." Another deep breath burst from his lips as he squeezed his eyes closed again. I could feel him shaking. "You should have told us, no question about that. But we can't change that…" Another pause and breath. "But if you hadn't acted, if you hadn't tried…Sarah Beth…might not have come home safe."

I looked down. I still didn't know what to say. He lifted my chin.

"You saved Sarah Beth's life. You…even want to save that…" He repressed what I guessed was a curse "…*kelpie*. And that, *that* is the choice of a *good person*. Do you understand what I'm saying?"

"I…think so." My heart pounded, and I felt a tiny smile creep to the edges of my mouth. Sarah Beth was alive, and the kelpie *would* become good—I believed that, truly.

He clapped his hands once more on my shoulders. "Now, let's see if we can save this Apology Breakfast. Did you set the table yet?"

I shook my head "no."

"Go do that, and let me see what I can do for the waffles, all right? When you're done, I'll tell you what I did, so you know. Okay?"

"Mmn-hmn." I nodded and left to fix the table with nice linen, all the proper settings, and every condiment I could think of arranged prettily.

When I came back into the kitchen, Dad said, "I see where you got mixed up. This is an American cookbook. I changed all the stuff to metric in the margins. You tried using both for, I guess, a double batch? I think I fixed it enough."

"Thanks, Dad." There was so much still on my mind that I wanted to know—and not about making breakfast. "Can I ask you a question?"

He paused as he closed the waffle iron. Heading over to the coffee maker, he finally said, "Yes, love."

"Why…? What…?" I started, but couldn't seem to find the words. "The pot. If it makes things worse later?"

He sighed. "Because I know…" He frowned, then just showed me the measurements of coffee for the pot and took the carafe over for water. "When I was…I don't know…older than Lily, I knew I reacted…differently…*emotionally*…than other people. Sometimes it helped for, like a play, or when I was on stage. And, because I could act, I could hide it when it wasn't helpful. My mum caught on, though, and she…she was a lot like your mum… I wish they knew each other, but, anyway, she had me try some meditation, and it helped. When I finally had to see a doctor, Dr. Snow, he gave me better exercises, and between that and the acting, I could hold off on *having* to take medicine. I was unusual, and he told me not to expect to be able to do this forever. I didn't want to take any meds, because I worried it'd mess with my acting. And it does, sometimes. I hate it. But…I'm not a good person without them."

He handed me the water to pour into the coffee maker and massaged his temples for a moment. I didn't push. I could feel he was still talking; he just didn't know the right words. I knew that feeling.

"Anyway, when I was in the Academy, one of my friends gave me a joint one time. I was too manic, I was fidgety, snappish, nervous—you know how I get. And it helped. Extra coffee at other times, that would help too. I could push off having to take meds. When I was younger, the disorder was mild, not like it is now…" He took a deep breath and stared at me for a long time. "Do you really want to try cutting that melon?"

"I cut one up once before with the big knife. Mum was watching."

Dad reached for the long chef's knife from the magnet block. I hadn't quite gotten tall enough not to need the step stool.

"Let me watch you." He leaned on the cabinet as I found the flattest spot on the melon. Fortunately, the melon was really ripe, which made it easy to cut.

"Very good," he said. "Give me half and I'll help you scoop the seeds." Dad met my eyes, and I couldn't read his face again. After a moment, he sighed again. "Ask."

I didn't know where to begin. "You… I heard you tell Mum you hadn't…messed with your meds since…you were dating Jess. I—Is…?" There were about five questions in my head. The one he answered was one that I was only barely thinking of.

"Heather, I would never lie to your mother, or any of you!" He sounded hurt and angry. "That is the truth. I have not done anything…like this…since I married your mother. I wouldn't do that to you. I *thought* I was making that clear!"

"I know—that, that wasn't what I was asking." I backed away, holding my de-seeded melon close. His face softened and he broke his eyes from me, looking guilty. "I-I thought, I…I thought that—that I made things worse with the kelpie and worried you and scared you, and that's why you had to…do drugs…"

I wouldn't have thought it possible for my Dad to look as guilty and horrified as he did when I said that.

"No, nonono, love, no! It's not your fault. Never, ever think it's your fault. How I am, my problems. Never!" He looked about ready to cry. "Promise me you'll never think that?"

"I-I promise." I continued cutting the melon while Dad grabbed something out of the refrigerator. We didn't say anything for a few minutes; I wanted to give him his privacy if he were crying. If he wasn't feeling so guilty about taking drugs or me thinking him messing with drugs was my fault, I'm sure I'd get a much worse lecture or guilt-trip for the whole eavesdropping thing. I'd heard from plenty of other kids about parents who listened in on phone calls or hacked their Facebook accounts or text messages. My parents had never done any of that. I also knew that when Dad was down, which is what he was trying *not* to be by messing with his medicine, he couldn't always keep from crying. The last thing I wanted to do was make him feel worse by not giving him his space. And the last thing he wanted was for me to think I made him feel worse. There really was no way around both of us feeling like complete rubbish at that point.

It wasn't until I heard the familiar sizzle of bacon and smelled it that I finally asked, "But…do you think it might be the kelpie…and it being around us?"

My dad was smart. While he didn't know as much as Mum did about magick, I know he knew that tides and really bad storms did mess with his moods, and since the kelpie was causing these things… "It crossed my mind."

A really big part of me wanted to ask if that was why he wanted to kill the kelpie so badly. I didn't. I'm not sure I wanted to hear the answer.

"I'm really sorry about Isis and Osiris," I whispered. This time I couldn't stop the sniffle. Both dogs were good about not outright begging, but their presence in the kitchen during cooking could not be helped. Dad would almost always—when Mum wasn't looking—throw each a slice of bacon. Amid the coffee and sizzling and occasional *ping* of the waffle maker, I felt an emptiness without the sound of their padding around underfoot.

Dad didn't answer, but I heard him try to hide a sniffle. Of all the animals around the castle, they were his the most. It had been Mum's idea to rescue them from the racetrack, but both of them had bonded with Dad.

"Thank you," he finally said.

It didn't make me feel *better* that he acknowledged my fault in that, but I did feel relieved. I knew that he'd lose them again if it meant that me and Lily were alive, but that didn't mean that he'd ever wanted to think of the dogs dying.

I heard silence from him for a moment. Then he said, "One more thing, Heather."

I turned around to face him. "A-aye?"

In his hand, he fiddled with a quarter-sheet of lined paper. He handed it to me. "This is Dr. Snow's number. I'll put it in your phone, too. If you want to talk to him about me, about anything…if Mum's not available, if I'm not listening, or if you're scared, he will answer."

I rubbed the paper in my fingers for a moment, too, lost for words. He gave me a nod, and we finished making breakfast in silence, but it was a mostly comfortable silence now. When we heard footsteps coming down the stairs, I turned around and gave him one last hug.

"Thanks, Dad," I said.

He hugged and kissed me back. "Thank you, too, love."

Breakfast itself felt weird. Dad did pull Mum aside to talk to her. She looked furious, but they didn't argue, and by the time she got to the table, she looked calmer.

Lily and Rowan kept looking at me (or in my general direction) for some sort of guidance, and kept complimenting breakfast. I appreciated their attempts to keep me out of further trouble. The twins were also surprisingly quiet, glancing at each of us in turn.

When Anita came in and Mum and Dad tried ushering them out, Ivy said, "One minute, please," and she and Ash ran over to me and Lily to give us hugs. "We're glad you're not hurt really bad."

I glanced at Lily, who smiled. We hugged each back.

"Thanks for looking out for us," I whispered back. The result was them beaming like I'd just crowned them prince and princess for the day.

"Rowan, go—" Mum began.

"No! I want to help this time. The kelpie cannot hurt me!"

"Rowan!" My dad's voice and eyes were angry.

"Please? This is important! And it really can't hurt me. Heather, did you tell them? Mum's spell and Dad not wanting any faerie or goblin near me? And how I helped with Monkey-Tom?"

"I did," I said. "I don't even think any faerie can touch him. Tom was even nervous." I looked at my brother's face and understood wanting to be let in on something this important. "Maybe it would be good to bring him, just to show that…we can do magick that made them unable to hurt us?"

Dad raised his eyebrows and sat back in his chair for a moment, then looked at my mother. She gave a slight nod.

"Me too, right? I was right there at the loch!" Lily said.

With a sigh and more of a slump, Dad closed his eyes. "Fine. But your mother is doing the talking. You three follow her lead and don't say or do anything without our direction."

"But the kelpie is Heather's." Lily frowned. "She put the soul-bridle thing on it…"

"Soul-bridle thing?" my brother asked.

"Mum and Dad are talking about the meeting with Lady Fana and Lord Cadmus," I told Lily, then turned to Rowan. "And Joe got a magick bridle that was supposed to make us control the kelpie, except it works because it took a piece of my soul and gave it to him—the kelpie, him." Looking at Mum and Dad, I further explained, "I didn't get a chance to tell them everything else since yesterday."

Mum nodded. Dad was still slumped with his eyes closed, wrinkles showing more than usual. I recognized his breathing as the exercises we always start with in karate and remembered our conversation. All his tools and tricks, prescribed drugs and illegal ones, seemed to be failing him now.

"As they are nobility, I'm guessing meeting them in jammies is not the best idea," Mum continued, putting a hand on Dad's knee. "So, get dressed in…I don't know…we're meeting them in the stable…"

"Dress nicely." Dad's voice was deeper and rougher than usual. Without opening his eyes much, he reached for the water on the table and wet his lips with it before taking a sip. "We have more leverage in whatever they want to talk about if we look and act like nobles ourselves." He opened one eye at Mum a little, squinting like the sunlight coming in from the windows hurt.

Mum nodded again. "What your father said. Now, go get ready."

Chapter 22

Where the point sometimes isn't the obvious one

Just yesterday, I was in the stable in a fancy dress with Joe, but it still felt massively weird to be all prettied up as Mum pushed the stable door open while trying not to permit dirt or pock marks on her dress suit or hat. She muttered something about convention garb and corsets, but Dad didn't respond. He was holding Lily's and my hands very tightly. While I was pretty sure most of it was him being afraid of what the faerie might do, I was also pretty sure a part came from him losing a battle to the depression and knowing it. Rowan padded behind us, his own brow wrinkled in worry. I'd faced off against the kelpie, I'd sort-of won, and things were *still* Not Right.

Tom was leaning on the office door, dressed in a blousy shirt with a vest and matching trousers that must have had some sort of hole for his tail, as it curled down his leg into a fluffy, twitching tip at his feet. His cat ears perked in our direction and his eyes widened.

"Well, I don't think we were expecting this," he said, walking over and bowing. "Family MacArthur." He stood, eyes lowered respectfully, but with a slight smirk. He made me think a bit of the Cheshire Cat from *Alice in Wonderland*. "By your leave, I will fetch my lord and lady."

"You have our leave to fetch the Lady Fana and Lord Cadmus," Mum said.

"My Lady." Tom bowed again, gave my silent father a curious look, winked at me, and then walked a few steps before disappearing from view.

"That was…interesting." Mum cocked an eyebrow at me.

My dad made a "hm" noise in his throat. I wriggled my hand in his and mouthed, "Ow."

"I'm not going to run off, Dad," said Lily on his other side, also wriggling her hand.

With a sigh, he let go of our hands and crossed his arms over his chest. Rowan hovered just to my left, close, but not touching, and rocking from foot to foot.

The air around us shimmered like it had by the castle ruins. Mum took half a step closer to us protectively. Dad took Lily's and my shoulders in his arms. He kept his eyes on Rowan, who he couldn't reach. As if they were walking from behind a curtain, Lady Fana and Lord Cadmus approached. Tom trailed behind them and resumed leaning on the office door. He met my eyes briefly, and I could sense his nervousness.

"Coooooool," breathed my sister.

Rowan said nothing, but I saw how wide his eyes were as he watched. I'd seen this before, but that didn't make it not-awesome to see again.

Before the shimmer faded, we heard a familiar jingle and padding paws.

"Isis!" I called as the dog ran over to us all, sniffing and wagging her tail. Even Dad dropped to one knee to hug the greyhound, who proceeded to thoroughly wash his face with her tongue.

"Family MacArthur." Lady Fana looked over us. I panicked for a second. Did Dad or Lily know not to look them in the eyes? Rowan wouldn't anyway, I knew. A quick glance at my father and sister calmed me. They were avoiding her eyes. "Well met. We found this one and were able to heal her. Her mate, I'm afraid, was beyond our abilities."

"Lady Fana, Lord Cadmus." Mum dipped her head in a half-bow. "Well met, as well."

Lady Fana's eyes looked past my mother and to my dad. "Well met," he said guardedly. "And, yes, th-" He caught himself; Mum must have coached him some on how to talk to faerie. "We appreciate the return of our dog." The daoine síth lady looked between him and my mother curiously. Dad stood up and Isis promptly stood at attention beside him. "Aimee can speak for the family," he said. "I trust whatever she says."

"You are unusual humans," Lord Cadmus noted, glancing at his wife, who nodded. "But we've already begun our negotiations with your daughter, and we'd prefer to continue."

"Heather is eleven years old," Mum said coldly. "She's in no position to represent our family or the village. You've already done enough damage setting her up against the kelpie."

"We did not 'set her up' as you say," said Lady Fana. "It was entirely her own choice to take on the responsibility. We were there to support her at the same time you arrived. Had you needed our assistance, we would have intervened."

"You have no children of your own?" Mum asked.

"Why do you ask?" It was Lady Fana's turn to take a guarded tone. Lord Cadmus pressed his lips together in a tight line, as overtly glaring as one might and still look properly noble and aloof.

"If you did, you might have thought twice about letting someone else's child risk her life for you. Or at least I'd hope so."

It was a subtle movement, but I saw Lady Fana brush Lord Cadmus' arm as he tensed even more. "Heather made her choice when she originally found the beast, and then snuck into our castle. My husband even offered to take it from her hands and suggested a contract with the beast on our terms, but at that time, your daughter was intent upon using the bridle and seeing to its destruction. We respected her choice. We pledged our assistance to her and kept the other human child safe until we saw that the creature was subdued and would harm no one else." She looked between my mother and me.

I clenched my hands into fists at my side. That wasn't quite how it went! Mum turned just a little to see me and held out her hand for me to join her, sharing another look with Dad. I stepped up beside her and she put her arm around me.

"So, the kelpie truly cannot harm someone else?" she asked. "How sure can we be of that?"

"Based on what little I know of the bridle, I know he must follow any and all commands given by your daughter to the letter." Lady Fana glanced at me. "Of course, that depends on how clearly you word your commands, and if you truly do intend to keep him enslaved as such rather than destroy him."

"So would you suggest we destroy him? What does that do to Heather's soul?"

Lady Fana looked at Lord Cadmus, who frowned, though he looked calmer. After they shared a look, she answered. "We don't know what that would do to your child's soul. Our preference would be that the beast is destroyed, but…" She looked at me for a long time. "As far as our understanding goes regarding human souls, only Heather truly has the choice of whether or not to take that risk."

Mum squeezed me, then asked, "What does it mean for Heather now that the kelpie has a piece of her soul?"

"Fey folk, by our very nature…do not have souls as humans do," said Lady Fana. "So our experience comes merely from observation and when circumstances would inflict a soul upon one of us." She looked again at Lord Cadmus, then nodded.

Lord Cadmus continued, "As I'm sure you're aware, any magick drawn from the essence of the human soul is extremely powerful, and completely dependent upon who is wielding that magick as to whether it is a great good or a great evil." He spoke slowly, almost empathetically, but for some reason, his voice still made me shiver and press closer to Mum. "While the bridle was made long before even my time, the belief was that it was made of pure intentions. The human who made it forgave the kelpie its crimes and wished to 'redeem' the beast." While he didn't actually roll his eyes, his voice hinted he would if it would not appear so *common* a gesture. "In effect, it seemed to work at the time. When a less-than…kindred soul…inherited the poor beast, it begged for the bridle to not be removed, to no avail. It was sent on its way. Later on, the bridle changed families, and the bridle was used to capture another kelpie for entirely selfish means. *That* story, I believe, has come down through the human tales relatively intact?"

"The last Graham of Morphie?" both Mum and I asked.

Lord Cadmus nodded.

"So, that story *is* true—sorry." I slapped a hand over my mouth from speaking out of turn, then glanced at my mother, trying to read if she were surprised to know she was right.

There was a little twinkle in my mother's eyes, as if she had just learned she'd gotten a school question right. She finished, "And he was cursed by the kelpie after he let it go."

"He abused the beast most cruelly," Lord Cadmus continued. "It is near impossible to kill one of them, as you saw, but more than a generation's abuse all but destroyed it in body and spirit. From thence, the beast and his kin wore the wounds of a tainted soul and took it out on the race that had been so destructive to them." His deep violet eyes glanced between me and my mother, calculating. It made me wonder how much the lord and lady knew about my family, that every animal we had was a rescue. That Mum had ended up being friends with the princess because of her work in horse rescue.

"So," I stopped myself this time, but Mum nodded at me to continue, rubbing my shoulder again. "What *does* that mean with regards to my soul? Will I go to Hell because it's attached to the kelpie?" My voice trembled more than I wanted it to.

I didn't expect it to be possible, but both Lord Cadmus and Lady Fana seemed surprised at my question. They looked at each other for a moment before Lady Fana said, "We have no way of knowing the destiny of your soul. All we do know is that it's strongly affected by your own actions and desires."

She paused, brow furrowed in thought. "Believe me, we wish you had killed the beast. Neither of us expected that you had actually obtained *that* bridle. But…as we understand it, to kill it now, or to let it be killed now…" She pursed her pretty pink lips.

I looked up to Mum again. She rearranged her "hug" so that she was holding both of my shoulders in her hands and she was behind me. She was letting me talk. I glanced back at Dad, who was keeping his face unreadable. I cleared my throat. "To kill it now…would be murder?"

"If you were to judge it that way, then yes," she said. "It's your own conscience you are judged with. In any case, it's no clean killing."

"But, if I let it live, if I keep it, could it get loose? Could it kill more people? And would that be my fault?"

"It cannot break the bridle on its own, nor can it remove the bridle. That I would vow with complete faith," said Lord Cadmus. "Another person might, but then, most likely, your soul would reunite, carrying only the weight of the kelpie's actions while you were joined. If the kelpie were released, it might very likely go back to killing. Or, perhaps your influence may have changed it to its core and it will merely retreat to solitude. As for fault, that would go back to your own conscience."

"You mean I really could make it…not evil?"

"That was the original intent when the bridle was created," Lady Fana said, though there was something off in her voice.

"The original intent was that it would make the kelpie not evil?" I pressed.

"The original intent was to stop it from killing and…have it adopt a particular set of beliefs."

Mum tightened her lips; I recalled the disagreement between her and Dad last night.

"Of course," Lord Cadmus added, "you're still imposing your will upon it. It *wants* to kill. I can't imagine it being happy with the processed flesh you feed your other carnivorous animals."

"If you were around to see when a kelpie was captured before," I said, "what did other people feed it?"

"I was alive, but not part of that mess." Lord Cadmus lifted his chin and looked down his nose with a sniff. "I'm sure the best way to find that out would be to discuss it with the beast. If it's bound to you, the kelpie would want to make that as pleasant for himself as possible."

Mum sighed, but nodded.

"Then things are in your hands now." Lady Fana's eyes covered all of us, but landed on me. "You captured the kelpie and it is bound to you. Unless someone does free the creature, my worries are assuaged that it will not threaten the safety of our relations."

"What does that mean?" I frowned.

"It means she trusts your soul." Mum kissed the top of my head.

Lady Fana nodded. "My lord and I will take our leave so you can discuss with your new ward the terms of his stay. Do keep in mind his lifespan, though." She and Lord Cadmus turned to go. The air around us began to shimmer.

"Wait, wait…please…" Mum gave me a sharp look. I met her eyes and pleaded. "One more question? That contract thing that Monkey—Tom—mentioned with the whole family?"

Tom shot almost a hiss in my direction. I had no problem glaring at him. *He* had brought it up in the first place.

"Oh, that." Lady Fana, who had obviously overheard what I said to Mum, turned only her head and a glint sparkled in her violet eye, making my stomach clench. "We can discuss it at a later time. You have a lot of work on your hands. As you humans say, 'we'll be in touch.' Blest day to you."

With that, the shimmer seemed to collapse in on them. Tom gave me a frown, but then mouthed "Good luck" before following them into the last waves of magick.

After almost a minute, Mum let out a big, long breath and wrapped me more tightly in her arms. "I don't even know what that got accomplished."

Dad glanced between where the shimmering curtain disappeared and Mum. "I hope it accomplished them staying out of our business."

My parents shared a look that was interrupted by a percussion section of hoof beats as the family herd decided to join us. We hadn't seen them all meeting; the sense of magick had probably had them all avoiding the stable. Now that Lady Fana and Lord Cadmus were gone, I'm sure they wanted to know if we were going to feed them or something. All of us, even my parents, jumped a little at the sound, then burst into laughter at ourselves that, I'm sure, only confused the poor horses even more.

I noticed Mum glance at Dad, as if looking for further approval, and he pulled her into a kiss that, while not one of their gag-inducing sessions, was still far too long for any offspring to witness. As they embraced, Lily ran over to me with a hug. Rowan was at my other side. He nodded, too, giving me a little smile. Isis started dancing between the group of us kids and my parents, licking whoever she could reach. I squatted to hug her, too, and kissed her around her face and neck. Her fur sort of hid the tears that ran down my face as this whole new reality set in.

I was the soul caretaker of a kelpie.

Chapter 23

Sorta-kinda tying loose ends, picking up pieces, and one more "royal" challenge—by yours truly.

A lot of stuff happened over the next few days that was too much to describe. We had a small service for Osiris and buried him in one of the back gardens. We let the twins choose where because, in my purging of truth over these days, I outed their pixie companions. Ivy and Ash were inconsolably betrayed, afraid their little friends would never speak to them again. (Dad clearly preferred the no-speaking-to-faerie-ever-again potential, but he insisted the twins not be mad with me.)

Tea with Shari and Sarah Beth was also mostly uneventful. It hurt more than I expected that she didn't remember my visit in Faerie or how I had stood up to Lord Cadmus. I kept my promise, though, and suggested that she have free use of Clint Eastwood whenever she liked. Her glee lit up the entire parlor.

Horse camp was back on, too. That morning, with the news release of the kidnapper's "body" being found and Sarah Beth's only-partly remembered accounts of what she thought had happened, most of the parents started calling and emailing Mum to see when they could send their children. (Sarah Beth was also invited to camp—but that was normal.) Now, we had a little over a week to prepare for that.

We also spent two days building a new, small stable and corral for Ehrwnmyr. Mickey was more than happy to help, but Mr. McInnis was not. Neither Dad nor Mum made him. We also hired a few contractors from the village. Ehrwnmyr chose the location and specified how much room he would need. It seemed large, but Mum and I agreed to it.

What made this endeavor particularly amazing, even to Dad (who'd spent the day in bed, but saw the result) was Ehrwnmyr calling the water. When the contractors left at sundown after the second day of work, the kelpie started trotting a circle on the side furthest from the stable. Picking up his hooves almost to his stomach, mane and tail flying high, he beat out rhythms and hopped diagonally and in turns that would make Olympic dressage horses look like they belonged in training camp. Below his hooves, the ground grew damper, but his steps never slipped. He danced the perimeter of his soaked ground from fence to fence. The mud grew wetter. Then a mini-earthquake nearly knocked over the bunch of us watching: me, Mum, Mickey, Lily, and Rowan. The slick mud began to bubble like water coming to a boil, only without the heat. Water, smelling of salt and brine, overtook the area until a brackish pond covered more than half the paddock. The kelpie nodded, looking satisfied, jogged a small circle and dove into the water, getting all of us quite soaked from the splash. He nickered and I could feel the first spark of happiness I'd ever noticed in him. The water must have been deeper than it looked, or he could liquefy himself or something, because he actually dove underwater a few times. He emerged with even more splashes, entertained as we ran from the flying water. Eventually, he came out and lay on his side, glistening green and black, at the edge of the water, content. Although he was hardly glamoured, for the first time, I didn't think he looked quite so terrifying. He was almost beautiful.

It was the fourth day after capturing the kelpie that the royal family came to visit.

This visit had been gnawing at my brain for days. Being so busy building a proper place for Ehrwnmyr had kept my mind mostly occupied. But I was never distracted enough to keep from reeling at the thought I might be banned—quite literally at the mercy of royal bodyguards—from ever seeing my best mate again. In church, on Sunday, I figured I ought to be praying for the kelpie and my soul. All I could focus on, though, was that God not take away my best mate—and, of course, thanking Him that my family and Sarah Beth were safe, and asking him to bless the souls of the other children.

But could our parents separate me and Joe? *Would* they? I was pretty sure the decision lay with his parents—his parents to whom I'd lied, who knew I'd lied to the queen herself! No matter what Joe said, I'm sure they must have thought that I'd put their son in danger; it was my fault. Parents were like that. That fact left me shaky and weak and sick.

Only two royal cars pulled up in the driveway—bodyguards in one, Prince Christopher, Princess Maryan, and Prince Joseph in the other. I recognized Jonathan and his partner, Joe's usual guards, by now.

As soon as Joe was out of the car, he ran right for me and grabbed me into a big hug that he held for a while. All my bruises smarted, but I didn't care. I hugged him back, trying not to imagine the angry looks his parents might be giving us. If he were breaking protocol like this, it didn't bode well, so I didn't want to let go any sooner than I had to.

"I'm so glad you're all right," he said.

"Mostly," I said.

He pulled away and scrutinized me with his green eyes. "Mostly? Did I hurt you? I'm sorry—I just…"

"No, no…just bruises. I got X-rays and managed to not break any ribs, the doctor said. It's just…"

He took a deep breath and nodded, offering his hand. I took it. We headed to the front of the castle.

"So…about…you know…" I managed to stammer in a whisper.

Joe avoided even looking at his bodyguards. "I don't know," he said, understanding my unspoken question. "They won't even talk to me." He squeezed my hand, and I knew he was as scared as I was.

At the main door of the castle, someone opened the door for us. Joe kept his eyes lowered, so I followed suit. I heard our parents' voices in the parlor.

Miss Eliza was serving a very early tea. We waited for Prince Christopher to acknowledge us by standing. He was talking with my dad, who, over these few days, had moved mostly past his depressive episode. I had a feeling he'd be climbing to the manic part shortly; there was a look to his eyes that I always noticed when that happened. I could have been imagining it, but it felt like Prince Christopher took his time before he acknowledged us. Gracefully standing, he invited, "Have a seat, please."

Lily sat on the furthest end of the couch, leaving room for me and Joe to sit next to each other. Miss Eliza poured us each a cup of tea. Fortunately, she noticed my shaking and poured me only half a cup, minimizing my chances of messing myself. It wasn't like I could actually eat or drink anything at the moment, anyway.

The thing with tea, of course, is you can't actually discuss anything important *while* having tea. At least not if it's a formal tea. With Important Royals.

I managed to eat half a cucumber sandwich because it's also considered terribly rude to not eat, either. And I drank a quarter of my tea. It was jasmine, which I liked and knew Princess Maryan liked. There was a second pot, too, that smelled like Earl Grey, which I was pretty sure was Prince Christopher's favorite. The menu included Mum's rose geranium cake that she knew Princess Maryan liked, and her spiced chocolate cake that I had heard Prince Christopher once say had yet to be duplicated by any fancy bakery. I almost wished for a momentary psychic connection with my parents so I could secretly thank them; they were pulling for me!

Finally, finally, the *tea* part of tea was over. "I suppose we should get to business," Prince Christopher called us to order. His eyes, clear blue but even more intense than Joe's, fell on me.

It was all I could do not shrink into the couch. Taking a deep breath, I sat up straight, ankles properly crossed, hands folded in my lap, eyes respectfully lowered, and said, "Your Royal Highnesses, I am so, so sorry for being dishonest with you, and with-with Her Royal Majesty Queen Margaret, for-for using your property without permission, and most of all for putting J—Prince Joseph and anyone else in danger. I-I know you have no reason to believe me, or-or forgive me, but…but I beg you to, please." By the end, I could hardly keep my voice above a shaky whisper. I squeezed my eyes shut and lowered my head for judgment.

I felt beside me the slightest shift in the cushions from Joe. He'd edged closer to me, but I knew he didn't dare show any affection at the moment. That would earn neither of us any favors.

"Mr. and Mrs. MacArthur," Joe's clear voice spoke and I nearly jumped as he addressed my parents. "I also owe you the deepest apologies for conspiring and putting your family and friends in danger. For convincing Heather that we should keep things secret. But most of all, I—neither of us…wanted anyone to get hurt. We mistakenly thought we would be able to help the situation, help the kidnapped children…and it was on my advice that we took the measures we did."

I looked at him, mouth open. We were equally at fault! He met my eyes briefly, begging me to be quiet, to trust him. I did. Taking a deep breath, I glanced at the adults in the room, but I couldn't focus on any of their faces. It was painfully silent.

My dad was the first to break it. "Of course, we accept your apology, Prince Joseph." His tone was even; it would be rude not to accept a royal apology. And, it set a precedent for Joe's parents.

"And we accept your apology, Heather MacArthur," Prince Christopher said. Like my dad, his voice was even, sure not to give *too* much, leaving room for conditions. I was very glad Miss Eliza had taken my teacup; it would have been rattling terribly by then. The crown prince continued, "Of course, now there is the question of the beast, itself."

"Would you like to meet him, Prince Christopher, Princess Maryan?" my mother asked.

"Meet?" Prince Christopher raised a brow at my mother.

"He's sentient. He can speak with you himself."

"Is it safe?" Princess Maryan asked.

"He's bound to obey Heather."

"Exactly how well is it bound?" Prince Christopher didn't sound convinced.

"He's bound by Heather's own soul," my mother stated solemnly, eyes challenging the prince to question that.

"What?!" Joe looked at me, grabbing my wrist.

"It's...complicated." I looked at Mum. Her lips were tight. I didn't know how much she'd told them already.

"Enlighten us, please," Prince Christopher said.

"We've discovered a lot since we spoke on Thursday."

Thursday? Mum hadn't talked to them since we took in the kelpie?

Prince Christopher looked between us and my father. Dad looked at Mum.

Mum would take forever to explain, so I spoke up: "When I touched the bridle, it absorbed a piece of my soul—I don't know how, some ancient magick—and when I put the bridle on the kelpie, it transferred that piece of my soul to him. The way that works is that his fate is tied to mine—so, if he's killed... *something* happens to me, and probably the other way around, too. But, also, that piece can kind of grow and end up being his own soul, too. So, he could change and become not evil, maybe a good being."

"Heather..." Joe whispered, his hand squeezing mine hard. "I didn't know—"

He stopped short, glancing at his father, who was giving him a *look*, and removed his hand. I wished he hadn't, but I figured he knew more about what he was "supposed" to do in this situation.

Prince Christopher, frowning, sighed, then said, "Well, I suppose we should go meet this…"

"Ehrwnmyr," I said without thinking. "His name's Ehrwnmyr…Your Highness," I added quickly, seeing my dad give me a *look*. "I didn't mean to speak out of turn. I'm sorry. At—at your leave." I looked back down at my feet.

The crown prince stood, and we all exited the castle in an orderly fashion, which seemed to take far too long for just heading out to the stables.

We pretty much fell in behind Mum, who seemed even more impatient with the formalities than I was. Dad walked behind her, holding her hand tightly. He hadn't gone near Ehrwnmyr in days, either, and I remembered our discussion over Apology Breakfast. The new stable and corral were farther from the castle than any of the others, but now Dad was headed closer to the kelpie, which might throw him into another massive mood swing.

Joe and I were somewhere in the middle, but it was a place where I was able to notice Prince Christopher nod at one of the bodyguards, who proceeded to take a rifle out of the guards' car.

"No! Wait! You can't bring that down there!" I stopped, heart pounding.

Prince Christopher's glare ought to have frozen me in my place, but I had made a promise to Ehrwnmyr. He was my responsibility—and it was my soul at stake!

"He doesn't want to die. You'll scare him and destroy any trust we've started to make! You can't bring the gun…Your Highness." I just barely managed to add the title, and it really only seemed to make things worse.

"Heather," Joe hissed at me. I shook my head and stepped away.

"No guns!"

"You do not have a say—" Prince Christopher began, but I did, possibly, the worst thing possible.

"I do so have a say! It's *my* soul. If you kill him now, he'll end up in Hell—and so could I!"

I don't know what my dad might have been thinking as I faced off against the crown prince of our sovereign nation. I don't know what look of horror Joe might have been giving me. I couldn't see anything but Prince Christopher's eyes, and their lightning blue was terrifying enough. My face burned, and my heart was pounding as if I'd run all the way across our property.

"Could…" he began, lips twitching.

"Could. Yes. But would you really take that chance, Your Highness?" I asked. My voice felt soft in my mouth, but it sounded loud in my ears.

Joe grabbed my hand again. "Father, please? Please?"

Prince Christopher closed his eyes before I did. All of a sudden, I could breathe. I looked at Joe, who looked pleadingly at his father.

"Heather MacArthur," Prince Christopher addressed me. My attention snapped back to him like a shock of electricity through my muscles. "You take full and complete responsibility for the actions of your kelpie? You would ensure the safety of anyone you bring near it?"

"I do, aye." I spoke without hesitation, surprised at myself that I didn't doubt my own words.

He sighed. "Christopher, Graehme, Jonathan, come with us. The rest of you stay here and lock up the firearms."

"Your Highness," the guard with the rifle began.

"That's an order." Prince Christopher looked at me with a mix of curiosity and challenge that reminded me a lot of Joe. I glanced from him to Princess Maryan. Her lips gave the slightest hint of a smirk, another expression I normally tied to my best mate. For his part, my best mate was trying very hard to neither smirk nor appraise my outburst. "Let's continue."

Prince Christopher walked down the access road, gesturing for me to lead with my parents. I kept my eyes straight ahead, and I still held Joe's hand, but I could feel the crown prince watching me.

As we approached Ehrwnmyr's paddock, his self-made miniature salt pond shone in the sun. Ripples grew and he burst from the water, shaking. Beside me, Joe hesitated and gasped. I heard his parents do the same.

The kelpie faced us, curling out his lips in our direction.

Prince... I didn't like the emotions tied to the kelpie's observation.

"Stay here for a second," I told Joe, pulling my hand away. Fortunately, the rest of our families stopped as I approached the fence.

You're cruel.

I put my words into thoughts so the others—particularly Prince Christopher and Princess Maryan—wouldn't hear. You're *cruel. He's my best friend and I may lose him because of you! Don't think what you're thinking about him right now!*

It's my nature to be cruel. You're supposed to be more kind. How kind would it be to have food you find delicious paraded in front of you while you're told you cannot have it?

My stomach turned at his equating Joe to a favored meal. *I went out on a big limb just to make sure they didn't kill you outright! They were going to bring guns! Can't you try and help me out here?*

What are you ordering me to do?

I sighed. *Are you really going to make me give orders? I don't want to have to boss you and constantly be afraid you're looking for every little loophole to get around. Why can't we be a team? Just for now? Please?*

Ehrwnmyr paced in a circle, head down, chewing.

I want peafowl for dinner. You just need to chase one into my paddock, maybe two. Something I can kill and eat in my own way.

I considered. *Deal.*

He lifted his head, looking for me, for some condition, some catch.

Two peafowl. I'll chase them in when they leave. Promise.

The kelpie jogged in one more circle, then stopped, head lowered in submission.

"You can come over now," I told them.

After my initial outburst with Prince Christopher, the rest of the royal viewing of my kelpie was mostly uneventful. I expected them to grill him with questions like my parents did, about how safe he was or how he might possibly escape me and go on another killing spree.

None of them asked about that. I felt both honored and terrified that they put that much trust in me.

In fact, after the initial introductions—and them making strange faces upon "hearing" Ehrwnmyr in their heads—most of the conversation was Prince Christopher and Princess Maryan having Ehrwnmyr do horse stuff: walk, trot, canter, stand. They did ask that he drop his glamour entirely, too. The appearance of black draught horse melted off him, revealing a lanky, angular beast with matted weeds for a mane and tail and those awful shark-like teeth that stuck out from ragged lips. That lasted a whole five minutes, which included them shrinking back and then Prince Christopher, who obviously had to be brave and all that, insisting on touching the unglamoured kelpie's nose.

Princess Maryan, who reminded me a lot of my own mum sometimes, wasn't to be outdone by her husband and also insisted on running her hand down the muzzle that only barely concealed his jagged teeth. Of the two of them, I gave props to Princess Maryan doing a better job of not being squicked out—or, at least, not showing such—when his weedy fur wiggled around her hand.

"It…feels softer than I imagined." Princess Maryan gave Ehrwnmyr one last stroke after Prince Christopher pulled his hand away and did his best to not overtly shake off the sensation of writhing fur.

In my head, I felt the kelpie more entertained than offended.

Joe stayed just behind me and did not reach for the kelpie. I noticed Ehrwnmyr look at him several times, and I sensed more curiosity than animosity now—and, thank goodness, no thoughts of eating anyone.

After a few more minutes of everyone just kind of looking at Ehrwnmyr, my dad suggested we retire to the house. He was the farthest way, though his posture and face appeared more relaxed than I figured he actually felt.

"I could go for another spot of tea." Prince Christopher backed away to join my dad.

"Or a beer?" my father offered.

"Or a beer."

"You're welcome to stay for dinner, of course," Mum also added.

"I wouldn't want to impose," said Princess Maryan.

"It's not an imposition at all. There's plenty of leftovers after Sunday's dinner."

"I'll speak to my husband." The princess smiled, putting a hand on my mother's arm. "You always serve some of the best food." Her eyes—Joe got his green eyes from her—alit on the two of us, then moved to my sister. Lily had always had better manners; she'd been quiet and demure this whole time. "Lily, dear, you must tell me about California. I have yet to visit."

"Of course." My sister beamed.

"Heather, Prince Joseph," my mother said to us.

"No, don't worry, Aimee," Princess Maryan said. "We're off to visit my family in a few days and getting back just in time for school to begin. It will be a while before they see each other again."

Joe and I both sucked in our breaths, eyes glued on our mothers. Mum smiled at us as Princess Maryan turned back to Lily. "You were in L.A., right?"

"Yes, Princess Maryan, I was…"

Once we saw they were back on the access road (Jonathan, of course, stayed behind), Joe and I turned to each other and hugged again. In the corner of my eye, I noticed Jonathan deliberately looking away from us, the very slightest hint of a smile showing beneath the dark sunglasses that hid the rest of his face.

"Oh—ow, okay, that really does hurt."

"Sorry!" Joe stepped back, looking sheepish as I ran my hands over my left ribs. Not broken, but definitely bruised.

"'S'okay, really. God, I'm glad!" I couldn't keep from grinning madly. "I was afraid they'd never let me see you again."

"Me, too." His face was also pasted with a huge smile. We just stared at each other for a moment.

Behind us, Ehrwnmyr whuffled some air out his nostrils. His sentiments weren't words, exactly, but it was uncomfortably close to my sentiments when my parents decided to snog. I glared at the kelpie. "We're *friends*."

"Did he say something?" Joe looked more concerned than I expected him to.

"Not exactly."

"Do you think…Can we go over to him again?"

I won't eat you. Heather has commanded I not even think about it.

I glared again, but Joe squirmed beside me, lifting his fingers to his temple.

"You talked before," he said slowly, glancing over his shoulder at Jonathan. The guard approached but Joe shook his head. Jonathan frowned, but kept his distance. Joe looked back at Ehrwnmyr. "I heard you talk. Why don't you talk-talk now?"

The kelpie's eyes flicked between us and Jonathan. "Eet's… not…eeeeassiee," he said.

"You only do it to creep people out?" Joe frowned.

Without words, the kelpie expressed affirmation.

As if that knowledge were enough to bolster his own bravery, Joe started walking towards the paddock, though he hesitated until I was walking by his side.

"So…you really trust him?"

I opened my mouth. I wouldn't say I trusted him, exactly, but I didn't know what else to say.

Trust has nothing to do with it, Ehrwnmyr answered for me. *She* knows *I must obey her. I am at her mercy, so it is in my best survival interest to act as she would want me to.*

"Yeah…that's about it," I nodded. I'm glad at least one of us had a clear understanding of the situation. I just wish it didn't make me sound so horrible.

"So, he's…like your slave?" Joe's voice shared the discomfort I felt at that idea.

Ehrwnmyr answered for us again. *My choice was this situation or death, and I was granted my choice.*

Joe blew air out through pursed lips.

"Yeah, that, too," I agreed with my friend's unspoken sentiment.

He looked between me and Ehrwnmyr.

"Will…do I have to ask Heather to talk to you?" he asked.

I will speak with you, Prince. The kelpie was curious again, nose flaring in our direction and his right hoof lifted. The glamour around him shifted like the misty veil I saw that hid the faery realm.

"No, really, I'm good with you looking more like a horse." Joe tensed beside me as we stopped just before the fence. Ehrwnmyr took back up the mantle of a black draught horse, like pictures of knights' war horses that I'd seen.

"How…does it feel to have Heather's soul?" Of all the questions I thought Joe might ask, that wasn't among them.

There was a flicker in the glowing sea-colored eyes. I had a feeling he was answering only Joe, but then I sensed a response. Firstly, it was a complicated feeling for the kelpie, and then, in words, an admission, *It's not as…unpleasant…as I expected.*

"Heather's a good person," Joe said. "With a good soul."

There was another long moment of silence and a flicker in the kelpie's eyes. I half wondered if there were more of a conversation between them. Joe's lips tightened, and I sensed the kelpie communicating to both of us. *That may affect the experience, yes.*

Joe bit his lip. "Can…can I see you without the illusion now?"

In a shimmer, like heat coming up off Mum's truck in the middle of summer, the black fluffiness dissipated. He was less bulky, more wiry, and his weed-like coat was a mix of green and black. We were close enough to see the small writhing of his not-exactly-fur and the needle-edged tooth points. His hooves were jagged, too, like broken stones.

Beside me, I felt Joe press closer, just barely suppressing a shudder. Ehrwnmyr lowered his head, looked between us, and didn't come any closer. Joe checked over his shoulder again. Jonathan was still pretty far behind us.

I didn't drop the glamour for him. I thought that unwise. Was I wrong?

"No." Joe looked back. "Good choice."

Would you like to touch me now, too, Prince?

I didn't like the tone of the question, so I glared at the kelpie, but Joe put a hand on my shoulder.

"Does it bother you? To have us touch you?"

Ehrwnmyr cocked his head and licked his lips, taking a few cautious steps forward until his nose was at the fence.

"Your Highness!" Jonathan was walking towards us.

"I'm fine, Jonathan. Please, stay there." Joe turned around and looked at his bodyguard. The man did stop, but he folded his arms impatiently. "Really, I'm fine. My parents left me here with Heather. They trust I'll be okay. Please?"

His sunglasses hid a good part of his face, but not the frown. He folded his hands in front of him and assumed his usual bodyguard stance.

"Jonathan, please?"

I wasn't overly surprised with the confused furrows that appeared above Jonathan's sunglasses. It obviously wasn't normal for Joe to *ask*. With a sigh, the man stepped back a few paces.

"Thank you." Joe turned back to Ehrwnmyr, who had backed up a few steps. Taking a deep breath, Joe tentatively leaned his elbows on the fence. I did the same. The kelpie considered us. "Does it…bother you, though? When humans touch you?"

The kelpie approached us again, nose out, neck stretched, snorting. It showed his teeth more. While I felt Joe tense, he didn't flinch as the pointed nose drew closer to our two hands and we could feel the hot breath. Ehrwnmyr arched his neck and took one more tentative step towards us. Slowly, he relaxed his head, letting the tip of his nose brush my hands first, then Joe's, before snatching it back.

No. Touching you does not bother me. I dislike being an ornament, though.

"I understand," Joe said softly.

I suppose you might. As if to offer peace for the acidic tone, he reached his nose to us again. After a few more snorts, he touched my fingers, then moved his head and stepped closer so he was also touching Joe's hand.

I hadn't actually touched the kelpie since bringing him here. We'd talked a few times, and I was in charge of feeding him. I also cleaned the poop from his paddock, which was beyond disgusting, but he'd kept his distance from me…and I was okay with that.

Princess Maryan was right; the squirming…not-fur…was much softer than I had expected. And, to borrow Ehrwnmyr's own phrasing, it wasn't as unpleasant as I expected. It kind of felt cool.

I rubbed his muzzle gently, like I would for any new horse, slowly moving up to his forehead and around his eye, wondering if that released the same endorphins as it did for horses. Joe was doing the same.

The kelpie's lips twitched, and I got my answer as he now pushed against our hands. No words came to my head, but I could sense his own surprise that he found our touch…not unpleasant. Better than "not unpleasant."

I looked at Joe. He was biting his lip and smiling a little. So was I.

After a few minutes, Ehrwnmyr stepped away, and both Joe and I pulled our hands back, understanding he was done. He gave us a little nod and trotted in a circle, thinking about the experience. Next to me, Joe let out his breath. I looked over at him and he grinned again.

"That was…kind of wicked." His eyes were bright and he smiled even more.

"It was," I agreed.

"You've had him this whole time, and you haven't?" He raised an eyebrow at me.

"We're…going really slow with this whole figuring things out bit."

Joe just nodded. We heard the kelpie pick up his pace from a trot to a canter. He circled around and headed for the water.

"No! Nonono!" I grabbed Joe's arm, yanking him back from the fence. We did *not* need to go back in the house with soaked clothes.

Ehrwnmyr stopped with just the small splash of his front hooves into the water. Flying droplets landed on our shoes. He lifted his head, making a sound somewhere between a whinny and a cackle.

"Your Highness!" Jonathan jumped in front of us, glaring at the kelpie.

"We're fine, we're fine." Joe laughed. "He was just messing with us."

I'd sensed that in my head, too. The kelpie shook himself, sending a few more stray droplets our way, and made that laughing whinny once more. I couldn't keep from giggling a little, myself.

"Yeah, he's a piece of you, all right, Heather." Joe smirked.

"Oi, thanks." I stuck my tongue out at him.

"We should probably head inside, Prince Joseph." Jonathan looked over our heads and eyed the kelpie warily. Ehrwnmyr circled into the water, then out very quickly, shaking his head and tail. I ducked behind Jonathan to keep any droplets from falling on me. It was a taunt, but not a malicious one.

You promised me dinner! he reminded me, lifting his tail and showing off a collected trot in the other direction. *And* they *are not leaving soon.*

"I've got to feed him," I said to Jonathan.

"Can I help?" Joe asked despite his bodyguard's deepening frown.

"It's chasing two peahens into his paddock," I told him.

"I think we can manage that, right, Jonathan?" He grinned at the man, who looked less than amused.

With both Joe and Jonathan helping, it didn't take long to herd two of the peahens, one green, one white—I couldn't quite get myself to send any of the pretty cocks to their deaths—into the kelpie's paddock. I felt a little guilty. We'd had the peafowl for many years; they were as docile as any of the chickens and would even occasionally eat out of our hands. It was hardly a job to chase them.

Fortunately, they met a swift end. The kelpie moved faster than anything we'd seen. He snatched each within a few seconds, breaking their necks cleanly. He picked both up in his mouth and trotted them into the run-in stall we left open for him and began to tear the white one apart and eat its innards.

"Gruesome," Jonathan muttered.

"A bit," Joe said. His bodyguard, who'd taken off his sunglasses, raised an eyebrow. "I meant for that to have more sarcasm."

Shaking his head, Jonathan headed back to the castle. Joe jogged after and past Jonathan; I followed. After we were far enough ahead, he slowed down and gave me a different kind of smile, "So, about starting school next semester? Dealing with things…"

I sighed, but realized I could have this conversation now. After all, I'd captured a kelpie, saved a friend from being trapped in Faerie, stood up to the crown prince of England… and I still had most of the summer to go.

And I knew I'd still have at least one best mate I could count on for anything.

Yeah, I could handle whatever trouble my family or a new school sent my way.

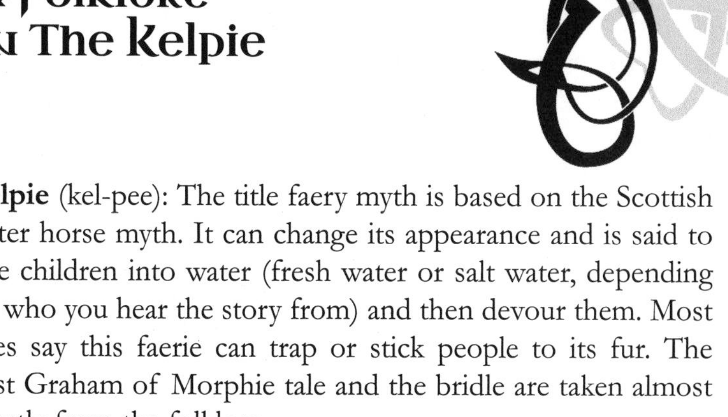

Some Author Notes on the Faery Myths & Folklore in The Kelpie

Kelpie (kel-pee): The title faery myth is based on the Scottish water horse myth. It can change its appearance and is said to lure children into water (fresh water or salt water, depending on who you hear the story from) and then devour them. Most tales say this faerie can trap or stick people to its fur. The Last Graham of Morphie tale and the bridle are taken almost exactly from the folklore.

Daoine Síth (dunnuh shee): Daoine Síth are the nobility of the Fair Folk—what people often call creatures of Faerie so as not to insult them. Their legends can be found all around Ireland (where they are better known as the "daoine sidhe"), Scotland (where it's "síth" not "sidhe"), Wales, and England. Often depicted as human-sized, they frequently also have the pointed ears and oversized eyes found in Tolkien and Dungeons & Dragons "elves."

Pixie/Nixie/Sprite (pick-see / nick-see / sprite): The small beings who talk to Ivy and Ash are similar to the small, winged folk that many more modern tales call "fairies", but less like Disney's Tinkerbell and more like some of the rascals crushed in *Lady Cottington's Pressed Fairy Book*. Folktales and faery tales about these beings are extremely contradictory; sometimes they define them as different types of beings and other times these terms are used interchangeably.

Animal Spirits: Animals that can speak and/or take on a more human-like form, such as Monkey/Tom, are found in myth and folklore all around the world...frequently starting all sorts of mischief.

The Angels Who Didn't Choose A Side: In trying to explain how soul magick might work on the kelpie, Aimee suggests the story that faerie are what became of the angels who didn't pick a side when Lucifer (Satan) chose to war against God. It's not a very common myth, but it is one that intrigued me when I first heard it at a science fiction and fantasy convention panel, "Faery Tales, Folklore, and Myth," and it's been wriggling around in my mind since. It's found more among Irish folktales than Scottish. It was most likely adopted when the Catholic Church was trying to convert the pagan tribes and clans from their faith to the Christian one.

Faery, faerie, fey (as opposed to "fairy"): There are several opinions on these terms describing beings that are "not of this realm" or a particular kind of supernatural being. I've jumped off from how Isaac Asimov defined them in the prologue to the anthology *Faeries*. "Fae" or "fay" or "fey" is derived from Latin meaning "faith" or "fate," and has been applied as a descriptor for someone or something that is otherworldly, something science cannot quantifiably prove. "Faerie" once would have meant the land from which "fey" or "fae" things came.

English is a forever-changing language, though, particularly in how we assign meanings and change spellings of our words. While actual fear and honor for fey beings existed for thousands of years, more recent changes in religion and science have either extinguished the faith and fear of such beings or aligned them with something evil that should be destroyed.

For some time, the term "fairy" became popular. One of the reasons I've heard that it came into use was from the term "Fair Folk," which many people called the (usually not very nice, but very powerful and easily offended) beings and adding the "-y" ending to lessen the fear and power associated with them. More recently, many people have tried to preserve the power of these folk tales and the beliefs behind them, so they returned to the more archaic spelling of "faerie" or "faery" to differentiate these beings from the cute, and mostly harmless, winged creatures many people still associate with the term "fairy."

For the purposes of Heather's stories, "Faerie" is used to talk about the place where the "faery" or "fey" beings live. "Faerie" also speaks about the beings as individuals or as a group, while "faery" is a descriptive word. Tom corrects Heather with the race's preferred form (at least in this novel's world) of "faerie" or "Fey Folk" for plural term. For the real story in the world you live in, it's best to ask them what they prefer. Just make sure you're polite!

Acknowledgements

I'm one of those geeks who always reads the "Thank You" and "Acknowledgements" sections in books, so I'm excited to write one of my own. I know I can't thank every single person who has helped me make my novel dreams real. Forgive me if I don't mention you; that doesn't mean you haven't a special place in my heart!

First, a big thank you to my parents, my brother, and my family, who gave me the "you can be anything you want" speech and not only meant it, but have helped me with as many tools and as much support as you could—and then some. I really am blessed with you all. All the *good* family moments are inspired by you. (The bad stuff is all totally made up!)

Just as important is my Husband-of-Awesome, Scott. He is my stable ground when my dreamy writer self needs it, and also the wings I need when I take a less-than-logical dreamer's leap off a cliff. I couldn't ask for a better soul mate. On top of all that, he let me plan our research/vacation to Scotland based on everything I needed for this novel. And he looks good in a kilt.

There is no measurement for the amount of thanks and love I can give to my Spencer Hill Press family. Vikki Ciaffone, you were the first editor to "get" and love my MacArthurs. Laura Ownbey, you put in so much overtime and love to help me polish Heather's story to the gem it is now. Both of you are awesome, and I cannot begin to say how much I appreciate all the work you put into my edits! Kate Kaynak, you do so much to help all of us achieve our dreams; we wouldn't be here if you weren't as magickal as you are. Rich Storrs, you keep all of us crazy dreamers in line with the important parts of reality through your almighty fact checking and stylistic knowledge, and I love it! And my copyeditors, Emily White and Shira Lipkin, thank you for catching all the little details. Thank you to my cover artist, Vic Caswell, for rendering my characters so well and being able to see into my head! Kendra Saunders, thank you for rescuing my cover reveal scavenger hunt and all your tips! Jennifer Allis Provost, thank you for helping me spread the word about *The Kelpie*! Anthony Francis, you are my formatting *savior* with your two-minutes-to-midnight rescue during my copyedits!

I also want to give special thanks to Catherine Maxwell Stuart, the 21st Lady of Traquair (www.traquair.co.uk). She kindly gave me an interview about living in a historical home (as Heather does) and a lot of insight about Scottish and British culture. Her hospitality, and that of all the Traquair staff, created one of the most magickal experiences in all my travels.

Similarly, the wonderful Michael and Fiona of Rhovanion Bed & Breakfast in Coldingham (www.rhovanion.org) were amazing hosts, great cooks, and extremely helpful in making Heather's life (I hope) authentic and real for readers. Visiting with them, talking about everyday life, and walking around the areas where Heather would walk, particularly the ocean trails and ruined castle, made my time at their home a particularly powerful visit.

In our modern world, no writer has to be an island, so I want to take the time to thank the writers' groups who have helped make my author dreams come true, particularly in helping raise

Heather to publication. Thank you to the Dragon*Writers who have been rocks for over a decade since we all met in A.C. Crispin's class at Dragon*Con. And thank you to A.C. Crispin for holding that class and continuing to be a mentor to so many of us. Thank you to the Traveling Java writers, who were the first to really get to meet and strengthen the MacArthurs and the kelpie. Also, thank you to my Southbridge writers' group who gave me some insight into Joe, politics, and his family.

I also want to give major props to Broad Universe (www.broaduniverse.org), an organization without which I'd never have started going to regular conventions, being on panels, and running book tables. I would never have met Kate, Vikki, Marlys (of Traveling Java), and so many other amazing women authors and editors without whom I would not have been able to travel the road I'm on now.

There are many fans, beta readers, supporters, and people lending me corners to write in who deserve massive thanks. These people include (but are not limited to) Del of Generations Gifts (www.generations-gifts.com) for being a fan and making my website awesome; Renee and Sean of Stained Glass Creations & Beyond (www.stainedglasscreationsandbeyond.com), who lent me a corner of their store to work in and helped me map out Heather's castle and find Traquair in my research; Darby Karchut (www.darbykarchut.com) for loving Heather and Joe as she does (and writing the awesome books that she does); Aimee Weinstein (tokyowriter.com), who I named Heather's mum after for good reason; Amanda and Amy Chickering and the Future Trainers of America (whipowillstables.weebly.com) for taking good care of my own horse and giving me plenty of horse and "target audience" feedback.

Lastly, thank you to all of you readers—especially you who go through the acknowledgement sections. :) I welcome more comments and dialogue from you on my website, www.anovelfriend.com.

A portion of the net profit of each copy of *The Kelpie* will be donated to the Bay State Equine Rescue, a 100% volunteer-run 501(c)3 organization in Massachusetts whose mission is to help abused, abandoned, and neglected equines through direct intervention, community outreach, education, and legislation. For more info: www.baystaterescue.org

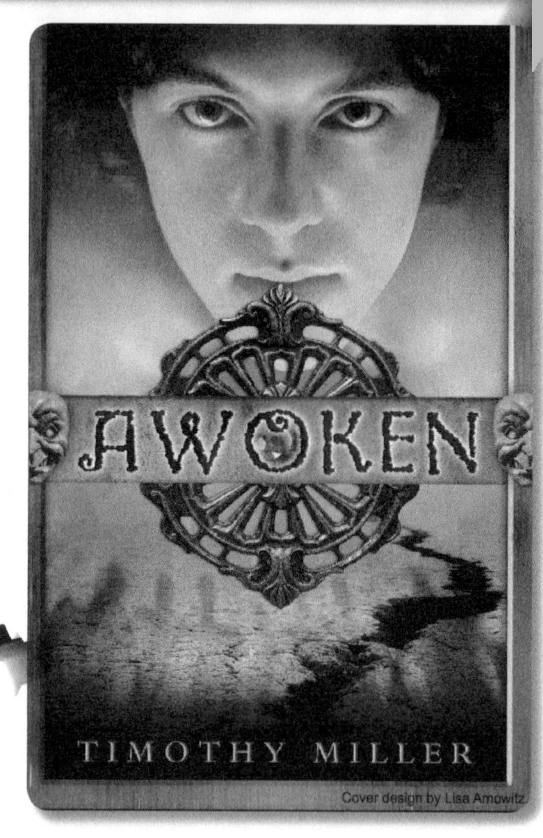

Fourteen-year-old boy discovers elemental powers and is caught in a war between frightening dollmen and a more frightening corporation that would use his powers to redefine "human."

As the tiniest Hapenny, a race of little people, Maewyn Bridgepost spends her days from breakfast to midnight nibble scrubbing the hearth, slopping the pigs and cooking for her guardian, Gelbane. As if life as a servant isn't bad enough, Maewyn learns that Gelbane is a troll—and Hapennies are a troll delicacy!

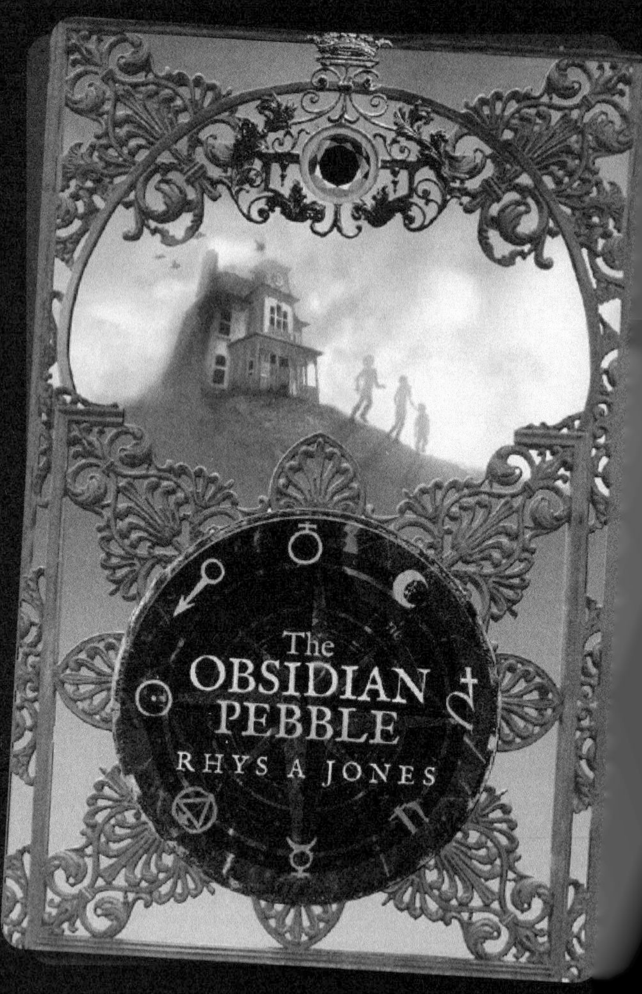
The
OBSIDIAN
PEBBLE
RHYS A JONES

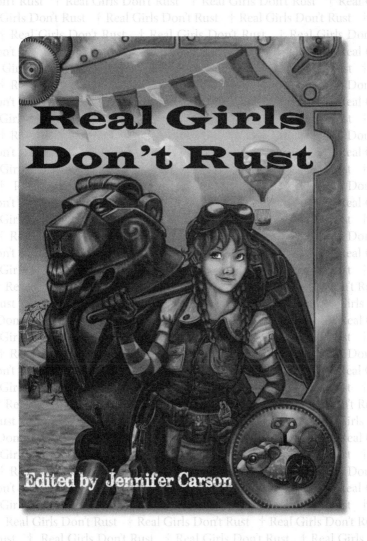

THE LOST IMPERIALS

The Tesla Institute is a premier academy that trains young time travelers called Rifters. Created by Nicola Tesla, the Institute seeks special individuals who can help preserve the time stream against those who try to alter it.

The Hollows is a rogue band of Rifters who tear through time with little care for the consequences. Armed with their own group of lost teens—their only desire to find Tesla and put an end to his corruption of the time stream.

February 2014

HEATHER McCOLLUM

SIREN'S SONG

Jule Welsh can sing. She enthralls people with her bel canto voice. But it takes more than practice to reach her level of exquisite song; it takes siren's blood running through her veins.

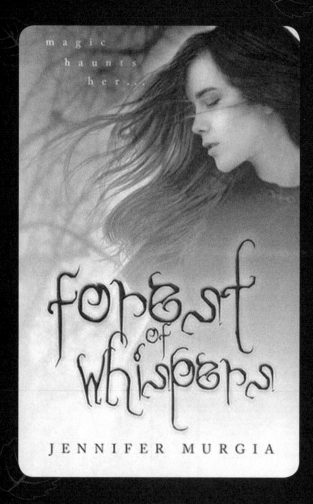

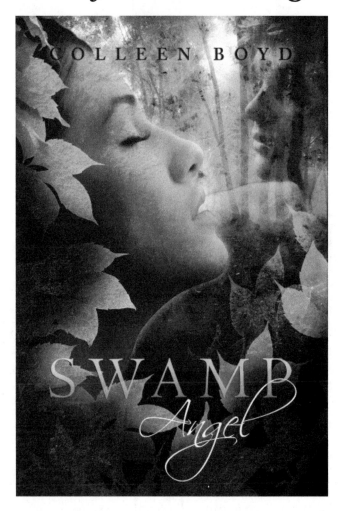

About the Author

T. J. Wooldridge is a professional writing geek who adores research into myth, folklore, legend, and the English language. Before delving full-time into wordsmithing, she has been a tutor, a teacher, an educational course designer, a video game proofreader, a financial customer service representative, a wine salesperson, a food reviewer, an editing consultant, a retail sales manager, and a nanny. While infrequent, there are times she does occasionally not research, write, or help others write. During those rare moments, she enjoys the following activities: spending time with her Husband-of-Awesome, a silly tabby cat, and two Giant Baby Bunnies in their Massachusetts home hidden in a pocket of woods in the middle of suburbia; reading; riding her horse (not very well); reading Tarot (very well); drawing (also not very well); making jewelry (pretty well), making wordy lists, and adding parenthetical commentary during random conversations. She also enjoys dressing up as fey creatures, zombies, or other such nonsense at science fiction, fantasy, and horror conventions.